LUST FOR

THE CRAVE SERIES
BOOK 1

J.L. STRAY

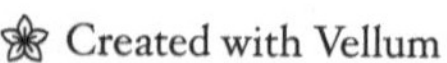 Created with Vellum

LUST FOR PLAY LIST

Interested in hearing what Crave sounds like?

Bleed It Out - *Linkin Park*
Careless Whisper - *Seether*
Broken - *Seether, Amy Lee*
Thinkin' Bout Me - *Drew Jacobs*
Papercut - *Linkin Park*
Burn It Down - *Linkin' Park*
Fake It - Seether
November Rain - *Guns N' Roses*
No Matter What - *Papa Roach*
I'll Follow You - *Shinedown*

CHAPTER ONE

The trip out to the beach was long. The traffic was so horrendous, the four-hour trip had turned into five. But what should I have expected at the peak of tourist season in Corolla, North Carolina? It's July and the tourists are flooding into the state for the beaches and other attractions it has to offer.

I put my Jeep into park and lean back into the leather seat. My limbs are stiff and sore from the drive. I still can't believe I came out here just because my mother asked me to, but the guilt in her voice was enough for me to know that she and my father weren't going to be able to make the trip anytime soon. Out of my brother and I, I'm the one with the more mobile career, so it made sense for me to come. After all, I currently have a gap in my commitments for my career in fitness. Normally, I wouldn't have minded coming, but it's not the season I enjoy most. Even though the town is small and quaint, I prefer when it's more private, like in early June or even late August.

But my parents are ready to sell this place since it doesn't get used as much as it did when us kids were younger. My twin brother and I used to stay every summer. Audrey and Aiden—a pair who did everything together, until he moved out to Los

Angeles full time to be with his band, Crave. I'm proud of him and the boys for finding success. However, it means we don't see each other as much as we'd like.

I get out of the Jeep and head toward the house, then take out my key and unlock the door. When I enter the house, I can see that someone is currently living here too. There are pizza boxes in the kitchen, a sweatshirt hanging over the back of the couch, and shoes lying in front of the back door. None of which should be here. This house should be empty and quiet.

I reach for the pepper spray in my purse, ready to zap whoever this fucker is. "Come out! I'm going to call the police," I call out to the intruder.

There's movement and noise coming from the back hall—either my room or Aiden's, I'm not sure. A dark figure emerges from the hallway and finally comes into the light. My shoulders slump and relax as I recognize the man standing in front of me.

"What are you doing here?" he grumbles.

I don't answer him immediately, because Derek Walsh is standing in front of me wearing only a towel. It's slung low on his hips, so I have a view of absolutely everything. Well, expect maybe the good stuff. He's just like I imagined him to be, all hard lines, muscles, and tattoos. Some are colorful and others are black and white, and I wonder what it would be like to trace each one with my tongue. His body looks like the most beautiful canvas I've ever seen.

His spiked black hair is disheveled and dripping with water. His brown eyes are wide and staring at me. I can see that his mouth is moving, but I honestly can't bring myself to pay attention to the sounds that are coming out. He looks almost angry at me. Although, that wouldn't be new for Derek. He always had a mean streak a mile long.

He and Aiden have been best friends since they were in middle school. Aiden is only older than me by two minutes, but one would have thought those minutes were hours, or even years, with the way Aiden made them sound. He always made me feel like the dorky little sister growing up.

"Jesus Christ, Audrey. What in the actual fuck are you doing here?" he asks, when I finally decide that I should listen to the words coming from his perfect lips.

The thing that Derek's never known is that I want him. I always have and probably always will. When my brother and his bandmates are one stage, he's all my eyes can focus on. No matter how many times I try to watch Aiden play bass, I always go back to the lead singer.

"I'm here to get this place fixed up. My parents are selling," I respond. Then I find my bearings, remembering that this is my family's house, and he shouldn't be here. "What are *you* doing here?"

He runs his hand through his hair. I watch the water slide down his strong forearms. Again, I fight the urge to walk over to him and run my tongue along the path that the droplets are taking.

"They're selling the beach house?" he asks, leaning back against the counter.

"Well, yeah. I mean, I don't come here all that much. Neither do they and you guys are always in LA. Why are you not in LA?"

He sighs and pinches the bridge of his nose, not saying a word. The silence stretches between us longer than I'm comfortable with.

"Derek?" I prompt, annoyed that he hasn't answered my question. "How did you get here?"

"Aiden," he says, making it sound like the most natural thing in the world. "Aiden gave me the key the other night. I flew in and I've been staying here for the past twenty-four hours. He didn't mention that you were coming or that Joe and Marie were thinking of selling the place." He throws out my parents' names like they're just our friends rather than the people who raised him while his mom was in and out of rehab. I never knew Derek's dad, and frankly, I don't think he ever did either.

"Oh. Well, you can't be here. I'm getting this place cleaned and seeing what repairs need done before we put it on the market."

"Your parents couldn't just hire someone to do that? Being the dutiful daughter, you had to come out here and box things up?"

"You're lucky they didn't." I roll my eyes, growing more annoyed with him by the second. "Whoever they would have hired might have called the police on you or shot you. So, you're lucky it's me."

It's been a long day, and I can tell it's about to get even longer. All visions of coming here, making a quick stop at the house before heading out for groceries, are lost. Even the plan of enjoying a pizza on the sand while the waves crash into the shore seems like something that won't be possible now.

Nope, not with Derek staying here. He'll probably try to get me to leave.

"Can't you do that another time?"

"I just drove for five fucking hours to get here and do this," I spit in his direction. My hands find my hips, and my chest juts out in defiance. No, I will not be the one leaving. "Besides this is *my* parents' house."

He shakes his head. "I know that. But Aiden gave me the key." He says it like that's all the permission he needed.

"It wasn't Aiden's key to give," I tell him.

He lets out a laugh. "Aud, are you really hell-bent on throwing me out of here?"

I stomp my foot on the tile. "Damn it, Derek. I can already tell you're going to be a pain in the ass about this."

"It's good to see you too."

"Is it? Or do you have someone coming here? Is that why you want to have the whole place to yourself?"

"No." His tone is sharp and short.

I must have hit a nerve.

I smile at him and push my own long brown strands out of my face. "Great, so beach time with Derek," I say dryly.

"We're both adults. I can stay out of your way, and you can stay out of mine."

"And what about me getting this place ready for sale?" I look around at the pizza boxes on the counter. The empty beer bottles in the sink. The trash can overflowing so badly that the lid won't even close. "This is a big mess for someone who hasn't been here that long."

He shrugs. "I was hungry. Come on, Audrey, once upon a time, you and I actually hung out together. It was civil," he reminds me.

"Yeah, it was." Little did he know, I was always staring at him a little too long and wishing that just once he would notice me as someone other than Aiden's little sister. But that never happened.

"I can help with some repairs if you need me to," he says. "How long are you planning on staying?"

He's staring at me so intently that it causes my cheeks to heat. I smile and look away. "Just for a couple of weeks. I have to be in LA for a shoot."

"Still doing that personal trainer thing, huh?" He throws the statement out there the same way my parents did when they first learned what I was doing—spending my time working with individuals who are either wanting to get stronger or wanting to lose weight.

It took off for me. The videos I used to shoot and place on YouTube found their way to Beachbody, who hired me as a super trainer and nutritionist. When I'm not working on getting workouts together for them, I'm training soccer players from the North Carolina Courage, a local National Women's Soccer League team. But everyone assumes I'm just playing around on YouTube because I heavily use social media to market my fitness groups, still place videos up, and even do live Q&As. I've found my fans really want to learn about me, so I do my best to be vulnerable and open, all while instructing them on nutrition and fitness.

"I am. Still doing that rock-star thing?" I throw back at him.

"Touché," he replies.

My brother and Derek had their share of naysayers when they were putting Crave together. Most people felt they wouldn't make it. Sure, they're talented, but so are a lot of bands. And with my brother's talent on bass, Brent's on drums, and Derek's smooth-like-honey voice, they really have something. Now it's about three years, two albums, and one tour later, and they're doing alright for themselves.

"So, are you out here to work on the new album?" I ask. I've heard rumors that Crave is in the recording studio after finishing up their tour. But Aiden hasn't mentioned it, and honestly, I haven't asked either.

I also heard that Derek has been seeing Serena Fox, a singer he performed a rather steamy duet with for her album. They get together and perform it as much as they can. The electricity and publicity it brings the band is worth the travel every time. Rumor has it that the chemistry between the two of them isn't fake; they're becoming quite the item both on and offstage.

It wouldn't shock me if that was the case. She's gorgeous. Serena is tall and all legs. Her large blue eyes, pale skin, and long black hair with blue streaks running through it make her an absolute knockout. She really looks striking beside Derek too; I've notice that from the photos I've seen online. And the many hours that I've spent Googling Derek and the band.

"No, not what I'm doing here," he says, the sharpness returning.

I don't bother asking about Serena, but I make a note to save that one for another day. When he seems to be in a better mood.

"Okay," I reply, shifting awkwardly on my feet. "Well, listen, it's been a long drive and I'm really tired. I'm going to bring the rest of my stuff in and some food for me before heading off to bed."

He nods. "I have some food here."

"Thanks. I think I wanna grab some of my essentials."

He nods again. "Need help bringing anything in?"

"No, I've got it. Which room are you in?"

"Aiden's."

"Okay, great. Then I can go in my old room."

Another nod. Then he turns and walks away, leaving me standing there.

"Great. This should be fun." I roll my eyes and take my bag to my room.

CHAPTER TWO

I wake up as the early morning sun shines angrily through my window. I don't want to get out of bed. I don't want to face the day. I don't want to be the one who's responsible for cleaning up this house. Only I know the reason for the cleanup and sale, but I'm sure it'll only be a matter of time before Derek does too.

I rise from my bed and pull on my workout clothes. It's time to get in a quick run and then a core workout before I start my day. I make my way from my bedroom and down the long hallway to hear that the house is quiet—I'm grateful for that—then take my pre-workout fuel and ready myself for a sweat session.

Most people think I've been fed the Kool-Aid or that I'm just trying to help my Beachbody family make more money by drinking all the shakes, taking the workout fuel, and following the eating plans. But I truly believe in their mission. The few online dietitian courses I've taken taught me quite a bit, and I know what they're preaching will help my clients lose weight and feel better about themselves. They just have to trust in themselves, follow the plan, and allow themselves to indulge every once in a while. I've written many blog posts on that last part.

The salt air is welcoming as I breathe it in before my run. I try to keep my mind blank and avoid thinking about the issues back home. Instead, I focus on the beach. I remember all the ways we used to play, swim, and build huge castles on it. We even had an annual summer touch football game the whole family played in. Aiden and I always had our friends over for it too. Some of them flew in special for it. My parents made a big deal out of it and made the trip worth their while—the same way they did anytime friends came over to visit.

I have such fond memories of this place, and now I have to pack it all up. The only comfort I have, or at least what I keep telling myself, is that another family can take the house and make their own memories. It's bittersweet, but it's what's best for my family. I've considered buying it. I do well enough with my business and my contract at Beachbody, but even this would be a stretch if I bought it at market value. I could ask Aiden to go in on it together, but I'm not sure he would like that. His life is in LA. He's embraced the fast-paced environment and California surfing.

When I get back to the house, my legs are burning and so are my lungs. It's already hot outside. I look out at the surf and think about running in to cool off, but I stop when I spot Derek a few feet in front of me. He's doing push-ups, working hard and sweating, his hair soaked. He must have been out here just as long as I have. Or his workout has been strenuous. Two bottles of water are up on the deck.

I move to head into the house, but he shouts, "One of those is for you, Aud."

I wave a thank-you and chug it, heading down to the sand so that I can lay out my yoga mat and work my core. We work out in silence, him focusing on his chest and back and me focusing on my abs—doing crunches, sit throughs, mountain climbers, and other moves. At one point, I look over and see he's doing some of the same things I am.

"Are you trying to get a free workout out of me?" I tease when we've both stopped.

He just laughs. "Something like that."

I sit on my mat and watch the surf come in. He's sitting directly on the sand. We don't say a word as the beach comes to life with the other residents who own houses on this strip. So many of them have changed over the years that I don't recognize many of them. Mom and Dad used to have friends that owned the house beside ours, but the wife died unexpectedly in a car accident and the husband sold it. My parents still see him in the city. It's too painful for him to be out here. Maybe that's why Mom is having me pack this place up for her. The memories will just be a bit too much.

"You okay?" he asks me.

"Yeah, just thinking about the task ahead for the day."

"Ever the dutiful daughter," he states.

Derek mentioned something similar when I got here. I'm not sure if he knows that something is going on and this is his way of getting it out of me, but I don't react or reply to him. I just keep looking forward at the horizon, cataloging in my head all the things that need to be packed up and shipped back home. All the things that need to be sent to the secondhand store. It's too much and yet just enough to help keep my mind off the reality of why I'm here.

I'm almost glad that Derek is here. He'll be a nice distraction and someone to talk to—or not *really* talk to. The light, everyday conversation will be a welcome to the silence I usually have in my life. Twenty-four years old and I'm still single. Not necessarily something that makes my parents happy, but they always want me to live my life and my dreams. My schedule with filming and taking clients can be hectic, and I prefer the company of a gym or a good book over hiding out in a bar. The only time I'm heading out is with my castmates after filming or if Crave is in town. But that's more like watching family.

"What's got you so quiet?" he asks me.

I look up at those big brown eyes and melt. I want to tell him that it's him. He has me so quiet. It's the smell of the sweat mixed with the smell of the sea. It's his body being so close to me that I want to lick it that has me tongue-tied. But I don't say any of those things.

"Just lots of things to do today is all. There's a lot of work and clearing out that needs done with this house. It's almost a daunting task."

"I can help where you need me. I just might need some notice to get my butt out of bed," he says with a chuckle.

Images flash in my head of Derek lying in Aiden's room. I want to join him in that bed, but I can't say that. "I'll remember that. You've got your own work, though. Don't let me keep you from it."

"I won't," he says with a wink. "Just let me know when you wanna tell me what's bugging you. I can tell something is up. More than worrying about this house."

"I'm fine," I lie. Denial isn't just a place in Egypt, but rather one I'd be happy to live in. I wonder what he would think if he knew what was really plaguing me.

He smirks and shakes his head. "Sure, keep living in denial, if you'd like. I'll be here when you're done." He walks off down the beach and lets the surf lick at his calves.

I watch him walking around down there, enjoying life and being so carefree. Maybe having Derek here will provide the perfect distraction to all my troubles.

The message on the fridge just read "Beach Day?" I guess he figured since I had been working so hard boxing up some of my parents' items and readying the house for sale that I would need a beach day. And he was right, as usual.

It's Sunday, and I was already planning on taking a break from cleaning up and packing. It feels weird being the one doing it. I had hoped my parents would end up wanting to be more involved, but they've just asked that I get the house packed up and told me that the movers would come take care of it. The real estate company will be putting some furniture in for staging. I just have to choose it.

I pull on a hot pink bikini and head down to the beach. He's not here yet, but I have no idea what time he got in last night or where he even goes when he does leave. It's a constant thing. Maybe he found some tourist or townie to hook up with. After all, being the lead singer of Crave has to have its perks. And judging by the throngs of screaming fans at every concert, he must have a few willing participants.

Aiden—or Ace, as most people call him—has apparently embraced this portion of fame. At least that's what I've gathered from the rumors I've heard. I try not to pay too much attention to my twin brother's sex life. No sister wants to know about those sorts of exploits.

I grab my book from my beach bag and settle in for some reading time. It's nice to relax. Lately, it's been crazy with cleaning out cabinets, closets, and anything else that I can find. We've owned this house for almost twenty years, and it's hard to imagine how even though it's a summer house, we could possibly have so much crap here.

Just as I'm getting into my book, there's a thump beside me. I look over to find Derek gazing out over the ocean. The sight of him takes my breath away, the same way it used to when we were teenagers. He's all hard lines and tanned and toned skin. His black swim trunks hang low on his hips, giving me a view of the *V* that leads down to somewhere I've always wanted to explore. A black Nike ball cap is pulled down low over his eyes, probably in an attempt to conceal his identity.

"You okay?" he asks, snapping me back to reality.

"I'm sorry?" I'm not sure if this is the first thing he's said to me or how long I've been staring. Looking down at Derek's body is enough to make me go stupid.

"I was asking if you were okay. You had this dumbfounded look on your face while you were looking at me. Is this not what I'm supposed to be wearing? It is a beach day."

I flush and turn what must be sixty different shades of red. "You look good." I realize my blunder when a widened smile comes across his perfect face. God, I'm so screwed.

He laughs. "So, I've been told."

I'm sure he has. I attempt to look back at the ocean. I feel his eyes on me, but I don't dare turn around.

"Make sure you put sunscreen on. That's an awful lot of skin showing," he comments as he lowers himself into the chair I set up for him.

"Thanks, Dad. I'll be sure to get on that," I quip and shake my head.

He chuckles. "Just trying to look out for you. You know, more like a brother than a father."

"Right," I say. It's a simple statement, but it's enough to remind me that of how he sees me.

"Are there any beers in that?" He gestures toward the cooler I brought.

"No, there are not. I didn't think about it."

"So, what is in there?" he grumbles as he continues looking around the beach.

"There's some watermelon, strawberries, granola bars, and water."

"Always so health-conscious," he remarks.

"It's part of the job," I remind him.

"Don't you tell your followers they should eat everything in moderation?"

I take in a sharp inhale of breath. "You watch my reels? I thought you had people in charge of your account." I don't know why such a simple statement causes such a big reaction inside me, but I just always assumed when he 'liked' my posts or commented that it was someone from their band's promo team or an assistant dealing with his social media.

"Nah, that's me. That account is all mine."

I love the way his voice is velvety and sweet, wrapping around the words *all mine*. I imagine what it would be like to have him refer to me that way. I swallow audibly, and out of the corner of my eye, catch him watching me.

"You seem quieter than normal," he says. "You okay?"

I smile at the memory of what a normal beach day was like when we were kids. It would be all of us—my parents, Aiden, Derek, my best friend, Emma, and sometimes Brent. There was always music playing and a lot of laughter and roughhousing on the beach. Those were the days. I miss them.

"I'm just tired from getting things together at the house."

"I'm sorry I haven't been more help with that," he says sheepishly.

"It's okay. I know you're working." I've been able to hear the strumming of his guitar through the walls, and it sounds beautiful. He's working on new music, I think. I recognize some of the chords from existing songs, and I swear I can sometimes hear his voice singing along. But most of the time, it's something new. I always strain to hear the words, but most times I can't.

"Trying to," he says.

"How's it going?" I ask, thinking it's a normal question to ask him.

"I don't want to talk about it, Audrey." His tone is sharp, and he rises from the chair. "I'm going to go take a dip and cool off. Do you wanna come along?"

I try to process the invitation, but my mind is still reeling from how he answered me. I wonder what that's about but decide not to say any more.

"No, not quite yet. I wanna sit here for a few more minutes."

"Suit yourself," he says and begins making his way to the water.

"Derek," I call out after him.

"Yeah," he says, turning toward me. The scowl from earlier has faded a bit.

"Hat." I motion to my head, as if he doesn't know where his hat is.

"I need this." He turns on his heel and heads into the water.

I watch the muscles of his back move and flex as he attempts to get out into the water. The beach isn't very crowded today, which is nice. These beaches tend to be more for the residences of the houses behind us. But every once in a while, the tourists will come down here to play. I guess that's why he feels the need to have his hat on to protect him from unwanted intrusions from fans.

Derek walks out into the water and dives forward. He's fully submerged. Coming up, he pushes his hair off his face and replaces the hat on his head. I watch him stand there, taking the moment in. I can barely see his face from where I'm sitting, gawking, and not reading my book. But if I had to guess his expression, I would imagine he is scowling. He has been doing that a lot lately. There are rumors swirling around the internet that he's dating Serena, the girl who sings "Call Me From the Darkness" with him. I wouldn't be surprised if the rumors are true. She is also absolutely gorgeous and almost the same height as Derek. They make a striking pair when standing beside each other.

Serena's a solo act and goes by just the one name onstage. She doesn't need the rest; she puts on a hell of a show herself. I enjoy listening to her songs. She has a bit of an edge to her songs. I'd classify her as rock, the same as Crave. Some of her songs are great ballads. The one she does with Crave has a bit of a ballad feel to it, but my brother adds some awesome bass guitar to it, giving it more grit.

I hear my name being yelled, and it pulls me from my thoughts.

"Aud! Get out here!" Derek is shouting at me, motioning for me with his arms flailing wildly.

I nod and rise from the chair, then discard my white shorts and head down to the sand. He's watching me as I come toward him. I swear he bites his lip, and I hiss as the cool water hits my skin. I thought it would be warmer than it is, but I haven't been in yet this year, so how would I know? The water temperature that's posted on the boardwalk never really means much to me. I can't equate it to how the water will feel.

"Doesn't it feel nice?" he asks me when I reach him.

He's standing in waist-deep water, and I'm having trouble focusing on anything other than how the water is rolling down his chest.

"Why do you keep spacing on me, Aud? Is something going on I should know about?"

"I should ask you the same thing," I tell him.

He just sighs. "What's with you today? I keep talking to you and you don't respond."

Because I'm busy admiring you. "Sorry, just tired."

"You're busy being the dutiful daughter," he remarks. He's teasing me and I love the smile that is spread wide across his face.

I flush and hope he doesn't notice. "I guess so," I reply. I push the water back and forth with my hands and splash it up on my arms. It'll soon be time for more sunscreen. For just a second, a fantasy pops into my mind of Derek rubbing the sunscreen on my shoulders and making his way lower. It causes me to shiver despite the coolness of the water.

He's watching me and I love how he looks at me like he's really seeing me. There's a softness in his eyes that I haven't seen before. It makes my warm all over. We continue to stare at each other. It's not weird like I would have imagined it would be. He opens his mouth like he has something he wants to say to me. Like it's on the tip of his tongue, but the words aren't leaving his mouth. Instead, he pulls his lower lip between his teeth and hisses out a breath.

"Say what you wanna say," I challenge.

He smirks and dunks his body under the water. When he comes back up, he asks, "Why do you think I wanna ask you something?"

"The look on your face," I tell him.

He shrugs. "Well, I'm not sure what that would be."

I giggle and a wide smile crosses my face.

"What?" he asks. "What's that for?"

"I'm wondering something." I feel bold out here in the water.

"What are you wondering?" he asks in a playful tone.

"When does Serena arrive?" I wish I could snatch the question back as soon as it leaves my lips. He looks sad and a bit annoyed with me. I ruined our moment.

"Do you see any camera crews around here, Audrey?" There's bitterness in his tone. Gone is the playful boy that was here a few moments ago.

"No," I reply lamely.

"Then you won't be seeing her." He dunks down into the water and swims a few paces away from me.

"So, it's an act?" I call after him.

He swims toward me. "Her people called my people and thought it would be good for the song. So, we pretended like we were together."

"Oh" is all I say.

"Yeah, oh."

"I had no idea."

"It's the magic of show business, Aud. No one really cares for anyone." His tone is full of malice. I can't tell if he's upset that it was all a ploy or just annoyed by it.

"Do you like her?"

He laughs. "Oh yeah, she's a fucking delight."

I just stare at him, waiting for him to give me more.

"Serena has been around a while. Her parents are actors."

I already know that, but I like the fact that he's letting me in. So, I listen to him.

"She's pretty spoiled and used to getting exactly what she wants. Serena has been handed everything that she has because of who her parents are. The fans eat her up, which helps. But Crave needed her more than she needed us. So here we are."

"I'm sorry," I say.

"It's okay. I just hate that I was the one that had to be used. I don't like playing their games and putting on a show. All I wanna do is play my music and have people enjoy it. The machine that is the music industry makes that so much harder than it has to be."

The vulnerability in his eyes makes me want to swim over to him and wrap him up in my arms. But I've never really touched Derek like that. Sure, there have been hugs on holidays or birthdays, but right here in this moment, it would feel too intimate, so I stay where I am.

"So yeah, Serena will not be coming to visit us." His voice

trails off, and he turns his back to me, looking out into the vast ocean.

"Where do you go at night?" I finally get up the courage to ask him.

"What do you mean?"

I smile because he's great at answering a question with a question. "When you leave the house, where do you go? You usually don't return until after two in the morning."

He nods, but he's still not facing me.

"I'm just out. Checking out some local places for music. Listening to the tunes and trying to get inspired." He turns and looks me dead in the eye and says, "You know, looking for my muse."

I freeze and watch him. I wonder if his last words were meant for me. Could I be his muse? I have serious doubts about that, but there's an insinuation in his voice that makes me think differently.

We're quiet for a bit. I watch the back of his head as he studies the horizon.

Finally, he turns around and says, "Alright, let's get you inside. We have to get some more sunscreen on you before you turn. You're looking about as hot as that swimsuit."

With that, he's off to the shore. But I can't stop replaying his words in my head. Derek Walsh thinks I'm hot. The thought brings me more happiness than it should. I don't second-guess it or overthink it in the water; I just paddle into the shore, staying close to Derek and hoping that when we reapply sunscreen, he'll be the one to rub it all over my shoulders, back, and maybe even my legs.

CHAPTER FOUR

Being at the beach for the day has made me sleepy. It always did when I was a kid, and right now is no different. I'm lying stretched out on the sofa, being lazy. My wet hair is fanned out over the back of it, and I'm in sweat shorts and a tank top, sans bra. I'm guessing Derek is gone for the night. It's only ten o'clock, but it is a Sunday, and the night life tends to quiet down early here in Corolla, even though it's summer.

"What are you watching?" His voice startles me from my thoughts, and I jump. A tiny squeak escapes my lips. "Easy there, fraidy cat. It's just me."

I flush and shake my head. "I know."

"Sure, you did," he says with a chuckle.

I turn my attention back to the TV to see what he was questioning. There are two detectives on the screen checking out a dead body. "It's *Criminal Minds.*"

"Ah, okay." He takes a seat on the sofa beside me.

I steal a glance over to see he's sitting beside me in a pair of gray sweatpants. I've seen him like this before but being here alone with him in the beach house is having an odd effect on me. It could just be because it's been month's since I've been touched by a man. My libido is going crazy.

"Are you not headed out tonight?"

"Nope," he says, looking over at me.

I sit very still, like I'm afraid any sudden movements will cause him to know what it is I'm thinking.

I don't say anything for a few moments, wondering if he'll talk to me. But he doesn't. Eventually, I groan, stretching my legs out in front of me and finally causing him to speak.

"Stiff?" he asks.

"Yeah. I gotta get to bed soon. I plan on waking up early tomorrow, getting a workout in, and then working on the house again."

"Always the dutiful daughter," he says.

I want to ask him why he keeps saying that to me. A flick of irritation wells up in me. I'm not sure if it's because I know it's true or if it's because I'm irritated that my parents would never think to ask Aiden to come here. Although he could have, if Derek is here. But he wouldn't. It's a trivial task he would say he doesn't have time for. His music, his fans, his band—all of that is what's most important to him. Whether one of his band members is here is beside the point.

"Does Aiden know I'm here?" I ask him. The question has crossed my mind a few times.

"He knows. I talked to him the other day."

I raise an eyebrow. Not that he would be playing the overprotective brother because I'm here all alone with his hot bandmate. No, he wouldn't even consider that. I shake my head. "Of course, he wouldn't come here to help me."

"I think he's trying to give me some space," Derek admits.

"From what? Serena?" I ask.

"No, not Serena. The band knows that it's bogus. They were naturally jealous that I was picked to do it. She was interested in me, but she would have taken Aiden." He rolls his eyes.

I've turned my body so that I can face him through the shadows. "Well, she sounds just delightful," I say, a hint of sarcasm dripping from my words.

"Oh yeah, she's a real peach. Completely and totally bitchy. And do not get her drunk. Then she becomes super whiny and clingy and immature. I don't have time for that." He shakes his head and runs a hand though his hair, his muscles flex as they move with his arm.

I take a moment to gawk at the tattoos on his body. He has quite a few—a tribal symbol wrapped around his bicep on his left arm, some symbols and words on his left forearm, the word *Crave* down his right. All the band members have that same tattoo. They got them together once the band hit number one on the chart. I can't make out the words on his left pec. I swallow as my eyes keep exploring, but I don't get to finish.

Derek clears his throat. "Whatcha doing?"

I look over and he's smirking at me. I've been caught with my hand in the cookie jar.

"Just admiring your tattoos," I tell him.

"Admire away." He holds his hands out so that his chest is in full view.

"No, thank you," I tell him with a shake of my head.

He laughs at me. "Most girls would love to be in your shoes right now. An unimpeded view of my chest. Well, damn, they would particularly be creaming themselves thinking of it."

The crassness in his words causes me to flush all over. "Charming," I tell him, pretending to be annoyed. But instead, I'm more curious about him than anything.

I've known Derek almost my whole life, but something about the man in front of me, the one who is famous and has throngs of women screaming his name, feels different. There's more of an edge to him than there used to be. He doesn't want to be vulnerable with anyone except the boys from the band, and even that might get him called a pussy.

"Sorry, Aud. I don't mean to be an ass," he admits with a shrug.

"It's okay. I've gotten used to the way you boys speak. Remember, I've been around you a long time."

"Yeah," he says, then swallows audibly.

It's then I remember that I'm not wearing a bra. The air conditioning has been turned down since the warmth of the sunburn is heating my body. I had welcomed the cold air when I did it, but now it's making my nipples stand at attention.

Without thinking, I jut out my chest a bit more to give him a better view. He smirks at me, and my tongue darts out to lick my lips.

"Do you wanna do something?" he asks.

I have no idea what he's referring to, but a million dirty images flash through my mind. *God yes, I want to do something with you. I want you to climb on top of my body and ravish it. I want to place my hands all over the hard lines of your body.*

Instead, I reply with, "What do you have in mind?"

"Tattoos," he says plainly, like it's the most natural thing in the world for him to be asking me to do.

"Tattoos?" I ask him, making sure I heard him correctly.

"I have an appointment scheduled for tomorrow, up in the city. I bet he could fit you in too. Would you like to get a tattoo with me?"

"You mean like matching?" I ask him. The response is dumb, and I'm pretty sure I know the answer before the words slip from his lips.

"Uh, no, not matching. But I have this lightning bolt design he's going to do on my back. I thought maybe you'd like to come along and get some fresh ink."

I just nod, not really answering his question.

"Do you even have any tattoos?" he asks me.

"You know I do. Aiden and have I have a matching jellyfish." Mine is purple and sits on my hip. Aiden's is blue and green, mean looking, and on his calf. We were supposed to get them on the same place, but I wasn't as established as I am in my career now. I was afraid putting a tattoo in such a visible place could jeopardize my relationship with Beachbody.

"Ah, yeah, that's right. Do you have any others?" His voice

comes out low and sultry, like he's asking me an intimate question. And I guess in a way it is. Tattoos are an intimate part of someone, and they have very personal meanings to them.

"N-no," I stammer out.

"Would you like to get one with me?" he asks.

"What would I get?"

"Get anything you want. Get a music note for me, get a pretty little flower, get some waves to signify the house. Just come with me and get something."

I barely hear the rest of his suggestions because he told me to get something that signifies him. It makes my stomach do a little somersault.

"Why would I get something to symbolize you?" I ask him.

He just shrugs it off. "Does that mean you're going to do it?"

"Maybe," I reply.

"What's stopping you? Does your work not allow you to have them? Are they asking you to uphold some squeaky-clean image?"

I consider his words for a moment. They aren't making me uphold anything. It's more me than them. I want to make sure I look the way they want me to, so I'm not dropped. The Beachbody family has all kinds. But going and getting something like this done has always made me nervous. "Not that I know of," I final respond.

"Great, then it's settled. You'll come with me tomorrow," he says with a quick smile.

I get ready to protest, but all my mouth does is open and close. I can't find the words to tell him no. And I'm not sure I want to. Not the way he's looking at me right now. Like he could just take me and swallow me whole. I can see why the women are so memorized by him when he's on stage. He's downright charming and demanding. It's incredibly sexy.

The doorbell rings and it startles me. Derek just laughs. "That'll be my pizza." He pulls cash from his sweatpants and goes charging for the door. I can hear him faintly talking to the delivery person. "Don't tell anyone, will ya?"

The delivery person must have recognized him. I wonder how often that happens to him. I think back to the low-slung baseball cap on the beach and sigh. I should have offered to get the pizza.

"You okay? I ask him.

"Why wouldn't I be?"

"It sounds like that person recognized you," I explain.

"He did. But I'm pretty sure my big tip bought him off," he says with a chuckle. "Want some?" He opens the box, revealing a pizza that's fully loaded with veggies. "I even got veggies to make it healthy for you."

My stomach growls at the aroma filling the room. The bowl of fruit I had for dinner is certainly not cutting it. "I usually don't eat this late at night," I admit sheepishly.

"Come on, Audrey, you can't make me have a couch picnic all by myself," he tells me with a wink.

The pizza box is set between the two of us, and he sits cross-legged in front of it, ready to share.

I sigh, giving in. I move over closer to him and mirror his seating position, then grab a slice of pizza from the box. I groan when I take a bite. It tastes like heaven.

"See, this was a good idea," he teases, eating his own slice.

"Where is this from?"

"Georgio's," he replies.

I should have guessed. Every time my family and I were here, we always got Georgio's. It's tradition.

"Are your parents okay?" he asks me out of nowhere.

I wondered if this question was going to come up. He's a smart man. The beach house has meant so much to them, so it makes sense that he'd expect them to be selling it for than the reason of no one using it.

"You're perceptive," I say in return. I finish off my slice and go to reach for another, but he closes the box on me.

"Audrey."

"Are you going to hold the pizza hostage until I talk?"

"Maybe," he says before opening up the box. "I don't want you to tell me anything you're not ready to."

I should tell him. I should tell *someone*. God knows my parents aren't talking. I'm not even sure that Aiden knows yet. They've been keeping the secret until they see him in person.

"My dad has cancer," I say shakily. "Pancreatic cancer. I stumbled across that news on accident when I came home for a surprise visit. But I was the one who received the biggest surprise of all. I found my dad in the bathroom puking. My mom had run out for a bit, not expecting him to need her in her short trip to the store. So, I helped him back from the bathroom and into his bed on the sofa."

I swallow audibly. I hate that I've told Derek, because telling someone makes it real. I also hate that he found out before Aiden. It doesn't seem right that my brother is still in the dark. But living with this secret is tearing me up inside.

Derek is sitting frozen, staring at me, mouth agape. There's a heavy silence stretching between us, so I fill it with more thoughts from that awful day.

"He told me everything, and my whole world crumbled down around me. When you're a kid, your parents seem invincible. But not anymore. Now this horrible disease is destroying my father's body and taking the only man away from me who promised to love me forever. Now, I carry the burden of being the only twin who knows. My mother was upset when I discovered the secret they had been keeping. She didn't want us to know just yet, but I think they were in denial. Like they thought the more people they told, the more it would become a reality. And now it has. And I'm pretty sure there's not much they can do. He's fighting, and they are trying, but..." I can't even say the words.

"You're not going to tell him?" Derek asks. "He'll know as soon as he sees you. It'll be written all over your face. You two have always had that psychic twin thing happening."

"I know, but they asked me not to. I have to keep my word and make sure he doesn't find out," I say quietly. "But he will soon."

He gets up without warning and comes over to my section of the sofa. Strong arms wrap around me and haul me into his chest. All I can smell is Derek. He smells like the sun and a woodsy musk that must be his cologne. I take a moment to breathe him in, but he must mistake it for tears.

"It's gonna be okay, Audrey. It's going to be okay," he keeps repeating.

I wanna ask him how, but I don't want to be a jerk to him when he's being sweet. We both know there's probably nothing they can do for my dad. But nonetheless, the words bring me some comfort.

"We're getting tattoos tomorrow. You get something for him, and I'll get something for you," he says.

"You'll get something for me? Why?"

"Something in solidarity, to remind you of your strength. Something to remind me that I'm your sole corrupter," he says with a chuckle. I can feel the vibrations in his chest when he laughs.

"The corruptor of me?" I ask him, trying to remember back to our childhood together. I don't think he corrupted me. I was just one of the boys.

"Here I am, with you for only a few days, and I've got you getting a tattoo and eating pizza at this late hour."

"You don't have to do that," I tell him. The gesture is so sweet. It makes me uncomfortable because I don't like people making a fuss of performing grand gestures for me. But I also feel honored that he would want to have a permanent reminder of me on his body.

"I want to. It'll be an homage to you and Aiden. You know, like some badass sea thing or something. An homage to all the times we've spent here on this beach. How much you both saved me over the years."

I smile. "I think that's really sweet."

"When are they telling him?" he asks me.

"I'm not sure. Soon, I think. I hope. I told them they have two weeks to tell him, or I will."

Derek gets up and heads back over to his side of the couch. He opens his mouth to say something and then snaps it shut. He repeats the action again and again. I can't see his eyes, but I'm betting his brow is furrowed.

"Damn, you think some people are invincible, but they're not."

"No, they're not," I say, swallowing the lump that has settled in my throat. "He's my father. I just assumed he would always be there. He's so young. This shouldn't be happening."

The words come out a jumbled mess, but I say them anyway. The thoughts have been weighing on my mind a lot lately. Derek has been a distraction—ogling him has been taking my mind off it. The thought makes me smile.

"What?" he asks me. "What put such a big smile on your face?"

I chuckle. I can't tell him the truth. "Just a memory of all of us being here like this."

We finish our pizza picnic in a comfortable silence, then I head off to bed.

"Don't forget tomorrow, he calls after me as I head down the hall. "I'm getting your ass inked."

"Okay," I reply, replaying his words over and over again in my head as I get ready for bed.

CHAPTER FIVE

We arrive early for our appointments. I would have rather shown up just in time, but Derek has this weird thing about being early everywhere he goes. He has since we were kids. I'm never late, but he takes early to a whole new level. Our appointments aren't for another twenty-five minutes, but here we are anyway, in Inked Men and waiting on Derek's buddy Rooster to be ready to tattoo us. I asked him what Rooster's real name is and he just laughed at me.

The shop was about two hours away from the house. Back in the city just to get tattooed.

"How did you hear about this place?" I ask him.

"I've been coming here for years. Rooster has done all my ink. If I can't get to him, I bring him to me." He says it so naturally while I stand there gaping at him with my mouth open. "What?"

"I didn't know tattoo artists did that," I stammer.

"If you pay them enough, they will. And once you find someone who does a great job on your ink, you gotta stick with them."

"What is it that you like so much about this one?"

"His fine line work is amazing." Derek leans over so that our shoulders are touching. He drops his tone real low and says, "So tell me, Audrey, where are you getting your tattoo? Do you have to hide them for shoots?"

His tone sends a shudder throughout my body. I swear he must feel it, because he snickers while I struggle to find the words to tell him.

"No, I think I can pretty much get it wherever." The words come out dirtier than I meant them too. I love the way his eyes widen when I say them. Like he caught some double meaning I didn't even realize I was slipping in.

"Where are you thinking?" His voice comes out like velvet. If we're playing some kind of flirty game with word play, it's lost on me. But I feel it.

"My ribs," I reply, then I lick my lips. He watches the motion, and I swear his chocolate orbs darken. Or maybe I'm dreaming. Either way, if I'm having an effect on Derek Walsh, I'm here for it.

"Nice." The words come out a whisper. He swallows audibly, his Adam's apple bobbing up and down. "Are you wearing the right bra?"

"Huh?" The word slips lamely out of my mouth.

"Aud, if you're getting your ribs tattooed, Rooster is going to need access to them. You'll most likely have to remove your top," he explains like he's talking to someone who is impaired.

"Oh," I say, grasping his point. "Will you be in the room?"

"Of course. Unless you request I go, I wouldn't leave you in there alone." He squeezes my thigh once, his arm brushing my nipples, which harden as he moves his arm across my body. "Rooster's a good guy, though. You don't have to worry."

I just nod.

"Don't be nervous," Derek continues. "He'll take good care of you and so will I. We'll get our tattoos and then we'll head over and get some breakfast."

"It'll be after lunch when we're done here." I'm not sure why

I feel the need to correct him about the appropriateness of a meal, but I do.

"Breakfast for dinner was always one of your favorites. Did that change?"

I smile at him remembering something so simple about me. He's known me most of my life. I shouldn't be this surprised that these kinds of details haven't slipped his mind. But he's gotten quite the fan base, and girls are literally throwing themselves at him, so why would my life's details matter to this man?

"No, it didn't change."

"Good."

We're both quiet while we wait for Rooster to be ready for us. Suddenly, a man appears before us. "Hey, dude."

He looks nothing like I expected him to. There's a swirl of color covering both arms, disappearing under his plain white T-shirt and up his neck. His legs have ink on them as well, even trailing up his shorts. He's bald, with a few earrings in his ears. There's a bullring through his nose, and he looks like he dwarfs me in size.

I slowly rise and make my way over to this large man. I remind myself over and over again that Derek wouldn't do anything that would cause me harm. He's got me, and this man does all of his ink, so I'm sure I'm in good hands.

"Hey there, little one," Rooster says when I finally reach him.

My palms begin to sweat with fear of the pain. I only have the one tattoo, and I got that quite a while ago. "Hi," I finally mange to say.

Rooster laughs—probably at my timidness. "Is she old enough to get a tattoo?" he teases me, but he's looking at Derek.

"She is," Derek replies with a smile. He reaches out to squeeze my hand, and I hate that he can feel how sweaty my palm is.

"Let's get back to my station." He turns and heads into the back of the shop.

I follow along, my breath picking up as we make our way through. There are six bays in Inked Men. All of them have thick black curtains surrounding them, offering the clients privacy. I expect Rooster to lead us into one of those, but instead, he opens a door and gestures for us to go inside. It's all white and sterile looking. I can smell the alcohol from the equipment he surely just cleaned. The walls have a couple of posters of rock bands hanging on the wall. There's even one of Crave hanging in the center of the back wall. It makes me smile to see my boys on the wall of this shop.

"Really, dude?" Derek remarks, pointing out the poster I was just admiring.

"Hell yeah. All of you have been inked by me, so of course I'm gonna show off that poster. And it helps with the ladies too."

Derek rolls his eyes but doesn't say a word. It's clear he's fond of Rooster, but I wonder if it bothers him that someone else is using him to get something, just like Serena does.

"I have everything ready and drawn up for you, Derek. This lightning tattoo is going to look so sweet on your back." Rooster is pulling up the template he'll use to trace it out on Derek's skin, but Derek is shaking his head. Rooster frowns. "Did you change your mind? We've been plotting this one for months," Rooster reminds him, apparently confused by Derek's sudden change of tone.

"Look, I need you to do something special for me. I need some waves and a shark fin right here." He pulls up his shirt and displays his impressive physique. He's pointing to his left pec. There's already a verse written there, but I guess he's going to keep filling it up. "It's important," Derek tells him.

"Okay. Whatever you say, man. What about you?" He gestures toward me.

"Rib tattoo," Derek tells him.

"Of?" Rooster asks me pointedly. "You're gonna have to talk to me, sweetheart. I don't bite."

I flush at being called out for my shyness. "I'd like a wave similar to his, with three little hand-drawn fish."

"Three?" Derek asks.

"Aiden, you, and me," I tell him plainly. "I wanna remember those summers."

"Who is going first?" he asks.

"She is," Derek replies. "We don't want you chickening out if you have to wait."

Rooster laughs, starting to leave the room. "Okay, give me a few minutes to get something drawn up. Make yourselves at home."

Once we're alone, Derek turns to me. "It'll be fine, Audrey."

"I know it will be, and it'll be worth it. Just nerves," I say, lying down on the table. I'm glad I went for comfortable today. I've got a white crop top on and black biker shorts with flip-flops.

Derek's outfit reminds me a bit of Rooster's. He's wearing a white T-shirt and black sweat shorts. I wonder if when you have tattoos, you dress plainly so those are the star of your outfit. I stare up at the white ceiling, where there's a mural of lightning and motorcycles. I chuckle at the sight of it.

"What?" Derek looks up from his phone and watches me with raised brows.

"Just thinking about how gynecologists doesn't have things like this on their ceilings."

Derek smirks and shakes his head. "I bet not."

We're quiet for a while, waiting for Rooster to return with our designs. Finally, the door clicks open, and Rooster enters.

"Lose the shirt," he tells me.

Despite being so shy and timid by the nearness of the attractive man in the room with me, I'm used to having my shirt off and being just in a sports bra. Most of my shoots are done in just a bra and leggings. It leaves nothing to the imagination. I toss the shirt off and, feeling bold, throw it at Derek. His eyes widen, but he catches it. Rooster chuckles.

"Alright, honey girl, lie down."

I do as I'm told and wait for the buzzing to start.

"Just try to relax," he tells me. "This won't be a piece of cake, but it's not the worst spot to get tatted."

He starts up the gun, gets it loaded up with ink, and then presses it to my skin. It feels like more than a pinch, but he gets underway.

"How do you know Derek?" Rooster asks me.

"Rooster," Derek warns.

I giggle.

"Don't move," Rooster commands.

I flush at the correction. "We sort of grew up together. I'm Aiden's twin sister." He said he's done work on all the guys, so I'm assuming that includes my brother.

"Oh, yeah. Now I see the resemblance." He looks at me for a moment and then winks. "I never knew Ace had a twin sister," he mutters as he continues to prick away at my skin.

I flinch a bit and try to not to think about it. I distract myself as best I can by staring at the posters that adorn the walls and looking for shapes in the textured ceiling.

"So, you and Serena, man..." Rooster comments with a snicker. "She's a hot piece of ass."

"Fuck you," Derek says, punctuating his words with a middle finger in Rooster's direction. He pushes his hat down over his eyes and slumps lower in his chair.

"Guess he's done talking to me," Rooster remarks.

"I'll talk to you when it's my turn in the chair and you're not being an asshole."

More snickers erupt from Rooster, and he turns his attention to me. "So, brother is a bass player. What does little sister Audrey do?"

"How do you know I'm the little sister?" I ask.

"Lucky guess," he tells me.

"I'm a fitness instructor."

"I can see that." His eyes lazily take in my body as he laughs.

"Knock it off." Derek's tone is sharp, but it only causes

Rooster to laugh some more. "I'm only pretending to sleep, but I'm not deaf."

Rooster ignores him. "What do you do, work in a gym or something?"

"I train clients either in gyms or out of my home, and then I'm also on Beachbody with a couple of fitness programs that anyone can do anytime they want. I have a few smaller classes up there too."

"Nice. Good for you." He's quiet for a bit, concentrating. He already has the waves done, and soon he'll be working on the fish. "Would you like me to shade those waves?"

I stare at my arm, not sure what to say. I haven't really thought this tattoo through as thoroughly as I normally would have. "Uh…"

Derek rises from the chair and looks at the ink on my ribs. "Yeah, shade them. Sorry, Aud, this part is going to be kind of painful, but it'll be worth it in the end."

He's right. When I'm all done and bandaged up, the pain was worth it. I really like Rooster's work, although I had a feeling I would based on what Derek had said about him.

Derek is now in the chair, ready to get inked. I study his chest and his hard, toned stomach. His whole body is a work of art, not just the tattoos he has but all those muscle and lines. He clears his throat, and our eyes meet. Derek snickers.

Great. Caught ogling him yet again.

Derek's eyes stay on me the whole time he's getting a tattoo. He stares at me so intently that my mind starts to play tricks on me. I think the look in his eyes is lust, and maybe the foolish way I've been feeling at him catching me staring at him was all for nothing. That he realized I have this stupid little crush on him and that it's okay because he feels it too. Just as those thoughts are going through my mind, Derek winks at me. Like he can read my mind and he's agreeing with everything I'm thinking and feeling. I clench my thighs together. I'm getting wet from just one look.

I bite my lip to keep from saying or even doing something stupid.

Rooster breaks the silence with some stupid conversation about Serena, and the spell is broken. His eyes may be focused on me, but that look is gone. He's busy bristling over the shit Rooster is giving him for dating Serena.

"Tell me something though, man. Is she really as vapid as she seems?" Rooster asks, pausing the gun over his pec for a moment.

Derek just shrugs. I think it pains him that he can't come clean about the lie. But with the way his life is, you never know who's listening, and I have a feeling that while Derek may like Rooster, he's not sure how much of his confidence would be kept. So, Derek keeps up the lie in front of him and steers Rooster to other topics, like the rescheduling of the lightning tattoo.

Once our tattoos are done, we make our way up to the counter. I go to pull my card out to pay, but Derek stops me.

"I made you get this, so my treat." He hands Rooster a black card, and he immediately runs it. I don't even have time to protest.

"Thanks," I say.

"You two have a great day," Rooster says as he hands Derek the card back. "Enjoy your time together." He winks at us like he knows. Like he's been let in on our little secret and is dying to torture Derek with it later.

"See ya, man." Derek takes my hand and leads me out of the parlor.

"Thank you," he says when we're out on the street. He kisses my hand. "This was perfect."

I don't want to say anything stupid and ruin the moment, so I stay silent. He leads me to his black Jeep, and we're off to find breakfast at two in the afternoon.

CHAPTER SIX

My muscles are exhausted from a long day of clearing out closets and boxing up items that are personal to my family. I wish someone else was doing this work. But at the same time, I don't want someone else going through all my memories and deciding what gets kept or tossed. I just don't want this to be something I have to do. I don't want this to be my new reality. But here we are.

Sitting on the hardwood floor sorting through our memories is not only starting to take a toll on my mind but my body too. I pull out a box that was way in the back of the closet and pull the lid off it, unprepared for what I find inside.

Finding all our old sand toys causes my heart to squeeze in my chest. It's silly to get upset over sand toys, but my mind flashes back to a time when we were all on the beach—Mom, Dad, Aiden, and me. I sniffle, blinking at the tears I hadn't realized were escaping down my cheeks. I hear a noise behind me and rapidly begin wiping at my face.

"Audrey," Derek says, making his way over to the closet. "You okay?"

"Yeah, I'm fine. Just clearing this out." My voice is shaky, so he probably knows I'm anything but okay. I hope that he just goes on with whatever it was he was going to do. It's late after-noon, so I'm not sure if he's headed out already or just going to the beach.

He doesn't leave, though. His footsteps continue in my direction.

"Audrey," he says again.

I freeze and will him away from me. It doesn't work.

"Look at me, please."

I shake my head. "I'm fine."

Derek lowers himself to the floor and sits beside me. There's not a lot of space where I'm at, so our knees are touching. "Talk to me." His voice is low, quieter than it needs to be, given that we're the only two in the house.

I look over at him and attempt to smile. "What do you want me to say?"

It's a lame attempt at humor and sees right through it.

"Talk to me. Tell me what's got you so upset."

"Nothing."

"You're crying," he says, reaching his hand over and wiping a tear from my cheek.

I wipe at my cheeks with both hands and then show him the box. "Sand toys. I found sand toys in the closet, and it upset me."

"Oh, Aud," he says, pulling me in close. "Come here."

"It's silly. I know it is." I sniffle.

"No, it's not silly. You're packing up a lot of memories. I'd be worried if none of them upset you."

"Really?" I ask him.

"Yeah," he replies, "Come here. Let me hold you."

I freeze, unsure what to do. I don't know that I can handle being this close to him. The toys shrave me so upset that I know if someone touches me or hugs me like that, the tears will come faster. I don't want to break into uncontrollable sobs.

"I'm not going to do that," I tell him, my voice shaking again.

"Please let me help you. I know I haven't been much help

getting this place boxed up, but I'd like to help you now, when I think it counts."

I glance over and see his shoulders are slumped, his eyes frantically searching mine.

"The sand toys are from when we were little," I say quietly. "I hadn't seen them in years. It was the fourth of July, and we entered a kids sandcastle building contest. Dad had run out that morning and picked up some new shovels, buckets, and molds because he said we needed to be prepared. I remember my mom pretending to be annoyed by the whole thing, mostly because we already had a million sand trinkets and definitely didn't need any more." I sniffle and push away some more tears, and his arms wrap around me tighter. "We went out there and worked for hours together, just the four of us. It was blazing hot that day. There were so many trips into the water to cool off, but we never gave up."

"And you won," Derek finishes for me.

I laugh. "No, we didn't win. We actually came in third, I think. But it didn't matter. We all worked together, laughing, and having fun. My dad would chase us around and spray us with water. My mom made us snacks and helped where she could. She wasn't the best with building castles out of sand, but neither were me or Aiden. That's probably why we lost."

"Sounds like a great day," Derek replies.

"It was." The lump in my throat grows until a fresh sob breaks free, and I let go for the first time since I arrived at the house.

Derek moves swiftly, holding me close. I fall apart in Derek's arms. He does his best to soothe me, rocking me back and forth.

"It's okay, Audrey. It's okay. I'm here. And somehow—I don't know how—but it's going to be okay. I'm here." He keeps repeating that he's here, and I cling to those words like a beacon in the night. They're enough for me.

I'm not sure at what point I stop crying, but he's still sitting here with me on the floor, arms wrapped around me. I pull back slightly. "Thank you, Derek."

"You're welcome. If I could, I'd do anything to take this pain away from you."

I shrug. "It's your pain too. He loves you too."

"That he does." He smiles at me and pushes a stray hair from my face. "I haven't been much help lately, so let me do this for you. Let me pack up this closet. You go sit and relax for a bit. I can take care of this one for you."

"Thanks," I mumble, standing up on shaky legs.

"Look, I'm not going to tell you that he's going to be okay from all this, because we don't know. But just know that you don't have to go through this alone. I'll be with you every step of the way. That much I can promise you."

I offer him a weak smile. "I'm glad you're here."

"Me too."

I move and stretch my sore muscles, then head into my room and close the door. Placing my body against it, I listen to the sounds of Derek packing the box for the next several minutes.

Then his cell phone rings in the quiet of the house. I hear him move down the hallway and enter Aiden's room. I freeze and move myself off my bed and over to the wall where our rooms are connected. I wonder if he'll head out for the night again. It's early for that, but who knows; maybe he has further to travel tonight. It's only been a few days of him being here, but I'd love to know where he goes and what he does. Part of me thinks that's stupid because I might not want the answer. My heart might not be able to take it—the same way it ripped in two when I found out he might be an item with Serena. His denial of it, though, sewed it back up and made me whole again. I'm not sure how much more ripping my heart can take when it comes to Derek. Maybe it's time to let childhood crushes die. He might never want me as much as I want him.

I can just barely hear him greet someone on the phone through the wall. From what I can hear from his side of the call, it doesn't take me long to figure out he's talking to the guys.

"I'm working on it, okay?" he says.

The tone of his voice has an edge to it, and he's rapping his knuckles on every surface in the room, I think. He's unsettled. I hear the creak of the floorboards and wonder if he's pacing. I can almost picture him running a hand through his hair.

"I've tried that. It's not working." He chuckles before adding, "I'm not like you, Ace. I can't just find some random person and hook up with her right now."

I smile at the start of his sentence, but by the end, I'm cringing. *Right now?* So previously he could? And apparently my brother can do that now. That's a disturbing thing to learn about your twin brother. I sink onto my bed and go back to listening. He's saying something about Serena. Of course, that would be the reason that hooking up with random girls would be the problem. If anyone ever found out, saw them, or took pictures, it would be a media shitstorm.

I've noticed there has been some speculation on gossip news sites and the Reddit feeds about where Derek is. Serena has been out doing her thing, promoting her new album. Everyone keeps assuming that Crave will be a surprise guest at one of her shows to sing the duet. I've wanted to ask him more about her, but she's been a touchy subject for him. I can't say that I blame him. And I can't explain the relief I felt when I found out that it was all a hoax.

I've texted Emma a few times about Derek being here. She knows all about my little crush on him, but she figured that out long ago. Apparently, I'm about as subtle as a gun when I like someone. But he has never picked up on it, oddly enough. Or maybe he has, and he just doesn't feel the same way. Maybe he's being a gentleman and not embarrassing me. Emma keeps reminding me that he's with Serena and I'm setting myself up for heartbreak. I know that. The thing with Serena may not be true, but there's no way someone like Derek would want to be with me. He could have anyone he wanted. And the thing is, even presented with the chance, I'm not sure the person he wants is me.

"Well, I don't know what you want me to say!" Derek yells. "We're going to go back to LA for *The Late Show*. I've already promised that and I'm not backing out. Right now, I just need to write a song and we need to make it bigger than that fucking song, so I don't have to do this anymore."

There's silence in the room, where the guys must be talking to him now.

"She calls all the time. I barely ever pick up, though. The last time I did, she told me how people are screaming at her shows for her to play the damn song."

He sounds defeated. The guys must be pushing him to take part in the media circus surrounding Serena and his supposed relationship.

"Does she have a show near where I'm at now?"

I cringe at the idea of the two of them together. Nothing has happened between us, just a few glances and a brush of the hand or two. But I've liked the time we've spent together, here in our little beach bubble. He's still heading out at night, and I'm more of homebody. I don't like going out into crowded bars or smoke-filled rooms. I fall asleep every night hoping that when I wake, he'll be home and alone. So far, so good.

"I guess we could arrange something with that. I can call her and talk to her tomorrow. From what I remember, she's playing right now."

More silence in the room.

"No, man, it's fine. I know, I know. I want to capitalize on this too, I do. I just hate that it involves me pretending to me something I'm not. But we'll make it work. We always do."

He taps the wall a few times, causing me to jump. I wonder for a second if he knows I'm listening to him. And if so, does he care? I move farther away from the wall and hope that he hasn't figured it out.

"Thanks. I'll get in touch with her tomorrow and then get back to you all. It would be great if you guys came out anyway. I think Audrey could really use some help packing and fixing up this house. Unfortunately, I'm shit at helping her with this stuff. Maybe if we're all here pitching in, things would get done faster."

My heart squeezes at the thought that he's worried about all the things I have to do. I do wish he would help me, but I don't want to push him. I know he's here trying to get some new songs written for the album. Trying like hell to write one that's a bigger hit than the one he sings with Serena. When I'm cleaning out a closet or working on boxing up all the memories, he's strumming on his guitar. I know he's working, and I don't want to bother him, so I keep my mouth shut. Besides, boxing up all this stuff and preparing the house for sale is hard enough. I don't want someone like Derek Walsh watching me do it. There are constantly tears in my eyes as I place all of our precious memories into boxes, and the ache in my chest grows more and more each day as I consider a world that may not include my father.

"Things are going to get done, okay?" The annoyance from earlier is back in his tone. "I already agreed to sing that fucking song with her. I'm not sure what else you'd like me to do."

More rapping on the wall next to my ear. I wonder what that's about. Is it a nervous tic or is he mad and trying not to punch the wall? I'm betting it's the punching-wall thing.

"It usually doesn't. There are no distractions. I just can't focus. But I'll get it done. I always do," he reminds them. "You're just going to have to wait a little bit longer. I think maybe if you came out here, that would add in some pressure."

He pauses. "I suggested that you come out here to help Aud." Another pause. "Sure, yeah, just do it. And I'll do my best to have something ready for you to lay some cords onto." One last pause. "Yeah, we will. See you guys."

He gets quiet now, and I hear him kick the wall. I feel bad for Derek. I know he's under a lot of pressure. But right now, I'm hoping his kick didn't add another task to the list of things to call the local Mr. Fix It to come take care of. I'm not handy enough to do any more than painting, and Derek isn't either. Plus, I know he has his own stuff that he's supposed to be doing, so I don't want to bother him with the trivial shit.

I decide it's best if I'm not in my room when he comes out. I'd rather be in a common area of the house so I can talk to him. He sounds like he could use a friend, and I'd like to be that friend. I grab my book from the bedside table and head out to the living room. Flopping down on the couch, I open my book and pretend to be engrossed in it until footsteps echo down the hallway.

CHAPTER SEVEN

"I'm taking a walk down the beach," he says as he peeks his head into the living room. He has a bottle of something with him as he storms out of the house.

"There's no alcohol allowed on the beach," I call after him, but he doesn't seem to care. "I better go find your ass and remind you," I mutter.

After finding my shoes, I follow him down the beach. He's just walking. The bottle he took with him must be in the canvas bag he has with him. His guitar is strung over his shoulder too. I think about turning around for a second because I know if he's writing he'll want some privacy. But against my better judgment, I follow.

It's not too far down the beach until it switches from public to private. We were one of the first houses that was built on this stretch of land, which is why he can access the public beach so easily. It's just over the broken-down bridge. I watch as he expertly makes his way over. In that instant, I know where he's headed. The first lifeguard tower is never occupied and certainly not at this time of night. We always used to come out here and play games of *never have I ever* with bottles of booze we were able to steal from my parents. Or that we had scored downtown from a visiting vacationer that didn't think twice about supplying a minor.

I make my over the abandoned bridge, careful not to step on any of the exposed nails or splintery pieces of wood that are sticking up. The city hasn't fixed it, and I'm guessing it's because no one is claiming ownership of it. The city argues that it's the private communities, and the community is saying it's city property. Either way, it's not getting fixed, and the bridge that I used to walk across and look out over the water on is in sad shape. It's not safe to be out there. I glance over at the opening and see that someone had the good sense to put a chain and 'stay out' sign across the entrance. You could easily go under it to access the bridge, but at least someone is trying.

He's making his way up the ramp, looking around as he goes. I chuckle to myself. Some things never change. It's the same thing we did as teenagers, or even in our early twenties when we just wanted some space—slipping inside the guard shack and disappearing. It'll be dark in there because the sun has almost set and there are no lights inside.

No swimming is allowed at night, or if you do, it's at your own risk, so no one ever really knew we'd come here. At least that was our thought. And it worked most of the time. Sometimes a random vacationer would be out there and yell us, not realizing we were locals and knew this town better than them.

Only once did an officer chase us all out of there. Derek, Aiden, and I ran into my dad as we were running up the deck steps to our house, a fit of giggles escaping us. He only wanted to know if he was going to have an officer coming to his door. I still remember Derek looking over at him and saying, "No, sir." Dad nodded and let us be. No officer showed up at our door, and Dad never talked about it again.

I make my way up the ramp, but there's no sound coming from inside. He's either still setting up or he hasn't gotten to the writing or singing part of the evening. I pull the door open slowly and see him cloaked in darkness, leaning against the back wall.

"Aud," he says, a hint of surprise in his voice.

"Hey." I come all the way in and take a seat on the side wall so that I have a side view of him and he of me.

"What are you doing here?" he asks me.

I can't see much in the dark shack, but I can see the bottle of alcohol between his feet.

"I thought you looked like you could use someone to talk to," I tell him.

"Ah, I see."

He doesn't say anymore; instead, he goes for the bottle. He unscrews the cap and takes a swig before wincing. I guess it burns, whatever it is.

"What are you drinking?"

He says nothing and just hands me the bottle. I take it and examine it. It's a decent bottle of whiskey. Not Jack Daniels, but the expensive shit I'm used to seeing my dad drink or order when we're out.

"Are you gonna take a sip?" he challenges.

I sigh. "I'm not much of a whiskey girl."

"What kind of a girl are you?"

I know he's only talking about booze, but for a moment, I pretend that he's asking me a different question. My stomach does a flip as I think of how I could cleverly answer this.

"What's your poison?" He asks the question a different way, I guess assuming the words went over my head.

"I like cocktails on occasion, and mixed drinks or seltzers." I can almost hear him roll his eyes at me. Derek Walsh is all hard lines and rough edges; he doesn't drink the same type of cocktails I do. No, there are no dirty martinis or Cosmo's in his future.

He laughs like I knew he would. "Take a sip, buttercup. It won't hurt you."

"I know," I stammer out.

"Drink or hand the bottle back," he orders.

"Are you going to tell me what's going on?"

"Drink and I will," he goads.

"I don't wanna get shit-faced," I tell him.

"Split a fifth with me, Aud. I need this."

There's a level of pleading and vulnerability in his words. I want to. I want to do a whole lot more than that with him, but that's not something he'd entertain. Especially tonight with the way he's feeling.

"Drink with me and I'll tell you all about my problems. After all, isn't that why you followed me out the door in the first place?"

"I wanna help," I tell him. Even though I can't see him, I can feel his eyes on me.

"I wanna drink. So, if you drink with me, I'll tell you all about the problems that the ever-popular lead singer of Crave is having."

His words come out bitter, and I can tell that all of that has him fucked up. Not like, *Oh, woe is me. It's hard being a lead singer with all the girls that want me.* But more like, *Things aren't easy right now.* And I know all about that.

"Fine, I'll drink with you." I unscrew the cap of the bottle and take a sip. The liquid is smooth all the way down. I swallow and appreciate the woodsy taste of it.

"See, it's not so bad as long as you don't chug it," he remarks. Must have been why I heard the wince in the air after his sip. "Bottle," he orders, snapping his fingers.

I hand it back over and he takes another sip, then I wait for a bit. The bottle is passed back and forth at least five times before I have the courage to speak again. The liquor is making me feel all warm inside and making my tongue a little looser.

"Okay, out with it. Lead singer of Crave, what is ailing you?"

He laughs at my choice of words but then sighs. "I can't seem to find anything good to write about. The boys are hoping that me coming out here meant I was taking a break and getting some real writing done. They want to put out another album. And believe me, I do too. But Aiden needs the words so he can work up the arrangement."

"Your new album hasn't been out that long."

"No, it hasn't." He takes a sip before adding, "But you don't wait a year before putting out more workouts after you complete one, do you?" The bottle is passed to me, and his fingers brush mine. "Slide closer," he orders me. "I'm getting kind of fucked up here, and I don't want to drop it."

"Then maybe we should stop," I suggest.

"I just want the music and the words to be good, you know? I know that everyone thinks I'm with Serena. I can't do anything about that now. But I want a song or an album that's bigger than that so I can come out of the shadow of the lie. I want to be able to say to her, 'No I can't come to that, we're promoting our own album.'"

"Is there anything I can do?"

"Do you wanna be my inspiration?" He's teasing me. It's either the alcohol making him seem a bit lighter, or talking is helping. My money is on the alcohol. He's not passing it very fairly, and Derek has had more sips than me.

"Would that help you?" I ask him.

"Little Audrey, always wanting to be the one helping every-one," he says with a bit of edge.

"Yeah," I say sadly. I hate that people see me that way. I don't want to be this Little Miss Handle Everything. But those are the roles Aiden and I have been cast with. He gets to go out in the world and explore because he has responsibilities to the band. Ones that are greater than mine. And I'm forced to help clean up messes and hide dark family secrets.

"Sorry, I didn't mean to say that." His tone is low and apolo-getic. If I could see him right now, I imagine his eyebrows are furrowed in concern or guilt.

"It's okay. It's the truth." I shrug it off. Rising for the first time since we've been drinking, I stumble forward. "Woah!" I yell before falling forward.

I crash into him. In his drunk state, he does his best to catch me, but we're just a tangle of arms.

"Ouch," I say, a pain in my knee registering.

"You good?" he asks with a chuckle.

"Just knocked my knee on the ground," I tell him, laughing a bit too.

I go to move, but he's holding onto me. His hands are on my shoulders, and I'm holding myself up because if I weren't, I'd be lying on his chest. I want that more than anything. I can see the new tattoo on his chest, and I remember the way I felt watching him get it. His eyes were locked with mine the whole time the waves and shark fin were inked on his chest.

"More whiskey will cure all that ails you," he says.

"It just might." We lock eyes, and I bite my lip, wondering what he would do if I placed my lips on his.

He clears his throat, and the next sentence comes out low and sexy. "I think you better get some, then. It'll make you feel better."

I want to pretend that he's not talking about the whiskey and dive in, but I don't. I sit down beside him so that our knees are almost touching and take a swig from the bottle.

"Maybe you're overthinking it," I tell him.

"What?" His head swivels in my direction. "What am I over-thinking?"

"The writing of the songs. It's great to have a goal or some-thing that you're working toward. But I think you're putting too much pressure on the songs to be great. Maybe you should just relax a bit. Have some fun."

"With you?"

I swallow audibly—I swear the whole beach can hear it. I have the worst case of cotton mouth right now. Any words I want coming out of my mouth are getting caught. Which is probably good because I'm not one to always have a filter. I'm afraid what I would say to him right now, buzzed on whiskey with my libido going crazy at the nearness of him.

I settle for a nod.

"Audrey, are you saying you want to have some fun with me?" He must have been unable to see the nod of my head, or he wants me to say the words.

"I am."

"I think I would like that very much," he replies. "What did you have in mind?"

"We should go jet skiing. Or the carnival is getting ready to come into town. We could go to that together, like old times," I tell him, bumping his shoulder. Although I hope it won't be like old times because that would mean trailing around after him, watching all the girls hit on him. It would mean pretending not to care or being out there looking for someone to hang out with too. Although, my pursuit of a guy was always useless. Aiden and Derek would scare anyone away if they tried talking to me. My parents would yell at them for it, but secretly, they were glad they did.

"Just like old times. Do we need Aiden down here too?"

"I was hoping to have you all to myself for once." The words spill out, and I want to snatch them back up. I freeze and await his reaction.

There's something in his tone I can't quite place, an emotion of longing or happiness. Or maybe I just want there to be so that I'm not the only one attempting to play with fire. "I like that idea."

"You seem to be saving me in more ways than one this summer, Audrey," Derek says, returning my shoulder bump.

"How am I saving you?" I stammer out the words.

"You're making it more bearable. And I forgot about how good it is to just sit and talk to you. It helps."

I flush, thankful he can't see me doing it. "I'm glad to be of service." The words come out all sultry, and I laugh once I hear them.

Derek just chuckles. "I wasn't aware this was a full-service summer."

I don't dare say a word, because I know no matter what I say right now, he'd probably reject it. He didn't actually mean that he would kiss me, let alone let me service him. But man, after ogling his chest while he got inked and staring at him on the beach, I can feel my self-control wavering. I hear him take another swig of the bottle.

"We should get you back soon before I have to carry you," I tell him.

"I guess we should."

"Unless we're sleeping here," I tease, remembering the night when we were teenagers that we all camped out in one.

"Nah, I'm too old to sleep on this hard floor." Derek stands and extends a hand to me. I take it, and he gently pulls me to my feet. "Let's get back."

I follow him out of the shack and down the beach. Derek keeps his hand in mine the whole way. I relish the feel of his hand in mind. I think it's the buzz he has going on. Or maybe he feels like I'll fall over if he doesn't have a hold on me. That might be true, but this buzz is less from the whiskey and more from the nearness of him.

Derek keeps my hand all the way inside the house. It's not until we're at the hallway where both of our rooms are that he drops it.

"I love you, Aud." The words are the only sound in the quiet house.

I want to think this means more than it does, but when you've known each other as long as we have and spent so many summers together, those words have been said a time or two. And not in the way I wish he would.

"Love you too, Derek," I tell him.

He turns and heads down the hallway.

"So differently than you do me, though," I whisper into the

quiet of the house, knowing full well that my voice was too low and he's too drunk to have heard me.

"Aud." His head pops back out into the hallway.

"Yes?" I squeak out, wondering how he could have possibly heard me.

"You working out tomorrow?"

"Uh...y-yeah," I stammer.

"Great. Well, since it's going to be a rough morning, why don't we do it together?" He flashes me that panty-dropping, million-dollar smile I've seen directed at fans a million times.

I melt.

"Sure, that would be great. See you at seven."

"Seven it is." And then he's gone.

I make my way to my room and throw myself onto the bed. It's only a little after one, but he's right. It'll be rough getting up tomorrow, and maybe more so now that I know I'll be working out with Derek. It's something we've done a million times, but lately, keeping my wits about me is proving to be harder than I thought.

CHAPTER EIGHT

I walk out into the kitchen, dressed and ready for my workout. I wonder if my workout buddy will be here waiting for me.

He is, leaning against the counter holding a cup of coffee in his heads. "I know I shouldn't. Not right before I work out. But I need it. My head is kind sore." He shrugs apologetically.

I wave him off. "Don't worry about it. I'm planning on having some iced coffee too." I reach into the fridge and pull out the Starbucks caramel iced coffee from the fridge. "My head is a little sore too."

"You're not an old pro at passing around a fifth?" he teases.

I chuckle. "No, I'm not."

He watches me as I pour some coffee into the glass I retrieved from the cabinet. "What's on the docket for today's workout, coach?" His tone is playful, almost mocking me. But I kinda like it. "Am I supposed to call you coach? Are you a coach? Are you *my* coach?"

I don't miss the dip in his voice. It makes me flush.

"Sorry, I'm not trying to embarrass you," he says with a chuckle, turning his attention back to his coffee.

"No, you're fine. You can call me coach. Most of my clients just call me Audrey. I'm not a coach or anything, though. That makes me sound like some kind of weight loss coach, and you certainly don't need that." My eyes linger too long on his body. He's wearing a black tank top and gray running shorts. The fabric of that tank top is already clinging to his body. What I wouldn't give to trade places with it.

"I guess I don't." He watches me closely. "Do you do a lot of that?"

"Not really. I do some with the Beachbody platform because they have a dietary program I have to promote with each of my workout programs. But I really just preach moderation, you know? It's easier on everyone. It's hard for me to take on weight loss clients because I'm so busy training members of the North Caroline Courage, either as a team or individually. But I do consult when I'm asked to. It's kind of a fine line I have to walk with Beachbody, so I do what they ask of me but never anything more."

He nods in response to my rambling. I realize that I gave him more details than I needed to. I usually do that. Sometimes I can be a bit of nervous talker, and I guess this is one of those moments. Standing here in this kitchen with him isn't something I haven't done before during all those summers we spent together here as teens. It's been a while, though, and maybe that's why I ramble.

"So, what type of workout are we going to be doing today?" he asks. "Are you taking me on a run?"

I watch him for a second before answering. I've been contemplating that since I woke up this morning. I don't want to run him again. We've already done that. "Let's do some light cardio and then look at some core exercises and maybe some strength training."

"I didn't bring a weight bench."

"I have core balls."

"Oh, do you now?"

I laugh at the inflection of his words. I guess I made that sound a little dirty. "We can pass them and use them in place of weights. But first we've gotta stretch out. So, let's get to it before it gets too terribly hot outside.

He agrees, following me outside to the deck and onto the sand. It's going to be a beautiful day; the sun is shining warm and bright. The fluffy white clouds certainly won't be providing any shade. I lead him through some stretches, and I can't help but stare.

"How long are we holding this for?" he asks me, bringing me back to reality and not his body.

"Oh, sorry. Yeah, we can let go now. Let's just kick one leg out and bend over as far as you can to touch the toes on that leg. Should give you a nice stretch in your hamstring," I tell him.

Derek does what I tell him to, and I lead him through a few more stretches. He must think I'm a complete idiot with the way I keep stammering over my words as I watch his strong muscles move and flex.

Then we begin working through the routine I'm developing for my next shoot.

"You don't seem so sure of yourself with some of these moves. Or am I making you nervous?"

"Well, I'm still working on this routine. This is something I have to head to LA to shoot in a bit. So, I'm not as familiar with the flow and the moves as I normally would be."

He nods. "I'm like your guinea pig, then?"

"I guess so."

"Nice. I like that I'm getting a sneak peek of all your moves." He winks at me, and I blush yet again. I'm hoping I can blame all of this flushing on the fact that I've been working out.

We move on to crunches and sit-ups, and he adjusts so he's sitting in front of me. "Here, I'll hold your toes while you do your sit-ups."

"You really don't have to do that," I say. "I can do them just fine."

"I want to," he replies.

He positions himself in front of me and holds onto my toes.

I begin doing my sit-ups. Each time I crunch up, I end up looking him directly in the eyes. The heat of his stare is making we warm all over. I almost wish I had the courage to crunch up and kiss his lips. I wonder if he knows what he's doing to me. I think he might and he's just having fun with me.

We switch positions and I hold onto his toes while he sits up and down. I think about biting that lip whenever he comes near me. The images flashing through my head get more and more vivid as he keeps going, and suddenly, I let out a low moan. I want to cringe, hoping he didn't hear me, but judging from the chuckle, it looks like he has.

"Getting a leg cramp?" he asks when he sits up again.

"Sure," I stammer out. "Let's move to the cool down."

We begin stretching out our muscles again. I walk closer to the water to splash some water on my face. I need a cold shower based on the number of times I've envisioned myself biting Derek or licking his sweaty skin. I should get a medal for that.

I notice that Derek has joined me on the surf and is now doing the same thing. *Wet Derek only adds more images to my fantasies.*

"I'm sorry, what did you say?" he asks.

Fuck. Did I say that out loud? I go to make an excuse, but our eyes flash to a loud motor sound coming across the ocean. It's a plane flying across the surf. They mostly advertise restaurants or events on the island. However, this time it's the carnival. The same carnival that we used to go to when we were kids. I watch it and smile, remembering back to all the times we spent there. When we were little, my parents let us ride all the rides and have all the sugary treats that only carnivals can provide.

Once we got older, it was "Here's some money, go play." Those were the days we brought Derek with us. The times we spent raising hell and having fun, playing games, riding the rides, and staying out as late as we could. My parents would still make an appearance at the carnival but only to hang out with their friends and see the exhibits. They would check in on us and make sure we had enough money or that we weren't on too much of a sugar high, or worse yet, in some kind of trouble. We never were in any trouble, but they always teased us that trouble would find us wherever we went. More like trouble would always find the boys. I was just along for the ride. And if Derek was there, I didn't care if it was going to get us in trouble with Mom and Dad —I was in. I would do whatever involved spending time with Derek.

"Look at that. We're both here at the perfect time for the carnival," Derek remarks, pointing at the sky.

"I enjoyed those so much," I reply.

I catch him watching me, a wide smile on his face.

"What?" I ask.

"We should definitely do anything that makes you smile like that."

"I was just remembering all the good times we had there together." I wonder if it that was a bad idea. Did I make him think of Aiden and how he might not like this interaction that's been happening between us? But I don't necessarily care. I've lusted after Derek Walsh for as long as I can remember.

"We did have some good times, which is why we gotta do it. Plus, I think you could use a good night out to get your mind off things. You keep staring off into space, like you're not quiet in the same room as me. Maybe this will help."

"Absolutely," I say with a laugh. But the selling of this house isn't the reason I've been so distracted in his presence. It's the man whose sweating body is in front of me.

"What? What's so funny?"

"Nothing," I reply, but I don't sound very convincing.

He advances on me and gets into my space. "You can tell me."

I want to lean into him and lick the sweat lines running down his chiseled chest. "I'm okay," I finally get out.

He smirks and backs up, and I can feel my pride deflate a little bit. That might have been a chance to try something with him. Maybe get him to see me as more than his best friend's little sister.

He chuckles. "You just let me know if that changes."

We stand there chugging down the water and staring out at the sea.

"So, the carnival—that's a plan for tonight, right?" he confirms, looking over at me.

"Yeah, I think it'll be fun."

"You and I could both use some fun." He wiggles his eyebrows in my direction, smiling.

I flush as my gaze travels up and down his body. I look up to see he's staring at me with raised eyebrows, seemingly waiting for me to say something. Instead, I just bite my lower lip, and his eyes dart down to them. I swear his breath hitches just a bit, but he looks away first and breaks the moment.

CHAPTER NINE

I loved the carnival as a kid—the cotton candy, the smell of fried foods, the rides, and of course, the fireworks display. There weren't any concerts like some venues had. Corolla is small and has a nice hometown feel to it, which is a little out of character for a beach town. But I think that's what makes it that much more special.

Now here I am many years and carnival trips later, getting ready to head there with Derek. Even though we've gone together before, something about this feels different. I definitely spent a little extra time on my appearance. I'm wearing jean shorts that are just a little tighter and shorter than what I've been wearing around him so far. My white tank top is tight across my chest and grazes the top of the shorts, bearing just the right amount of skin. My long hair hangs long and straight down my back. The humidity of the night air will make me pull it up, I'm sure. But for now, I want to leave it down.

"You ready?" he asks me, knocking on my bedroom door.

"Yeah, let's go." I head toward the door, tripping on a sneaker in my path. "Crap," I yell as I fly forward.

Derek steps into action and grabs my forearms. He steadies me, snickering. "You okay there, Aud?"

"I'm fine." I turn fifty shades of red.

"Still so graceful." He's still teasing me, and I loathe it.

I didn't want to make an ass out of myself in front of him. I wanted him to see cool, fun, and sexy Audrey, not the one who also trailed after him as a kid hoping for some attention.

Yes, I am only Aiden's younger sister by a few minutes. We share the same birthday and are the same age. But I've always felt like the little sister who was trailing after him, begging Aiden to include me in his fun.

"Let's just go already," I say, trying to shake it off. But my face is still red when we climb into my Jeep. "Okay, passenger princess, let's get to the carnival."

He just shakes his head and makes himself comfortable in my front seat. There's a black ball cap in his lap, which I'm sure he's going to be wearing in order to keep himself from being noticed.

I ease my way into the busy parking lot. "We should have gotten here earlier." It's the only words that have been said during our fifteen-minute drive over.

"I suppose we should have. But you know someone was so busy getting ready," he mocks me yet again.

I just shake my head.

"You look pretty damn good, though," he remarks, shooting me a wink.

That wink heats my cheeks and core, making my stomach flutter a little bit more than it should. "Thank you."

"There's that flush," he says, running the back of his hand along my cheek as I pull into a parking space. "Do I make you nervous?"

I put the car into park and turn to face him in the car. "You have no idea how intimidating you are, do you?"

"Me?" He places a hand on his chest. His eyes are wide, like he couldn't imagine that someone who spends his life serenading screaming crowds could possibly make me and every other girl in the world speechless in his presence.

"Yeah, you. Come on. Have you not seen yourself?"

"I have no idea how to answer that question," he says with a chuckle.

"Then allow me to elaborate a little bit for you. You're one of the most beautiful men I've ever seen and the fact that you have no idea makes you that much more attractive to me."

He stares at me, mouth agape for a moment.

"Really?" I ask him. I'm not trying to call him on his bullshit, but that's exactly what I do.

"Fine, I know that I'm an attractive man. Women wouldn't be throwing themselves at me if that wasn't the case. But they have no idea who I am. They're just looking at me because of the way I'm dressed, the way I sing, and the way I look. You, however, actually know who I am. You have seen me at my worst and maybe even my best. So, hearing you say that I'm attractive makes me think there might be something to it."

"For a moment there, I almost believed you weren't feeding me a line. But Walsh, you, and I both know that those type of lines don't work on me. You're as confident in your looks as you are your singing voice." I roll my eyes and exit the Jeep.

He's laughing when I find him on the other side of the Jeep, pulling his ball cap down over his eyes. "It didn't even work just a little bit on you?"

"Nope," I say, popping the *P*. "It wouldn't work on someone like me. But you know one of those bus bunnies that show up hoping for the thrill of a lifetime might actually believe it."

"Who told you we call them that?"

"Ace," we say at the same time.

I laugh and bump my hip into his. I almost wish he hadn't been bullshitting me back there in the Jeep. I wish he thought I really saw him. But I know that's not the case. I wonder if the farce that he put on in the car was just his way of distracting the both of us from the tension I felt bubbling up. I'd like to believe that it's not all in my head, but I wouldn't put it past me.

"Audrey. Earth to Audrey," Derek is saying when I finally bring myself out of my thoughts.

"I'm sorry, what?" I ask.

"Where did you go?"

"Just deep in thought."

"Thinking about your dad?" he asks me.

"Mm-hmm." I lie so easily because why bother saying to him that I was thinking about how I wish he saw me as more than Ace's little sister.

"Any news from home?"

"They're going to tell Aiden. You know, when everyone comes in to visit you," I say, glancing at him from the corner of my eye. He tenses. I know he's worried about that. He hasn't made much progress on the songs he owes them. "Apparently, my dad is up for traveling, but that won't be the case when he's deep in treatment."

I don't say any more as I scan the carnival attendees. No one is paying attention to Derek, and they haven't figured out who he is yet.

"You ready for that?" he asks, pulling me closer to him.

"No, I'm not."

"You don't think Ace can handle it?"

The way he slips from my brother's name to his nickname makes me smile. To me, he's always Aiden, and I like that Derek usually refers to him as how I know him when we're together. Calling him Ace is something for the band and bus bunnies. He's my Aiden.

"He can. I just hate that he has to."

"I hate that you both have to."

"Me too."

"It must be a lot to know this secret about your family but not be able to tell the one person that you tell everything to." He's right. Aiden is the one person I can confide in.

"It is. We talk mostly through text, though, so at least he can't hear the tone of my voice. I'm sure that would give it all away. I'm not that good at keeping secrets."

"I don't know. I remember many a time when you had to hide

where Aiden and I were. We would sneak out, and somehow we trusted you not to tell your parents. That was no small feat."

"It wasn't. And I had to do that so many times because the two of you were always sneaking out."

"If your parents wouldn't have freaked about us going to those parties, you wouldn't have had to."

"They wouldn't have let us out of the house with what was happening at those parties."

We both laugh, and I can tell by the sparkle in his eyes that we're enjoying the same memories.

"Are you going to tell him or are your parents?" he asks me.

I sigh, wishing we could change the subject. I know he's only trying to help me and give me someone to talk about this huge secret with, but it's killing my buzz and the butterflies I'm feeling about being with him like this.

"We're telling him together," I finally say.

"You don't want to talk about this, do you?"

"Not really."

"Alright, well, let's go get some fattening food and watch the fire in the sky." He pulls me into him, and I smile, loving the way his poetic mind works.

"That sounds amazing."

He looks over at me, and my stomach flips and flips, tricking my mind into thinking that this might be the moment something happens between us.

"What are you hungry for?" he asks after we've made our way past a few food stands. Both of us examine the menus as we make our way past them.

"I was thinking of some funnel cake."

"Perfect." He leads me over to a stand that claims to have the world's best funnel cakes. "I think we need to try these out and see if they in fact do have the world's best funnel cakes."

I laugh at the mocking tone of his voice when he describes them.

"Let's do it."

I decide on a plain one, whereas Derek's is covered in cinnamon sugar and has apple pie filling in the center. It looks amazing. I almost got a similar one with strawberries, but I was afraid I would end up with it all over me.

"You know you are so giving me a bite of that," I tell him as we get settled in for the fireworks.

"I figured as much. I thought you were getting the strawberry one. You were particularly drooling when she handed the lady in front of us one."

I nod. "I thought about it, but the original ones have always been my favorite." It's a lame excuse, but he seems to buy it and doesn't say any more than that.

We're eating in silence while the sky turns darker. He finally breaks it and says, "Here." He's holding out a piece of his fried dough covered in sweet sugar and dripping apple filling. My mouth waters at the sight of the bite he's holding out to me. "Come on, you know you want to."

I lean over and take the bite into my mouth. It tastes like heaven. My teeth brush the fingers he's holding the dough with. I moan at the taste of it as I chew and swallow.

"You missed a spot." His eyes look hooded. The bite tasted like sugar, apples, and Derek. He holds out his fingers, waiting for me to suck the apple glaze from them.

I grin and lean back over, deep throating his fingers a little more than I need to, but I take them into my mouth, close it around them, and pull my mouth back off them of as I suck the apple up. I swear a moan escapes Derek's lips as I do it. I know there was one coming from me.

We stare at each other. My stomach is wild with desire. I got a little bit of a hit from him, and now I want more. He's watching me with the same intent—eyes are still wild with desire, and his mouth hanging open. There are words he wants to say; I can tell by the way his lip is trembling. But he doesn't, at least not right away.

"Audrey." My name comes out of his mouth and sounds all

breathy and needy. I wish I had my wits about me more than I do, because I might have responded. Instead, I just swallow and watch him, waiting for him to make the next move. I feel like I've forced his hand a bit and made him see me as more than Aiden's little sister. He hasn't said a word, but a shift is happening. I can feel it in the way he just keeps staring at me.

The moment is broken when a loud boom explodes in the sky. A flash of light now illuminates Derek. I hadn't realized they turned off the streetlights that allowed me to have such a beautiful view of this man. But they've replaced it with the fire in the sky. The way the pinks and blues are flashing over his dark brown hair and tanned features is making him look even more dangerous and forbidden. As if that weren't already possible.

The fireworks eventually break the spell, and we turn to watch them. My stomach feels warm, and not just from the food. I abandon my funnel cake and can see that he has too. Instead, he's watching the fireworks display above. He moves over closer so that our arms are touching. Music begins to play from a band that's set up in front of us. I have no idea when that happened. But when I'm with Derek Walsh, the whole world clearly just falls away.

The fireworks play on and on. The band is playing cover songs. The one they're playing now is "Don't Stop Believing" by Journey. I smile and begin to sway a little bit. I feel like whenever this song comes on we're all that same small-town girl. I move my hips a bit more and bump into Derek. He looks over, eyes still hooded from our earlier exchange, and that's when I see it—the crack in his resolve. Derek can't hold back anymore, for whatever reason, and I don't want him to.

He leans in, grabbing my face with his strong hands and hungrily puts his lips on mine. It takes my mind a minute to realize what is truly happening. But eventually my body catches up with my brain, and I join in on the kiss. It's not soft at all; he's going for it. His tongue is begging for entrance into my mouth, and I allow it, a moan escaping my mouth. My hands have a mind of their own. They take advantage of our chance to explore his hard body and how hard it is. I brush down his back and grip at his ass, then pull him closer. I can feel the hardness of his cock against me. Up his back, my hands wander, until they find their way to his neck, and I hold on for dear life as Derek continues his delicious assault on my mouth.

When we finally break apart, we're both panting.

"Audrey." This time, my name comes out like a prayer. His eyes widen and his body stills. Watching for a moment, and slowly breathing in and out, the reality of who he kissed sets in "I'm so sorry. I shouldn't have done that."

"I wanted you to," I tell him. "Please don't apologize, and please don't act like I'm someone you can't have or shouldn't be kissing."

"That's exactly what you are," he says, taking a step back. "But..."

I love that last word that comes out of his mouth. It gives me hope that the next few words are going to be exactly what I've wanted to hear.

"I want you. I'm not sure when it started. I'm not sure if it's because I've been here all week trying to write some silly songs and all I can see is you. Or if my life is just that damn hard and it needs you as a distraction."

"I'm happy to be that distraction," I tell him with a giggle.

He pulls me in for a hug. "That's not fair to you."

"What wouldn't be fair is you not kissing me at all. I've wanted you to do that for so long."

He's smiling widely back at me now. "Really? I thought I was just your brother's annoying friend and bandmate."

"You definitely were, but I always thought of you as my friend, too. You have no idea how long I've watched you and wanted you to do just that."

The fireworks continue above us, lighting up our faces. This feels like one of those huge moments I'm going to remember for the rest of my life. I know he might not, with all the shows he performs and moments that are going to be bigger than this in his career, but right now it doesn't get any better than this for me.

"I had no idea."

"Well, now you do," I tell him. I lean back in and give his lips a quick peck because I feel like I can now. The ice has been broken, and the first kiss has been shared. Frankly, I want more, so much more. Especially, since I could feel how much he wanted me when his cock pressed against me.

"Okay" is all he says. He pulls me back into him, and we watch the fireworks display.

Our touching doesn't stop the whole way out of the fair. I'm waiting for the other shoe to drop, and I feel like it just might on the way home in the car. But it doesn't; at least not completely.

"We can't tell Aiden about this," he begins before adding. "At least not yet. Not until I figure out what's happening here."

"Do I get a say in this?"

"Of course." He reaches across the shifter and squeezes my thigh. "What do you want to say?"

"I don't want to go backward. At least not yet."

"Okay," he says again. I like the finality of his words. "But remember, the rest of the world thinks I'm seeing Serena, so while I want to keep kissing you, the band will kick my ass if they figure out I'm screwing that up for them. This fake relationship isn't just about me, and that's why I agreed to go along with it."

"So where does that leave us?"

"Let's go somewhere tomorrow night and get some dinner. I wanna get to know the Audrey whose lips were just on mine."

"I would really like that."

"Good."

"Good," I repeat.

We head back home in silence. Once we reach the front porch, he stops me from going in by grabbing my arm and jerking me back toward him. My chest runs into his while his arms are wrapped around me to steady me.

"I'm a little traditional, and I'd like to end this evening by making out with you on the front porch."

I giggle, biting my lip. "I'd really like that."

"I can tell," he says, teasing me just before his lips take mine.

The kiss is softer this time. He lightly takes my lips and lets them dance with his. His tongue slowly moves against mine. It's everything a first kiss should be. The kind I know I'm going to be reliving. I'm dazed when we break apart.

"Good night, Audrey," he tells me before opening the door and motioning for me to follow.

"Night." It comes out all dreamy and dazed. I float on a cloud back to my room.

I hear his bedroom door close, and it makes me happy to know that he's not headed out tonight. Instead, he's in his room, slowly strumming on his guitar. I allow the soft sounds to lull me to sleep.

CHAPTER TEN

I wake up early the next morning to go for a run and clear my head. My dreams were full of Derek Walsh. Some of them were *very* exciting and others were disturbing. There was one where my brother punched Derek out until there was nothing left. I know that's a real possibility. Aiden has never liked it when his friends have paid that type of attention to me. It was like an unspoken rule.

As I make my way back to the house, I wonder how Derek is feeling and if I'll run into him and if it will be awkward. I hope not. I make my way up the deck steps and through the glass patio door. My eyes are drawn to the bright yellow Post-It note attached to the coffee pot.

I have some things to take care of, but I'll be back.
Make sure you're ready for our date tonight. It'll be casual fun.
Can't wait for more fireworks.

-

My stomach flips at the message, especially at the last line. Those were the best fireworks I've ever been to. I giggle out loud like a schoolgirl as a read and reread his note. I'm guessing there's no buyer's remorse from last night. I'm glad about that. I had considered the thought that he may have come to his senses and realized that it wasn't the best idea to date his best friend and bandmate's sister, but apparently not.

A new wave of anxiety hits me as I stare at the clothes I brought. None of them are too sexy or anything I would normally wear on a date. I brought a few nice things, but I thought I would be here alone. I hadn't planned on Derek, and my wardrobe is showing it.

"Ugh!" I scream aloud and throw myself back onto the bed. Emma. I need Emma. Without a second thought, I call her cell. Of course, being my very best friend, she answers immediately.

"Hey, girl. How's tricks?" Her tone is playful. It sounds so light that I bask in the warmth. Even over the phone, she makes me instantly feel better.

"Tricks are for kids, sunshine," I tell her, using the nickname she's had since she was a kid. Because that's what Emma is—pure sunshine. Her warm blue eyes, sunshine-blonde hair, and sunny personality make her my favorite person in the world to speak to.

"How goes the great clear out, then? And the alone time with the hunk?" She giggles, referring to Derek.

I called her and told her the morning after I arrived that he was here. She's been sending me little notes of encouragement on seducing him. Little did she know, I would do just that—without having to result to any of her tricks.

"He kissed me last night. At the fireworks."

"Seriously?" She squeals so loudly into the phone I have to pull it away or I'll go deaf.

"Easy there," I say with a giggle.

"I'm sorry, I just can't believe it. Really? Oh, my goodness, you have to tell me absolutely everything!" Her voice comes out in a rush.

I laugh. "Okay." I fill her in on the funnel cake, the kiss, and how good it felt to have him against me.

"I'm so freaking excited for you. And now you're going on a date with him? This is huge. I thought Derek would have second thoughts, and then you'd be having to convince him that, Ace's little sister or not, you're worth it."

"I'm not totally convinced we won't be having that conversation at some point. But for right now, he seems to be onboard with going on a date with me. So, we shall see."

"What's wrong?" She knows me so well. "I can tell by your tone of voice. It's like you want to be excited, but you won't let yourself. And now your voice is coming out all flat, when clearly you should be on cloud nine because you've wanted this boy since you could walk."

I have wanted him for a long time, but it hasn't been since we could walk. I met Derek Walsh when we were twelve. His mother moved to my hometown, Cary, when she finished up her latest stint in rehab. Something about a fresh start. Derek was none too pleased to have moved again. But him and Aiden became fast friends. Everyone did with Aiden; he was so warm and welcoming. I, on the other hand, was always shy. So, when I met Derek, it was a little bumpier than Aiden's introduction to him.

I sigh, thinking back to that day.

It had been a normal summer day. I was out on the back porch, sulking. We were going to the beach house again, so I should have been happy. Most girls my age would have killed for a beach house in Corolla. But Emma and I had just been invited to Bree Summers thirteenth birthday party. She was one of the cool kids, and as we were going into middle school, Emma and I were determined to go to all the important parties. We wanted to start our middle school years out on the right foot. Well, my parents were on the verge of ruining that for me. Emma would still go, and of course I wanted her to, but I was just sad that I couldn't go too.

"What are you doing here?" I asked the boy who climbed up our back steps. He looked all disheveled and like he could have been crying.

"Aiden here?" he asked. No hello for me. Just immediately wanting to know about Aiden, and it pissed me off.

"Who wants to know if Aiden is here?" I asked, getting to my feet. I placed my hands on my hips and stared him down.

He laughed, pushing his black hair from his eyes. "I'm Derek, his friend."

"No, you're not. I know all of Aiden's friends, and he doesn't have one named Derek."

Derek chuckled again. "You must be the twin sister," he said matter-of-factly.

"Oh, and you must be the new kid that moved next door to us, huh?"

"At your service." He tipped an imaginary hat at me.

"You're so weird. Who speaks like that?" I shook my head and moved toward the house.

"What's up your ass?" he called after me, making me pause. He sounded so arrogant when he spoke. "You know, your brother is nice and friendly. But you, man! It's like someone pissed in your cheerios."

I whirled around, my eyes burning with fire. "I'm not sure who you think you are, but I don't owe you an explanation for anything."

He just laughed at me again.

"Why are you laughing at me?" I screamed and stomped my foot. This only caused him to laugh harder. "Stop it!"

"Okay, okay." He held up his hands in surrender. "I'm sorry. I just think it's funny. You're cute, but you're not at all like Aiden described you."

"I'm sorry I can't be on all the time. My parents just appear to be hell-bent on ruining my life right now."

"How are they doing that? Are they making you move for the umpteenth time?"

I furrowed my brows. "No."

His brown eyes turned sad as he sat down on one of the patio chairs, leaned back, and let his arms prop up his head. I watched his arms flex, and then my eyes did an exploration of the rest of his body. He had definitely been hitting the gym or working out. He was broader than the rest of the boys my age, and I could see his six-pack starting to form as his stomach peaked out from the bottom of his T-shirt.

Lowering myself down onto the chair across from him, I asked, "How many times have you moved?"

He sighed. "This year or in my whole life?"

"This year," I said, though I wondered what the total number would actually be. There was a pain in his eyes that made me think I shouldn't ask how many times he had moved in his whole life.

"Three," he said.

I stare at him in shock. I can't believe he's moved that many times. "Army brat?"

"If only." He sat up, staring at me intently, and let the story of his life spill out. "You see my mom has a problem with recreational drugs. It makes it difficult to keep a job and a stable place to live. She's been in and out of rehab, so I've spent a lot of time with my grandparents. So, we'll just have to wait and see if things work out for us this time."

"What about your dad?"

"What about him?"

"What does he say about all of this?" I asked him. I instantly felt sorry for him. I could tell by his glare that was the last thing he'd want from me. I imagined with the life he had described to me; he must have seen a lot of things. Things that someone like me had only seen in movies or on TV. My parents had provided us a pretty good life and weren't doing drugs. They only had the occasional alcoholic beverage, and even that never got out of hand.

"Not around," he said, as if it was an obvious answer.

With that, Aiden came flying out of the house. "Would you please stop giving Mom and Dad a hard time about going to the beach this weekend? I really wanna go, and if you acting like a brat spoils it, I'll deck you."

My eyes snapped to Aiden's and then back to Derek. It was then that Aiden realized Derek was there.

"Hey, man. What's up?"

"Not much. Just getting a chance to meet your little sister."

"I'm only younger by a few minutes," I protested.

They laughed at me now.

"Ready to head out?" Aiden asked, and Derek nodded. Before leaving the deck, Aiden turned to me. "Give Mom and Dad a break, will ya?"

"Whatever," I said, rolling my eyes.

"Good to meet you," Derek said, tipping an imaginary hat before following Aiden around to the front of our house.

I would learn more about the horrors of what Derek had gone through and what brought him to us in the coming months. Derek's mom wouldn't stay sober. But this time, instead of moving him, his grandparents came and stayed at his mom's house, giving him stability. I didn't see his mom a whole lot after that. But I never again asked about his dad.

"Hello, are you still there?" Emma calls into the phone. "Talk to me. What are you so worried about?"

"Sorry," I stammer, trying to bring myself back to reality and not to thinking about Derek and his painful past. "It's just like you said, I'm worried he's going to have a change of heart when he realizes that Aiden will kick his ass. Or that he'll have some kind of text exchange with the band and that'll be the end of our date. I don't want him to give up on this. I've wanted Derek since the minute I saw him."

"I know you have. But you just have to give him something he can't say no to. You have to be so fucking hot that it takes all the strength he has not to want to rip your clothes off. Give that Serena bitch a run for her money."

"I'm pretty sure I can't compete with her. And I wouldn't want to."

"Well, no one is hotter than my best friend. Except for maybe me." She giggles into the phone. "How is your brother, by the way? Has he come down to the house yet? Should I come down there and, you know, go down?"

I can almost see her waggling her eyebrows at me as she's sexualizing my brother. "Oh God, Emma, please stop. You're going to make me puke. I don't know what it is you see in him."

"You're not supposed to, silly," she tells me. "Besides, he's a fucking rock star. The likes of Aiden Zaks are never going to look my way."

I can tell by the way her voice fades off that she's not happy about that reality. "I'm sorry, Emma."

"It's fine. Let's go back to talking about your upcoming date with Derek. Now, what are you going to wear?"

I put her on FaceTime, and we decide on a plain black tank top and the blue denim jean skirt I brought, along with my Birkenstock sandals. It's simple but she's right, that's something he'll like about it.

Before we hang up, Emma says, "Call me if you need anything, and don't forget to take some protection." She throws in that last part with a chuckle.

"Isn't he supposed to provide that?" I ask, letting my ignorance of dating shine through.

"We can never be too careful. Besides, we wouldn't want any little Derek Walshes or Audrey Zaks walking around. That would surely send Serena over the deep end."

"No, we wouldn't." I can't tell her that the thing with Serena is fake. I promised Derek I would keep that knowledge close to the vest and I plan to. Emma may have already figured it out on her own because she hasn't batted an eye at the fact that he's going out with me tonight and not Serena.

"Have a good time, girl, and call me tomorrow."

"I will."

"Oh, and Aud," she says, catching me before I click off the line. "Call me if you need me, okay? I'll come help you box the house up or hold your hand while they tell Aiden. And then I'll do my best to console Aiden...with my boobs." She throws in that last part while cackling into the phone.

"You are so gross."

"You only say that because it's your brother."

"True."

"Be safe and I love you."

"Will do. Love you too," I reply before hanging up the phone.

I go with the outfit Emma helped me pick out and ready myself for our date, giving myself pep talk after pep talk.

Once I'm dressed, I head out into the living room. I heard Derek come in while I was fixing my hair. I've spent most of the day obsessing over this date, so I feel a little bit of a relief when it's finally here. There he stands in black board shorts and a gray polo shirt, with checkered Vans on his feet.

I take a moment to gaze at the perfection that is Derek Walsh. All of the feelings from last night come rushing back, and I want to run over and kiss him senseless again. But I'm afraid that attacking him before the date even starts would not go over so well. So, I settle for a lame greeting.

"Hi."

"Hi," he replies back, his eyes roaming my body.

Good outfit choice, I think to myself. I'm so glad I didn't have any of my minidresses with me. I think Derek likes the more tamed-down version of Audrey, and that makes me happy. I like these clothes better too; they're more comfortable.

"You ready to go?" he asks, smiling at me. He must think I'm a bit crazy for the way I just keep openly staring at him.

"Yeah, I'm ready. Where are we going?"

He clears his throat before saying, "There's a cute taco place I found the other day, and then I thought we would go listen to some music."

"Sounds perfect," I tell him. I'm rewarded with a megawatt smile from him. I've seen that smile before, but it's never been aimed at me. I'll give him those kinds of answers all the time if I'm rewarded with a look like that.

"Perfect. Let's go." He extends his hand out to me, and I take it. We walk hand in hand out to Derek's Jeep. He opens the door for me like a perfect gentleman before running around to the other side and getting in himself. Once we're both inside the car, he grabs my hand. "This is going to be fun, Aud."

I just smile back, unable to speak, afraid I'll ruin the moment as he backs out of the drive.

CHAPTER ELEVEN

The taco restaurant Derek found is perfect. It's a little out-of-the-way place I've never been before. The name is in Spanish, and I can already hear the Spanish music that's loudly playing inside. I love the ambience.

"How did you find this place?" I ask him.

"A bartender told me about it. I was looking for some tacos, and she said they have the best ones."

My smile falters at the mention of the bartender being a *she*.

"I didn't fuck her," he tells me.

My head snaps over to look at him.

"I could tell you were wondering." He shrugs and laughs. "I know what you think of me. I know the image I portray when I'm on stage, but I'm not always that person."

"I know." But even I know my tone isn't convincing.

"I'm not sure that you did." He leans over in the car and gives me a quick kiss. "Now let's go get some grub."

We order our tacos and head to a picnic table to sit and wait for them to be ready.

"I've never met anyone who eats their tacos so plainly," he says. "Like damn, woman, do you want anything else on their other than meat and cheese?"

I giggle. "There's salsa, queso, and lettuce on there too, you know."

"Oh yes, let's not forget the lettuce, you little rabbit." He leans over and taps my nose with his finger.

I love this side of Derek. It's not one I've seen many times. Mostly, he's serious, or lately, moody. I think the situation with Serena and how to get out of it with everyone's reputations intact is weighing heavily on his mind.

The counter girl calls our order.

"Be right back," he says, going to retrieve our food. He stops and has a conversation with her. "But you won't tell anyone," I hear him say.

She's nodding vigorously.

"Do you want me to sign something?" he asks.

More nodding. She leaves the window and comes back with something. Derek chuckles and signs it.

"Let's not tell anyone that you saw me here, okay?" he says, pointing at me.

More nodding.

I just laugh at him as he's making his way over to me. He's shaking his head and laughing as well.

"Get recognized?" I ask him.

"Yep. I asked her not to say anything, though." He divides up the food while I stare at him. "Don't worry. We're safe, I think."

I dig into my tacos. They're a lot plainer than his. He left the radishes, jalapeños, and sour cream on. None of that stuff appeals to me.

"What did she ask you to sign?" I finally ask him. I wasn't going to, but curiosity got the better of me.

"A magazine with Serena and I on it," he tells me, his face falling.

I don't say anymore because I can tell he doesn't want to talk about it.

"Mmm," I moan after taking a few bites of a taco. "This is

incredible." When I look over at him, he's just staring at me with his mouth agape. "What?"

"I've never heard you moan before."

"Um, I think you have. I did last night when you kissed me," I remind him.

"I don't think much was registering other than 'Holy fuck, I'm kissing Audrey,'" he tells me with a smirk.

"No way you felt that about kissing me."

"Why wouldn't I?" He puts his taco down and studies me.

A woman from the restaurant comes over and places a bowl of chips and guacamole down on our table, breaking the moment.

"Thank you," Derek says, "but I didn't order this."

"Oh, I know, I know," she says in broken English. "But I wanted to." And before we can say another word, she's gone.

"Thank you," I call after her. She turns and waves, reentering the taco truck.

"So, tell me why I wouldn't be so distracted by the fact I actually got to kiss you that I wouldn't register your moans." His voice is so low that no one else can hear him speak.

I smile and lean in closer to him. "Because you are Derek Walsh, the lead singer of Crave, and I'm sure you had many a woman throw themselves at you, and a lot of pussy at that. Why would I even register?"

"Say that again," he commands, leaning in further.

"Say what?" I breathe out.

"Pussy."

I flush red. "Pussy."

He squirms in his seat, and I swear he just adjusted himself. "That's hot. I've never heard you talk like that. And for the record, Audrey, it doesn't matter how much pussy I've had or who I am, you do things to me." He takes a bite of his taco.

I get warm all over and just stare at him, not sure what to do next. The things that come out of Derek's mouth turn me into putty.

"Eat your dinner, Aud."

We finish up our food mostly in silence. I moan every once in a while at the taste of the delicious food, and Derek keeps adjusting himself as he we eat. Apparently, I'm making things hard for him.

"That was so delicious. Thank you," I say once we're back in his Jeep.

He looks over at me and smirks. "I could tell that you were really enjoying it."

I blush and shake my head.

"Stop," he commands, making my head snap over in his direction. "Don't be embarrassed. I thought it was really cute." He captures my lips in his, and I resist the urge to moan into his mouth.

When we finally break apart, I ask him, "Where to now?" My voice comes out all soft and breathy. Darkness pools in his eyes, and I wonder if I'm affecting him the same way he's affecting me.

"Well, it's not home yet," he tells me, gripping the steering wheel. "If that's what you were hoping for."

I giggle. "Well, at some point, I'm hoping for that."

He snickers. "I'm sure that can be arranged. But for night now, we're gonna head downtown and listen to some music."

"I wasn't aware Corolla had a downtown," I tease him. It's such a quaint and quiet beach town. I didn't imagine or remember it having much of a nightlife.

"Okay, well, maybe the next town over." He rolls down the windows and begins to drive. The smell of the sea air fills the car. I lean back in my seat and breathe it all in. As he drives, his hand rests on my thigh. We ride in silence the entire time, but it's a comfortable silence, like we've been doing this for years and could do it for the rest of our lives. I know I could.

We pull into this little hole-in-the-wall bar. It's down by the water and looks like someone has repurposed a building that was down by the docs for a bar. I almost expect to see some boats and jet skis when we walk inside. Derek takes my hand and leads the way into the bar.

I don't miss the jolt of electricity that shoots through me when he takes my hand. He must feel it too because he looks over his shoulder and shoots me a wink. I melt inside. I don't care if this is the only date we ever go on. I want it to last forever. It want to be able to take these moments and commit them to memory. I don't ever want to forget the way it felt when he told me what I do to *him*, the way he kissed me in the car, and how his hand feels rested in mine right now.

We reach the entrance, and a man is standing there at the door. Derek goes up to him, still holding my hand, and they have a few words. I have no idea what's being said, but eventually he pats Derek on the back, and we make our way inside.

"Everything okay?" I ask, confused by the whole interaction.

"Yeah, just had to inquire about who was here tonight. Gotta make sure it's no one that can blow my cover."

I'm suddenly so glad that he planned this date night; those are things that I never would have thought of. Although my idea of a date night would be dinner, drinks, and maybe a movie.

We make our way over the bar. He turns to me, asking, "What will you have?"

"I..." I stammer. I'm unsure what I want right now. My stomach is full of the tacos, chips, and guac we consumed, and I'm not sure I could eat much more. "Something light?" I ask him, brows lifting in question.

"I've gotcha," he tells me.

I smile because I feel like he really does. He has me in more ways than one. He is going to take care of me tonight, that much I can tell, but I'm also wrapped around his finger. If he told me to go down on him in this bar, I just might do it. That's how much of a fool I am for this man. I've got to get a grip before I do something stupid.

Derek turns to the bartender and places our order. The music coming from the stage is so loud that I can't hear what he says. I'm guessing there's no chance of us talking while we're in here. I can barely even hear my own thoughts.

As if he can read my mind, he leans and in and tells me, "This band is going to be taking a break soon. Then the next band, the one I want to see, comes on. We'll have some time before it gets loud in here again."

I just nod.

"Relax, Aud. It's just you and me." His voice in my ear sends vibrations down my neck and gives me a chill. I lean in closer to him.

"I know, it just feels bigger than you and me."

He turns back to grab the drinks from the bartender, his stoic expression giving nothing away. I rock back and forth on my heels, staring at the drink he's about to hand me.

"It's a whiskey sour."

I start laughing, remembering the last time we drank these together. He has one too, and it makes my heart so happy that he remembered. Derek and I got so drunk on these on my and Aiden's twenty-second birthday. We laughed all night together. Aiden thought we were nuts. But we didn't care. Nothing happened, much to my drunken dismay. But I've always loved the memory of when he treated me more like a friend than his bandmate's twin sister who he's known since he was twelve.

"Figured you could use something good," he whispers in my ear. The music has stopped. He was right, we didn't have much time left on that band's set. But I love that he whispered anyway. Like it was a secret just for him and me to keep.

We make our way to an empty table. I watch as Derek cases the place, making sure everything is just as it should be. I'm assuming he's also checking that he hasn't been noticed. I don't think he has. At least, if so, no one has approached us. I guess time will tell.

"Do you ever get sick of it?" I ask him.

He smiles, watching me carefully before answering. "Only when I have a secret I can't tell anyone else."

I take a sip before I answer. "Are you referring to the truth of you and Serena?"

"No," he says, shaking his head. "I'm referring to you. I wouldn't mind if the whole bar—hell, the whole town—knew I was out here with you. But that would bring on some many complications that I wouldn't do that to you, or the others."

The response smacks me in the face. "You mean Serena?"

He shakes his head, laughing. "I don't care what that spoiled bitch thinks. She would rain a shitstorm down on me, sure. But she's not the one I'm worried about."

"Who are you worried about?"

"You," he says, as if the answer is just that simple. "I wouldn't want things to get harder for you. I don't want to jeopardize your work or your life. Fans can be mean, Audrey, and I don't want them coming for you because they think they have a right to do that."

I nod, reaching across the table and giving his hand a reassuring squeeze. He kisses my knuckles before releasing me. I've known Derek Walsh for a long time, and I thought I knew everything there was to know about him,. But this, this level of honesty and sincerity from him, isn't something I was expecting.

"You're not what I thought you'd be like tonight," I finally tell him.

He smirks. "And what were you expecting?"

"I'm not sure," I admit, realizing I should have known he was going to ask that, and I would have no answer for it.

"Okay, then," he says, letting the subject drop.

"Who is this band you want to see perform?" I ask him, effectively changing the subject.

"They're called Legend, and I've seen them a few times on YouTube. I've always wanted to see them in person." He smiles. "Apparently, we're near their hometown," he adds in, and then he continues to talk about their sound. His eyes light up when he talks about music, and he's the most adorable man when he does. He's so animated and passionate; had I known this was the result

I would get, I would have asked him a thousand questions about it.

"So, what's new with your work?" he eventually asks. "You mentioned that you didn't have to shoot anything yet, but what about your clients?"

I smile when he asks me about work. Most people just refer to it as "That little fitness thing." And by most people, I mean my parents.

"I have a few workouts to film for the Beachbody platform, and then I have some clients I've been checking in with via email and Instagram. I do have to film some more reels, like the one you appeared on. My manager is also hammering out some deal for protein bars she'd like me to endorse. As long as Beachbody doesn't care, then I will."

"That's so cool. I love that you were able to build something you love."

"Thanks," I say, blushing at his offered praise.

"I know it's easier for some people to give praise to Aiden because of the band going on tour and winning awards, but what you do is helping people too. I can tell by the posts you make and the way you speak about it. You're incredible."

"You're not so bad yourself."

"Oh, I know," he tells me.

I laugh as Legend takes the stage.

We fall into a comfortable silence, listening to them play. He orders me one more whiskey sour, only having one himself. He says it's because he's driving.

We're on our feet by the middle of the set, dancing and swaying to the music. I take this opportunity to let my hips grind up against his. I get bold and push my back into him, taking an arm up and draping it around his neck. I pull him close while he kisses the exposed skin on my neck, and I grind against him, a hardness forming in his board shorts. I take full advantage and continue to grind and tease him. By the time we leave, his eyes are full of lust.

Back in the car, his hand rests on my thigh again, where he draws small circles with his fingers. I smile over at him, and he returns it. We say very little on the car ride home. It's like we can both tell that whatever happens next is going to change everything.

Either he gives in, or he doesn't.

He lets me have him or he doesn't.

It's like a game of poker. I've played the best hand I could. Now it's time to see if he's bluffing or not. Will he really take me home and ravish me? Only time will tell because we've just pulled into the drive.

CHAPTER TWELVE

I get out of the Jeep and head inside, hoping that he follows me. I can feel him on my heels when I open the door. I don't turn on any lights, leaving us covered in darkness.

"Derek," I say to the silence.

He's staring at me, chest heaving. He's probably either trying to talk himself out of this or promising himself that it won't ruin everything. Either way, I want this, and I want him, damn the consequences. He just needs to see that too.

"Yeah," he finally says.

"Don't overthink it. Be the guy you were on the dance floor. Be the guy who held me without any regard. Please." I walk over to him, and he leans his forehead against mine and lets out a tortured sigh.

"What are you so worried about?" I ask him.

"You know what I'm worried about."

It's Ace. It's the band. It's my parents, to some degree. As much as Derek likes to play himself off as a manwhore to the thousands of fans that scream at his feet, he's trying to do right by me. But I don't want that Derek. I want the Derek who is willing to give into the lust.

"Just let go." There's very little distance between us now. I don't think my body could get any closer to his without having him inside me. And right now, that is what I want. The way he held onto me on the dance floor, the way our hips moved in time to the music—I want that now. I want it all in a tangle of arms and legs.

"If you don't put your hands on me soon, I'm going to explode." My voice comes out all throaty and sultry. I'm hoping it's his undoing.

And it is.

"Fuck it," he says, throwing all caution to the wind. He picks me up and carries me back into my bedroom.

The heat from the fire burning between us is strong, and it threatens to torch everything we've built and destroy anything in its path. And boy, could it ever cause destruction. But Derek doesn't care about that right now, and neither do I. I've said what I needed to say to push him just far enough over the ledge that he's willing to take that next step with me.

He tosses me onto the bed, and I land with a soft yip escaping my lips. Derek smirks at me and then removes his shirt. I stare at him; my mouth open wide. I'll never tire of the sight of those defined muscles and the stupid little *V* I want to touch just so I can learn what's below it. Subconsciously, my tongue comes out, and I lick my bottom lip as I stare at him.

"Audrey," he says as he comes over to me on the bed. "You have entirely too many clothes on for what I'm hoping to do to you. Let's get rid of some."

I've never pulled a tank top over my head faster than in that moment. A wicked grin covers his face as I keep going, popping the buttons of my jean skirt. I stretch out my legs so that once my ass is lifted, it can easily slide down my legs. I do all of this while he's watching me.

"I feel like you owe me some clothes," I tell him. I'm surprised by the boldness of my tone, but he doesn't appear to be. He just grins at me, a wolfish grin that says I'm in big trouble. He does as he's told and removes the board shorts. I'm rewarded with the site of him standing there in black silk briefs. His erection is strained against the fabric. I want to put my hands on the length of him and see what he feels like. Eyes trained on me, he takes his hand and strokes his dick. I let out a low moan as I watch him.

"Is this what you'd like to be doing right now?" His voice comes out hoarse and sexy as he continues to stroke himself.

"It is," I tell him. "I need you, Derek. I've spent so many nights thinking about what this night might feel like, and now I need you to come over here and show me."

He smirks and says, "Well, we wouldn't want you to have to wait too much longer to find out if I can live up to your dreams."

"Oh, baby, I'm sure you will," I reply.

He smirks. "Do you want me to come over, or are you coming here?"

"You should come over here. Isn't that why you threw me on the bed?"

"Sex doesn't always have to be on the bed. In fact, I think you need to come here. Let me teach out a thing or two."

My sex grows wet with his words. I can barely manage to get myself off the bed and go over to him. On wobbly legs, I stand before him. I bite my lip to keep from moaning at the sight of his hungry eyes.

He closes the distance between us and kisses my lips roughly. "I wanna kiss these lips first," he tells me when he pulls away. "Then I'm going to kiss there." He taps my pussy with his fingers, and I feel like I could come with that simple touch.

I'm a ball of want and need, and he hasn't even touched me beneath my clothes yet. "Derek," I murmur.

"I'm going to take care of you. Just be patient for me, baby."

His lips are back on mine, and they thrust forward. Grinding his hips slowly, I push myself further into him. I need to get closer, and I need more friction. His hand comes down and brushes my wetness.

"Already so ready and eager for me, Audrey. You're not the

only one who has been dreaming of this. Of how that sweet little cunt is going to feel with my dick inside it. It's taking everything I have right now to not bend you over your dresser to fuck you. But I want to make sure you're ready for me."

"Stop talking and just touch me," I pant out. I feel like I'm going to explode. I need a release. The kind of release that Derek Walsh is promising. The one that only he can provide.

Dropping to his knees, he looks up at me with hooded eyes. "May I?" he asks, eyeing my thong and then looking back at me.

"Yes," I whimper out.

He chuckles. "Oh, don't worry, baby. I'm going to take care of you now." With that, he moves my thong to the side and dives in.

I jerk forward and hold onto his shoulders. "Derek," I cry out.

He continues to explore my folds with his tongue as I'm crying out in pleasure. He inserts a finger and then another until there are three fingers inside me. My knees begin to buckle.

"Hold onto the dresser," he commands as he pushes his face back into my pussy.

Sucking on my clit this time, he drives me over the edge. My whole body convulses, and I cry out a string of curse words. But Derek doesn't stop; he keeps his assault going, licking up every last bit of my release. Finally, he pulls away and sits back on his heels with a proud smile.

"Wow," I say, gazing at him with half-closed eyes. I can barely stand; my orgasm was that powerful. "It's never felt like that before," I admit sheepishly.

"Then you haven't been with the right kind of men," he tells me.

Derek stands to his feet and grabs my lips for a forceful kiss. Our tongues dance together for a brief moment, then he trails kisses down my neck and to my breasts. Reaching around my back, he pops the clasp of my bra, letting my breasts free. His hands take the place of the bra, and his touch feels so good.

"So good, so good," I say while he's circling my nipples with his tongue. "Fuck," I cry out, holding onto him for balance.

He pulls back and smirks at me. "Oh, you're going to be so much fun to fuck. I can't wait to feel that sweet cunt around my dick."

Normally, I don't like when someone talks dirty to me like this, but with him, I want to hear all the dirty things that come out of his mouth. And I want him to teach me to talk dirty to him too. I've never been a talker, and I'm not sure what I should say.

"Baby, stay here with me," he says. "Stay here in this moment."

He captures my lips again. His hands have returned to my breasts, and I feel like I could come again just from the ministrations he's performing on them. I moan and convulse around him until it's too much. I'm screaming his name as he sucks on my right nipple while kneading the left. It's too much, and it's just fucking perfect. I fall over the edge a second time, holding onto him for dear life.

"Fuck," I say when I come down from my high.

"Yep, that's what we're gonna do next. And you're going to watch me fuck you. I want you to see how beautiful and wild those brown eyes become when I'm giving you pleasure. Because, baby, it's a thing of fucking beauty. Take your thong off," he commands.

I do exactly that as Derek removes his briefs and then goes for his shorts and retrieves a condom from his wallet. I try not to think of how natural this action is for him.

"I want to be inside you so bad. I'm going to fuck you from behind. It's going to be so deep. It's going to feel amazing. Put your hands on the dresser and stick your ass out."

I quickly do as I'm told.

"This ass is so fucking perfect, Audrey. All those fucking squats are paying off." He bites my ass cheek, and I yip in response. He slaps the spot where he bit as I push my ass out to him. "That felt good, huh? We're going to have to play with that later."

With that, I hear the ripping of a condom wrapper. I look over my shoulder and watch as he rolls it on his length. "You ready for me?"

I look him in his hooded eyes, which I'm sure match mine, and nod.

Derek wastes no time separating my legs. Before I know it, he's lined up with my opening and driving in. I let out a yelp at the burn. He's getting so deep, hitting me in just the right spot. I moan and push my ass back further, begging him for more. I'm so greedy, so desperate.

He's pounding in and out of me like he's punishing me, but I love it. If I knew what I did to have him take me this way, I would do it over and over again. I'd do anything if it ended with me getting railed by Derek Walsh from behind. I look at myself in the mirror, and like he said, my eyes are wild with desire.

"I'm so fucking close," I whimper out.

He lays his back on mine and reaches his hand around to the front of me. "Let's get you there, baby. I can't hold out much longer." He begins rubbing my clit.

I whimper and moan, pushing back further and further. I come undone when he does. "Fuck, Derek," I scream out.

He bites down on my shoulder and empties himself into the condom.

"Wow," he says once we've come down from our high. "That was unexpected."

"It certainly was." I'm standing on wobbly legs, so I use my dresser for support. I'll never look at that thing the same way again. "I needed that."

"Been that long?" he teases.

"Yes," I tell him.

"Glad I could help you out." He pinches my clit.

"Let's get you cleaned up." He takes my hand and leads me to the shower connected to my room.

We climb in and I lean back into the spray. He follows, kissing me gently. We go at it two more times in the shower before finding our way back to my bed. He wraps his arms around me, and finally, we sleep.

When I wake up the next morning, he's gone. I'm immediately sad. I wanted to wake up beside him, but the soreness I'm feeling between my legs lets me know that at least last night was real. There's a clanging of dishes coming from the kitchen, so he hasn't gone far, and we can still have our morning together. I climb out of bed and head toward the noise of Derek preparing breakfast for me. Something I never considered happening in a million years.

When I walk into the kitchen, he's in just a pair of low-slung shorts as he toasts bagels.

"Good morning," I say. My voice comes out a little throatier than I mean for it to.

"Morning," he says, looking over at me and smiling. His eyes travel up and down my legs. They're exposed because all I've got on is the oversized T-shirt I put on before falling into his arms before sleep. "Bagels are all we had." His voice trails off, and he suddenly looks so much like a little boy.

"Bagels are great," I tell him. I walk over to him slowly. We're both being tentative with our movements, neither one wanting to scare the other. "I woke up without you."

"I wanted to do something nice for you."

"I feel like you did plenty of nice things for me last night."

And with that comment, we're back. Back to that comfortable space we had last night. Derek pulls me in and gives my lips a quick kiss, but before he can pull away, I deepen it. He lets out a low moan.

"Careful or I'll drag you back to bed," I tell him.

He winks at me, going back to readying our bagels. "Wanna eat this on the deck?" he asks.

I follow him out there. I see he figured I would agree, because beside the two Adirondack chairs facing the water, he has two glasses of orange juice, an iced coffee for me, and a hot one for him. I smile. "This is perfect."

He seems to relax a bit and lowers himself onto the chair. Once seated, he hands me my bagel—plain with strawberry cream cheese. His own has cream cheese and peanut butter mixed.

"You still eat it that way?" I ask, shaking my head. I've never understood that combination.

"This is delicious. You just don't know what's good."

"I think I know what's good," I tell him, waggling my eyebrows at me. He just laughs and watches me. "Why is this awkward?"

We seem to be tiptoeing around each other this morning. Not that I expected everything would be completely normal when we woke up. This man, who has never once seen me naked before, just had his tongue and hands in and all over my body.

"I think because neither one of us knows where we stand after last night."

"Was that a one-time thing?"

"I hope not," he replies.

"Are we hiding us from more than Serena?"

"You're talking about your brother."

"I am."

"I think we have to for a bit. He's going to be so pissed. I promised him I'd keep my hands off you, and well, look at me. He's the one man I've always called my brother."

"Stop. You're making this sound a little incestuous."

He laughs. "I don't mean to. I want you to know that this wasn't just a roll in the hay for me, Audrey. Last night meant a lot to me. And not the sex. It's been a long time since I was on a date with a girl, and I could be myself. Hell, it's been a long time since I was on a date."

"I know that for reasons different from mine, it's been a while for you," I begin. "But it's also been a long time for me too.

Ever since that guy who works at Beachbody, I haven't really had the desire." My voice trails off at the end.

"That was almost a year ago?" he asks.

I nod. "It was. Look, I don't want to be some complication that breaks up the band or the relationship that you have with my brother. I just know that last night, I got everything I've been dreaming of since I was sixteen."

His eyes widen at my admission. He's quick to school his features, but some of the shock is still written on his face. "Okay," he starts slowly.

"So, what happens now? Because damnit, Derek, I have no intention of going back to acting like things didn't happen last night. I want to keep going forward with you. And if that's not what you want, then screw it. This," I say, gesturing between him and me, "is over. I won't be jerked around." I can see he's getting ready to protest. "But I will respect your decisions when it comes to Serena and the situation with the band and my brother. Just as long as this never becomes a farce."

"You will never become a farce to me, Audrey. I'm not sure how this will shake out with the band, but please know you are real to me. The only thing in my life that is real."

He leans over and kisses me tenderly. I kiss him back. When we pull away, our faces are inches apart. "I can't believe this. That you're real and we're here like this."

He smirks. "Believe it. You may have had these dreams about me when you were sixteen, but what you never knew is that I had them too."

"Really?"

"Really, baby. You are everything to me."

I want to ask him more about that. I want to know how long his feelings have been more than platonic. But instead, we finish our breakfast while watching the waves crash against the shore. I have some filming things and workouts to do, and Derek agrees to hang out with me and do them too.

Today is going to be a good day.

CHAPTER THIRTEEN

After changing, I head back onto the deck. I take a sip of my water and admire the view. The sun is up, burning the sand and sparkling off the water.

"Are you ready to do this?"

I look over and see him standing there in black workout shorts and a dark gray tank top. He's always dressed in black or dark clothing. I'm not sure if it's the persona of a rocker or if it's what he prefers. I'm thinking back, trying to remember what he looked prior to the launching of Crave, when he interrupts my thoughts.

"You doing alright, Aud? You're studying me awfully closely." He's watching me with concern, and I shake my head to clear the fog in my mind.

"Sorry."

"You good?" he asks, making his way over to me. His arm comes around my shoulders, and he pulls me into this chest.

I relish in the smell of him, taking a moment to inhale deeply.

"Okay," he says, "Well, maybe when you're done getting high off me, you can tell me where you went."

I laugh and pull back just enough to see his face. "I was just thinking about how I've never seen you in anything other than dark colors."

"I tend to wear only dark clothes because that's what I wear on stage."

"You're gonna be hot when we're working out," I point out.

"Then I'll just lose the shirt." He places a quick kiss on my brow before releasing me and heading down the steps. "Now, if you're finished with your ogling, my trainer promised me a session."

I shake my head and laugh. "Well, then your trainer better get to it." I follow him down to the sand and begin stretching.

Derek mimics my movements. "Don't we need weights?"

"You've seen me out here using weights before, huh?"

"Yeah, maybe." He grins, and I swear it's the cutest I've ever seen him look. There's a shyness written all over his face that makes me think he'd rather die than admit that I caught him looking at me.

"How long have you been watching me?" I ask, stopping my movements and bringing my arms across my chest like armor.

"How old are you?" He asks the question like he doesn't already know the answer.

"Derek."

"How old are you?" He makes his way toward me like a lion stalking his prey.

"You know how old I am."

He raises his eyebrows as if to say, *Out with it.*

I sigh because I know he's more stubborn than I am. I won't get out of this conversation without answering him. "Fine. I'm twenty-four."

"Twelve years. That's how long I've been watching you," he admits.

The admission knocks the wind out of me. I take a step back and stare at him. "Are you serious?"

"Oh, come on, did you really think it was all so one-sided?

Did you really think I was just that hard up or so easily seduced that I fell right into your bed?"

"We didn't use a bed," I quip.

He smirks. "We recently did not."

I flush and he's watching me intently. "I had no idea."

"You weren't supposed to. And besides, if there was anything happening there, Aiden would have cut my balls off." We both laugh at his statement. I know he's right. "Hell, he still might."

"But you're risking it anyway?"

I feel like I'm waiting for the other shoe to drop. Like I'm waiting for him to tell me no, he's not putting his relationship with Aiden and the band on hold. This is more than me just being his best friend's little sister. This is his bandmate's sister and his livelihood that we're both screwing with.

"I think I am. Because why the fuck not?"

I'm not sure I like that response. Makes it sound like he was bored or just wanted to see what it would take to fuck Aiden's little sister. Apparently, it doesn't take much.

"Don't look like that," he says. "I get tired of people telling me where I can and cannot go. I get tired of people designing my life. I get tired of people telling me that I need to pretend to date someone so that a single will go well. I want to take some control, and you"—he cradles my face in his hands—"seemed like the perfect place to start."

I nod in understanding. I'm not sure what to say to that. Derek is a lot of things, but the biggest thing I'm finding is that he's so unexpected. In all my wildest dreams, this was never how I thought he would talk to me. I never expected him to be so open and honest with me. He plays the role of the moody rocker very well, but that must be all it is—an act.

I lean over and close the distance between us, brushing our lips together ever so slightly. I pull back just as quickly as I pulled in. "You didn't wear a hat today, so I better not get too lovey with you," I tease.

He nods, not saying a word.

"Let's go for a run," I tell him and take off down the beach.

We run on the sand down by the water, where the tide came up and made the sand hard, making our run a little easier. Sometimes when I'm trying to give my legs a serious workout, I'll run where the sand isn't quite as packed. But today, I want to take it easy on Derek, because if memory serves, he's not a runner. We make it all the way down to a pier before he's signaling me that he needs a break.

"Jesus, woman," he pants out. "How in the hell are you just jogging along like nothing is happening?"

I laugh. "I'm in shape."

"Fuck," he screams up at the sky. "I thought I was too, but it's like you're trying to kill me. How far was that?"

I look at my smartwatch. "Only two miles."

"Only two miles," he says, mocking my voice. "Fuck you. That was hard." He lets out a laugh and continues to attempt to catch his breath.

"Put your hands above your head and breathe in and out slowly. Stop gasping for breath. It's not going to help you catch it any faster."

I lean against the pier as he moves around, attempting to calm his breathing. The tattoos on his body are on full display. I didn't get the chance to examine them that closely last night; he was behind me most of the time. I smile thinking back to it all. I never thought I would be one to like doggy style, but there was something about fucking Derek that way... It was so primal, so dirty, and very much needed.

"See something you like?" he asks, breaking me out of my trance.

"As a matter of fact..." I make my way over to him.

He chuckles. "You're insatiable."

"Only when it comes to you."

"Well, you might get to go for another round. That is, if you don't kill me first."

"We're not done yet. We have some body weight work to do. Or at least I do. I have some filming."

"Work stuff, huh?"

I nod in confirmation. I wait for the witty comeback about it not being real work, but then I remember I'm with Derek and he doesn't judge like some guys do. "Do you want to be in the clips as someone I'm training with?"

"Sure, just don't make me look so old and out of shape. Fuck, I'm only a year older than you and I feel like I could die."

"How much cardio do you normally do?" I call as he works out. His body is all hard lines, toned arms, and sculpted legs. That body was made from hard work.

"Well..." He wiggles his eyebrows at me suggestively.

"Are you telling me that sex is your only cardio?" The admission makes me take a step back. I'm not sure that I like that the only form of cardio he does is fucking other women.

"No, but you should see your face."

"Asshole," I say, pushing his shoulder.

He gathers me up in his arms. "Rowing machine," he tells me. "That's how I get the cardio in. I have a machine at my house."

I nod in understanding.

"The things that you must think of me," he says, throwing his head back and laughing. "I'm not all that bad, you know."

I smile, looking up into his brown eyes, which right now, are full of worry. "I know that you're not all that bad. You forget something, Derek. I've known you since you were thirteen. You left a string of broken hearts back there in Cary, and throngs of girls scream your name every time you sing —"

He cuts me off. "I'm not coming off so well here, Aud."

"You're coming off just fine." My voice drips with innuendo. "But what I was going to say is that I think a lot of that is just you being a tease. I know you. You don't take a girl home every time you have a show. Yes, you've had some fun, but who hasn't? Relax. I'm not worried about who you were before this started. I worry about who you'll be with me now."

"I think you might be the single greatest woman I've ever had the pleasure of fucking."

I throw my head back, laughing. "I'm so honored."

He captures my lips with his, and I moan into his mouth just as his tongue begs mine for entrance.

Suddenly, he sobers up and pulls away. "We can't be doing this out here. What if someone sees us?"

"Very true. Wouldn't want your other girlfriend to find out."

He doesn't say a word about that. Instead, he tags me and yells, "Race you back." Derek takes off running for the beach house.

Laughing, I chase after him and end up catching him pretty easily. We run back side by side to the house and chug some water when we get there.

"Alright, lady. What do we need to film?"

I snicker. "Well, there are a couple of positions I'd like to try out." I mean it as a tease, but with the way his eyes widen and study me, I can't help but wish I wasn't kidding.

"I'm all up for experimenting." He comes up behind me, encircling me in his arms.

I look at him over my shoulder. "Later. But right now, I gotta run in and get my tripod to get some of this done."

Derek is actually a better sport than I thought he would be. I film us doing push-ups, burpees, lunges, and sit throughs. He does his best to keep up with me, only faltering on the sit throughs, which aren't the easiest move. But he takes it all in stride. Once we're done, I show him the results and get his permission before posting.

It's not until later that I check the comment section and I'm reminded of just who he is. Derek finds me sitting out on the deck watching the ocean.

"I thought after you showered you would come find me," he says. "I thought I was going to help you clean."

I just shrug. He hasn't seen my face yet, so he can't see the tears.

"Aud, you okay?"

"Yeah." My voice comes out soft. I'm trying to hide the tears, but he must hear them anyway.

Derek walks around to my front. I hide my face, but he lowers himself on the hassock in front of me. My legs are pushed to either side, and he's in between them. I can feel him watching me.

"Audrey, what's going on? Is it your dad?"

I shake my head, although I can see why he would think that. But as far as I know, there's been no change in that area.

"So do you want to tell me what's going on?"

I shrug.

"Baby, what's got you so sad?" He begins rubbing his hands on the underside of my calves. "I can't fix it if I don't know what it is."

I sigh. "I don't think you can fix this."

"Show me," he commands. "Don't tell me what I can and cannot fix."

I shake my head and thrust my phone in his direction.

He looks at it. "Unlock it."

I shake my head and lean forward, grabbing the phone from him. I unlock it and hand it back. "Here, look at this."

He takes the phone from me and stares down at my Instagram comments. Not even twenty minutes after I posted the video of Derek and I, the nasty comments started pouring in. He reads them and shakes his head.

Some of them are surprised to see him there. There are some encouraging ones, so I'll give my fans that. But the ones that are causing the tears are the ones that make me wish I could take the video down. But I can't. It's the cowards way out. I just need to get a thicker skin. A thicker skin against things like:

Who does she think she is?

Why is Derek working out with her?

Serena's body is way better than hers. What does Derek see in her?

Why did she feel the need to post that he's her friend? Like someone like Derek would ever be interested in her.

Okay, Exercise Barbie, stay away from Serena's man.

"Those little bitches. How fucking dare they." He's seething, his jaw clenched. There are words on the tip of his tongue—I can tell by the way his mouth keeps opening and closing. But he doesn't say a word.

I grab the phone from him before he can.

"Can you delete them?" he asks. "Or reply and set the fucking record straight?"

The last thing out of his mouth shocks me to my very core. "What do you mean set the record straight?"

He pulls me to him. My face is buried in his chest while he strokes my back. "You could tell them that Serena doesn't hold a candle to you. Or that I'm not Serena's. Better yet, I could do it."

I shake my head. "No, this happens every once in a while. It happened the last time I let Aiden on my story. I should have learned from that, but I thought it would be harmless."

I look up and he's watching the story. It's replayed at least twice by now. "I like that you used a Crave song for this. It looks really cool."

"Thanks," I say meekly. At this point, I couldn't care less that he's impressed with my editing and filming skills. "I should have turned the comments off, learned from the last time that I put something like this up."

"You shouldn't have to censor yourself to make them feel good about themselves."

"I know, I know." I shake my head. "It's stupid that I'm so upset over it. It's not like they know anything about me."

"They know nothing about you. They only know the you that you should show. They have no idea how big your heart is. Sure, they can see this amazing body, but they have no idea how amazing it is when that gorgeous smile is pointed at them."

"You're sweet. It's a good thing you're a songwriter."

I get up and walk to the rail. I'm being silly. I know that I am. I just hate that all the things that have lurked in my head are now splashed on my social media.

"I'm not bullshitting you, Aud." He comes over to the railing and puts his arm around me.

"Where's your hat? Shouldn't you be making sure that no one can see you?"

"Private beach," he spits out. "What would you like me to do, Audrey? Do you want me to hop into the comments section and defend the shit out of you? Do you want me to have the band's agent send out a press release saying that you're just a childhood best friend and to leave you the fuck alone? I mean she could, but she'd be lying. You're more than that."

"I'm being stupid."

"No, you're just new at dealing with this shit. Believe me, I've dealt with it for a few years now. The best thing you can do is live your life and stay out of the comments section. That, and apply some alcohol to the situation, because it tends to help you forget why you were so upset in the first place."

I nod and look over to find him smiling.

"There's my girl."

I lean into him. "I'm sorry I'm such a baby about this. It just hurt."

"I know it did. And it's okay that it hurt you. Just don't hide it from me." He starts messing around on his phone.

"What are you doing?"

"Sharing your reel to my story and adding in a comment."

I gasp and grab my phone. Sure enough, there's a notification from Instagram. And sure enough, it says that Derek Walsh has commented on my reel. I open it and look for the comment.

Crave_DerekWalsh: Thanks for the great workout, Aud. You're an amazing trainer. :)

I smile. "Thank you."

"Welcome. Now what are we doing today? Are we tackling some closets?"

"No, no more closets. I can't tackle another one," I say, sighing as I look out over the ocean.

"You okay?"

"Yeah, I'm fine," I lie, my eyes remaining on the ocean. I refuse to meet his.

"You know you've said you're fine so many times, I'm starting to see through it. I know you're not fine. Jesus, Audrey, how could you be? I just wish when I ask you, you'll be straight with me. I wanna help. These next few days are going to suck, and I would like to be there for you."

I sigh. I'm a bitch. He's only trying to help. "Sorry, it's just a lot."

"I know. How are you doing with Aiden coming to town and your parents? Have you spoken to them?"

"My parents?" I ask him, ignoring the first question because I'm not really sure how to answer it. Every time I think about them coming and telling Aiden, I get sick to my stomach. This will kill Aiden, like it's slowly doing to me. Thankfully, I have Derek to help distract me. I'm not sure how Aiden will react.

"Yeah," he confirms.

"No, I haven't really talked to them. Just a text here and there. My mom says he's doing well enough for travel and that no one will notice anything's wrong." I shrug.

Derek pulls me into him, and I rest my head on his shoulder. He leans over and kisses my head. "We're all here for you," he reminds me.

"I'm glad Brent is coming with Aiden. It'll be nice to see everyone. It just sucks that this is why we're all coming together. Especially because Aiden has no idea." I feel like I'm deceiving my brother.

"It's going to be okay. You're honoring your parents' wishes. He may be angry at first, but he'll understand."

"I hope you're right." I'm not sure that he is, but I don't bother saying anything. I don't want to ruin the nice morning we've been having. "We have so much to do today. We need more food in this house."

"I can be here if you want me to be. Hold your hand through the whole damn thing." He grabs my hand and places a kiss on my knuckles.

My stomach flutters with delight. "I appreciate that, but won't Aiden think it's strange?"

He looks over at me and shrugs. "Alright, baby, let's go get some dinner and then stock up the house."

CHAPTER FOURTEEN

I wake up in complete darkness, and it feels like I'm lying on the sun. There is a heavy arm draped over my shoulder. I smile, remembering that I'm waking up next to Derek. He chuckles behind me.

"Good morning," he says, pinching my ass. "How did you sleep?"

"Well, once you let me go to sleep, I slept pretty well." I roll over and face him.

He chuckles. "I don't remember you complaining last night. I mean, there were moans coming. Should we do it again this morning and find out if those moans were you complaining or you enjoying things?"

I giggle. "No, those were not moans of complaining."

"Does that mean you don't want to do it again?"

"Aren't you worried about my morning breath?"

It's his turn to laugh at me. "Baby, I'm not worried about a damn thing when I'm between your legs."

I flush at his words and bite my lip. I grow wet at the thought of it.

"Oh, you must think that's a good idea," he says.

He doesn't wait for me to answer, rolling over and covering

my body with his. The hardness of his erection presses against me, and I roll my hips in anticipation. He moans and begins kissing down my neck to where my breasts are covered by a long T-shirt.

"You really need to lose this." He pulls the T-shirt over my head, and I'm bare for him. "This just happens to my favorite outfit of yours."

"Uh-huh." I can barely get words out. He's stroking my clit with his fingertips while he's talking to me.

"I think you're just about ready for me." He inserts two fingers inside me, and I lean into him, moaning.

"So good, so good," I mutter while he pumps in and out of me. His mouth comes down and covers my breast, biting the nipple just a little bit. I arch into him further.

"Someone is greedy this morning," he says.

I grab ahold of him, and he removes his hand from my wetness and uses it to pull me flush against him. I grind my hips into him, rolling us so we're on our sides. It's my turn to make him moan. I pull back and run my hand down his chest and stomach until I'm gripping him. He jerks into my hand. Slowly, I stroke him and look at his eyes. They're hooded and his head is lying back. I smile, enjoying the way I'm making him feel. I feel like I'm the prop most of the time. Derek does amazing things to my body, and I'm just there for the ride. But I'm happy to reciprocate.

I begin kissing down his chest.

"Where are you going?"

I look up at him meekly. "I was thinking I would..." I'm not as bold as he is; it's hard to say the words.

"You were thinking you would, what, suck me off?"

I flush at his directness and shrug. "Well, yeah."

"You don't need to do that."

"I know. You don't need to eat my pussy, but you do it."

"Baby, I love it."

"How do you know I won't love sucking you off?"

He smirks at me. "I don't."

That ends that conversation because he rolls us so I'm on my back again. "You don't need to do that now. Right now, I'm going to come inside that magnificent pussy and make you come several times over."

I smile wickedly at him. I love the thought of it. In no time at all, he has a condom on and is pushing into me. The pace he sets is quick. Derek likes it hard and fast. I'm not used to this, but I like it. The thoughts fly out of my mind when he kisses down my neck and to my breast. He grabs my breasts and pushes them together, kissing both my nipples at the same time. I moan and grind my hips deeper into him, trying with all I have to get him deeper inside me.

"I know what you need," he tells me. And just like that, he flips me over so that I'm lying on my stomach. He pulls on my legs until I'm at the edge of the bed. "Stick your ass up in the air."

I do as he asks. With the way he grits out commands while we're naked, I would do anything he wants me to.

In one swift motion, he enters me. I cry out in both pleasure and pain. Derek drives in and out of me while I push back into him. It's hard and fast. I can feel myself teetering over the edge.

"Fuck," Derek mutters as he places featherlight kisses on my spine. "You are so fucking beautiful. I love the way you feel. I love the feeling of you squeezing the hell out of my dick with your pussy. Goddamn, Audrey, I'm not going to be able to hold out much longer. You're gonna have to come soon."

Derek pinches my clit, and that's it. That's all it takes. I fall over the edge and collapse on the bed from an orgasm stronger than anything I've felt before.

"Fuck," he says, covering my body.

"That was amazing," I tell him.

"Why, thank you." He kisses my neck, and I roll over so that I'm facing him. "How did I get so lucky?" he asks when our eyes meet.

"I've been wondering the same thing." We lie there watching each other for a bit. "What time is it?" I finally ask him.

"Almost nine."

"Ugh, they'll be here around eleven. I'm not ready."

"Why's that? I thought you were looking forward to seeing your family. You haven't been together since Christmas."

It has been a long time. With Aiden being on tour and my work, we don't get together as much as we used to.

"That's part of it."

"What's the other part of it?"

"You," I tell him. I feel silly saying it, so I focus on his lips. They're covered in a smile, and I get the courage to look him in the eye.

"Why me?" he asks, stroking my leg. Derek's eyes are shining. He looks so content and peaceful. I wish we could stay here all day long.

"Because when everyone is here, we won't be able to be together like this. This is Aiden's room," I remind him, gesturing around us. "He'll be taking it. And you'll be heading to the guest rooms or something."

There's plenty of room for the band to sleep here. Someone could bunk with Aiden, and there are two twins in another room, and a sofa bed in the living room.

He shrugs, a sly smile on his face. "You know, I could always sleep in your room."

"Do you have a death wish? Aiden would not be pleased," I remind him.

"Yeah, that would be an understatement."

"So, what are we going to do?"

"You're not ready to not fuck me while they're here, huh?" He's teasing me and I don't care. He's right, I'm not. "Maybe we could play a game. See how quiet we can be. Make it a challenge."

I flush at his words, and he laughs.

"Do you think you could do it?" he asks.

I shrug. "I don't know."

"I could give you my leather belt to bite. See if that would help things."

I suddenly get images of me on all fours with a leather belt around my neck, him holding the other end of it, pulling it tightly. I swallow loudly.

"I would give anything to know what is going through your head right now."

I snicker. "Oh, the images I have of you and a leather belt right now. I'm not sure you'd wanna know."

"Trust me, I wanna know."

I sigh. "It's gonna have to wait. I have bedrooms to make up and a shower to take. Guess you'll just have to hear all about my dirty kinks later."

"That's a conversation I'm looking forward to."

After showering, eating, and straightening up a few things, Derek and I are waiting for my family and the band to arrive.

My parents arrive first. Nick and Anne Zaks make their way up the walk, and I smile, thinking of the number of times I've seen this sight before. It stings a bit, knowing soon I might not see the two of them together.

My dad looks tired, and he's thinned out a bit. It must be the treatments. He's tall like Aiden, the salt and pepper in his hair turning more salt than pepper. His brown eyes match mine and Aiden's. He's the parent we resemble most. Anne Zaks has the blonde hair I used to always want, along with the prettiest hazel eyes I've ever seen. The only thing I got from my mom was her short stature and curves.

"Hi, Nick and Anne." Derek is grabbing their bags and helping them in the door.

"Derek, what a lovely surprise." Dad pulls him into a hug and then comes over to me. "Hello, baby."

"Hi, Daddy." I give him a long squeeze. When we pull apart, tears have gathered in my eyes. "How are you feeling?"

"I'm having a good day," he says. There's a finality in his tone that warns me that he doesn't want to talk about it.

Mom comes over and pulls me in for a hug. "Hi, sweetheart. How are things?" Her hazel eyes are watching me with worry.

"They're going well. Not getting as much done as I thought I would be. Derek just gets in the way," I tease.

"Really, do I?" He stares at me, his eyebrows raised. "The other night you were just saying that—"

Before he can say another word, I cut him off. "That you need to pick up your shit."

"Can I take your stuff to your room for you?" Derek asks my parents.

"No, we can do that." My mom heads down the hallway, my dad in tow.

"What is wrong with you?" I ask him.

"What are you talking about?"

"Your comment earlier?" I remind him.

He snickers. "Relax, I think I could straddle you and no one would say anything." He pulls me in from behind, placing a kiss at the base of my neck. "It's going to be fine. Besides, they're not who I'm worried about."

I turn in his arms. "Ace?" I ask, and he nods in confirmation. "Relax, I can handle my brother."

"Oh yeah, because you'll be the one he's most interested in talking to." He releases me and heads into the kitchen.

"Having second thoughts about all of this?" I ask, following him.

"No, I'm not. I just...I don't know. I don't want to do anything that jeopardizes the band."

"I won't let this ruin the band. I'll leave you alone if it would come to that."

"That would be easier said than done." His voice is low in the empty kitchen. "For me, at least."

My palms start to sweat. I know my parents are right down the hall and could come out at any moment.

"You're like the best hit of…"

"Pussy?" I finish for him.

He throws his head back, laughing. "I love to hear you say dirty things. What other dirty things can I get you to say?"

"Derek," I murmur. "My parents are right down the hall."

"I know. It'll be like we're horny teenagers trying not to get caught."

"Aren't we, though?"

"Horny teenagers? Oh, abso-fucking-lutely when it comes to you."

I move to kiss his lips, but the front door opens, and a commotion comes from the living room.

"Fuck," I say, stepping out of his embrace.

"They're here," he says. A smile lights up his face, and he releases me immediately, rushing for the living room.

I follow him and in steps Aiden and Brent. He moves to them in quick strides and embraces Aiden first. The male version of me—taller than I am, but with the same brown hair and eyes. His hair is falling into his face as the white T-shirt stretches over his muscular frame. I make my way over and hug Aiden.

"Aud," he says, pulling me in. "Are Mom and Dad here?"

"They're in their bedroom," I tell him, giving him a tight squeeze.

"Got any hugs for me?" Brent asks. He's the tallest one in the band and looks the most intimidating. His head is shaved, and he's covered in tattoos, but he's the sweetest man you will ever meet. He barely speaks. I think in the four years I've known him; he's said about twenty words to me each time he sees me. But I love him all the same.

"Hi, Brent. Of course, I do." I hug him and he gives me a big squeeze that makes me grunt.

"Be fucking careful with her," Derek growls.

I freeze instantly, and all eyes snap to Derek.

"Okay," Brent says, slowly releasing me. "Everything okay, D?"

Aiden is studying him, waiting for a response. I swear they've been here for less than five minutes, and I've already lost five years of my life.

"She just got a tattoo. Her ribs are probably sore," Derek says coolly.

I nod and close my eyes, taking a deep breath. Then I immediately hope that no one noticed the action.

"Let's see it," Brent says, smiling brightly at me. Aiden is glancing between Derek and me.

"Who inked her?" Aiden snaps at Derek, glaring at him.

"Rooster," Derek replies.

"I'm old enough to get a tattoo, Aiden. Would you relax?"

He sighs. Hearing who inked me seems to relax him a bit, maybe since it's someone he knows and not from some hole-in-the-wall shop. "I know you are. I don't care that you have one. Have you seen me?" He gestures to the full sleeves he has on both arms.

I've lost count of the amount that he has—both of his arms are covered in the colorful artwork. They're all of the sea, and it almost makes me want to call him Aquaman, but I'm pretty sure he would kick my ass for the comparison. "I'm glad you got it from someone reputable."

"I'd never take her to a shady place," Derek says defensively.

"No doubt," Aiden answers.

"It's just three little fish with a wave," I say.

"Cool. Can we see it?" Brent asks.

"Who are the fish?"

"Duh!" I say with a laugh, gesturing toward him, Derek, and me. I pull up my tank top and put the tattoo on display, and Aiden nods in appreciation, eyebrows raised.

"Awesome," Brent says.

Derek's staring at me, his eyes darkening with desire. I shiver at the look he's giving me. Thankfully, no one notices, and my parents make their way into the room as I'm lowering my shirt.

"Did you say you got a tattoo?" Mom asks.

"I thought it would be something nice to commemorate the beach house and all."

She nods. "Looks nice, honey."

I figured she would have no issues with it. Neither would my father. My brother is covered in tattoos, and she has never said a word about it. My parents have always been very accepting, which makes me wonder what they would think about me sleeping with Derek. I look over and he gives me a slight shake of his head, like he can read my mind. A little piece of me dies inside, knowing that Derek will never want to tell my parents and Aiden what's happening between us. The judgment of my parents and the stakes with my brother are just too high.

"This is so nice having everyone under one roof. I love it," Mom says.

I walk over and pull her in for a side hug. "It will be nice to have everyone together."

"Do you know what we should do?" Aiden asks, looking around at everyone with excited eyes. When no one answers him, he just says it. "Let's have a bonfire like we use to for the Fourth."

"The Fourth is long gone, man," Derek reminds him.

"Dude, I know that. But I thought this would be a good time for it. We're all here. How often is this going to happen?"

"Sounds like fun."

"Yeah, man. Whatever you want to do," Brent says, slapping him on the back.

As far as Brent and Aiden know, this is just a trip that will mark the last time we're all together in the house. But it's more than that. I'm not sure when my parents are planning on spilling the beans, but I know they will. And it will crush Aiden. It will also make the writing sessions that the band has planned a little harder. I make a mental note to remind Derek of that. I can't stop my parents from telling him, though. They need to. Aiden spends all his time in LA, so this is their chance to tell him in person. It's just a shame that Aiden may not be in the right frame of mind for working. Or who knows, if Derek has some angry songs worked out, it might work for them. He was overly moody before we hooked up.

"Sounds like a good time, son," Dad says. He looks over at my mom, and they have a conversation with their eyes.

I saw them do it a million times when Aiden and I used to ask for permission for things when we were younger. They were always trying to figure out how to answer and make sure they were on the same page. Now I wonder if they're thinking that this bonfire will be the best place to tell Aiden. They may as well do it in front of everyone. Derek knows. I consider telling Mom and Dad that, when Emma comes barreling into the house.

"What's up, party people?" she shouts.

I laugh and make my way over to her.

"Hi, Emma. It's so good to see you." My mom follows me over, Dad trailing after her.

Emma, my little sprite of a friend, is much shorter than me. She's barely five feet tall to my five-six frame. We're polar opposites on looks.

"I've missed you." She pulls me into a hug.

"You too, sunshine," I say, giving her a big squeeze.

"This is a nice surprise," Derek says, making his way over to say hello, while Brent just waves from his spot on the couch.

I notice Aiden is staying away from her. I know he's figured out over the years that she has a crush on him. She's never too out there with it—only stolen glances when she's pretty sure he's not looking, or a derogatory comment here and there. But nothing he can't handle.

"Sorry to spring this one on you all," Emma says. "But I thought I'd come in and hang out with everyone one last time in this house."

"I'm so glad you did," I tell her, leading her further into the house. "It'll be nice to have you here."

"Absolutely. I love having all of you kids together in one

house." My mom hugs Emma and turns to my father. "This will be a great way to say goodbye to the house."

"Do you two think you'll be putting it on the market soon?" Aiden asks.

"I think so," Mom replies. "As soon as it's done being cleaned up and cleaned out."

Derek shakes his head. I know he has feelings about this being placed on my shoulders. It's clear from the way he's called me the 'dutiful daughter' on more than one occasion.

"I'm working on it, Mom," I tell her. "But now, with everyone here, maybe Aiden can do his room and the guys can chip in a bit. I have to head to LA in about two weeks. I have a shoot to do."

"Well, let's hope it's done by then," Mom replies. I know she doesn't mean anything by it, but it burns me the wrong way. Same with Derek.

"I'll be of more help, Aud," he says. "I wanna see you get this done so you can take care of the things you need to do."

"Totally. I'll help too," Aiden replies.

I just nod in their direction, my way of saying thanks. But I think to myself that if this is done, then Derek will go back to LA, and I won't see him anymore. We haven't talked about what will happen when we leave this house. And the answer might be nothing.

That's why I haven't asked the question; I'm not ready for the answer.

CHAPTER FIFTEEN

T he sun has fallen, and the air has gotten a little cooler. But it's still a warm summer night. I bask in the glow of the fire as the boys make it just right. I look up and catch a glimpse of one of the dancing flames against the backdrop of the starry night. It takes me back to the last time I saw fire in the sky. I smile at the thought. Looking over, I see Derek is watching me. I wonder if he's thinking the same thing I am.

What I wouldn't give to be able to go over to him right now, place my arms around his waist, and pull him near me. But it would raise too many questions, and Aiden would surely punch him in the face. I don't want any harm to come to him. It's been slightly frustrating. There hasn't been any time for us to sneak away. He's been talking a lot with the band in Aiden's room. When we all had pizza on the deck, he didn't come near. But that didn't stop us from watching each other. I think the only one who noticed was Emma, and that's because watching us has become her new favorite pastime. I think even more than watching my brother.

"So, are you two gonna get some sexy time while everyone's here?" she asks me in a low voice.

I flush and look back over at him. He winks at me, and Emma squeals.

"Could you please just chill?" I reprimand her quietly. "You're going to get us caught."

She snickers. "I'm sorry, but Goddamn, the looks he's giving you. How has Ace not noticed all of this?"

I shake my head. "Probably because he doesn't think Derek would be stupid enough to touch his sister."

"Thank fuck that he was because damn, girl, it's been forever since you've gotten some action. Were there cobwebs growing down there? Were you trimmed and ready?" She lets out a fit of giggles at her own jokes.

I give her a shove, almost sending her off the bench we're sitting on. "Knock it off. Yeah, I was ready for him."

"Oh, I like how dirty that sounds. So, you never have told me, is he good? Because he looks like he'd be good."

I clench my thighs together to fight off the wave of desire that has bubbled up from watching him. He's standing in front of the fire, poking at it with a stick to keep it going. The flames are dancing off his dark features, and it's making him look so sexy and forbidden. I want a taste.

"I think that look on your face is my answer," Emma says and laughs at me. "Would you like to take a dip in the ocean to cool yourself off? Take a moment to yourself to freshen up the down-stairs?" Emma finds herself hysterical and is cackling now.

"What's so funny?" Aiden asks, coming over to us.

"Nothing," I reply a little too quickly.

"Was she making comments about me again?" Aiden asks. Sometimes I think he enjoys the little bits of attention he gets from Emma. It gives him a much-needed ego boost.

I swat him playfully. "You know not every interaction we have is about you."

"Should be." He shoots Emma a wink before walking away.

She just sighs and runs a hand through her blonde shoulder-length hair. "I wish he wouldn't play with me like that. Makes me want to mount him."

"Oh, I know you do. *Everyone* knows you do."

"Even your parents?"

I shrug. "Maybe to some degree."

Emma sighs, looking sad that she might be the butt of jokes sometimes because she hasn't been very subtle with her attraction to my brother.

"They look so happy over there," I remark, drawing her attention to something else. My parents are seated on a bench across from us. They're sitting so close, talking in low, hushed tones. I'm pretty sure it's not about my dad and the fact that he's sick, because they're smiling and holding hands. "I want that," I admit.

"Think you'll ever have that with Derek?" Emma asks me.

I shake my head and turn to her. "No. Even if Aiden knew, I'm not sure he's the type to want to hold someone for the rest of his life, you know? Too many wild oats to sow out there on the road."

"He just might surprise you." Emma gets up and heads over to the cooler the guys dragged out here. It's got water, beers, and seltzers. She picks up a few drinks and then drops them back in there, so I'm guessing she's looking for something alcoholic.

I want to do the same, but Derek comes over and drops down beside me.

"You okay?" he asks.

Surprised by his question, I look over at him. "Why wouldn't I be?"

"You just looked really sad. One moment, you looked like you could jump my bones right here, parents and band be damned. The next minute, it looked like you could cry."

"My parents," I say, gesturing over to where my mom has her head resting on my dad's shoulder. "Look how happy they are."

"They've had a lot of wonderful years together."

"They have. I just wish it wasn't ending."

"Me too," he says, quickly pulling me in for a side hug before releasing me just as fast. "You sure that's it?"

"Yeah, that's it. I need a drink," I say, heading over to the cooler. I can't tell him that I was wishing that would be me and him someday. I know that's not the life he would want. Besides, he's always on tour. I don't want to hold him back, and I'd like to date someone I can actually see. I've done the long-distance thing in the past. It hasn't gone well. I just assumed this might fizzle and fade when we leave Corolla. But I've just not wanted to let on that I feel that way, at least not to him. I'm sure he'll agree. I just don't want him to feel like he has to make any declarations of love or commitment when I know that's not what he wants.

My mom clearing her throat brings me out of my thoughts. I know instantly why she's doing that. It's time to let everyone know what's happening with my dad. Derek must sense it too because I see him move over to stand with Aiden. Brent is looking from me to Derek, his brow furrowed.

"We have something we would like to tell you all," she begins, her voice trembling a bit despite her best efforts. Mom keeps wringing her hands, leaving her eyes trained on a spot on the floor.

My heart squeezes in anticipation of the words she's about to say. I hate that she's about to crush Aiden's world, but I'm happy he'll know so that we can lean on each other. Emma comes over and guides me to the bench we were sitting on. I pop open my seltzer and wait for my mom to change our worlds.

"Everything okay, Mom?" Aiden asks.

She sighs, and Aiden rubs the back of his neck, his shoulders slumping forward. He lowers himself onto his own bench, and Derek and Brent join him, waiting to support him in whatever is about to happen.

"I hate to ruin this wonderful night before it really even gets started, but there is something you should know," she continues.

"Something that might help explain why we have decided to sell the house."

My dad stands up beside her and holds her hand. I steal a glance at Derek, but he's too busy looking from Aiden to my parents to notice.

Mom takes a deep breath. "There is no easy way to say this, so I'm just going to come out with it. Your dad is sick. He has pancreatic cancer. The doctors aren't really sure how much time he has left, as treatments aren't going as we had hoped." She pauses, looking around the fire.

My eyes shoot to Aiden. His lip is quivering, and he quickly hides it by placing his head in his hands. Emma wraps her arm protectively around me.

"I'm sorry that you had to find out this way, but I couldn't bring myself to tell you over the phone or when we've been on FaceTime." She's looking solely at my brother now. He looks up at them and then over at me.

"Did you know about this?" he asks me.

"I did."

"Why didn't you tell me?" He gets on his feet.

Derek and Brent have flanked him. Brent has a supportive hand on his shoulder, but Derek looks like he might be ready to hold him back.

"Because we asked her not to." My mom speaks up, saving me. "You want to be angry with someone, please be mad at me. She wouldn't have known anyway had she not just dropped in on us."

Tears fill my eyes. "I wanted to tell you. I wanted to talk to you about this for so long."

He makes his way over to me and hugs me quickly before grabbing my hand and taking me over to our parents. "Dad." His voice comes out in a rasp. He's openly crying as we all hug. "I love you."

That's it. That's the line that makes my tears turn into sobs. I lose it right there. My parents and Aiden do their best to hold me up. I feel someone hug me from behind, and I know instantly it's not Emma. It's not Derek. His hard body is lined up with me, and he's doing his best to comfort me while my family holds onto me too.

"Fuck, guys, I'm so sorry," Derek says.

"Me too. So sorry," Brent echoes.

"Me too," I hear Emma pipe up, but I'm not sure where she is.

"It's going to be okay," my mom says, comforting us. "Your dad is seeing some of the best doctors, and they are doing everything they can to help him. We'll get through this, kids."

We're a mess for a while, the four of us just standing there holding onto one another, murmuring *I love yous* and trying to get it together. It takes some time, but we finally do it.

"Fuck, the fire," Derek says. He's no longer behind me, and my body registers the loss immediately.

Pulling away from my family, Emma comes over and gives me a hug. She knew, of course, but in this moment, she wants to provide comfort too.

"Love you," she says quietly.

"Love you more, sunshine."

Aiden and Brent are quietly talking. Brent is doing his best to comfort Aiden with words of encouragement, and Aiden slaps him on the back and turns to look at me. He simply nods, but I know him well enough to know that he's not mad at me for not telling him and we're going to get through this together.

"Let's bring this up a bit," Aiden says, shaking his head.

"Yeah, totally," Emma agrees.

"We could roast s'mores," Dad says.

Everyone agrees. I want to get this night back to what our bonfires always were before the sad news broke. There was always singing and storytelling, and roasting s'mores has always been one of my dad's favorite pastimes. It's his favorite treat, and every year for his birthday, my mom would find some type of s'mores-themed dessert to celebrate with. In that moment, as I watch my dad put a marshmallow on his stick, I know I will never look at a s'more without thinking of him. As if he knows, he looks over at me and winks.

"You good?" a voice asks me quietly.

I smile at Derek. "I'm good," I reply lowly. I'm not really and I think he knows that, but what else can I say at this point? My dad will more than likely die, according to everything I've Googled, and my family will cease to exist as I know it. Right now, in this moment, it's my job to just enjoy them.

So, I do it.

I sit back down on the bench with Emma, and everyone else takes their seats too. The conversation starts slowly at first, but eventually, it's boisterous and loud like the old days when we would have bonfires. Aiden is regaling us with the time that a drunk and naked chick walked onto their tour bus. We're all laughing, even my parents. These are the moments I will remember with my family.

I'm torn from my sentimental thoughts when my dad turns to Derek and says, "So where's Serena tonight?"

"Ugh," Derek says, looking up at the sky. "You heard about that too, huh?"

I wonder if he'll come clean with my parents and say it's a farce.

"I think everyone has heard of that, son," he comments, causing us all to laugh.

"I guess so." Derek looks over at Aiden as if asking for permission, and my brother nods. "Can you all keep a secret?"

He looks around the circle and we all agree. I don't miss the way his eyes linger on me. I flash him a quick smile.

"It's not true. There is no relationship with Serena," he says in a low voice. There aren't too many people on the beach, but he doesn't want to risk being heard by anyone just happening by. "It's all a lie drummed up to help sell the single."

Mom is the first one to react to the news. "Can I just say that I'm so happy to hear that?"

We all laugh and Derek stares at her, mouth agape.

"I'm sorry, Derek," Mom says. "But I really don't like her. She seems a bit spoiled. I really think that fame has gotten to her head. Not like you boys."

"Well, thanks," he replies. "But we're not nearly as huge as she is."

"I think you're underestimating yourself, but I'm thankful to hear she won't be showing up."

My dad laughs and nods. "I'm a little relieved too. She just doesn't seem to be your type."

"Who seems like my type?" Derek asks.

I don't miss the way his eyes dart over to me when he asks the question.

My dad shrugs. Unfortunately, Aiden has an idea to share and speaks first.

"Oh, I see him with some girl he picked up on tour. At least for a few hours. Then we'll move onto the next city, and he'll find another one."

Everyone is laughing except me. I forget that I'm supposed to be. This isn't supposed to bother me, but it does. I look at the ground. Emma notices and places a hand on my thigh. When I look up, his eyes are burning into mine.

"I'm sorry," he mouths.

I look away, but I notice Brent is watching me. He gives me a slight shake of his head, like a warning. I implore him with my eyes not to say anything. Unsure of whether or not he'll listen, I see that my mom is watching us too. *Fuck, so much for privacy*.

"I want to hear you guys sing," Dad says. "I haven't heard you in a long time. Is there a new album coming out soon?"

My eyes snap to Derek. I know what trouble he's been having with this lately. He just groans.

"Yeah, brother, how have the songs been going?" Aiden teases him.

"Getting a little better," Derek tells him. "I'm getting my block all worked out."

I can't help but wonder if the innuendo in his voice was meant for me. I don't dare look at him, though. I'm pretty sure Brent is suspicious, and I don't want to create any in Aiden.

The guys grab their guitars from the deck, because of course they were ready for this. My parents have often asked Derek and Aiden to sing. When this happens, Brent has a pad that he plays on. It brings in the perfect beat for the songs and keeps him included. They set up and we all sit back and enjoy the soft tones of their voices.

I love watching Crave perform. Every time they have a show near me, I make it a point to attend. And when a new tour starts, I will head out and watch them too. Even if it means traveling. Aiden has been supportive of me with my Beachbody career and other training that I've done. I feel like I owe it to him to do the same thing for him.

It's a beautiful night, and the gentle strumming of guitars makes it all that much more perfect. Crave normally has a harder sound, so when they sing and do this acoustically, it's just that much more special. My brother's voice is the first one I hear. I smile and watch him. His eyes are closed, and he's really focusing on the words coming out of his mouth and on his guitar playing. I bump Emma's leg with mine because I know right now she is homed in on his singing too.

I look over and catch her beaming. My eyes drift over to Derek. He's staring at me while he plays. His expression is so intense that I can't bring myself to look away. Then he begins to sing.

People see what they want to see
But you
Never you
Only you see me

I swallow audibly, thinking that those words are meant for me. I keep watching him as the song continues. His eyes never leave mine. The song ends and we all clap. It's then that the trance is broken. Derek looks around the fire, making sure no one else caught our moment. I take a look at my parents, and I'm pretty sure my dad caught it. He's watching me with a raised eyebrow. I shift uncomfortably before getting up to get another drink. Anything to distract myself and to keep my dad from looking at me like that. He better not ask, because I don't want to have to lie to him.

The band continues to play, and I stay over by the coolers where it's darker. The fire isn't heating here, keeping our drinks nice and cold. It allows me to cool off just a bit too, from the heat of his stare.

My dad comes up and stands beside me.

"What are you doing over here, Audrey?"

"Just getting a break from the fire. It's getting a bit warm over there."

"What are you doing, sweetheart?" he asks me.

I look over at him. He knows. There's no point in denying or pretending like it's not happening.

"I don't know, but please don't tell Aiden or Mom."

He sighs. "Okay, but if I'm asked, I won't lie."

A loud cell phone cuts through the night air, making the calm sounds of guitars and drum stop.

"Fuck, man. I thought that was on silent," Aiden says.

It's Derek's phone. He pulls it out of his shorts pocket and glares at the screen. "Of course, it's fucking her."

My blood runs cold. I hadn't realized that she reached out to him on his personal cell phone. For some reason, I thought their conversations were strictly through their agents.

"Hey," Derek says into the phone. He scrubs a hand down his face and grimaces. Whatever she said must be working on his nerves. "Hang on, hang on. Let me talk to the guys." There's more silence on his end. "Because there's more to the band than just me, and I have to make sure they're okay with it."

Pulling it away from his ear, he hits a button on the phone

and turns to the guys. "She wants us to hang out at her next show, which is in Cary, so that we can sing our song."

"Just your song?" Brent asks.

"Are we allowed to do any other songs?" Derek asks Serena. The stress and irritation are written all over his face. You can tell he hates dealing with her, and if she can't see that, she's blind. Or just self-centered enough that she doesn't care.

"We can do two others," he tells them.

"When?" Brent asks him.

Derek asks her, then replies with, "Tomorrow."

Aiden looks over at Mom and Dad, waiting for their opinion.

"Do what you need to do," Mom says in way of answering.

"We should do this," Aiden says to Brent, and then he turns to Derek. "You know we have to do this. It's good for us. And for once, her tour stop is close to where we are, not thousands of miles away."

"He's right, man," Brent tells Derek. "Just play the dutiful boyfriend for one night, and then we can hide away again and work on the album."

"And help Audrey pack up," Mom adds in.

"That too," Aiden says.

Sighing, Derek puts the phone back to his ear and walks away from the rest of us, figuring out the details.

"Where is this show?" Emma asks. "You know we wanna go."

"Wouldn't have it any other way," Aiden remarks. "It's at the Aster Theatre. It will be nice for you ladies to come see us play."

"Yay!" Emma squeals.

I just roll my eyes. As much as I like hearing them play, seeing Derek with Serena isn't something I'm looking forward to. And knowing that it's not a big deal if she touches him when I can't, may just kill me.

CHAPTER SIXTEEN

Emma and I are lying on the beach enjoying some much-needed sun and girl time. We spent the morning packing up some things in the house and helping my mom. She's going to have a donation place come and pick up some of the goods before she leaves—or I leave; that's not quite clear. But now my dad is resting, and she suggested that we go enjoy some time together.

"Thank you for coming out here to be with me."

"Are you kidding me? It's been fun watching you squirm and Derek eye-fuck you from across the room."

I pick my foot up and smack her leg with it. "Jerk."

She just giggles. "I'm glad I could come out here and help you. I think your mom was a bit disappointed with the progress that you made. I think she thought more would be done."

"She definitely was. But we made headway this morning."

"Guess you were fucking Derek more than cleaning up, huh?"

My face heats, and I keep my eyes pinched shut so that I don't have to look over at her. "My dad may know something. Think he'll say something?"

"How does he know something?"

"He caught us watching each other last night when the guys

were playing." I peek over and see her nod. "I hope he keeps his mouth shut to Aiden. He said he would, as long as he didn't have to lie."

"He shouldn't."

"Nope," I agree.

"Are you going to be okay tonight?" Emma asks me, propping herself up on one shoulder to get a look at my face.

I open my eyes and watch her for a moment before answering. "I don't care about the fans staring at him. He'll just be doing his job."

"And Serena?"

I sigh. "I think I may want to rip her hair out. Although knowing how he actually feels about her should make me feel better right?"

"It should, but will it?"

"No, because he'll have to act like he likes her. He'll have to play the role of the dutiful boyfriend. You heard Aiden last night when she called."

"I did, but you also saw his face, right? He didn't want to do that, but he did," Emma reminds me.

"But why did he walk away to talk to her? Why couldn't he talk to her around the rest of us? What if he really is starting to like her?"

"You can't honestly believe that. I think you know Derek well enough to know when he's actually into a girl and when he's not."

"I would like to think I do, but maybe it was all just an act to see if he could nail his bandmate's sister. And oh, look, it worked." I sit up and chug a sip of my seltzer, letting the burn of it go down my throat. I'm going to need a lot of alcohol to get through this evening. Might as well start as early as I can.

"I think you're being dramatic. Maybe we shouldn't go tonight. Tell them we'd like to stay here and make sure your parents are okay. Help a bit more with the house."

"No, we can't do that. I made my bed and now it's time to lie in it. Plus, I know you wanna see Aiden play."

"That I do. But I don't want to go if it's going to hurt you."

I smile warmly at her. "I appreciate that. But you're right, I'm just being dramatic and letting her get to me already. It's going to be hard knowing she can touch him if she wants to. And no matter how much *I* want to, I can't."

"True, but you're the only one who knows what his touches really feel like."

I grin. "Thank you for making me feel better."

"It's what I do," Emma says, lying back down.

I join her, and we soak up the rays until a dark person-shaped cloud looms over me. I open my eyes and stare into a familiar pair of brown ones.

"Hey," I say to Derek.

"Hi."

I sit up and look around, seeing he's the only one out here. "Where are the other guys?"

"Getting ready to come for a swim. I got ready faster than them."

"Is that so you could come out here and see this girl?" Emma teases.

"She knows?" He directs the question to me, but Emma answers for me.

"Did you expect me not to?"

"I don't know what I thought. You excited to come to the show tonight?" His eyes are currently roaming up and down my body.

I'm wearing a hot pink two-piece. I can't wait to see his reaction when I stand up and he sees that most of my ass is showing. I decide to test that little theory. I stand up and take a few steps toward the water, then turn around to face him. "Yeah, I am."

"What the fuck are you doing to me in that bikini? Jesus Christ, woman, I'm sporting a partial just staring at you."

I smile. "Well, that seems like a you problem, because this is my suit."

"I love it." He takes off his sunglasses, and his dark orbs stare directly at my ample cleavage.

"I can see that," I tell him.

"You must love torturing me" is all he gets to say on the matter, as Brent and Aiden join us.

Neither one pays attention to the way I'm dressed or says a word about my suit or Emma's, which is a pale purple two-piece that's much cheekier than mine.

"You all wanna get in the water?" Aiden asks.

The boys must want to because they start toward the water. Derek turns before leaving us and asks, "Are you coming with us?"

Emma sits up on her elbows. "Oh, were you talking to us too?"

She pushes her chest out, attempting to give Aiden a show, but unfortunately for her, I don't think he's paying attention to her.

"I meant anyone who wanted to come to the water," Aiden replies loudly.

"Come on," Derek says, motioning for us to follow.

They turn on their heels and head for the water, all three of them in black trunks with baseball caps drawn over their eyes in an attempt to hide their faces. The beach is a little more crowded today, so there's more of a chance they would be recognized than when it was just Derek and me. Especially with all three of them being here.

Emma gets up and runs down after them without warning, beating them to the surf and splashing around. Most of her ass is on display, and I wonder if she did that so that Aiden would notice her. He's watching her, that much I can tell. She's saying something, but I'm not sure if he's noticing her the way she hopes. I sit there for a moment, watching them and wondering what I would think if she ever had a shot with him. It's easy to say I would be fine with it considering what I'm doing with Derek, but I wonder how I would actually feel about it.

Aiden is definitely more of a player than the rest of the guys. He's my brother, so I don't have an opinion on his looks, just on Derek's and Brent's. If you ask me, Derek is more attractive than Brent. Not that Brent is a slouch in the looks department. But Emma says that out of the three of them, Aiden is the hotter one. She told me this even before her crush had fully developed on my brother. There have also been magazine articles and polls done on the boys on Instagram. Aiden typically comes out on top. However, I'd bet if one was done now, Derek would come out on top because of his relationship with Serena.

"Audrey, get out here!" Aiden is calling to me.

It makes me smile. It reminds me of my first beach day with Derek. It feels like it's been ages, when really it's only been a few days—not even a week—since all of this started. It happened so fast, and I fear that it'll end just as quickly.

I get back to following them out into the water. I don't miss the way Derek's eyes follow me the entire time. He's watching me and biting his lip. What I would give to have his mouth on me right now, or at least hear what he's thinking. I dive deep into the water and pop up a few feet from them. Derek hisses out a breath, and it makes me smile. Clearly, me coming out of the water soaking wet with my breasts on full display is affecting him.

Emma snickers, and I give my head a slight shake, hoping she takes the hint.

I look over and see Brent watching me. Not in a creepy way or like he's enjoying the view, but more like he's trying to figure out what my game is. He's perceptive, that one. I'm going to have to remember that.

"What time do we have to leave tonight?" he asks.

Aiden, who was splashing around in the water, turns serious and comes closer to the group. "I figure we have about an hour here and then we should be on the road around three. That'll get us there around five. She doesn't go on until eight. Plenty of time for sound checks and all that."

"Fuck, we don't have much time in the water then, do we?" Brent says.

He looks a little relieved by that. I think it's the way Derek is staring at me and I'm looking at him that is giving him pause.

"Well, we could show up at six. That would still give us enough time to do all that stuff. Plus, I told her she probably wouldn't see us before six. That also keeps us out of her meet and greet bullshit."

"You don't think we should do that?" Aiden asks. Aiden is always up for meeting and interacting with his fans, and Derek may have bailed because he would have to spend more time in front of Serena and the fans, pretending.

"We don't have our security team, Ace. I don't want to be out there unprotected. Especially since some fans get a little extra charged when we're with Serena. Her team will be worried about her and shouldn't have to worry with us too."

Aiden nods, considering all of this. "Okay." He's quiet for a moment and then asks, "How have things been going here? Have you been recognized?"

"Once or twice, but nothing I haven't been able to handle. Audrey and I went to hear Legend, and the doorman recognized me but promised me he'd be cool about it."

I freeze for a second, not sure how Aiden will feel about that. But of course, I worry for nothing.

"That's cool. What did you think of the band?" he asks Derek.

"They looked good. I liked them. I didn't stick around to talk to them, because I wanted to talk to y'all before we offer anything. But if we can, I think we should tell Dale to talk to their manager. See what they'd be down for."

Dale is Crave's manager, and he certainly enjoys pulling all the strings for them. He's what got this whole Derek and Serena thing happening in the first place. Which is partly why I'm not a fan of him. Plus, I've heard Aiden bitch about him on more than one occasion.

He turns toward me. "What did you think?"

I smile, surprised that he wants my opinion. "I thought they sounded good. Seemed like they had a similar sound to you guys."

"Not too similar, right?" Brent asks.

"No," I tell him. Derek is watching me, and I wonder if he's also thinking that we were more preoccupied with each other than the band that was playing. He mentioned checking them out on YouTube and Spotify to be sure he was giving the guys a good review. I smile at the memory.

"Are you all riding with us?" Aiden asks, gesturing between Emma and me.

"Is that an option?" I ask.

"Wouldn't have offered if it wasn't. Besides, we have the Audi we rented, and it'll seat enough. Back seat might be a little crammed, but I think you can manage."

"Shotgun," Brent calls.

"Great, that leaves me in the back with the girls," Derek says, pretending to be annoyed.

"Nah, man, I was going to ask you to drive," Brent says. "We need to talk about some of those new tracks you sent over. I wanna get your thoughts on some of the beats I laid down before we left LA."

"Cool," Derek says.

Brent managed to burst my bubble as soon as it formed. I was really looking forward to being crammed in the back seat with Derek. No such luck now.

"You and me, hanging out in the back seat like old times," Aiden teases, splashing water at me.

I kick my feet in their direction, hitting all three of them with water.

Derek lunges forward and grabs my foot, then pulls me toward him. "You're gonna pay for that."

My stomach flips because I know how I'd like to pay for it. But that isn't happening out here in the ocean with Aiden and Brent watching us. Derek drags me to him and lets his fingertips graze my breast under the water. My nipples harden instantly at the touch. His hand drops lower as he pretends to attempt to dunk me, and I fake fight him off. Fingertips brush my sex, and I have to bite my tongue to keep from dropping my head back into the water and moaning with pleasure. Without warning, he dunks my head back and I get a mouthful of sea water. I come up coughing to find that everyone, but Emma is laughing at me.

"You good?" she asks, swimming over to me.

"Yeah," I cough out.

Derek comes over and puts his arm around my shoulders, pulling me toward him. "Are you okay, Aud? Sorry, I didn't mean to make you choke." Under the water, his hand is brushing across my hips, from one to the other, before he releases me.

"I'm okay, just wasn't expecting it. I turn toward him; his back is to everyone, and he winks at me. It dawns on me that he did that on purpose so that he could throw them all off. I swim closer to Emma again.

Aiden and Brent start talking with Derek about tonight and the two songs they're going to perform.

"You guys haven't figured that out yet?" I ask. "What were you doing all morning? I thought you were rehearsing and not helping Emma and I?"

"Relax, Aud," my brother says. "I'll help tomorrow and get my room all packed up, okay? It'll be fine."

I shake my head. "Okay. Well, I'm gonna swim in. I've gotta get ready for tonight."

Emma follows me, and we make our way back to shore. No words are spoken as we make it back. It's not until our feet hit the sand that she says, "Was he touching you under that water?"

I smirk. "Think it was noticeable?"

"Nah, Ace isn't watching you two for that. However, I think Brent may know a thing or two."

"He squashed that riding in the back thing real quick."

Emma laughs. "He did. But he could have legitimate reasons for it. Don't get paranoid yet."

We head back into the house so we can get ready.

———

I'm back in my room after my shower, with just a towel wrapped around me. Emma is in our shower now. I'm thankful for the solitude so I can mentally prepare myself for seeing Derek with Serena. I lean over the dresser and close my eyes. Images of him taking me from behind flash through my mind. I squeeze my thighs together at the memory. I feel lips pressing on my spine, and my eyes snap open.

There he stands behind me, still dressed from the beach in his black board shorts and no shirt. I lick my lips at the sight of him.

"Hey, baby. Whatcha thinking about?" he teases.

"Oh, I think you know." I smirk at him and spin around so that we're facing each other. "Where are the guys?" I look around and listen for the sounds of anyone.

"Aiden is on the deck with your parents, and Brent went to get in the shower."

"You don't think they'll come walking in here?" I ask.

"Maybe. Maybe not." He smirks at me. "But the possibility of getting caught makes it that much hotter."

"Makes what hotter?" I ask him.

I don't have to wait long for the answer. He brings me closer so that my body is flush against him. His lips come down on mine, and he kisses me gently. I think he's trying to be quiet. When we've kissed before, there's always been a rush or some bite to it. He's never been quite this gentle. I let out a low moan.

He pulls back and chuckles lowly. "You've gotta be quieter than that. Do you want Ace to come in here and see us?"

Afraid my voice will betray me, I just shake my head no.

He places featherlight kisses on my neck and makes his way down to my breasts. "Do you think I could get a nipple in my mouth without getting caught?"

He's already playing with the left one; I'm sure soon the right will end up in his mouth. My hips push forward. I'm getting so worked up that I'm going to need release, or I'll explode.

"Derek...we can't do this," I say between pants as his lips close around my nipple. He bites down lightly, and my head rolls back in pleasure.

"I love seeing you this way," he says quietly. "I love how responsive and turned on you look right now." He kisses my lips hungrily and pulls me close, circling his hips into mine. I jut mine forward, trying to get more friction.

"Goddamn, Derek."

He lets the towel drop to the floor while pinning me to the dresser with his body. "Remember something. When I'm up there on stage with her or when you see us interact, please know I'm *only* thinking of you. I'm *only* thinking of you. I have never touched her body or held her the way I have you. I have never tasted her the way I've tasted you."

Derek drops to his knees and gives my center a lick, and I bite my tongue to keep from screaming out. He inserts one finger into me while sucking my clit, and that does it. I come instantly, my legs shaking as I'm seeing stars. The things this man can do to my body... I almost can't take it.

"Derek," I breathe out as he hands me my towel. But I don't cover myself. I just stare at him in a daze.

"Please remember that tonight. Promise me you'll remember that."

"I promise," I pant.

"See you in a bit, baby." With that, he leaves the room, leaving me with legs that are still shaking.

CHAPTER SEVENTEEN

The ride to the venue is pretty uneventful. I spend it in between Emma and Aiden. Emma offered to sit between the two of us, but she had a bit of drool on the corner of her lip that told me she would enjoy that just a bit too much. So, I sat in the middle seat, trying to catch Derek's eye in the mirror. It doesn't work for most of the ride, though, because he's engaged in conversation with Brent.

I love watching Derek talk about music. He's really into it, talking animatedly with Brent, one hand on the wheel, another making guitar motions. Aiden jumps in from the back seat when he can get a word in. I love watching their creative process, especially when it involves Derek.

The closer we get to the venue, the larger the lump forms in my stomach. I wonder what Serena will look like and how Derek will have to act around her. I've never really paid attention to the press surrounding them. It stung too much then, but now that he's actually touched me, I know it would sting even worse. And I wish I had looked when it wouldn't have hurt as much. But we're here, so I'm about to find out what it all looks like. I'm sure I can do this. I'm hoping there's alcohol backstage. I know there's a pre-show ritual of shots, and I hope I get to partake in that.

While Aiden and Derek are talking to Serena's sound guys, I stand there with Emma and Brent. I finally work up the courage to ask him a few questions.

"So, what does he have to do with her that he hates so much?" I ask. I sneak a peek over at Brent, and he's giving me a knowing smirk.

"Well, they don't kiss or anything, if that's what you're worried about."

"Brent, come here," Derek calls.

"Sorry, kiddo, gotta go."

"It's gonna be okay." Emma does her best to reassure me, but I'm not so sure. This is going to be rough.

"Sure, it will."

"Hey, we're at a Crave show together. This doesn't happen often. Let's hang out. Don't let that bitch get you down. He has a job to do. Let him do it."

I nod. "You're right. You're right. Sorry, let's get out of this funk and go have some fun."

"Hey, girls." Aiden stops and puts his arm around both of our shoulders. "We have to go take care of some stuff—sound checks and all that. If it's alright with you, this guy"—he gestures to the large, unfriendly-looking security guard—"is going to take you to your seats. There's a box that you sit in while we get ready and play."

"Wait, there's a box?" Emma squeals.

"Aiden, where are we really going?" I ask him. I know this theatre. I've been here a million times for shows. I've even seen Crave here before a host of other bands.

"There's a separate row section they roped off for family. Serena doesn't have anyone coming here, but she always has it just in case. So, if you don't mind, please go with him and he'll take you to your seats."

"What don't you want us to see, Ace?" I tease.

He grins, knowing I'm onto him. "Serena and a couple of girls are coming back here. I thought it would be best if you just left before they got here. I don't need you here while I talk to them."

"Are you worried about me embarrassing you?" I say with a giggle.

"Yeah, and Derek asked that I send you to your seats. He said you can come back after the show."

He's sending me away so that I don't have to see her with him. "Okay, fine. But I want to come back for the after-party."

He smirks. "Sure, I'll make sure you get back here for that." He turns to the security guard. "Did you hear that? Make sure they come back once the show wraps."

"Will do, sir," the security guard replies.

I almost hate that Derek's getting rid of us, but I'm not going to fight it. I know why he's doing it, and I don't want to cause a scene. I do wish I could wish him luck before I leave, but I can see that's not going to happen. So, I settle for saying it to Aiden.

"Go get 'em, Ace." I lean over and pull him into a hug. "I love you."

He smiles and pulls me in for another hug. "Thank you, Aud. I love you too. And I'm glad you're here. I know the guys are too. It's just preshow stuff. Easier to do it alone."

"You don't have to explain. I get it. Don't worry, we'll go." I turn to leave with the guard.

"Good luck, Ace," Emma says to him.

"Thanks, sunshine." He leans over and gives her a half hug before heading back to the guys.

Emma's smile is huge after Aiden's hug. I'm sure he doesn't do it on purpose—tease her and make her think he likes her too. Aiden's just a friendly guy. He's friendly with a lot of girls. I always try to avoid him when he's drunk and attempting to hook up with one of the bus bunnies. It's not something I'd like to see.

The security guard who leads us to our seats is tall, has a bald head, is covered in tattoos and wearing all-black clothing. He looks like he'd make a good fifth band member of Crave; however, I'm sure his size and stature effective as a security guard. He leads us down long hallways, where I can hear people getting ready to enter the venue as we make our way through the special entrance to the theatre. Just before he opens two metal doors, he turns to Emma and me.

"Have you ever been here before?" he asks.

We both nod. Emma takes a step back, shrinking into herself as she avoids eye contact with the large man in front of us.

"Okay, then you know there's a pit section. That's not where I'm taking you. There's a wide walkway between the pit section and the grandstands. In front of those grandstands is a roped-off seating area we reserve for VIPs. That's where you'll be. You will not make your way to the pit area. You will not venture into the grandstands. You will stay seated, and you will not cause an issue."

"What about when our boys take the stage?" Emma asks him. "Do we have to stay seated then?"

He glares are her before answering, "Princess, I don't care what you do when the band starts playing, but you will not cause a scene during it. And you will not move seats. You are close enough and where the rest of the security team can look after you. Got it?"

We both stare at him, afraid to say anything. He looks so angry and menacing.

"I need you both to say that you understand in order for me to open this door." We must not answer fast enough because he says it again. "Say you understand."

"Yes, sir," we say at the same time. Emma and I giggle over our identical responses, but he doesn't seem to care. He just opens the door.

The Aster Theatre looks just as I remember it. The guys played here a time or two, more so when they were starting out. This is a smaller venue than I expected Serena to play in. It makes me wonder if this spot was staged or if it was part of the originally planned tour. But judging from how packed it is, it must have been planned.

Emma is bouncing with excitement beside me. She loves going to events like this and seeing the guys play. I love watching them play, too, but I'm not very comfortable in crowds. Also, if all of these people are here to see Serena, then I'm sure she'll be all over Derek.

"So, I'm pretty sure you don't want to talk about this right now, but I've been wondering what happens when Derek goes back to LA? Have you guys talked about that at all?"

I sigh and turn toward Emma. She's right, I don't want to talk about it. "We haven't had that discussion."

"Is this something permanent? Like, are you his girlfriend?"

I flush at the word and Emma grins. I tell her about what he said while she was in the shower, and she nods eagerly and takes in all the details. The area around us fills up, and then we have to start talking in code.

"If D is saying things like that, then there must be some type of a future there, right?"

"I don't know," I tell her honestly. I don't even know how that would work. "I'm not even sure he's going to tell Aiden."

"He'll have to if things move forward."

"Aiden will kill him. Especially with the media circus involving Serena."

Emma nods. "I saw that he appeared on your story, and you got some hate for that, girl."

"I didn't know so many trolls would come for me with that video. I didn't even tag him. He commented and some of the haters stopped, so at least there was that."

"How will you handle it if this is real?"

I lower myself into the chair and think for a moment. Emma joins me in her seat, watching me intently as she waits for an answer that I don't have. "I haven't really thought of that because I'm not sure what this is. Or if he's even serious about me. Or if this is just one of those summer flings. I mean, he says all the right things."

"Maybe you should talk to him."

"Maybe that will scare him away."

"Isn't it worth finding out?"

I shrug, smiling at her. Just then, the house lights go down and Serena's opening act takes the stage. They're pretty good. We enjoy listening to the band play and dance around to songs we've never heard before. Then it's Serena's turn to come out. After a twenty-minute break in music, she emerges.

Coming out of the smoke, she stands in black platform heels, purple leather pants, and a black leather bra. Her abs are on full display. She looks incredible, with her long black hair straightened and hanging down her back.

I shift uncomfortably in my seat before rising like the rest of audience. I don't cheer, though. Emma yells out a few Woo's, but I just stand there, sizing up the competition. Serena's beautiful and so talented, making her a hard person to dislike. Sure, she's demanding and works on the guys' nerves, but man can she sing.

I can tell she's getting ready to bring the guys out when the house lights start to go down. Serena sits on a stool that was brought out for her.

"I have a very special surprise for you all tonight. There's a song that has been burning up the charts from me and the boys of Crave. Well, I got them to come out here to Cary, North Carolina, and see you all."

I shake my head. This is where Aiden and Derek are from. She didn't get them to do anything. II roll my eyes and look over at Emma. She misses my glance; she's too busy bouncing up and down in excitement.

I hear the beginnings of "Memories" as the house lights come up, and Derek sits beside her on a matching stool. He's smiling at her.

"Look who came to visit me?" she croons into the microphone. "Isn't he just the sweetest?"

Derek just smiles and waves at the crowd. He's scanning it, and I imagine he's looking for me. But I doubt it.

When the intro finishes, Serena and Derek begin to sing. They look so perfect together. He's wearing a matching black ensemble and moving closer and closer to her. I've seen them sing together before, on YouTube. I know this is part of it, but it stings all the same. The crowd goes crazy, and Serena plays into it, running her hands on his body.

He lets her, of course.

I die inside a little bit as I watch it. Emma is lost in the performance, dancing around and screaming. Derek gets so close to Serena; their bodies are practically welded together. I decide to turn my attention to Aiden. He looks so happy playing his guitar and bopping along to the beat that Brent is providing. It's actually great that she included the whole band in the song. She could have used her own. I wonder if that was part of the deal Derek struck. I make a mental note to ask Aiden later.

"Your brother is so fucking hot!" Emma yells in my direction.

I make a face and turn my attention back to the performance.

When the song ends, Serena and Derek both take a bow.

"Alright, since the guys of Crave were so nice to come out here and sing this song with me, I thought I would let them sing two of their own songs. Would you all like that?"

The crowd goes wild. I join in because yes, I want to hear them sing some more, especially if Serena won't be a part of it.

"Take it away, Crave," she yells, backing up to stand on the side of the stage. She doesn't leave it, but she's just far enough away to let them take center stage.

The boys play "The Cure, and stwe all dance along. And then I hear the cords for the song Derek was singing last night. The one that made me think he was singing right to me. I get warm all over, and Emma bumps me with her hip.

Derek begins singing, scanning the audience. I wave my arms in excitement, hoping he finds me. Once he does, he sings the words to me, and I melt inside, getting lost in his voice. I feel like he could have written it for me, because it's about a girl who truly sees a man in a way that no one else does. And I think it's almost a perfect fit for us.

But the moment is ruined when Serena comes over as the song finishes and kisses him right on the lips.

It shatters me. I stand there dumbfounded. He puts his arm around her and squeezes her to him. The crowd goes wild, and I die inside.

"Fuck me, Aud. I'm sorry," Emma says.

But I don't respond. I just stand there watching them. Derek is smiling at her, like he welcomed the kiss.

"Thank you everyone for a great night," Derek tells the crowd, then he turns to Serena. "See you backstage."

The words are like a gut punch as I watch Crave leave the stage. I don't register anything that happens for the rest of the concert. I just stand there in my own world while Serena finishes her show.

CHAPTER EIGHTEEN

The surly security guard comes back for us and leads us backstage. I don't even want to go back there. I don't want to see Serena and Derek together. I just want to go home. But the boys are our ride home, so I have to. Plus, Aiden would think it was strange if I avoided going back to see him. I know he'll be excited to see me. I just know that I don't want to see Derek. I want to punch his stupid face instead.

We're led back into a room that smells like sweat and smoke. A few of Serena's band members are smoking. There are bottles of alcohol being passed around, and I immediately wanna grab one and chug it down. I see one that looks like the bottle Derek brought for us the night in the lifeguard stand. I want to chug that bottle. I head straight for it.

Aiden intercepts me on my way to it. "Hey, what did you guys think?"

He's so excited and I feel like an ass for having my own personal crisis right now. The guys are hyped. The show, while shorter for them, went so well. I can't bear to bring him down now. "It went great, Aiden. I'm so proud of you. You were incredible."

"Thank you." He picks me up and spins me around in a hug.

I'm laughing by the time he puts me down. "Emma!" he calls, placing me down and picking her up.

His excitement and laughter are contagious as he hugs Emma and spins her around in his arms too. She's grinning from ear to ear, looking like she hopes he never puts her down.

Brent makes his way over, and there are more congratulations and hugs given to him as well. I look over and see that Derek is standing by Serena's side. His arm is around her waist, gripping her hip. I look away the second he catches me watching them.

Derek doesn't come over to us. He just stays with Serena while all of her handlers come in and out of the room. There are a few fans that got a backstage meet and greet after the show. She's asked Derek to be a part of it. There are times when he calls the guys over for a group picture. To her credit, Serena obliges every fan request for a photo with Crave, never seeming to mind the attention the guys are receiving from her fans.

A giant table of food is set up in the center of the room. I make my way over to it. I'm starving and it looks like it has some tacos, nachos, fruit, and drinks all over it. I need a drink, that's for sure, but I also need something in my stomach, so I don't make an ass out of myself. Like start crying uncontrollably because Derek hasn't stopped touching Serena since they got backstage.

I take a plate and start putting a few of the nacho chips and fixings onto the plate. My stomach growls, reminding me that I haven't really eaten too much today, so I grab a few strawberries and a seltzer, then turn to make my way back to Emma. But I'm blocked.

Serena is standing right in front of me.

"Hi," I stammer out.

"Hi," she says in a sugary-sweet way that lets me know I'm not going to enjoy this conversation.

"Great job. Your show was amazing," I tell her, hoping a compliment will win her over. No such luck.

"I know" is all she says in return.

I'm not sure what's going on. I look around to see that the guys have left the room. *Fuck.* What am I going to do?

"Are you looking for Derek?" she asks. "I sent them all to the merchandise table. I wanted them to approve some new designs. So they went with my manager out there."

I simply nod and wait for the other shoe to drop.

"I see the way you look at him," she tells me, jutting her breasts in my direction.

"I'm not sure who—"

"You know exactly who I'm talking about. I saw him on your stories. My people alerted me to it, so I checked you out." The way she says *my people* makes my stomach turn. She takes her fame very seriously and uses every bit of leverage that brings to her advantage.

"It was a reel actually." I don't know why I correct her, but I do.

She simply laughs. "Yes, well, I saw you there. I saw they came for you in the comments. Derek of course, being the gentleman that he is, stuck up for you. So, I decided to see who you were." She watches me like she's waiting for just the right moment to strike.

I don't know when that will be. But fuck, I'm not looking forward to it. She looks like she could make a meal out of terrorizing me and then go back to her adoring fans with a smile on her face, all the while cleaning her claws.

I finally get up the courage to speak. "I'm not sure what you want from me."

She snickers like the idea that she would want something from me is ridiculous. It kind of is because she has everything. "I don't want anything from you. Well, not really." She pauses. "It's really quite simple. I know you won't go away, and I get that. You're Ace's twin sister. I'll be seeing you at Crave events and parties. And you should be there. Your brother is a great guy. I almost struck this deal with him, but Derek was all too eager, so I went with him."

Hearing her say that about Derek makes my stomach twist. I'm suddenly not hungry. But I don't dare move to put my plate down.

She continues. "But you need to remember that he's with me. You can fantasize about him all you want. You can stare at him from across the room, you can hate on me, but he's mine. For. As. Long. As. I. Say." She punctuates each word with a pointing of her perfectly manicured black fingernail.

I want to deny it all, but I don't.

The nastiness continues. "Sure, he may fuck you. He does that, dear. He picks random women all over the world and has his way with them. It's just what he does."

My mouth opens to defend him, but I snap it shut.

She lets out a malicious giggle. "Oh, you didn't know? You thought you just might be special? Well, you're not. Derek needs someone like me. Someone who can help his career and not hold it back. After I'm done with him, Crave will be huge. And you want that, right? For your brother? So do us all a favor and stay away from Derek.

"Take your moony eyes somewhere else and leave him the fuck alone. Or I will come back and put you in your place. My fans will put you in your place and you will not have that little fitness site to fall back on. Are you understanding me here, baby?" She uses Derek's nickname for me in the cruelest way. "I will ruin you."

"Got it," I croak out.

"Good. Glad we've come to an understanding," she says with a playful laugh. And then she has the gall to lean in and hug me. "Now that we have that out of the way, enjoy the party."

With that, she walks away. On shaky legs, I make my way back to Emma.

"You okay? That didn't look friendly."

"I'm fine," I tell her. I lower myself into a chair, place my food onto the table beside me, and concentrate on breathing in and out. I can't believe what just happened. The things she said can't be right. But in the back of my mind, I know they are.

"Hey, earth to Audrey," Emma is saying. "You good?"

"Oh yeah," I tell her. "I'm good."

Derek might be just playing with me, and that's fine. Because I can play with him too. I can get what I need from him and move on, just like he can with me. He can have Serena because from the sounds of it, they're cut from the same cloth.

Aiden comes over, so they must all be back. Sure enough, I look over and Derek is back on Serena's arm. He raises his drink to me. I just smile and look away. I can feel his eyes on me, but I don't ever look back over. Instead, I focus on Aiden.

"Serena said she came over and met you. How did that go?"

I lie so easily to him, and if he can tell, he doesn't let on. "Oh, that was fine. Yeah, Serena's great." There is only a touch of sarcasm in my voice.

Aiden picks up on it and laughs. "She's quite full of herself."

I nod in agreement. Clearly, he thinks our exchange was about something entirely different than it was. I don't want to burst his bubble, so I let him go on thinking that. "She certainly is."

"How was the merch she brought in for you?" Emma asks him.

His eyes light up and he goes into a whole description of all of it. Apparently there are T-shirts, sweatshirts, stickers—all with the likeness of Crave on them. There are even some pieces with Serena and Crave.

"It looks so awesome. You should run out there and check it out. But don't worry about buying anything. I'm having a few pieces brought back with us. Something for both of you plus Mom and Dad."

"Thanks," I say, hoping my smile meets my eyes.

"That's amazing," Emma says. "Thank you. I need a new Crave hoodie. My old one has been getting a lot of use."

"I'm sure it has," Aiden teases. Brent calls him over and

Aiden tells us, "I've gotta run, ladies. But hey, make sure you get some food or something. We'll be heading out of here in a bit."

Emma makes her way over to the food and starts piling some on a plate. I just push my food around and wait for it to be time to leave.

Derek makes his way over once Serena leaves for a bathroom break.

"Hey," he says, dropping down beside me. "How are you holding up?"

I roll my eyes and reply, "Peachy."

"She said she talked to you. Was she friendly?"

"Sure," I tell him, the irritation seeping in. "You two seem to be getting along pretty well. She doesn't seem to be annoying you too much."

"It's called acting, Aud," he reminds me.

"Then you deserve an Oscar."

"Come on, Audrey," he says, leaning into me. "You know it's just an act."

"You guys did great tonight," I tell him, trying to change the subject.

"Are you okay?"

"You looked great, and I hear the merchandise she's providing fans is great too. Will that be at all her tour stops?"

"I think so. But what's going on? Why won't you let me check on you?"

"You did. I said I was fine. Now can we drop it?"

"I just get the feeling that you're not," he tells me.

"Well, that's your issue, not mine," I spit at him.

"Fine. If this is the way you want to play it, go for it."

"I will," I reply.

"I didn't do anything wrong."

"No one said you did."

"It just feels like—"

I catch Serena walking back into the room. "Look, your girlfriend is back. Better be a good puppy and trot on back over there."

He sighs and rises. "This isn't finished."

"But it is." I'm not sure what I'm saying is specifically finished. Is it this conversation? Is it him and me? But the longer I sit here, the longer I wonder how this could have even worked between us anyway.

The rest of the party is uneventful. Emma and I sit alone in the corner and pick at our food. I'm starting to get tired, and I'd like to head home, but I know the boys aren't quite ready. They seem to be having fun talking to Serena and her band. It's nice to see them in their element, and I don't want to be the bratty little sister who says it's time to go home. But man do I want to.

Finally, around one in the morning, the boys rise and stretch.

"We should get going," Aiden says.

Thank God.

"It was so nice to have all of you here," Serena says while clinging to Derek. "If you decide there are other parts of my tour you'd like to join me on, then please do. There's plenty of room on my bus."

He smiles warmly back at her. "Thanks, we'll keep that in mind."

This doesn't look like the way I pictured it would. I thought he'd be more annoyed with her. I thought he'd stay further away from her and not let her touch him.

"You ready?" Brent asks after making his way over to Emma and me.

"More than ready," I say, not bothering to hide my yawn.

"It was so great to meet you, Audrey," Serena croons. "It was nice of you to come out and support your brother."

I just nod and gather my things, then Aiden and Brent lead us from the room. I imagine it's so that Derek and Serena can say goodbye without us watching them.

"I suppose that fake relationship is going well," I bite out in a low tone.

"Easy there, killer. It's still just as fake," Brent assures me.

I'm not sure about that, but I don't object or say a word. In fact, I'm quiet until we hit the doorstep of the beach house, only pausing to say goodnight to everyone before heading into my room. I don't even bother to give Derek a passing glance before closing the door.

CHAPTER NINETEEN

It's three a.m. and I can't sleep. I got tired of tossing and turning, so I left my room and headed out to the kitchen. Now I'm sitting here at the island, cradling a hot cup of tea. I was so tired at the venue, but now in the comforts of home, sleep is the last thing on my mind. Instead, I keep replaying all the images of Serena and Derek together. I'm trying to reconcile all of that with the things he's told me, but I just can't seem to.

A creaking comes from down the hallway. From the way the hairs on the back of my neck are standing up, I instantly know it's him. He either knows I'm here or he can't sleep either. I turn to him just as he reaches the entrance of the kitchen, shirtless and in a pair of gray sweatpants that are slung low on his hips.

God, he looks incredible. I look away from him, unable to stand his perfection in that moment. I unwrap my hands from the cup of tea and wrap myself in a hug. The stool beside me squeals lightly on the floor as he pulls it out. Out of the corner of my eye, I catch him glancing my way.

"Sorry," he says.

I don't say a word. I just look straight ahead.

"Couldn't sleep either?" he asks. Again, I don't answer. He sighs heavily. "Are you really not going to talk to me?"

"No, I couldn't sleep either." It's not much but it's something.

"Thank you," he says.

I look over and give him a half smile.

"Just how much trouble am I in for tonight? I meant what I said before I left. That was all an act. It had to be the whole time. But I hate that it hurt you."

I sigh. I'm not sure if I want to tell him what she said. But he beats me to it. "She was nasty to you, wasn't she?"

"She was," I say. "But that's to be expected, I guess. She wants this to be real, I think."

"She does, but it won't be. She's a spoiled bitch and I can't stand her."

"Didn't look that way tonight," I remind him.

"She has redeeming qualities. I like to believe that everyone does. But there's no way I would actually date her, Aud. I meant what I said to you. I just had to play a role tonight. And for longer than I would have liked. When Aiden went over to you and was able to wrap you in a hug, lifting you off the ground, I envied him. I wanted to be the one to do that. But I couldn't."

I don't say a word.

"Audrey. Are we done?" he finally asks.

My head snaps over, and I look at him with wide eyes. "I don't want that. I just know that she'll…"

"So will Aiden," he reminds me.

We both sit there for a moment, neither of us speaking. I'm processing the situation we're in. I'm not sure what he's doing, but he's the one who breaks the silence.

"We both agree, though, that this isn't done." It's more of a statement, not a question.

"Yes," I say softly.

"Good."

"Good," I say in return. I shoot him a half smile and lean closer to him, taking in his warmth.

"You know, I was fully prepared to grovel," he tells me.

"Oh, shoot that would have been fun," I say with a giggle.

He laughs and bumps me with his shoulder. I lean back into him, and he speaks again. "What are you out here thinking about?"

"You," I tell him.

"What about me?"

"Whether or not you're worth it."

"Come to any conclusions?" he asks.

"You are, but you already know that."

He laughs. "See, you would think I would, but I don't. I never have felt worth it."

I get the feeling we're not just talking about tonight and the events between him and Serena. He means more than that. "I think that's why I behave the way I do sometimes. The reason I take the random girls backstage and have my way with them. Or let them have their way with me. It's what I'm good for. It's partly why Serena has me in this arrangement. Aiden has principles and morals, more so than I do. Even if he doesn't always show it."

I laugh and cringe inwardly, thinking of things I've learned about my own brother and his sexual antics.

"This little family you've got here," he continues, "as burdensome as it may be sometimes, it's more than I have. My mom has no idea what I even do for a living."

"I was going to ask about her, but I wasn't sure if that would upset you."

"You mean you were going to ask if she's still alive?"

I nod slowly and shoot him an apologetic look.

"It's okay," he says, reading me perfectly. "She is. I just think she's strung out again. I don't know what the hell's going on. The guy she's with seems alright, and he's trying to help her. But she may just be beyond help. Her sponsor will call and update me. I've asked her to do that much. And Mom lets me know when she needs money for her medications or her treatments. I call the pharmacy or the rehab center and pay all of that for her."

"Does she know?"

"No, probably not. I'm not sure if anyone tells her. I just do my best to keep money out of her hands. I don't want her using it to score drugs. And she probably will. My mom will probably always be sick, Audrey. The drugs have too strong of a hold on her. She may never be free. Or maybe she doesn't want to be. I'm not sure."

I reach over and squeeze his thigh, and he covers his hand with mine.

"I never knew who my dad was," he says. "He was never around. Hell, I'm not even sure my mom knew his fucking name. He may have just been some dealer she fucked in order to score some weed. Because that's what she was into before I was born. The harder shit came later, after she had me and life got harder."

"I had no idea."

"Aiden does. I got drunk one night and told him." He scrubs his hands down his face, seeming to be struggling with what he's going to say next. "The point I'm trying to make here, Audrey, is that I'm used for what I'm good for. And that's what's happening with Serena. I recognize that it might be different with you. Believe me, I do. But where can it even go? Aiden will never be okay with this."

I've thought about that. I had hoped that maybe one day he could just understand that we're consenting adults who care for each other, but I'm not so sure now, hearing Derek talk.

"We're doomed before we start?" I ask.

"No," he says, shaking his head. "Not us. Not you. But me. I was doomed before I even started. Good things always seem to fall apart on me. And I don't want this band to fall apart. I don't want it to be the one good thing I lost. Which is why I agreed to the whole Serena thing to begin with. Who cares if they fuck with the broken boy? No one cares about him anyway."

"Derek..." I'm not sure what to say to him. How do you console someone who has thought their whole life that they're not good enough? "You have us—Aiden, my parents, and me. Always me." I turn toward him and grab his hand. "Regardless of how this goes down with you and me, you will always have me. I'm not going anywhere."

He shakes his head slightly. I get ready to object, but he removes his hand from mine and holds it up. "I was just going to say that you and Aiden are my family. And how do I repay that man? I sleep with his sister."

I snicker. "Pretty badass of you."

"More like stupid," he says. "And the worst part of all of this is that I'm dragging you down with me. I've got you sitting out here at three in the morning feeling bad because of the way I acted."

"Want some tea?" I ask him lamely.

He looks over at me and smirks. "Yeah, sure."

I get up and put the kettle on and prepare the bag with the mug. There are no words spoken while I fix him his tea. It's not until I put it down beside him that he speaks.

"Thank you. I heard you say that you have to go to LA in a few weeks. What's that for?"

"I did say that." I admit, but he looks like he wants more. "I have to film some workouts for the platform."

"Are the NWSL games done for now?" he asks me. "Aiden told me all about it. He was proud of you. Fuck, I'm proud of you too. You're training a women's soccer team. That's a big deal."

"Thank you."

"I don't get any more than that?"

"What do you want me to say?"

"Fuck, I don't know. Tell me about it. Tell me when LA is. Tell me what you're doing there, and how long you'll be there. Give me something."

"You really wanna hear about my work?"

He looks at me like I'm crazy. "Goddamn, woman, you're either making me work for it tonight or you think I'm not being sincere when I ask you about it."

"I should know better than to think you weren't actually

interested. It's just that not everyone sees what I do as real work. I think my parents are starting to because I'm training the team or because I appear on the platform. But most people think I'm just a personal trainer, something that could easily be done as a second job. There's not a lot of respect for it. Not like what you do."

"Oh yeah, baby, please respect the hell out of my job." The sarcasm is thick in his voice, and I laugh.

I remember when they were teased about wanting to be rock stars. How my parents suggested going to college or having fallback plans. They had for me too. But Aiden wasn't one that could be bullied. I, however, studied Exercise Science just to appease them. But Aiden and Derek took their own paths, and it paid off.

"You've made yourself into something. Look at the way the throngs of fans come out to see you. You were a late add and had very little publicity but look at how well tonight went. Crave has a following, Derek. You're amazing up there."

"You really think so? I never did get to ask what you thought."

"Are you fishing for compliments?" I tease.

"Would it be wrong if I was?" He snickers and bumps my shoulder with his.

"Only a little bit, sir."

He just shakes his head. "God, you sure do like to make me work for it."

I laugh a little louder than I should, so I cover my mouth with my hands to try to stifle it. He grabs my hands and uses them to pull me to him.

"What's so funny?"

"The fact that you think I make you work for it. I don't know, D. I think I've made it pretty easy for you."

"That part has been pretty easy, but I mean like the talking thing. Getting you to open about anything other than the surfacy shit has been hard."

"I didn't know you gave a shit about anything other than the surfacy shit."

"Well, now you know." He pauses for a moment, taking a sip of his tea before continuing. "Okay, so LA—give me the details. You're shooting for the platform, but what does that look like? How long are you there? Can I see you?"

"Do you wanna see me after we leave this beach house?" I ask. I turn to face him so I can see how he's reacting to my question.

"I know I'll see you again, with Aiden and all. But you know I wanna see you more than that. I wanna see you naked and beneath me." His eyes darken as he speaks. "I wanna be able to taste you again and again."

I finally laugh and look away from him. "I'm pretty sure I'm always behind you. We haven't had sex once where I've been in front of you."

He winks at me and says, "No, we haven't. But does that bother you?"

"No, it's just different. I'm not used to that."

"Good. I like being different from all the other guys."

"There haven't been that many guys, Derek."

"Stop distracting me. Tell me the LA details, please."

I think for a second and then reply, "It's in two, three weeks, maybe? I'm not really sure. I'd have to look at my phone. But I'll be there for about a week. I have some workouts to shoot. I do two a day, usually. They're long days and long hours because some of it is broken up. We don't just shoot for a half hour and then cut it."

He nods, listening intently to every word I'm saying. He's genuinely interested in what I'm saying, which is something I'm not used to. Unless someone's in my world or a close friend, I get a lot of judgment on the work I do. It's nice to see that Derek is different.

"I have promo shoots that I'll have to do and maybe an interview or two to be posted later on Instagram. So yeah, I'll be pretty busy."

"Any chance you would be able to see me?"

"Would you like there to be?" I ask.

"I wouldn't have asked if I wasn't wanting there to be. I have a lot going on, and the guys don't want me hanging out here much longer. They've given me my space, and they've respected it enough. But this little break is about to come to an end."

"And you'll be leaving here."

"I'll be leaving here," he repeats.

We sit in silence for a bit. Nothing really gets resolved or said. We're good at that. We just talk a lot—say a lot but don't really come to any conclusions. I wonder if he notices.

"It's almost five," he remarks. "Neither one of us has gotten any sleep."

"Nope. My parents will be up soon, I'm sure. Even though they're retired, they still wake up early. They don't like to waste the day."

"You'll have to start helping them with packing again."

"I will. Hopefully Aiden will take care of his room and some of the other rooms for me."

"I'll help him and get him to do that for you. When are they leaving?"

I sigh. "I'm not sure. I thought the whole point of them being here was to tell Aiden and then bolt. But I think they want to make some good memories before they go. So maybe another day or two. Unless my dad has an appointment."

"He seems to be doing okay," Derek remarks.

"He does. But when I saw him that day—the day I found out —it was brutal. He was vomiting blood. His treatments are rough on him, and he was so sick." Tears fill my eyes as I think about it.

Derek instantly moves off the stool and gathers me into his arms. "Shh, shh," he repeats as he rocks me. "I'm so sorry, Aud.

I'm not going to tell you it's going to be okay, because I can't say that it will be. But I'm here for you. For anything you need."

A sob breaks through and I cry harder. He keeps rocking me and attempting to soothe me. It's nice just having him near. It's all the comfort I need. But I also need this cry.

"I'll stay as long as I can," he tells me.

A familiar voice joins our little party in the kitchen, and I immediately freeze.

"What's going on, guys? Everything okay?"

It's Aiden. I pull away from Derek and start wiping my eyes. Derek goes over to the counter and grabs me a paper towel, then hands it to me. I smile in way of thanks and blot at my eyes.

"I couldn't sleep and came out here to find that she couldn't sleep either. Got to talking about your dad and..."

Aiden nods in understanding.

"Did we wake you?" Derek asks.

"Nah, I woke up and you were gone. Thought I'd come see what you were up to. You alright, Aud?" He pulls me into a hug, and I lean into him and accept his comfort.

I'm on high alert. I'm not sure why he came looking for Derek, or if he suspects anything. Technically, what Derek said wasn't a lie; it's just not the entirety of his and my conversation.

"I'm good. I was just talking to Derek. You know... a lot going on."

"I'm going to help you get this place cleaned out. Had I known what was going on, I would have come out here with Derek. I thought Mom and Dad were just saying they were gonna sell. I didn't think they actually would. But with Dad being sick, well, I guess they will."

"Looks like it. I should try to lie down a bit. Lots to do here in a few hours."

"Or we could make everyone a big breakfast," he says, waggling his eyebrows at me.

I remember doing that when we were teenagers, using every dish in the kitchen that we had. We would make Mom and Dad eggs, waffles, hash browns, and bacon. It was so much fun cooking with Aiden.

"That would be fun."

"Awesome. Wanna help, man?" he asks, turning to Derek. "I think we need to run to the store first, though. Then we can cook."

"Let's do it," Derek replies.

"Awesome." My brother turns to me. "Audrey, we'll see you in a bit, okay?"

I clean up our teacups. Maybe he doesn't know anything. Sometimes I think that would make two of us, because just when I think I've figured things out with Derek or have made a decision to stop, he reminds me of why we started. And, why I love him.

CHAPTER TWENTY

It's time for the band to leave.

All but Derek. It's weird and I don't get it, but somehow Brent and Aiden have agreed to go back to LA without him.

My parents have to head back to Cary too. Dad has some appointments coming up, and I think it's harder for them to be here than they thought it might be. But we've spent some quality time together as a family. There have been bonfires, big family dinners, beach days, and reminiscing as we pack up—a nice final goodbye to the house.

The morning everyone is leaving, Brent comes out onto the deck, where Derek and I are finishing our coffees. Emma is on the phone with work, letting them know she, too, is on her way back.

"Hey, guys," Brent says, joining us at the table.

My blood runs cold for an instant. I've been waiting for this, for him to tell us he knows.

"Hey," we say in unison.

"See, here's the thing..." Brent starts. "I know there's something happening here, so don't even try to deny it." He holds his hands up, stopping all rebuttals before we could possibly give them. "And I don't necessarily care. But I do know that this will end badly for both of you. Aiden won't like it."

"And what do you think?" Derek asks.

"I think it's the end of the band."

Brent is always direct. I'm almost glad he's not beating around the bush with us. However, I hate that he thinks that. It could very well be the truth, but I'm sure it'll spook Derek. It should spook me, but it doesn't.

I watch Derek, waiting for his reply. Emma comes over, her phone call over.

"You think so?" Derek finally asks.

"Yeah, I kind of do. He's not going to be very happy with this." He gestures between the two of us. "This band is our life, man. So, you better be so fucking sure that you know what you're doing here." He points to me, turning his attention my way. "And you better be so fucking sure that *he* is what you want because this is going to hurt Aiden and it will hurt your relation-ship with him. You are the one thing he always works to protect. And he'll beat the shit out of this man because of you. You better be ready for that."

We let Brent's dose of tough love sink in.

"I get what you're saying," I begin, "but don't you think he'll be a little understanding?"

"How naïve are you, Audrey? You can't honestly think he would understand this. How are you going to explain it? I remember the first day I met you. Aiden told me he had one rule for me, and that rule was to not touch his sister."

"But you won't tell him?" I get he thinks this is a bad idea. There's no way I'll be able to change his mind, but I just need him to keep our secret.

Brent scrubs a hand down his face. "I won't tell him, but Audrey, I'm not going to lie. I won't do that to him." He pauses and looks at Derek. "You're fucking with the band right now by doing this."

Derek closes his eyes and lets out a big sigh. When he opens them, there's turmoil in his brown orbs. I wonder how long it will take him to decide that he's ending this.

"I know, man, I know. But don't worry, I won't let it come to that."

I want to say something reassuring, but there's nothing I can say to change the situation we're in.

"Well, I'm not sure how you're going to avoid it, if you keep on doing this." Brent turns to me. "Look, I know you're having a hard time with everything, the moving and your dad, so if you need anything, please give me a call. I'm here for your brother, but I'm also here for you too."

As if on cue, Aiden makes his way out onto the deck. "What's everybody looking so serious about?"

I freeze, wondering how long he's been watching and if he could have heard. When we were kids and our parents were debating something out here, cracking the patio door open was one of our prime listening techniques. Makes me wonder if he's done the same now.

"Just saying goodbye to these two and letting your sister know I'm only a phone call away," Brent tells him. He sighs and glares in Derek's direction. "And reminding this fucktard not to do anything stupid while he's here."

Aiden laughs. "Yeah, don't go screwing any locals. After that kiss with Serena the other night, the internet is on fire with photos and theories about you two."

I die a little inside at that. I haven't looked or checked because I don't want to see what the press is saying. I've tried to stay in my lane and away from it while I'm on social media, but that might be harder than I thought now.

"You gonna be okay if I leave you?" Aiden asks. He steps closer to me and pulls me into a hug. "He's going to be okay, Aud. I promise you that."

I look over at him, dumbfounded, wondering if he's done the same research that I have. There is very little chance our dad will survive this. Or maybe my brother just likes the rose-colored glasses approach to this because he can't fathom that we will lose our father at such a young age. And that my mom will lose the love of her life. She'll be all alone, and life will certainly be different for all of us.

I just nod.

"What?" he asks me, leaning down so that he can look me in the eyes. "Tell me what you're thinking."

"Nothing," I rasp out. My voice is so thick with emotion, I could cry right now if I'd just let myself.

"I took care of everything I can here, Aud. But if you need me to, I'll stay here with you. I know Derek is staying, but hell, I'd probably be more fun to hang out with than him."

His statement makes me laugh. I don't say a word to contradict him. "You're probably right about that. But I know you're not a fan of being here right now. You like the fast pace of LA. Even though it's probably the last time you'll be able to stay in this house," I remind him.

"I think that makes it that much sadder but also easier for me to leave." He looks out at the ocean. "A lot of shit went down in this house and town. It's easier to remember it that way instead of the empty house you're about to have here in a few days."

I nod, thinking back on all the fun we had here.

"I wish I could have known you guys when you were younger," Brent says out of nowhere. "I know I've had my fun here too, but I started coming here like three years ago, maybe. Hanging with you all and hearing the stories... I don't know. I wish I'd been a part of it."

"We would have had a blast," I tell him.

Brent comes over and gives me a quick hug. "I don't doubt that. I always have so much fun when we're all together."

There's an air of sadness around us. Even though Brent hasn't spent as much time here as the rest of us, he's feeling the loss of the house too. While Derek, Aiden, and I feel the loss of the house *and* Dad.

"Are you sure you need to stay out here to finish writing?" Aiden asks Derek. "I feel like we could be so much more productive if we were together."

They've had this conversation many times. I'm not sure why Aiden can't let it go, but I try not to let my irritation show. I don't want to make him suspicious.

"I'm fine," Derek responds. "Plus, I'll feel bad if the donation people are coming and Audrey is the only one here to deal with them."

"They load it for you, don't they?" Aiden asks, looking over at me for the answer.

"They do," I confirm.

Derek continues. "I need to keep my head clear. Serena's fans will be all over me in LA. I think the best chance of getting anything done is staying here in Corolla for a few more days. Aud flies out to LA soon. I'll leave when she leaves."

"You're coming to LA?" Aiden asks me.

Shit. I hadn't realized that I never mentioned it to him. "Um, yeah. I have a shoot coming up."

"I didn't know that," Aiden says slowly.

I wonder if he's putting things together or just trying to figure out logistically if he can stay too.

"Are you gonna give me a ring while you're there?" he asks, watching me intently.

"Will you have time for me?" There have been many times when I've been in LA that we've been like passing ships in the night. There hasn't been time for either one of us to see the other.

"I figure your little shoots won't take up too much time, so you can come over and see me at the studio. At least I'm hoping that's where we'll be." He shoots a poignant look at Derek.

"They aren't *little shoots*," Derek tells him, looking irritated. "She's there all day long for days at a time getting things right." He shakes his head and heads over the rail.

Brent and Aiden are staring at him. Aiden looks confused,

his brow furrowed like he's unsure what he said that made his friend get so mad at him, especially when I seem perfectly fine. But I'm used to my brother thinking my shoots aren't as large as they are.

"What's the deal, man?" Aiden asks.

Brent shifts uncomfortably, like he feels that it's all about to come to a head.

"Nothing," he says, turning around and leaning up against the railing. "I'm just worried about getting all those songs over to you. You know since you're hoping to be in the studio."

Aiden stares at him for a moment. "Okay."

Thankfully, Mom and Dad come out onto the deck to say their goodbyes.

"Well, kids, time for us to be hitting the road," Mom says. "I want to get your father home so he can rest. He has an appointment tomorrow."

I move over to hug her. "Please let me know how that goes."

"Me too," Aiden says. "Just use the freaking group chat now that you've clued me in."

"We only wanted to tell you in person, son," my dad reminds him. "No one was trying to keep anything from you."

"I know. But just include me now, will you? I want to know how things are going."

"It was so nice to see you all," Mom says, looking around the group as her eyes fill with tears. "Thank you for coming out here to see us and spend some time here. I'm glad we got to share our last time with such great family."

Everyone goes over to Mom and Dad. Emma has thankfully hung up the phone and is able to hear all of this too.

"We wouldn't have missed it," she says softly. "Thank you for having me out here. Not just this time, but all those times. It really meant a lot to me that I could share this time with you all. You made me feel so welcome and like one of your kids. I'll never forget that."

"Aw, Emma, you're like another daughter to me." Mom wraps

her in a hug. "I'm glad you're here too. You've been a great friend to the kids, and a big help these last few days. Now you take care of yourself and don't be a stranger back in Cary."

Emma wipes at a tear, moving to my dad and wrapping him in a hug. "Go, fight, win," she says lowly.

He pulls her in for another hug. "Love you too, kiddo."

Everyone else hugs Mom and Dad, and then it's finally my turn.

"Take care, Daddy. I'll see you soon, okay?"

He gives me a big hug. "Be smart," he whispers in my ear.

I know he means about Derek. I simply nod and place a kiss on his cheek. "I love you more than anything, Daddy."

"I love you too, princess."

Teary-eyed, I make my way over to my mom. "Thank you for everything you're doing here. I couldn't have done this without you. I'm so glad I have you." She hugs me tightly, and it makes me regret feeling the sense of obligation and resentment toward Aiden for not immediately being here.

"You're welcome, Mom. Anything you need, I'm here."

"I know," she says over the lump in her throat.

"Let's hit the road, huh?" my dad says.

We all say our final goodbyes, then I take in the image of my parents leaving this house one final time and let the tears stream down my face.

"You know I hate to do this, but I've gotta go too," Emma says, wrapping me in a warm hug. "I've gotta get back to work."

"Thanks for being here."

"Wouldn't have missed this for the world." She squeeze me tightly and whispers, "Keep me posted." Emma hugs everyone else and then makes her way out of the house.

The guys say goodbye to Derek, making him promise to come back soon so they can get recording. Aiden says something to him that I can't quite here, and my nerves are on edge waiting for a blowup that doesn't happen.

Brent comes over to me and whispers lowly, "I hope you

know what you're doing." I promise him that I do, and to that, he says, "I hope it's worth it all."

I stare at him for a moment. I think it is but knowing everything that's at stake here—the band, the friendship—I wonder if I'm making a huge mistake.

The guys are gone, and Derek turns to me. "That look you have on your face tells me the same thing is going through your head that's going through mine. I'm not sure if this is the right thing anymore either. Aud, I need some time to think."

With that, Derek leaves me standing on the deck all alone. I look out at the waves as I hear the start of an engine out front, then tires are peeling out of the driveway, and I know he's gone.

I collapse onto the deck and sob. I sob for my family and wonder if that's the last time the four of us will all be together like this. I sob because I wish Emma was here to distract me with her humor or her warm embrace. I sob thinking about how Aiden may never understand how I feel about Derek, and that I just might be tearing apart the band that he helped build.

How can living out my dream with the man I'm so sure I love be the thing that could tear everyone else's world apart? There has to be another way.

With my newfound purpose, I finish cleaning up the house and getting things together for the movers who will show up the day after tomorrow. I get more done today than I needed to, and I'm nowhere closer to figuring out how Derek and I can be together. Because there is no way I can make the Aiden in my head see reason. I hope I'm wrong and all the walls he'll put up can be broken down. Because for once in my life, being the dutiful one, the one that always follows the rules, should end in some kind of reward. And in my mind that reward is Derek.

CHAPTER TWENTY-ONE

He comes back when the house is dark. I haven't bothered with any lights. It's late at night, around eleven o'clock, and I have no idea where he's been. He hasn't answered any of my text messages or phone calls, which has me really worried. Needing something to calm my nerves, I grabbed a bottle of wine and began drinking glass after glass.

He enters the quiet house and doesn't seem to see me sitting on the couch at first. My legs are curled up beneath me, glass of wine in hand. I'm sitting here in the dark contemplating every scenario that either involves him being dead, dumping me, or saying he's okay risking so much on a relationship with me.

"Aud," he says into the darkness.

"I'm here," I tell him, waving a hand in the darkness, hoping he can see it.

He comes over to where I am and lowers himself onto the couch. He touches my cheek, running his hand slowly up and down it.

"Hi," I say in a small voice. I can barely see him in the darkness, but I'm pretty sure he's smirking at me. I've seen him do it so many times, not always directed at me. But it's the sexiest thing I've ever seen him do.

The air feels charged with electricity, but it could just be the wine and the fact that I can smell the whiskey on him. The hairs on the back of my neck stand on end. I know something is about to happen, though I'm not sure if it's good or bad. I just know that, in his mind, a decision has been made. Hopefully, not one that ends us.

"Just say it," I tell him when I can't take the silence anymore.

He gets up and turns on a low light so that we're illuminated in a soft glow. When he joins me on the couch, he crosses his legs and faces me. I smile at him, but he doesn't react. He just keeps staring at me so intently, his eyes wandering over my body. He looks hungry, like a starving man finally sitting down to a feast. And I hope that means he's about to devour me. There's something pained in his expression. I feel like he's teetering on the edge of some internal battle. It's time to push him over the edge.

Placing my wineglass on the table, I lean over and run my hand along his thigh. His breath hitches at my touch.

"You're Ace's little sister. Tell me to stop, Audrey. I don't have enough fight in me to stop." The Devil is in his eyes, telling me that he would love to do some deliciously naughty things to my body. "I've been thinking about all the ways this could go, but I'm not strong enough to stop it. I want you."

I've always wanted to hear someone say those words to me. No one has ever told me that they wanted me quite like this. No one has ever made me feel so desired the way he has. I'm being selfish and I know it. There's so much at stake, but all of that be damned.

I want him more than I care about the consequences. Fuck the consequences.

"Tell me to stop," he hisses out again. He's tortured by this decision—it's written all over his face.

"Go," I say, knowing damn well it will break his resolve. It works.

"Fuck." He lunges forward, and we crash together in a delicious tangle of arms and legs.

Derek jerks me forward, then lays be back on the couch so that I'm flat on my back. He covers his body with mine. I love the feeling of the weight of him covering me. I buck my hips up at him as he attacks my lips. His tongue is begging for entrance. I moan and that's all the permission he needs. Slowly, his tongue enters my mouth, dancing with my own. Circling my hips, I let him know where I need him.

"I wanna go slow," he tells me, breaking our kiss. "I don't want to rush this."

We've never done that before. "Does that mean you won't be fucking me from behind this time?"

He smirks at me and taps my nose. "You don't like that?"

I smile back at him. "I never said I didn't like it. I've just never had sex with you while we were actually facing each other."

"And everybody else has fucked you that way, huh?" he asks. There's no anger over the mention of others—more like curiosity.

I shrug and look away from him, embarrassed to say it. My sex life has always been full of missionary. He's the first one to show me something different.

He kisses my lips quickly. "I can fuck you that way if you'd like. Doesn't always have to be from behind."

I flush at his words. I look down so that I'm staring at his neck. I've never known what to say when he says things like that to me. I don't know how to talk dirty to a man.

"You don't have to respond," he says. "Not tonight, anyway. But just let me go a little slower tonight. I really want to feel you."

I nod, and that's all the permission he needs. His lips come down and recapture mine. His kiss is no longer urgent and full of need. It's slower and softer. I almost miss the urgency, but I lie there and enjoy the way his lips move with mine. The easy way in which his hands travel up and down my body. He pulls at the hem of my T-shirt and up it goes. I lean forward a bit to help him in its removal. He takes a moment to look at my bra and brushes his fingertips over one of the cups. I arch into him.

He shifts to the side so he's now lying beside me. "Do you like that?"

I whimper in response.

Derek takes the cup of my bra and pushes it to the side. His mouth covers my breast, and I let out a louder moan.

"It's a good thing we're home alone, because people would surely know you're gonna get fucked," he teases.

His hand slides around to the back, and he pops the clasp of my bra. "You won't be needing this anymore." Once it's discarded, he turns to both of my breasts, working one over with his mouth the other with his fingertips. I'm a ball of need and want, squirming around the couch. He leans down and kisses my lips, swallowing all my moans and kneading a nipple with his hand.

I need him close to me. I need friction, or I just might explode. I grab him and pull him back on top of me. Circling my hips on his, I try to get some much-needed release. He pushes his hips into mine, letting me feel the full weight of him. It feels so good that I moan.

"Derek, I want to feel you," I tell him, pulling at the hem of his shirt. He maneuvers over to the side and pulls off his shirt, and I marvel at the sight of him. He's a thing of beauty, with his tattoos and recently tanned skin under the soft light. I can't bring myself to look away, but when I do, he's smiling at me.

"Are you enjoying the view? You've got a little drool there." He motions to the corner of his mouth and laughs at me.

I just smile back at him and shrug. "What can I say? I like to look at your body."

"I'm glad." He goes for the string of my shorts and begins untying them. "I wanna play with what's beneath here." Leaning down, he places a featherlight kiss on my core through the shorts, and I buck my hips up in appreciation. "Lift for me," he says, dragging the shorts and my thong down my legs.

I'm naked before him and can smell my arousal.

"You are so ready for me," he comments. "But I'm not ready for you yet. I want to play with you a little bit more."

Lying back down beside me, his fingers dive into my folds, and he inserts two fingers inside me. I cry out in pleasure.

"Let's see if you can take three." He inserts another one and begins twisting them ever so slightly.

I squirm with pleasure. "Oh God, Derek. Take your pants off," I command.

"Why?" he asks, still working me over with his fingers.

"Because maybe I want to play too." I really haven't touched him much since this whole thing started. He's made it more about me and giving me pleasure. I want to do the same for him.

"Okay," he says, standing up and discarding his shorts and boxers. He moves naked throughout the house and goes back to his room, then returns with a foil packet.

Ah yes, protection. At least we don't have to worry about him getting me pregnant.

My thoughts are immediately cut off from their practical path when he's standing in front of me naked. His dick is hard and already standing at attention. I love how big he is. How deep he gets and how it rides the line of pleasure and pain.

"Come here." I beckon him over with a finger. "Are you going to make me beg?"

"Why would I do that?" He smirks at me in the dim lighting but doesn't move.

"Because you like to torture me and having me at your mercy. It's time you were at mine," I say to him, sitting up and grabbing for his hips. I get a hold and pull him toward me.

"Audrey," he says in warning, like he knows what I have planned for him. "You don't have to..."

"I know I don't, but I want to."

I lick my lips and take him into my mouth. I almost fear that he won't quite fit without seriously testing my gag reflex, but I manage to guide him to the back of my throat and then slide forward. I love the moans coming from him. I pull back so that he slides almost out of my mouth and then circle the tip with my tongue. I peek up and see he's struggling to keep his eyes open. He grabs ahold of my hair and forces himself further into my mouth. He's setting the pace now, working himself in and out of my mouth. I'm just along for the ride at this point.

Giving his balls a squeeze, I feel him tense and that's it. That's what takes him over the edge. I do my best to swallow all of him. Once I wipe the corner of my mouth, I look up at him and see he's staring at me with admiration written all over his face.

"Wow," he says. "It's been a long time since I let a girl do that."

I'm surprised by his comment, but I don't have a lot of time to think about it. He grabs ahold of my wrists and pulls me to him, kissing me while reaching for a condom. He puts it on and then lifts me up, entering me in one swift motion. My legs wrap around his waist, and he begins driving himself in and out of me. It feels so good.

I can't move. I just hang on and place kisses onto his lips and mouth when I can. He's licking and teasing and touching my nipples. I'm close, and I can sense by the pace he's setting that he is too. The only sounds in the room are our moans and the slapping of skin. Derek has set a rough pace and we come together in a string of grunts and moans.

He lowers me to my feet, and my legs are shaking. I stand there while he discards the condom, then comes over and places a kiss on my lips.

"I'm sorry," he says. "I know I promised slow. There's just something about you—I'm hungry when I'm inside you."

I flush at his words. "I don't mind." It's never been like this for me before. I've never had someone need me and want me so animalistically that they couldn't control themselves.

Derek sits down on the couch and pulls me into him. I cuddle up beside him while he strokes my hair.

"So, are we doing this?" I ask him.

He sighs. "I don't know. I'm worried."

"I can tell. Did that help clear your mind at all?" I tease.

He chuckles. "Yes, it did."

"Where did you go? I tried to get in touch with you."

"I know. I saw." He doesn't answer the question, which makes me almost afraid to even hear it. Did he find someone else to also help clear his head in the moment?

"So where were you?" I ask again.

He sighs. "I was just out driving around and clearing my head. I needed it."

"There's that phrase again," I remark.

"Which one?"

"Clearing your head. I thought that was what we just did. Do you have someone here in town that helped you clear your head too?"

"No, no," he says. His mouth is agape, and he's staring at me like he can't believe I would think that. "How can you ask me that?"

"I'm just asking a question. Just trying to get a little bit of information out of you. I didn't realize it was such a big deal."

He rises and begins to put his clothes on. I sit there dumbfounded as he gets dressed and heads out the back door. I throw my clothes on quickly and follow him.

"Derek, what the hell?" I call.

He's down on the beach, just before the surf, standing on the hard sand and staring out at the ocean. I go stand beside him, unsure of what's going on.

"Derek," I say in the quiet of the night, hoping for some kind of an explanation.

"I shouldn't have reacted like that. I just feel this strong sense of pressure. This big sense of responsibility to do the right thing here. And I'm not sure that I am doing the right thing."

"We're consenting adults," I remind him for what feels like the hundredth time.

"I know that. But Ace will never forgive me for this."

"I thought you weren't worried about that right now."

"It's so easy to say when you're lying beneath me, but the reality of it all smacks me in the face as soon as our clothes are back on."

"What happened in there?" I ask him.

"The picture of the three of us playing in the surf. The canvas that your parents had made that you haven't taken down yet."

I nod, knowing exactly which one he means. It was taken the first summer we met Derek. My parents took him to the beach with us. He hadn't been on a vacation in years, and they wanted to do something nice for him. I felt bad for him when my parents told me the reason why he was coming with us. He was such a fun-loving kid, so easy to get along with. I couldn't believe that someone who was so fun to be around and smiled the way he did had such a life. The picture was taken while we were running the surf. My mom called our names, telling us it was time to come in for dinner. At the exact moment we turned to look at her, my dad snapped the picture.

I love the photo. I have it hanging in my own house, too. I know I need to take it down in the beach house, but it's always made anywhere I am feel like home.

"I'm sorry. I wasn't being fair to you tonight," I remark. "I'm being selfish here. You stand to lose your livelihood. That can't be easy."

"It's not."

"Do you think he'd really turn his back on the band? On all that you two have built together?" I ask.

He shrugs. "I'm not sure. The one thing I've known is that I'm not supposed to touch you."

"Well, there was touching," I tease.

"I know and the worst part of it is, Aud, I feel like an asshole for it. It was so easy for me to touch you that first time. It was so easy for me to take you to bed. It should have been harder than that after all Aiden and your parents have done for me. What are your parents going to say about this?"

"Honestly, I think Aiden is the only one with the caveman bullshit about not touching me. My parents won't care as long as you're respectful to me and you don't make me cry."

"I think I may have ruined that one already. Pretty sure I made you cry." He bumps my shoulder with his and I shrug. "You are way too easy on me and way too forgiving. Why?"

I shrug again. "I don't know. I think because I see a different side of you. You don't give yourself enough credit, Derek. You don't see what an amazing person you are. But I always have. And that amazing body and dick you have don't hurt either."

"Did Audrey Zaks really just say the word *dick*?" He says with a laugh.

"You act like you've never heard me say anything crass." I shake my head and turn toward him.

"It's been a while." He pulls my body into his. "Let's go get some rest. It's already the next day, and yesterday was a hell of a day."

I let him lead me into the house, and then we fall asleep in my bed, wrapped around each other. I'm so exhausted that I let sleep take me immediately. I can worry about all our problems in the morning. There always seems to be time for that.

CHAPTER TWENTY-TWO

I wake up to Derek staring at me.

"Good morning, baby," he says. He looks at peace. Settled. I'm hoping that's a good sign.

"Good morning," I say back to him. My voice is less certain than his, but that's because I'm not sure if he's flipped on me again. The last few times we've talked, I feel like I gain him but then lose him all over again. Not like a breakup, but like we're dancing through this relationship, and he keeps making moves that are backward and forward. I want to go forward and stop with the back and forth.

"You okay?" he asks.

I smile. "I was going to ask you the same question, actually." I stretch my tired muscles. "Is this a happy wake up, Derek? Or is there something we have to talk about?"

He shakes his head, and I fear we have a lot to talk about.

Again.

"I think"—he moves closer to me and hauls me onto my side —"this is a good wake up. I'm not going to go back and forth with you anymore. There's a lot of risk here and I know that. But I want this. I want you and I don't care what anyone else says. I've been lying here thinking about all of this for quite some time now, and I think I've decided…fuck it."

I laugh. "Fuck it, huh?"

"Let people have their opinions and say what we should and shouldn't do, but I'm done listening to them. All that matters is that I'm in love with you and I want you. Damn the rest of them. We're two consenting adults, and this isn't really their business."

My brain is still tripping over the fact that he just said that he loves me. "Derek…"

"Yes," he says, the low timbre of his voice vibrating against my chest.

"Did you just say that you love me?"

He leans down and lightly kisses me on the lips. "Yeah, I did. I love you, Audrey."

My voice catches in my throat, and I can barely get the words out. "I love you, too, Derek," I whisper.

"You don't have to say it just because I did."

I hold my hand up to silence him. "I do love you. I think I have since we were kids."

He laughs. "Oh man, I wasn't the easiest kid to love back then." He looks up at the ceiling.

"I've always found you lovable." I run a hand along his shoulder, down his arm, and squeeze his hand. "You dealt with a lot when we were kids. I think you forget that you were owed some grace with all of that."

He just smiles at me, his brown eyes shining back at me.

"The hell with what the band says or even Serena?"

His body stiffens at the mention of Serena. "You know she's not real. I'm not actually seeing her."

"I know you're not. But I just feel like she's going to have some feelings about you seeing me. She had some feelings about me being there the other night."

"What did she say to you?"

"It doesn't matter," I tell him, hoping he drops it.

"I feel like it should. But you're not going to tell me, are you?"

"It's no big deal. Nothing I can't handle."

"But you're worried about what she'll say when she finds out that we're dating?"

"Because you're dating her to help with her image. Isn't this going to hurt it?"

"No," he says slowly. "But I can see where this might hurt mine." I go to say something, but he puts a finger over my lips. "Although, you could help it too. Childhood best friends find love. Sure, some people will hate me for hurting Serena, but all press can't be bad for me, right?"

I laugh uneasily. I get a feeling in the pit on my stomach that his manager and other handlers are not going to see it that way. But I decide not to bring it up right now. He looks so happy and peaceful lying in my bed.

"Relax." Derek strokes my hair away from my face. "You're worrying about things that aren't even there yet. I have people who can handle this type of thing. It's what we pay them the big bucks for. Don't worry, we're not going to have to handle this on our own. Once we get the band on board, we'll get the rest of my team to follow, and life will be good. It might be bumpy for a bit, but we'll get there."

I'm not sure that he's right, but I let it go. My thoughts are interrupted, and the conversation is halted when the doorbell rings.

Derek gets up to get the door. "Who the fuck is spoiling my perfect morning with you?"

I scurry out of bed and follow him. Derek pulls open the door to find two men wearing jeans and black polo shirts. I immediately wrap my arms around my body. I'm in small shorts and a tank top sans bra.

"Go put some clothes on," Derek says over his shoulder.

I head back down the hall and change. After a minute or two, Derek comes back into the room. He pauses when he enters, his eyes trailing slowly up my legs and finally reaching my face.

"Are they still here?" I ask him.

"Who?"

I laugh. "The men at the door."

"Oh, them," he says, shaking his head like he's clearing it from a fog. I have him so distracted, and I'm only standing here in my tiny sleep tank and jean shorts. The shorts are open, and you can see my thong beneath them. "Yeah, they're here. It seems your mom asked them to come take some of the stuff you're donating."

"I thought they weren't coming until tomorrow?"

"Wires got crossed, I guess."

"Great," I say sarcastically. I do a mental inventory of what's finished and what needs to be done to determine if I'm even ready for that.

Sighing, I make my way out of the bedroom. "Hey, I have some things ready for you, but I don't have it all done. I thought I had today to take care of this."

"We can come back tomorrow, too, if that works for you."

"Like two separate pickups?" I ask him. He's not looking at me anymore. His eyes are fixated behind me. I know instantly that Derek must have come out of the bedroom and is standing there too.

"Are you...?" the guy starts.

Derek makes his way over. He's got a swagger about him, slow and sure. "I am." His voice is several octaves deeper than I've heard him talk to me.

Aiden has a voice similar to this. I always call it his stage voice. I look over at him and take him in. The way a cocky grin has slid across his face, his eyes dancing with amusements. The rock star has been recognized.

"You're Derek from Crave," the other worker says. They both look like they're about to start bouncing on their heels with excitement.

"That would be me." He grins at them.

"Wow," they say in unison.

He chuckles. "Tell you what, I'll sign whatever you two want if you promise not to tell anyone that I'm here. I'm just helping out a friend," he gestures to me, and my heart sinks a bit at being called a friend. But the facade must be kept up. "Could you not tell anyone that you saw me? Or that I'm here in town? It would really be bad for me if this place was swarmed with people. I just wanna help her pack up this stuff before I have to head back to LA."

"Sure, man, no problem," one of them stammers. "Happy to help you out."

"Great. Thanks. You want anything signed?" Derek asks.

One of them nods vigorously. "I'll just go to the truck and get it." And then he takes off.

Derek chuckles, looking over at me. "I hope they aren't bull-shitting me." He stares out the door.

"What's it like?" I ask him.

"What's what like?"

"Having grown men fawning at your feet in disbelief that 'Oh man, he's a rock star and he's standing in front of me.' What is that like?"

He shrugs. "It has its perks. Sometimes it's annoying if it's a bunch of people and they're mobbing me. But this is just two guys. Plus, I have to be nice, so they don't tell people I was here with you. Think about the way he saw us the first time." He winks, and I just shake my head. "Besides, it's not always that bad."

The two men return with napkins for him to sign. Derek looks at their excited faces and then at the napkins. He takes the sharpie from their outstretched hands and signs them, and they thank him profusely.

"Alright, let's get your stuff picked up, and we'll be back tomorrow free of charge," one tells us.

"Thank you," I reply. "That's so nice of you."

"Of course. Anything to help you guys out."

"And you'll keep your mouth shut about this?" Derek clarifies. He looks slightly intimidating as he puffs his chest out.

He looks so sexy; I wish he would stand over me and then fuck me senseless. I bite back a moan.

"Of course, yeah. We'll keep our mouths shut. It's so nice of you to help her out."

Derek reaches out to pound fists with them.

"You're so lucky that you're dating Serena," the other says. "She must be so chill if she's cool with you being here right now."

Serena. The woman that has the potential to be our undoing. Of course, they would mention her. It was such a perfect morning.

I freeze, not sure what to say. I awkwardly excuse myself and head into the bedroom. I have no idea how Derek replies to them. But then I hear him call my name. The tears want to come, so I swallow back the lump forming in my throat.

"That everything?" Derek asks me. The guys are standing there trying to see me from where I stand hidden in the shadows.

"That we have ready now," I say, wishing they would just leave, and I could go hide away. Even though I know chances are slim that he'll actually let me hide away from him, considering the reason.

"Guess we'll see you guys tomorrow."

They say their goodbyes while I just stand there. I kinda wish I could tell them that they can't take that stuff. We'll find someone else to take it. But I know that's silly. It's all loaded up, and this is what my mom wanted me to do. I head out onto the deck and stare out into the sea. It's a beautiful view. I'm going to miss this place when we sell. The door opens behind me, and a shiver goes up my spine when he brushes his hand on my hip. Gently, he tugs me to him.

"You good?" he asks.

"Peachy," I tell him.

"You wanna tell me the truth this time?"

"Nope," I say, leaning into him.

"So, is this about the fact that some of the things from your childhood home just left, or is it because they mentioned Serena?"

I smile. He knows me so well. At least he's given me a chance to take the high road on this one. I decide to be honest with him. "Both."

He sighs. "Do you want to talk about either of those things?"

"Not really. We could have sex instead."

I can feel him smirking when he kisses the top of my head. "I'm going to hate myself for saying this, but we should talk about it and not ignore it."

"You're turning into a woman," I tease him again, hoping he'll drop it. "The old Derek would have said that he'd rather have sex instead of talking."

"So, you think the old Derek only had sex with women? Maybe I did talk to some of them."

I snort. "Sure, you did, baby."

"Well, I would have at least offered, same as I just did with you."

I knew I was right. "I don't want to talk, Derek. I just want to stand here with you and stare out at the ocean."

"It's a beautiful view," he tells me.

I look over, and of course, he's staring at me. "That's a bit cliché." But I love that he said it at all.

"It's what I do. Turn beautiful women into putty in my hands."

"You're so cocky." I can imagine the look on his face, and it makes me feel weak.

"I know you don't want to talk about it, so I'm going to let it slide. I know part of it is because of what's happening with your dad, but we should talk about Serena. I don't want it to fester."

"You're sweet. There's nothing to talk about. It bugs me like a lot of things lately, but I'll get over it."

"I hate that you have to."

"I hate a lot of things. But it's okay. You'll make it up to me later." I bump my hip into his.

"Nice distraction. And yes, I will."

"Don't make me say any more. Just stand here with me for a bit."

"Deal," he says with a sigh.

I like that he doesn't push. He just lets me be me. And right now, with everything that's happening, I need that more than he knows.

CHAPTER TWENTY-THREE

ater that night, we're sitting outside together. The deck has always been my favorite place at this house, and I feel like we're losing it. I want to spend as much time out here as I possibly can. I have my bullet journal spread out in front of me, prepping for the upcoming week and also plotting out some videos I want to shoot.

Derek is still beside me, a notebook in front of him and his guitar in his lap. He's been strumming away and mumbling. I've enjoyed hearing the beautiful chords he's playing.

"Are you over there changing genres?" I ask. "The guys will be none too pleased to hear you'll be playing softer music now."

I catch him smiling at me from under his ball cap. Ever since the moving guys recognized him, he's been wearing the ball cap outside like it's his job. Anything to keep from being recognized. I don't mind it, though; I wouldn't want word getting out of where he is and risk someone else bringing up *her* name.

"Nah, just writing one little slower song. But the rest of what I'm writing will sound different with the boys. What are you up to over there?"

I look back down at my book. "Just planning out some things," I tell him.

He nods. "Do you wanna hear what I'm working on?"

My mouth is hanging open, catching flies as my mom would say. I have no words for the feelings bubbling up inside me. He actually wants me to hear what he's writing. I would be hearing something before the guys.

"You really want me to hear it?" I ask him when I finally find my voice.

"I wouldn't have asked if I didn't." He makes it seem like it's not a big deal, and maybe to him it's not. But for me, it's more than a little bit surprising.

"Oh" is all I say.

"Ace doesn't let you hear what he's writing, does he?"

I laugh. "No, he doesn't. But to be fair to Aiden, I haven't been around him when he's writing lately."

He shrugs. "I'd like you to hear what I've got going on."

I smile and turn my body so that I'm facing him.

He clears his throat and adjusts the guitar, sneaking a peek at me from behind his lashes as he begins. Soft strumming is coming from the guitar. I watch his fingers work the strings. He plays them just as well as he plays me.

There's a change in the air.
I can feel it building.
Something I've never felt before.
A love so pure and true.
Hiding from the rest
I would sacrifice my heart for you.
I would sacrifice my life for you.
For you

Derek continues to sing about love and what he would do for the woman in the song. I get the feeling he means me. I know I'm right when the song comes to an end. He looks up at me, shining bright with love. "What did you think?" His brows are furrowed in concern.

I smile brightly at him. "I loved it. Was that song about me?"

"Who else would it be about?" He sets his guitar down beside his leg.

"I don't know. I thought maybe—"

"No, don't you even say her name and ruin this moment for you. I can tell I'm about to score because you clearly loved that song."

I giggle. "I did. I loved it." I lean over and kiss his cheek, but he grabs me and steals a kiss from me.

I yip, lose balance, and end up sitting on his lap.

"Now, this I really like." He turns my body so that I'm straddling him. "Yep, this I *really* like."

He chuckles and begins trailing kisses up and down my neck. I moan in appreciation. "It looks like you really like this too," he teases.

"I do," I reply, leaning into him.

"Do you need to keep working? Or can we take this into the likes of the bedroom?" he asks me. I lean back, surprised by his question. I would have thought they would have just taken me right here.

"That's a cheesy line," I tell him with a giggle. I reach up and take the ball cap off his head. "There. I can see your eyes now."

He shakes his head, looking around.

"I'll keep you safe," I tell him. "Plus, I doubt anyone would come up here to see you. This is supposed to be a private beach."

"Supposed to be being the operative word there. You would be surprised what I've had to stop women from doing just because they saw me. Or the band."

"Oh, do tell," I say, waggling my eyebrows at him.

Shaking his head, he laughs at me. "Girls have scaled walls, they've interrupted birthday parties, weddings, and even pretended to be maid service just to see us."

"Oh, wow. You are *so* in demand," I tease him, my voice dripping with innuendo.

"Okay, okay, I hear you. You're just making fun of me now."

"I would never make fun of you, baby."

"Uh-huh. I think you're going to pay for that." He flips me so that I'm lying on my back and his body is covering mine.

"What if someone comes up here and scales the deck just to get a look at *the* Derek Walsh."

"Stop it," he warns, tickling my sides.

I squirm under his touch and try to get him to stop tickling me, but my attempts are all fought off. He moves quickly, tickling behind my knees, neck, and ribs. Bringing his lips to my cheek, he trails kisses down my neck.

The giggles quickly turn into moans. "Derek."

"Yeah, baby?" he asks, continuing his descent down my neck to my breasts.

"We really shouldn't do this out here," I warn him.

"It'll be fine. No one can see us from up here."

"I'm looking forward to people seeing your bare ass."

"What about your bare ass when I'm pounding you from behind?"

I flush at the thought.

"Oh, I see someone liked that. You like the idea of people seeing you like this?" He trails a hand down my body and into my shorts, where he grazes my wetness. "Oh yes, someone really does like that. You're already wet for me, baby."

I squirm under his touch. "Derek," I plead. I need him to touch me. I need friction or some type of movement or I'm going to combust. "Please, please. Touch me... or something."

"Or something," he says, stopping the grazing of my wet center. "What's the *or something* you'd like me to do to you?"

The shrill ringing of a phone pulls us from our moment. I whimper in disappointment as he reaches for his phone.

"Yep, it's mine. And it's Serena," he tells me, climbing off me and answering.

My body feels the loss of him immediately. I hate that he had to get up. I hate it even more that he's talking to her. And so far away from me too. I just leave it be, though, and let him have his privacy. I sneak a peek in his direction and see that he's pulling at his hair. Yep, she's frustrating him again.

I go back to working on some content creation schedules and hope that he's not on the phone long. My own phone beeps, and I look to see that Emma has sent me a message.

Emma: I would have called, but who knows if I'm interrupting anything. I wanted to check on you. How are you doing, girl? House all wrapped up?

I sigh and look over at Derek, who's pacing back and forth, talking lowly on the phone to Serena. I figure I can make a quick phone call myself. I dial Emma and she picks up immediately.

"Hey! I thought you would be hanging out with the hottie. I'm surprised you picked up."

I laugh. "Well, I was, but he got a phone call of his own." I decide to leave the part about Serena out. I don't want to give her too much info because there isn't anything to worry about. I know that. He never looks irritated when he talks to me like he does with her. "But yeah, things are moving along with the house. The rest of the stuff will be picked up tomorrow, and then the day after, I head out to LA for a little bit of filming. Derek is actually coming with me."

"Oh really? Does he live near where you film?" Emma sings with delight.

"No, he doesn't. But he's gonna stay with me for a little bit. There are some bands nearby that he can get away with seeing, so he'll do that while I film or sleep. We'll have a few days before he has to go back to the guys."

"Where will you go?" she asks.

"Aw, sunshine, is that your way of asking me if I'll be coming back to you soon? Do you miss me?"

"Yeah, of course I miss you."

I smile. I miss her too. When I'm living in Cary, we typically see each other a few times a week. Between her work, my training sessions, and my content creation, we can't see each other every day, but we make it work.

"I'm not going back to the beach house if that's what you mean. The realtor will be stopping by. Mom and Dad know her, so she can just meet with them via Zoom and get everything taken care of with an empty house. Thank God." I roll my eyes, and I'm pretty sure Emma can hear my irritation over the phone. I was so glad that Laura was able to work with us and do most of the work through Zoom. Because I have to get back to Cary. I have some new training sessions set up with the NC Courage. They're also hosting some camps with potential college soccer players, so they'd like for me to train them. I'm a little exited for this opportunity, and I'm hoping it leads to more training or a full-time position with them. Currently, I'm just rotated in with their other trainers."

"Oh, good. I need some girl time."

"Me too," I tell her. It hits me then that I'll be coming home without Derek. He'll be in LA, and I'll be halfway across the world with a three-hour time difference to contend with.

"Are you gonna miss him?"

I don't say anything; instead, I steal a glance at him. He's watching me and smiling. After giving me a wave, he turns back to face the beach.

"I'm guessing that silence is my answer," Emma replies. "Have you two talked about it at all?"

"Nope," I say popping the *P*.

"Afraid to ask him?" she says with a giggle.

"Kinda," I admit. "I know he likes me. But I'm not really sure how long he'll like having me around for, you know? Especially since the guys won't be too thrilled with this. Brent knows and he's probably ready to kill both of us."

Emma laughs. "They'll get over it. Like Derek said, you're both adults."

"True."

Emma's been texting me relentlessly, asking for updates and

just checking in. I can tell she's worried about me. With every-thing going on with Dad, then add Derek to the mix...it's been a roller coaster of a few weeks.

There's a rumble of thunder letting us know we're about to get some much-needed rain. It's been so humid out here lately. We could use the rain to cool things off, if only for a minute.

"Do you want me to let you get back to your man? You've gotten quiet over there," Emma says.

"Soon. I was just watching the weather. It looks like it might rain here soon."

"More like you were peeping on your man and hoping it's about to rain down some Derek all over you." She laughs at her own joke, and I can't help but join in.

"You're so subtle, Emma," I tease.

"But of course."

I look over when I feel a pair of eyes on me, and there's Derek watching me. His phone call is over. I move to turn around, but he juts his lips out, pouting a bit.

"Hey, did you hear me?" Emma is asking me.

"Crap. No, I'm sorry."

"Getting distracted over there, huh? I'm gonna let you go, but promise you'll give me a call. I just want to check on you and make sure you don't need anything, okay?"

"I appreciate it, Em. Thanks for everything."

"That's what I'm here for, babe."

I let out a scream when the sky opens up and begins pouring down rain.

"You okay?" Emma asks.

"Rain," I shout. "It's raining here."

"Oh, good. Talk to you later, girl."

We hang up and I turn to see him staring at me. My shirt is white, and so is the bra underneath. I can see his hooded eyes from here.

"We've gotta get inside," I call out to him. "We're getting soaked."

"Yeah, we really should." He stalks over to me, looking like he has no intention of going inside. "Come here, you." The thunder rumbles overhead.

"You're gonna get us struck," I warn him.

"That's what makes it so exciting. And besides, no one else is on the beach for us to worry about."

I giggle. I've never had sex in the rain. It sounds like it might be perfect, creating some heat of our own while the sky gets angry around us with flashes of lightning and the rumbling of thunder. Just then, a strike of lightning hits just a little too close to us.

"On second thought, maybe we should head inside," he says, grabbing my hand and dragging me to the house. "Wouldn't want to get you struck. I'd hate to have to explain that one to everyone."

I laugh, following him into the house. He stops me right beside the back door in the dining room. This is where he takes me from behind at the dining room table while the lightning and thunder crash in the background. Thankfully, that table is staying with my parents, because if they were getting rid of it, I would try to buy it as a souvenir. Now, I'll have something to remember him and our time together by whenever I come to the house.

I try to decide whether that's a good thing or not while he pounds into me. I lose all sense of thought when my orgasm rips through me. We fall to the table, sated. On second thought, I might need to keep it just for me.

CHAPTER TWENTY-FOUR

"American Airlines flight 495 to Los Angeles will begin boarding..."

I don't hear the rest. I just hold onto Derek's hand as he drags me through the airport. I swear my feet can't keep up with his long strides.

"Slow down, Derek," I tell him for what feels like the millionth time.

"If I slow down, we'll miss this flight." He barely looks over his shoulder as he drags me.

Well, if someone wouldn't have insisted on going for another round this morning, we might not be late. But I don't say that. I keep my focus on moving forward. I'm still a little sore from the way he pounded into me when he was going for round two. We have yet to have a slow session. He always tells me he wants to take his time with me, but that never happens.

We reach the gate, and Derek drops my hand. He's fishing for his ticket and ID. I do the same. I don't miss the way the perky blonde particularly eye-fucks him as he's scanning his ticket.

"You're in our first class, Mr. Walsh," she tells him.

He nods as if this isn't news to him. And it shouldn't be. He's the one that booked the flight. He also upgraded my ticket last night too. That was a fight because I don't like taking his money. But he insisted. I almost held my breath, hoping there wouldn't be any seats left in first class with him. Of course, there were and now we're going to be sitting together.

Her eyes remain on him while I scan my boarding pass. I wonder if she'll have anything to say to me. She doesn't. She's still too busy checking him out. I can't blame her. Derek's dressed simply for the airport—dark jeans, white T-shirt, and black baseball cap that he's been wearing all week. It's pulled down real low so no one can make out that it's him. I don't blame her for staring. The sight of him took my breath away when I saw. I almost pulled him back into bed to go for round four. But if I had, we would have missed our flight for sure.

"Am I in first class too?" I ask her. I want her to have to talk to me.

She looks over at me, seemingly annoyed that I would ask her a question. But she answers me almost as sweetly as she did him. "Yes, you are." Her eyes dart back over to him.

I roll mine and reply, "Why, thank you very much!" I lay it on sugary sweet, but it's a waste. She's not paying any attention to me.

Derek smirks. He must have figured out what I was doing. We make our way down the boarding ramp, and I've never been so happy to be headed onto an aircraft in my life.

I'm not a nervous flier, but the butterflies do kick up when we get close to takeoff. I almost grip the seat in trepidation, hoping that everything goes well. Once we're airborne, I calm down. I wonder if Derek will notice as I make my way onto the plane. He puts our carry-ons in the overhead compartment. We settle into our seats, and I finally ask Derek about it.

"Do all women look at you like that?"

He smirks. "Baby, you have no idea."

I punch him in the shoulder. He fakes hurt and I shake my head as he laughs at me.

"Oh, relax. I only have eyes for you." He leans over and gives me a kiss.

The rest of the flight goes by without incident. Once we arrive in LA, Derek leads me through the crowded airport and over to baggage claim.

"So, do they send a car for you? Or how does this work?"

I laugh. "Well, Mr. Famous Rock Star, it's not like when you travel to LA. I take myself to the studio, which we need to head to now so that I can get some filming in. I have a tight schedule."

He chuckles. "I'll bet you do. Do we have time to make out in the cab?"

I shake my head. "We do not. Now let's get a move on."

When we arrive at the studio, the crew takes me immediately to get me set up and ready. The producer is kind enough to give Derek a place where he can watch from. While I'm getting ready, he meets the rest of the crew and the small cast they've brought in for me to do the workouts with.

"How many will you do today?" he asks me when he sees me in my lime green sports bra and matching leggings. "I like this, by the way. Do you get to take it with you?"

"Sometimes I get to take some of my favorite pieces with me, but don't rip it. I might need it for reshoots."

"Oh, I make no promises."

"Well, then you can't take this one off me."

"Strip show, I like it," he says, squeezing my ass.

"Not while I'm on set," I warn him.

"Okay, fine. I'll be a professional. Wouldn't want you to look bad in front of your people."

I think he means it, but with the way his eyes keep wandering my body, I'm not so sure that he does.

I make my way over and we begin filming. We arrived in LA at three o'clock and at the studio by four thirty. I'd like to think they'll take it easy on me, but I'm seeing that's not going to be the case. But to Derek's credit, he's being so patient and watching and waiting. I make my way over to him on a break.

"Hey, I'm sorry this is taking so long."

"Why are you apologizing? You're doing your job. It's completely fine. Just keep on doing what you have to do, and I will be here waiting when you're done."

I smile at him, and I can't imagine how I got so lucky. It's been a long day, and he's in his hometown. He could easily go to his apartment or over to the studio or even hang out with friends. But he stays with me instead. No one is supposed to know he's here. So, we'll be lying pretty low in LA, which I'm okay with. Usually when I'm here, I don't go out to eat a lot. I spend most days filming and then eat dinner in my room. Or on set, depending on how late they keep me. Part of me thinks Derek is looking forward to this type of schedule, where we can just go from the hotel to the studio and back—no pressures or expectations for him.

The guys still think he's in Corolla. I'm just hoping the press doesn't catch wind of it. They know he'll be heading to LA in a few days, which is when we'll let them know he's here. Because Aiden has my schedule, he's asked me to stay in LA for a few days to hang out a bit. That's perfect for Derek and me. I wanted him to stay with Aiden anyway. I just hope we can keep everything from the band.

"Hey, a penny for your thoughts," he says, bopping me on the nose.

"Sorry, I was just thinking things over."

"You nervous? You seem nervous."

"On-set jitters, I guess." I shake out my legs and do a few stretches.

"You're gonna be great," he tells me, giving me a comforting hug. "I love you, and I'll be waiting for you as long as you need me to be."

"Thank you."

I love the support he's showing me by being here. Not

everyone would agree that this is as important as his work, but it is to me. This is only my third program shoot with Beachbody, and each time they ask me back, I'm so surprised. It's something I never just assume will happen. It doesn't feel like a given. It feels like I must prove myself each time I do it.

"Audrey," the producer calls with a wave.

I snap my head in his direction, holding my hand up to let him know that I'll be there in just one second. He nods.

"I gotta go," I tell Derek, leaning into him for one more hug.

"Go have fun. I'll be here waiting for you. No matter how long it takes." He slaps my ass when I walk away, and I yip.

I head over to my cast, and Natalie, one of my regulars, is waiting for me. I can tell she wants to ask me a million questions.

"Is that who I think it is?" she asks.

"That depends on who you think it is," I tease.

"Is he in Crave?"

I knew someone would recognize him. And we talked about the possibility of it happening. He told me to lie, so I do.

"No, he just has one of those faces," I tell her. "Believe me, I wish he was. The guy from Crave is super hot."

She nods in complete agreement. I've known Natalie for a while, but not long enough to tell her who my brother is and that he is in fact in Crave. That's one of those things I've learned to keep close to the vest. You never know who's being your friend for who you are or who wants to get close to your famous twin brother. Natalie doesn't come off as the type, but I've learned, unfortunately the hard way, that that's not always the case.

Thankfully, Natalie doesn't push the issue any further, and Derek stays in the corner with his standard ball cap drawn down, out of sight. We get through the shoot in a few hours and by nine that night, I'm on my way to the hotel with Derek in tow.

We get into our suite, and I immediately tell him that I need a shower.

"You were impressive today," he tells me.

I stop and smile at him. "Really?"

"Yeah, really. I'm not just saying that because I'm hoping for some shower sex. I had no idea what all goes into filming these workout programs. How many times they start and stop you. The amount of times they have you lifting and doing those cardio moves. You handle it so much better than I would. How do you put up with it?"

I sigh and look at him. I'm happy that he got to see me working today and that he seems proud of me. "It's not easy. My muscles literally feel like Jell-O, so I can't hold myself up much tonight. But it's what I love to do. It's not easy putting together a program, but it's one of the first times the director has seen the moves in person. I filmed and sent them to team. It'll all come together. It always does."

"You're amazing and I'm so proud of you."

I cross the room and kiss him tenderly. "You are amazing, Derek."

He smirks and lead me into the bathroom, then strips me bare. I step under the spray as he gathers my toiletries from the luggage we brought, and he washes me and rubs at my muscles while he uses the bodywash on me. I appreciate the time and attention he takes on each one.

We order room service that night and then crawl under the covers to sleep. He doesn't seem to mind that I pass out in his arms. I'm exhausted from the long day we've had, and I need sleep. It'll be a busy week.

And it is. He stays with me all week long while I film. We spend the nights making love since the first night was the only day it was long and grueling for me. When the spot is finished, we head over to his apartment to see the guys and try to hide the fact that we've spent four blissful days locked away undetected.

CHAPTER TWENTY-FIVE

My work is finished for the week, and somehow he convinced me to come stay with him. I have the time, and I want to be with him. My training with the Courage isn't starting for another two weeks, so why not? I'm not ready to leave him anyway. I don't want to think about what it will mean for us when I do have to go back. How will we manage? How will *I* manage without him? I like waking up beside him, cooking dinner together, or ordering takeout and hiding in a hotel room to eat.

Being in LA with him is different than being back in Corolla. Corolla allowed for him to roam around with just a baseball cap on. As long as he wasn't flashing a big sign that said *I'm with Crave,* then all was well. But here in LA, people are more likely to recognize him. There are women and teenage girls that travel to LA specifically to catch a glimpse of a star, and they would be all over these boys if they stumbled upon them.

"Do you miss it?" I ask him when we're lying in his bed.

"Miss what?"

"Being able to move around without having people swarming you."

He shrugs and sighs. "It's all a part of it. And frankly, when

I'm here in LA, I don't go out all that much. I make sure I hit the right events when Dale tells us to. I see the guys and we hang out at each other's houses as much as we can. But I was never one for going out much anyway. It's kinda why I have a full bar at my house. Why go out when you can bring the bar here?"

I laugh, thinking of the impressive bar he has off the living room. Derek lives in a studio apartment that only has separate areas for the bedroom and bathroom. The rest is an open floor plan. You enter into a living room with the kitchen directly beyond that. To the left is the bedroom and bathrooms, and on the right you have the dining area and bar. It almost looks like a professional setup, complete with a keg. The black mahogany bar allows for seating for five. Beyond that is an impressive liquor selection that only displays the top shelf items he's collected. Below that, there's shelving where the remaining bottles are stored.

The place is the typical bachelor pad, complete with black furniture and scarce decorations. But I like that his couch is long and U-shaped, and it's not leather. I fully expected leather, but it's comfy. There are some pictures on wall of the band and their album covers. It makes my heart happy to see that he has a picture of Aiden, him, and me on the wall from when we were kids. We're all in front of the ocean, and you can see the waves crashing behind us in the background. It makes my heart squeeze a bit knowing that if we do go back there, we'll be tourists and not locals who own the house with the nice private beach.

Derek leans over and blows out the candle that is lit beside him. "Do you wanna be a little bit adventurous?" There's a menacing look on his face. It's sexy, but everything about him is sexy. The dark clothing, he wears, the intense stare of his brown eyes, and his strong body. I love to look at him and marvel at his physique and the man he is. It almost makes me wish that some-one, some family, had stuck around to see how he turned out.

But I know he has Aiden and me. His found family has been there and is so proud of him.

"What did you have in mind?" I ask. I've never been very adventurous with sex. This is the most doggie style I've ever done. But it appears to be all he likes. He tells me it's all about the angles.

"Wanna play with wax?" He waggles his eyebrows in my direction.

I slink back, unsure.

"I would never do anything to hurt you," he reminds me.

"Sure." My tone is a bit shaky and uneasy.

"Relax. Nothing is on fire, and you don't have to worry about me burning you. I've done this before."

"Uh-huh," I reply. He's done this before. I wonder if there will ever be anything that Derek and I could ever do that would not be new to him.

"Do you trust me?" he asks. His voice is velvety smooth.

I do. I just don't know if I want him to play with fire or wax around me. Finally, I give in. "Okay, I'll give it a try."

"I think you're going to be pleasantly surprised." He grins, leaning over the bedside table. From the drawer, he pulls out a lighter and a candle. It's a funky—a black high votive that has a spout. It's not as decorative as others I've seen in his house.

"What is that?" I ask him, my voice trembling just a bit.

"It's a candle."

"I can see that, but I'm not sure you're supposed to pour hot wax on me from some random candle."

"Relax. It's a soy candle that's made for this sort of thing. I wouldn't burn you on purpose."

I watch all his movements, trying not to think about how natural that all looked for him.

"So, what now?"

"We have to let it burn for a little bit, and then I'll slowly pour it on you."

I feel myself begin to get wet with anticipation.

"I can tell you like the idea of it," he teases me. "Your pupils are dilating. See, baby, this is going to be fun."

He yanks me toward him, and I let out a little yip of surprise. It gets lost in the passion of his kiss. He rolls me onto my back, and I feel the full weight of him. I grind my hips against his while we explore each other. He removes his shirt, and mine soon follows. Before I know it, the only thing I'm wearing is a smile. I think maybe he's decided against playing with it. I'd be okay with that. I'm so wet and turned on just from him running his hands all over and me. I *need* him now.

"Derek," I gasp out. "I need you."

"You'll get me, but not yet."

I'm so turned on that at this point, I don't care what he has to do before he's inside me. I just want him to do it.

Derek rolls off me, sits up, and blows out the candle. He's leaning in front of me. "Just remember, this isn't going to hurt. I think it's going to feel good."

I nod.

"Put your hands above your head for me and just try to relax."

"Okay, I can do that."

"You look so worried. I need you to relax for me."

"I'm okay. Just nervous, I guess."

Derek leans down and kisses my lips tenderly. I relax and lose myself in the kiss. I feel the warm wax dripping onto my nipple. The bite of it feels good, and I moan into his mouth. Bucking my hips off the bed, I beg for more.

Pulling back, he says, "I see you like that. Good."

I just moan in response. He's twisting my nipple covered in wax. He moves to the other one and drops some wax on that one. It feels amazing. I had no idea it would feel this way. I imagined I'd feel like I was on fire when he dripped a flaming candle on my body.

"Derek," I breathe out.

He smirks at me and kisses me again before placing the

candle onto the table. Twisting both of my nipples, he moans, grinding his hips into mine. I think he's going to enter me, but instead, he reaches over and grabs the candle again. The wax is poured down my stomach, and he kisses his way down. I'm a ball of need. When he pushes his hips against mine while playing with my nipples, I let go, letting out a loud moan like a pornstar. Soon, I go weightless. I'm not sure what the better feeling is— coming apart like this or the way it felt when the wax covered me the first time.

He's a bit more adventurous with it than I am. Lying on his side, he drips the wax so that it's covering his groin. His hand comes up and gathers the wax, then he strokes himself with that hand. I just lie there watching. I want to touch him, and I want him to touch me.

"Touch yourself for me," he pleads, his voice strained. "Come on, baby, do it for me."

I hesitate for a second. I'm not a prude but touching myself is something I usually do when I know I'm all alone. I've never done it in front of a man before. He seems so comfortable lying there beside me, pleasuring himself.

"Touch yourself while you touch me." He grabs my hand and places it on his dick, then he strokes himself with my hand, showing me how he likes it. He moans. I look up at him through hooded lashes.

Letting out a sigh, I let my hand travel down my body and cup my sex. My hands find my folds, and I show him how I pleasure myself. I smirk and then let out a moan. I think back to all the times I touched myself and imagined that my hand was his.

I love the way he's staring at me right now. His lips are parted, and he's moaning lowly as I stroke him. His eyes are glued to where my hand is pleasuring me. He takes a finger and inserts it inside me.

"Don't stop touching either of us," he grits out.

That's it. That does it. Those orders and those sounds are all it takes. I come hard, screaming out his name. He kisses my lips tenderly when I stop moving and lie still.

Just when I feel like I'm coming down, he takes advantage. He rolls a condom on, moves me so that I'm on my side, and hitches my leg up over his. In a switch motion, he enters me. I cry out in pleasure. It's quick and furious. I can't keep up, let alone move. Derek is twisting my nipples and kissing on my neck. He's everywhere all at once. I just lie there and moan, attempting to push my ass against him.

With a pinch of my clit, he sends me soaring again. I let go and scream out in pleasure. Derek soon follows me. I lie there, my entire body feeling like jelly.

"We've gotta clean up," he finally says.

"Do we really have to move?" I ask with a giggle.

He slaps my ass playfully, and I let out a yip. I snuggle back into him. I really could lie here all day. I know we have things to do. Well, he does. He has to go to the studio and meet with the boys—more work on the album.

"Are you finished writing all your songs?" I ask him. He has been up late at night writing and working on songs. I think that's probably why we got busy this morning.

"It's going well."

"I heard you a few times last night. I thought it sounded really good."

"Am I keeping you up?" he asks, kissing my neck.

"No, you're fine. I can never sleep through the night."

"You don't seem to have a problem when I'm lying beside you."

"It's your hot body. Helps me sleep at night."

"You mean the way I look and not the fact that I smother you with my body heat, right?" he teases.

"I totally mean that," I say with a laugh.

"We really should move, though. Or we're gonna have a bit of a problem." He means the condom.

"Fine, let's get up. But I need a shower. Someone made me a little dirty."

"Fine," he says, mocking me playfully. "Let's get in the shower. We've gotta get ready. Are you coming to the studio with me today?"

"I was planning on it. I wonder what Aiden will say when he sees me, though." Aiden has no idea that I've been staying with Derek.

"I told you; we'll go get coffee beforehand, and I'll just tell him I ran into you at the coffee shop. Easy peasy."

"You don't think he's smarter than that?"

"Nah, I don't think we've given him any cause for concern. Brent might be suspicious, but I don't think he wants to rock the boat. So, we should be good." Derek gets up and discards the condom. "Come on, pretty girl, let's get you cleaned up." He stretches his hand out to me, his big brown eyes shining back at me.

A sexy little smile is stretched across his lips. He looks so alluring when he's like this. His walls are down, and he's not putting on a show. Not being Derek from Crave. Stage Derek's voice would be a few octaves deeper. His smile would be more guarded, and he would be choosing his words very carefully. But not when we're here. In the safety of his apartment, he's relaxed and more himself. I see peeks of the Derek I grew up with running in the surf.

We shower and get ourselves ready for the day. I choose some light and casual clothes, while he goes for an all-black ensemble, with his hat down low.

"Are you sure this is going to work?" I ask him, when we get out of the car and head into the Starbucks close to his studio.

"Yes, trust me. You worry too much." Before we enter, he gives me a kiss on the lips. The angle of his head makes his hat ride up.

His face is on full display, but I think he's too caught up in the moment to notice. I know I am. My arms come up and pull him closer. I moan into his mouth, hungry for more. Hungry for more of what we did this morning.

We break apart when a throat behind us clears. "Mind if I pop in here, guys?" the man in the suit asks.

"Sorry," we say at the same time. We move out of the way so he can enter.

I pull Derek's hat back down over his eyes. "We gotta hide you, Walsh. Wouldn't want the world to catch wind of us."

Oh, but they did. That was the end of our secret, and my life would never be the same.

CHAPTER TWENTY-SIX

It doesn't take long before we're called into his manager's office. It feels a little like being called into the principal's office. They send a car for us, and Derek and I rush from that car into the back entrance of the building. Derek's dressed in black jeans, a black T-shirt, and a gray hooded zip-up sweatshirt. The hood is pulled tightly across his face. He's trying to hide from the press and hope that no one sees him. He tells me to do the same. I don't have a whole lot, but I make do with one of his hoodies and dark jeans. The hood does help to hide my face. I also put on a ball cap because I can't bear to be caught.

The things that are being said about me online are harsh. I thought it might come to this if anyone ever found out about us. He's supposed to be with Serena, after all. Now it looks like he cheated on her. One of the headlines I saw said *Rock Princess Cheated on by Dark Rocker*. I'm not sure why they were referring to Derek as the "dark rocker," but I didn't like it.

"Think we're in trouble?" I ask him as we wait for the elevator.

He looks over at me, smirking. "How can this be good?"

The hoods have come down, and we're safe going the back way into his office. I've only ever heard Dale's voice on the phone, but he doesn't sound like a friendly man. He's always very short and direct on the phone. In all the times I've heard him speaking to the guys, I've never heard him laugh. The only time I saw him smile was when Crave hit number one.

This is a conversation I'm not looking forward to.

"We're gonna be fine," he says. He's trying to reassure me, but it's not working. I can't relax. My toe is bouncing. "Really want the elevator to hurry, do you?"

I look over at him and sigh. "What is going to happen in there? How bad is this going to be for us?"

He sighs and pulls me into him. Our faces are inches apart, and I can feel the heat coming off him. "Don't worry about a thing. That's going to be the easy part. You forget your brother is probably on his way here. We're going to have a come-to-Jesus moment with him at some point."

My mouth makes an *O* shape. I hadn't thought about the fact that Aiden would have been called. Brent will be here too. But they'll both be hopping mad at us. I check my phone for the millionth time, wondering if anyone from Beachbody is going to reach out to me. There's been several references to where I work in the articles that I quickly scanned on the way over here.

"But don't you worry. It's you and me in there. I'm not backing down. We will figure this out. Dale will yell and be all big and bad, but I'll smooth that over. Aiden will kick my ass and I'll probably let him. But eventually they'll calm down." He leans in and kisses my lips quickly. "Especially when they see that I have no intentions of giving you up."

I gasp at his words. I thought he would eventually just tell everyone that it was a fling, and we would be history. I would just be some girl he used to date or had a fling with. Things would be fixed with Serena and life would go on.

"Don't worry, Aud," he continues. "I'm not giving you up. It's you and me." He kisses me again and pulls me onto the elevator when it arrives.

"Okay," I mumble.

"Unless you want it to be different."

"No," I stammer. "I'm glad to hear that you're going to stand with me."

"Only place I wanna be is with you."

The elevator arrives at Dale's floor.

"He's expecting you," the bouncing blonde receptionist says when she sees us.

"Thanks," Derek tells her.

"Great," I mutter.

He stops and places his hands on my shoulders. "It's going to be fine. I've got you, baby."

I melt with the look of love on his face—the softness of his smile and way his eyes are shining at me. "Okay," I manage to say, but it's lost in the air. He's tugging me into the office.

Dale wastes no time when he sees us. "Derek, what the fuck, man? Do you have any idea how many phone calls my office is fielding because of this? The PR team is going crazy. How could you cheat on Serena? This wasn't part of the plan."

Derek is looking at him and smiling. I'm surprised and Dale is too. He's standing there staring at him, mouth agape. Apparently this isn't the kind of reception he thought he would get from Derek.

"Yeah, sorry. I know I kind of screwed things up with her. But in my defense, I never wanted to do that anyway, so..." Derek is so nonchalant that I fear for Dale's health if he doesn't start groveling soon.

"But you agreed to date her. You agreed that you would do it. You knew the stakes—for everyone." He throws his arms in the air, emphasizing his point.

Derek just smirks at him. "It'll be fine. We'll get through this like we always do."

"I'm afraid this is far more serious than this," Dale retorts.

"There were no contracts," Derek reminds him. "Serena and I never signed anything. We're good."

Dale lets out a sadistic laugh. "Yeah, you and Serena will

eventually be good. Or you won't be—I don't fucking know. But you put your career in jeopardy."

"How?" Derek and I say at the same time.

"Well, exercise Barbie," he says, turning and addressing me for the first time since I entered the room. "He jeopardized his career with the agency. He was supposed to run his decisions—like cheating on Serena—by me."

"Don't fucking call her that," Derek bites out. "And clearly I never planned on falling in love with Audrey, but I did. And I certainly never planned on getting caught. We—"

"What the ever-loving fuck, man?" Aiden screams as he and Brent storm into the room.

"That's what I've been saying," Dale agrees.

"How could you fucking do this? She's my sister!" Aiden shouts.

"Everyone just calm down," Derek says, holding his hands up.

"Fat chance, man," Aiden replies.

"We just need to do some damage control," Derek replies, attempting to settle things.

Dale pinches the bridge of his nose and sits behind his desk. "I think the best way we could do some damage control would be for you to release a statement saying this was a mistake." He gestures between the two of us. "Once we do that, we'll send you to one of Serena's concerts so that you guys can sign together. Bing, bang, boom all is well with the world again."

He says it like it'll solve everything, but the words crush me.

Brent is just standing there watching me. He has yet to say a word since he entered the office. I would give anything to know what's going through his head. Or to at least apologize for the way this has blown up in his face.

"Let's get to drafting that statement." Aiden sits down in front of Dale. "We'll deal with the 'my sister' of it later."

"No, that's not how we're handling this," Derek says. He comes over and places an arm around me. "This isn't just a fling, Dale. Guys, I'm in love with her. I don't want to explain it away as a mistake. So, you better figure out another way to deal with it."

"You think you're in the position to call the shots right now?" Dale asks, standing and approaching Derek. "You have royally screwed up right now. Do you know how many bands darken my door, attempting to get their big break? Do you know how many of them would have killed to be in your position? You barely made it pretending to date her for a month. Yeah, she's a pain in the ass, but she was helping you. Doors were opening because of her."

Derek shakes his head. "I don't want to get ahead in my career because of her."

"Grow up, kid. That's sometimes how it works in this business."

"I'm not okay with that," Derek says.

"What about the rest of the band? Did you even bother to consider what they think of all this?" Dale asks him. "No, you didn't because you were too busy thinking about her pus—"

"Don't you fucking—"

"Yeah, yeah," Dale waves him off. "You love her and all that happy horseshit. But imagine where you're going to be in a few months when you give up everything for her and your band is in shambles. Will it really have been worth it all? Think about it, man."

"It's not fucking like that," Derek grits out.

"He has a point," Aiden says. "Did you even consider what this would do to Crave? We've been working hard. Yeah, this thing with Serena isn't ideal, but it was helping. The albums were climbing the chart and people were listening to our songs."

"So, you're okay with people listening because they think I'm fucking Serena and not because they think we're talented?" Derek asks him.

"It may have started out like that, but they're staying for our music. They're staying because we built a following with them. It's just going to take some time. And we already talked about how you two would split amicably. That way no one was the bad guy. Well, you blew that shit to pieces."

"Ace, this is your sister's and my happiness you're talking about."

"You are *not* dating my sister," Aiden grits out.

"What does this mean for us?" Brent finally speaks up, and of course it's to ask the right question. He's a man of few words, but he uses them wisely.

Dale sighs and sits back down. "The internet isn't loving you right now. You're going to take a hit for this. I can try to run some damage control, but I don't know if it will work. Then there's the very basic and simple instructions he couldn't follow." He juts a finger in Derek's direction. "If I can't trust that you'll listen and do what I ask, how can this partnership go forward?"

"You'd drop us?" Aiden asks, shaking his head.

He and Brent make their way over to the desk and sit in front of it. Derek stays with me. He reaches out and grips my hand.

"What can we do to fix this?" Brent asks.

Dale sighs and looks over at Derek. "Are you going to continue to be a problem?"

"I won't be. Just don't make me go back to her," Derek replies.

"I'm sure rekindling your relationship with Serena isn't something that's in the cards. She doesn't want to look like she just goes back with man who would cheat on her—feminism and all that," Dale says with a roll of his eyes.

We've only been in his presence for a little while, and I can tell why Derek detests him most of the time. I detest him right now. He's slimy and exactly what you would expect an agent to be like. I'm sure he's very good at his job, but right now the only thing that he's good at doing is pissing me off.

I move forward and start to say something, but Derek yanks me back. "Go on," he tells Dale.

"So, we'll just have to do some damage control on that end of things and hope the whole world doesn't hate you for hurting her. Plus, there's the song you two have together. It's going to number one and there's talk about a Grammy."

"Dude," Brent says, shaking his head.

"Really fucking this up good for us, man," Aiden remarks.

"I'm sorry, guys. I'm sorry I fell in love," Derek says sarcastically.

"Don't. Just fucking don't," Aiden replies sharply.

"Career-wise, are you keeping us?" Brent asks, turning his attention back to Dale.

Dale sighs. "I want to. But..."

"Man, please," Aiden says, jumping in.

Derek looks at his band members and drops my hand. He heads over to the desk, and for the first time since we got in here, he actually looks sorry. His head and shoulders are slumped forward. "Please. I know I was idiot and acted carelessly and with no regard for them." He gestures toward Brent and Aiden. "But please don't punish them for my mistakes. I love this woman and I'm not giving her up. But I won't be the reason they lose their dream. Remove me from the band and let them continue Crave without me."

"There is no Crave without you," Brent replies, slapping him on the back. "We'll figure this out. Right, Dale?"

Dale nods. "There's going to be some rough times and very specific rules, but we'll see what we can do."

"Thank you," Aiden replies, shaking Dale's hand.

Dale smiles at him and accepts. I can't see Derek's face, but he mutters something to Dale that I hope is a thank-you.

"Can we go to a conference room alone and talk?" Aiden asks him.

"Yeah, I guess you all have some talking to do," Dale replies. "Go ahead and use the one attached to my office."

"Let's go," Aiden says, leading the way to the room.

I sigh and follow the guys. I'm not looking forward to this.

CHAPTER TWENTY-SEVEN

As soon as we enter the room, Aiden's fist connects with Derek's face.

"What the fuck?" I scream. I move to stand in front of Derek, but he steps in front me.

"You have every right to be angry, but can I please explain?" Derek asks. He's holding his cheek where Aiden's fist just connected. "We've been through so much together, and I would never hurt you intentionally."

Aiden is pacing now, clenching and unclenching his fists. Brent comes over to me and places his arm around my shoulders, leading me away from Derek.

"Let's just move you over here, just in case," he tells me.

I keep my eyes glued on Derek. I'm scared right now. I've never seen Aiden so angry.

"What is there to explain? I've told you time and time again that my sister is off limits, and you didn't fucking give a shit. You just fucked her anyway. Then you got her caught up in this media circus." Aiden swings and punches Derek again. I'm not sure where the punch lands at first, but I see Derek go for his mouth.

"Guys, you can't beat the shit out of each other. Remember, we need to play and all that..." Brent reminds them.

"The only one who doing the hitting is me," Aiden replies.

Derek storms over to Aiden and holds his hands up in surrender. His eyes beg Aiden not to hit him again. "I didn't do this to hurt you. I care about her. She's not like one of the bus bunnies."

That seems to tip Aiden over the edge. He hauls off and hits Derek in the stomach. "Fuck you. I know you. I've been there. I know how you operate. This isn't going to end any differently than the rest. You couldn't even fake a relationship with Serena. How in the hell are you going to do this with *my sister* of all girls? This is fucked, man. This is twisted. This is unforgivable."

"Come on, you don't mean that," Derek pleads. "There's no way you want to end the band over this..."

"How could I not? Look what you've done to her. Or would you like me to read the things that are being said about her online?"

This is not going well. I want to jump in and say something, but I know better. Aiden isn't just my brother; he's also my twin. I know better than anyone how to deal with him. There's no helping Derek right now.

My phone rings and I look down at the caller ID. It's my boss at Beachbody. "I have to take this." I hold up my phone. "Can you please make sure he stays alive?" I say to Brent.

Brent just grunts in return. I head into the hallway and answer.

"Hello," I say.

"Audrey, hi," Tina replies. "I've been seeing some things online. Care to help me out with this?"

"I'm so sorry. He's the guy I'm seeing."

"The guy you stole from someone?" she asks me, her voice emotionless, like she's simply checking questions she was supposed to ask me off a list.

"I didn't steal him. Or at least I didn't mean to," I tell her. "Are you going to fire me?"

She sighs into the phone. "No, I'm not going to fire you.

We're just going to ask you to lie low for a little bit. The recent videos you shot will be on a delayed release. Eventually, I think they'll release them, but first Ed wants to talk to you."

"The CEO wants to talk to me?" I shriek as quietly as I can into the phone.

"I'm sorry, but he does. When can you be at the home office?"

"I-I don't know," I stammer. "Let me check on a few things, and I'll get back to you."

"Okay," she says sharply. "But let me know sooner rather than later."

Just like that, Tina's gone. I exhale loudly and lean against the wall. Sinking to the floor, I take a few deep breaths. How can this be happening? When I woke up this morning, I was happy. Now I'm just the world's biggest whore because I took a singer's boyfriend—even though he wasn't. I don't know if I can tell people that, which is why I kept my mouth shut to Tina in the first place. I'm not sure she would have believed me to begin with.

I can hear the guys from inside the conference room. It sounds like a pissing match coming from in there, and I just can't deal with it. I sit there a little while longer, until Dale ends up finding me.

"Brent sent me out here to check on you. He said something about your job calling you."

"Looks like I just might need your PR services too. I have to meet with the CEO of Beachbody at some point, and the videos I just shot for my new program are being put on hold."

Dale nods. "Sorry," he says.

I'm not sure what else I can say. I doubt he'll sympathize with me any more than he already has, especially after the way he talked to Derek. "Things don't sound good in there."

He shrugs. "Not sure what you want me to say, kiddo. Big brother told everyone to leave his sister alone. Derek had the balls to not listen. I can't believe that didn't sit well with Ace," Dale says sarcastically.

"I've loved Derek since I was a kid. We've known each other for quite some time. This wasn't just a fling."

"So, you wanted him and finally saw the chance to take it when he was a rock star?"

"No!" I exclaim. "That's not what's happening here. I just never thought he'd look at me that way until he did. I didn't mean to cause this big of a mess."

"Well, you did." He laughs. "Big brother may calm down, or he may not. That's between the two of them. The one thing you need to remember is that Derek is who he is. I just hope *you* know who that is."

I go to say something, but he holds up a hand. "I don't need an explanation."

"Okay." I open the conference room door. Derek and Aiden are still shouting at each other. "Shut up, both of you," I say loudly.

Aiden's and Derek's eyes snap over to me immediately.

Aiden starts talking first. "Aud, I just wanna make sure—"

"What about *shut up* was so fucking confusing?" I shake my head.

"Nothing," he mutters.

Derek smirks and I just shake my head at him. "Aiden, why is this such a big deal for you? Is it because our faces are splashed all over the papers and social media? Is it because people are calling me a whore? Or a homewrecker? Or is it because I'm your sister and he's your best friend? Are you really that freaking possessive?"

"You're asking me too many questions," he replies, like he's trying to make light of the situation. I glare at him in return. "It's just that I don't want anyone to hurt you. And I definitely don't want it to be Derek. I've seen him backstage. I know how he operates. I don't want him screwing with you and then leaving you."

"So, you would rather some complete stranger do that? Because you know that could happen too."

"Then it wouldn't be someone I know. What if you ask me to stop being in the band if he breaks up with you?"

"We're both mature adults, and it's my life. If I want to make what you think is a mistake, then why can't I do it?"

"I know you think I'm being a caveman here, Aud. But come on, it's Derek. How can you want someone with his past?"

"You don't know him like I do, Aiden."

"I don't think I'm supposed to," Aiden quips.

We both share a laugh. I look over at Derek and wink, then I move closer and put my arm around him. "If he makes me happy, how can it really be that bad?"

"Sure, it's all great now, but what happens when he goes back to banging girls backstage? You act like he's never had a relationship before. But when he's on tour while he's dating them, all of that goes out the window."

My smile falters, and I look at my feet.

Aiden smiles triumphantly, like he's just made his point in the best way possible. "See, you had no idea about that, did you? Casanova never told you."

"I know you think I'm no good for her, Ace," Derek begins. "But no one will love her like I do. I would never treat her like those other girls."

"How do you expect me to believe that?" Aiden asks.

"You just have to trust me. You used to trust me."

"That was before."

"Really?" Derek shakes his head. "If you remember, I never wanted to do this with Serena. But you all thought this was the best idea ever, so I went along with it. And look how it turned out."

"You had one job, man. You were supposed to lie low. That's why we agreed to let you go out to Corolla in the first place. I had no idea you'd make a move on my sister."

Derek smirks. "Oh yeah, because I'm this horrible manwhore. There's no way your sister made any moves on me."

Aiden visibly cringes. I laugh and he shoots me a glare.

"Aiden, you gotta get past this," I tell him as I grab Derek's hand. "I love him, and you can't keep us apart. This isn't something you get a say in."

I lean in and give Derek a kiss. He kisses me back gently.

"Stop it," Brent says.

"I don't approve of this," Aiden says in a low voice.

"But you'll work on it once you see that I'm serious about her?" Derek asks.

"We'll see. I make no promises," Aiden says.

"Aiden, maybe give them both a break. Things are going to be hard enough for them. Let's let them breathe a bit," Brent suggests.

"What did Beachbody want?" Aiden asks me.

"Tina called to say that she's holding my new program. Ed wants to meet with me—as in the CEO of the company. So that should be fun," I quip, rolling my eyes.

"Think they'll fire you?" Derek asks.

"I have no idea," I admit, shrugging. My shoulders sag forward as I consider all the other ramifications this could have. I wonder what the NC Courage will think of all this. I hate to even think of that conversation.

"I told her our PR services could help her too," Dale says from the back of the room.

I'm not sure when he came into the room, but he's just that slimy that he comes into the room without being noticed.

"You know you could give her up," Dale tells Derek. "Make this a whole lot easier on all of us."

"Fat fucking chance," Derek replies.

"She better be worth it," Dale shoots back.

"She fucking is." Derek pulls me into a hug and holds me.

"I'll never get used to this," Aiden says, shaking his head.

We stay at the offices making a plan of action. I give Dale the information for my agent with Beachbody, hoping he'll help smooth things over, and I'll still have a job.

The day that started out lazily lying in bed with Derek sure turned shitty fast. Now I'm the most hated woman in American, and I'm not sure any amount of PR will fix that.

CHAPTER TWENTY-EIGHT

"Let me get her home," Derek says to Aiden when we leave out the back entrance of Dale's office.

"Home, huh?" Aiden growls out.

"Ace," Brent warns. "Let's just let them go so Audrey can get some rest."

Aiden shakes his head and turns to me. "Are you sure you don't want to come home with me? I live here too, you know."

"I know you do, but..." Considering the day I've had, the fight is draining out of me.

"You wanna go with him," he finishes for me.

"Just don't yell at me right now. I know you think this is a bad idea, and I know you're angry. But right now, just let me be with Derek. We've all had a long day."

"I'm not mad at you." He looks sharply at Derek. "It's he who should have known better."

"I'm not a child. I'm as much to blame as he is. He didn't seduce me or come after me. This is between two consenting adults. And you know what, Ace?" I say his nickname with malice. "If you want to know the truth, I pushed him. I pushed his buttons. I made it hard for him to say no because he's something I've wanted since the day I met him."

Aiden stares at me in shock. Brent is pacing. He hates conflict, and I'm sure he's worried about how this will blow up. Clearly, it's having ramifications for all of us. I hadn't thought about the effect this would have on the band's career or mine. Beachbody didn't cross my mind once when I was screwing Derek's brains out.

"I had no idea. You never said anything to me, and we share everything with each other," Aiden finally chokes out.

I can't tell if he's angry or more hurt that he never knew. As twins, we have shared everything with each other. It's true what they say—there is a twin bond. I always seem to know how he's feeling and sometimes what he's thinking. We've gotten the same scores on the SATs and written almost the very same thing to our parents separately. There's a mental connection. But this was one thing that he never could have guessed.

"I just figured you would be upset," I tell him. "You always warn everyone to stay away from me. I figured you would kill Derek if you even knew I had a crush on him. I just don't understand why you don't think I'm worthy of him."

He pulls me in for a hug. "It's not you, it's him."

"But he's good enough to start up a band with? To make your livelihood depend on?" I ask him.

"And look how that turned out," he bites back.

"All because he felt like he couldn't be honest with you. Because he knew this would happen. You can't expect me to not fall in love with someone like Derek, especially when you swear me off all our friends. But they're the people I spend all my time with. Some of them are the best people I know. Like Derek."

Aiden just looks away from me, lost in thought.

"Just get her home," he says, turning to Derek.

They stare at each other like they're having some silent conversation. It gives me a little reassurance that maybe things are salvageable. But it's almost like he's dismissing me. My shoulders sag and Derek wraps a protective arm around me, leading me away.

"It's going to be okay, baby. I'll make sure of it," Derek promises.

I want to remind him that he doesn't know that. He can't promise things will be okay. This has implications for both my career and his. It has implications for our family dynamic that we can't predict or control. It looks like Aiden may be on the road to acceptance, but I have no idea. He didn't tell him to stop seeing me, which I honestly expected.

"How's your face?" I ask. He has a little bit of a swollen lip, which I fully expect to get worse. His right eye has a bruise forming from where Aiden's fist connected with it.

"It's fine. I'm not worried about it. Collateral damage in the story of us," he says, holding my hand and helping me into the back of the chauffeured car.

I nod and sink into the seat, waiting for the car to pull away. Derek is staring at me. "What?" I ask when he's been looking a little too long without saying anything.

"Nothing. You've just been so calm for the most part," he says. "I just want to make sure you're okay."

I shrug and look out the window. The city is rushing by, and we're headed to Derek's, which I guess I'm happy about. "I just never imagined this could impact Beachbody, and now the CEO wants to talk to me. I have no idea what that's about. I'm just worried."

"Dale's people are going to talk to Tina today. He'll smooth things over. He's good at that. He can be a jackass most of the time, but this is why we keep him around. Have a little faith, baby."

I smile. I want to believe him. I just hope he's right.

When we arrive at his house, I go upstairs and lie down to take a nap. A few hours later, I'm woken up by the sounds of banging around in the kitchen. I lazily make my way toward the noise and find him plating some noodles. On the table is a salad and bread.

"How long was I out?" I ask when I join him in the kitchen.

"About two hours," he tells me, coming over and kissing me on the forehead. I notice his grimace. His lip is more swollen than I remember it being.

"Did you ice any of that?" I ask him, gesturing toward his face.

"Um, a little bit. It's just sore. Should clear up in a few days."

"He got you good." I stand there awkwardly. I can see the plates on the table, but he hasn't said anything about sitting down. "Smells good."

"Thanks," he says, and he smiles sheepishly. "I thought you could use a home-cooked meal. Wanna sit and eat? Or did you want to wait a bit?"

"No, let's eat. It smells delicious." I sit down at the table and breathe in the cheesy goodness of what he's prepared. I can smell the garlic from the sauce.

"It's alfredo," he says as he watches me smell it.

My stomach grumbles at the smells coming from the plate in front of me. It's been a long time since I've had Alfredo sauce and. Normally, I stick to proteins and veggies, but I don't want to tell him that. Instead, I dive in, moaning as soon as the cheesy garlic goodness hits my mouth.

"This is amazing. How did I not know that you could cook like this?" I ask. It surprises me. During all the time we spent at the beach house, either I cooked, or we ate takeout. And then there were those times in the beginning when he wasn't there. I never knew where he went. I want to ask, but I have other pressing questions.

"Don't let this fool you. I'm not some gourmet cook. I can make a few things—this being one of them." He gestures with his fork and takes a bite. I smile as I watch a noodle smack his chin. His tongue comes out to lick the mess off.

I lick my lips at the motion and shift in my seat. Everything this man does turns me on. I can't help it.

"How are you doing?" he asks. "With everything that's happening, how are you really doing?"

I sigh and put my fork down. "I'm really worried about my job, to be honest. Well, and yours. But beyond that, I think that Aiden will calm down."

"He just needs some time. We really caught him off guard, and then with the way the media is treating you and me, that's enough to piss him off."

"Have you heard from Serena?" I ask. His eyes widen at the mention of her name—mouth opening and closing but he speaks no words. "One of us had to mention her."

He smirks and shrugs. "I'd prefer to never mention her name again. But I know that won't happen because I made a deal with the literal devil. I haven't actually heard from her, and I don't expect that I will. Dale said he would contact her agent today. Tomorrow, I'll give her a call and apologize for blowing this up. But she's getting to play the victim, so there isn't any real damage to her image that I know of."

I nod, thankful for that at least. But I imagine she won't be too thrilled with Derek breaking up their fake romance so quickly. She seemed to be enjoying it, and I think a part of her had hoped that he would be with her for real. That won't be happening now. I think back to when she told me that he wouldn't go for someone like me. The fact that we were caught kissing, and the photo is unmistakably me can't be sitting well with her. I smirk at the thought.

"What?" he asks, studying me.

"I was just thinking that Serena can't be too pleased that you were caught kissing me in the photo. She said you would never go for someone like me. And she said she would ruin me if something happened between the two of us."

Derek slams his fork down. "She said what?" He shakes his head. "She's fucking unbelievable. I will *not* let her ruin you; I promise you that. Plus, Dale said his people would help too. I'll release the email that shows that her people requested this arrangement to repair her image, if I have to. She was becoming so fucking difficult, and people were starting to see the real her.

She was losing fans. I was the carrot that brought them back. Trust me, Audrey," he says with so much force, it scares me a bit. "I will ruin *her* if she does anything to you."

I simply nod, not knowing what to say to that. I wonder if he actually can or if the record label and his manager would allow for that to happen. She's the clear victim in all of this now. It's not something that can easily be turned on her. And her people will work to protect her too.

I'm so lost in my thoughts and eating that I almost forget that I had something I wanted to talk to Derek about. "Tell me about the relationship that you ruined on the road. The one that Aiden spoke about in the office."

Derek sighs. "I don't want to talk about that."

"I understand that you might not, but I do. I want to know what's happening there. Please," I beg. "I think I have the right to know, because it sounded like Aiden was worried that something like this could happen to me. I'd like to avoid that, please. Aiden said you were seeing someone, but all that went out the window when you what got around some girls backstage?"

"Thanks for the recap," Derek snarks.

"I know it's not something you want to talk about, but I would like to know. Don't keep secrets from me."

He sighs and pushes his chair back from the table. He scrubs his hands down his face, the turmoil shining in his eyes. He's weighing his options and how he can get out of this, I think. But I won't back down and I won't drop it. I'll just keep bringing it up because I want to know. This isn't a Derek story I've heard before, and it doesn't sound like my Derek.

"Fine." His voice sounds thick with defeat. I almost feel bad for pushing him to talk to me. "I was dating this girl I met in LA."

"How did you meet her?" I know it may hurt to hear, but I want all the details.

"I met her at a bar. I was there scouting some talent, and this guy was hitting on her hard. I saved her. We ended up spending the evening talking. I completely missed the band that was play-ing." He smiles at the memory, and it kills me a little bit. "We dated for about two months before I had to go on tour. It was just a short one, but she wasn't able to get away and come visit me."

He chugs his water, but it's not enough. He walks back into the kitchen, which connects to the dining room, and grabs two beers from the fridge and comes back to me. My body tenses, knowing this discussion will require alcohol. I don't think that's a good sign.

"I thought we both could use a drink after the long day."

"Is it that, or will we both need it for this story?" I come right out and ask it because there's no need to beat around the bush.

"Little of both, maybe."

"Okay, let's have it. What happened?"

"I was good for the few weeks on the tour. But one night I got particularly drunk, and I ended up having sex with the one of the bus bunnies that came backstage to see me." He puts it right out there, and even though I knew that was basically what he would say, it socks me in the chest. "She looked a lot like her, and I guess I was just missing her. I was drunk and it seemed like a good idea at the time.

"The guys tried to tell me not to. And of course, I knew better, but I didn't care. Not the in the drunken state that I was in. I fucked her. While I was doing that, Erin, that's the girl I was seeing, had flown in to surprise me. She walked in on it."

He hangs his head when he's finished talking, refusing to look at me, and I'm not sure which I'd prefer. I ask the question that's nagging my mind. Something I want to know but I'm afraid to hear the answer to. "If she hadn't walked in on you, would you have told her?"

He considers my question for longer than I'm comfortable with. So, I tell him, "You're quiet longer than I'd like you to be here, Derek. Just tell me the fucking truth."

"I think I would have told her. The guilt would have eaten away at me."

I get up and begin to pace, feeling like I need another nap. This day has been draining and I made it even worse by asking him this question.

"It will be different with you. It's not like that with you." He gets up and walks over to me, taking my hands. His eyes are pleading with me to listen to him. "What I felt for her wasn't even close to what I feel for you. You have to believe me."

"I do believe you. But the thing that gets me is that you knew it was wrong and you didn't care. I don't know. What would stop you if you were on the road and the same situation came up? What if you were drunk?"

"I'll be good. I'll be so good to you. Because you're someone I never thought I deserved, and I will do everything in my power to be the man that you deserve, Audrey. I really will."

I look at the man that I've loved since I was sixteen years old. He's finally mine and he's saying all the right things. I can't walk away. Not from a man that I've lusted after for all these years. Not from a man whose touched I've craved.

He takes me upstairs and we make love. It's slow and torturously good. It's the perfect way to end the day.

CHAPTER TWENTY-NINE

Derek has been taking me everywhere with him lately. It's only been two days since the news broke. Every time he has band practice, I go with him. If he has a quick errand to run, I go with him. But for the most part, we're huddled up in his apartment.

They're at practice now, and Aiden breaks away and comes over to talk to me.

"How are you doing?" he asks.

"I'm fine, Aiden. How are you doing with all of this? Are you going to be nice or are you still pouting?"

"Pouting," he replies. "If those are my only choices, I choose pouting."

"Aiden," I say, my tone conveying the warning coming.

"Don't, Aud. I know what you're going to say. But you're my sister. I've seen the way he operates. I don't want you to be caught up with someone like him. I think you deserve better than Derek. So no, I don't plan on playing nicely with the two of you anytime soon. You know Mom isn't happy about this either," he adds, looking over at me, letting it all sink in.

"I have to call her back. I talked to Dad, though, and he wasn't surprised. He guessed it when he was visiting."

"He did?" Shock is written all over this face. "Why didn't he tell me?"

"I think he wanted to let us figure this out. He just said the same thing as Brent, that he wouldn't lie."

Emotion plays all over Aiden's face—more shock, betrayal, and anger. "Brent knew?" he yells.

Brent comes over to where we're talking and glances from me to Aiden. "You told him?"

"It slipped out," I say, wringing my hands in worry.

Derek places his hand on the small of my back. "It's okay, Aud. Aiden will cool off."

"I can't believe that everyone I trust and love in this world was keeping a secret like this from me. Are you fucking kidding me, Brent? Why wouldn't you tell me?"

"Because it wasn't my secret to tell. I also kind of figured it would just run its course while they were at the beach house, and we wouldn't have to worry about it here in LA." Brent shakes his head. "You don't get to get all pissed off at me because you're pissed off at the world. Enough is at fucking stake here. We might not even still have a contract with the record company. Dale told me about that a little bit ago. He's coming here soon to talk to us. I suggest we all quit our bitching and moaning about who knew what when and get back to rehearsing."

"Dale's visit doesn't sound like a pleasant one," Aiden remarks, shooting daggers at Derek.

"Bitching doesn't change it," Brent says, shaking his head. "Let's just start rehearsing so he doesn't have concerns about *us* and our ability to do our jobs when he gets here."

I move over to the sofa that's set up near where they rehearse.

As I'm walking over, Brent mumbles to Derek, "I hope she's worth it."

I look back and see Derek nod. I want to think that nod is a yes, but I'm only guessing at this point.

The band takes their places and begins to warm up.

"Is any of the new music ready?" Aiden asks.

"Yeah, I have some arrangements together that I sent over to Brent," Derek replies. He looks at Brent like he's going to save him from some of Aiden's wrath. But I think it's past that. I think Brent is just sick of being the peacemaker, and he hates that his world has been shifted over this bullshit. I want to believe he'd be on Derek's side, but Aiden has made it perfectly clear how he feels about his friends touching me. It's annoying.

I sit there and zone out on the discussion over arrangements and think back to when Aiden almost came to blows over me when we were sixteen. That was the moment I realized Aiden was going to go nuts if I dated anyone he knew. The trend continued all throughout high school, so I dated guys from other schools. Aiden only intimidated them, and I learned to keep them away from him.

I lost my virginity in a car because I was afraid to go into our house or his. I thought for sure Aiden would show up wherever I went. It was weird and bumpy, but it was the one experience that Aiden didn't ruin. I shake away that memory and of all the crap I've dealt with over the years. Some things never change.

The guys have played a few of their hits. I like watching them play—whether rehearsing or playing live, they're something to watch. I hope the relationship Derek and I have doesn't ruin that. Derek is strumming his guitar and singing the chorus to "Incredible Sin." His eyes are closed, and he's getting lost in the music. He truly has an amazing voice.

Aiden is backing him up on vocals and playing his bass, dancing, and swaying to the beat of the music. He looks so happy up there. So does Brent. His head is bopping along to the beat as he plays the drums. These boys are so talented, and I don't just feel that way because one is my brother and the other I've known for forever and am now sleeping with.

Please let this all work out, I pray silently.

The song ends and Derek huddles close to Aiden and Brent. All I could make out was that they wanted to try something. The boys talk for a few moments, and then there's some agreement made. The guitar chords are soft, and so are the drums. Brent is only using the high hat and a cymbal. I've heard it before, but I can't quite put my finger on it.

It's not until the chorus really kicks in and the version of the song turns more rock that I pick out "I Want to Know What Love Is" by Foreigner. Crave doesn't do covers very often. A few are thrown into their shows from time to time, but none have ever made the album. I get the feeling that Derek chose this song on purpose. He's looking over at me while he sings.

I love the song he's chosen to give me this message. I know that he hasn't had it easy. He used to act out a lot as a teenager, stealing little things and cutting class. He would take girls home just the for the heck of it. That behavior has continued into his twenties, but he's never felt he deserved loved. And he's telling me that now, through song.

I see out of the corner of my eye that Aiden is staring at him. He doesn't look angry anymore. He's just watching him sing and stare at me, brow furrowed. Aiden doesn't join in on the song. I think he realizes what's happening here, and he doesn't want to step on his toes. I kind of love him for it. As long as he doesn't punch him out when it's over.

Just as the song is about to end, Dale walks in. *Oh good. This should be fun.*

"He changing genres or singing that for you?" Dale asks me.

"I think it's for me," I tell him. I refuse to look over at him or encourage him to talk about this anymore.

The song wraps up, and Dale claps. Derek, however, comes walking over to me and drops to his knees in front of me.

"I do love you. There isn't another woman in this world that is more tempting to me than you. No one holds a candle to you, and I will be true to you until the day I die."

Tears spring to my eyes. "You are so perfect," I tell him.

"He's just wonderful," Dale says, killing the moment.

I look over and catch Aiden staring at us. I wonder what's

going through his head right now, but he doesn't say anything. I knew the song wouldn't fix things or make him suddenly be okay with us, but at least he's not hitting Derek right now.

"We should add that one to our mix," Brent says, joining us. "I kind of like the rock version."

"I liked it too. That would be a good one for concerts," Dale agrees. "You guys sound great. I listened to some of those demos you sent over. I like them."

"Good, man. That's great news," Derek says, finally acknowledging Dale's presence.

He tugs on my hand, and I stand up with him. Wrapping me in a hug, he gives me a quick squeeze. I place a kiss on his neck.

"Please stop that," Derek whispers. "Or I'm going to have a big problem here."

I snicker. "Well, what would be the harm in that?"

He just shakes his head and kisses my neck. He's incredible and I don't know what I would do without him. I hope Dale isn't here to try to end things or terminate their contract. That will really ruin things with Derek and me. Their dreams would be crushed, and Aiden would never forgive us. Which means Derek and I would never be able to be together.

"Come sit," Dale says, gesturing toward the table and chair that sits away from the instruments.

It sounds ominous and I hate it.

CHAPTER THIRTY

We're all getting situated around the table. Derek goes to pull me into his lap since there aren't enough chairs around the table.

"Get Audrey her own fucking chair, you douche," Aiden growls out.

"Someone's grumpy," I tease. Aiden just rolls his eyes.

Brent pulls a chair from the closet and sets it up between him and Derek. "Here you go, kiddo."

"Thanks," I say as I lower myself into the chair.

Derek reaches over and squeezes my hand before asking, "What's the word, Dale?"

Dale sighs. "Well, I've got good news and I've got bad news. Which would you like first?"

We all stare at him. No one is in the mood for these games. We just want to know the future of the band. I want to know how this is going to impact me moving forward. Will my twin brother officially hate me? Or will I be able to be with the man that I love? It's all up to Dale, apparently.

"Okay, fine, let's start with the good news. Audrey," he says, turning to me. "We were able to talk to the CEO of Beachbody. Ed is a good guy. He agrees that you didn't do anything that would jeopardize your employment with them. They haven't been getting any hate. Someone did turn off the comments on your Instagram, though, and they will be taking a break from releasing your new videos. Probably looking at a March release for those, not September. So, sorry about that. But the good news is you can keep your job. The North Carolina Courage...we checked into them for you too because Derek said you really enjoy working with them."

Dale continues with his list. "They don't care either. You're actually coming out of this pretty unscathed, other than the obvious hate you're receiving online. You might want to lie low for a little bit. Also, if you need security, please let me know. Or let Derek know. He has agreed to pay for any additional security for you, regardless of the state of your relationship."

I see Aiden's eyes snap over to Derek. "Thank you, man. I appreciate you doing that for her."

"Least I go could do," Derek mumbles.

I take his hand to my lips and kiss it. Derek brushes his other hand up my thigh. I look over and wink.

"Aren't you two cute?" Dale says his voice dripping with sarcasm. "But that's the problem with it. People really hate that you're together. Or that you cheated on Serena." He gives Derek a glare. "There's going to need to be some damage control. I think you're going to have to release a statement or something. But that'll come when Serena releases hers. I should see copy of that today."

"What will hers say?" Brent asks.

"It's not pretty, boys." He looks around at all of them. "She isn't mad at you and you." He points to Brent and Aiden. "She's thinking of changing the song up so that she sings it with Aiden and is considering asking that Derek not even be on stage when it's performed."

"That bitch," Derek exclaims. "She can't do that. I'm in the band too."

"Yeah, well, she kind of can because she has her own band,

and when you all come on stage, they have to leave. So, she's looking at that option. But right now, she's just playing the hurt bunny card—very well, I might add. Her statement was horrible at first, but I got her to tame it down a bit. She's now going to say that she's heartbroken that you cheated on her. That she was looking forward to many happy years together, but that's not going to happen. She wishes you nothing but the best, but she feels very betrayed and requests time to heal."

The guys hang their heads. It's not the worst thing she could have said, but it's not the best.

"Can you ask her to add something about how dating was never going to work because our schedules were just so different?" Derek asks.

"I tried to get her to work that in, but it's her statement. Ours will include something like that. It's going out today," Dale says.

"Can we see it?" Brent asks.

"Sure, I'll get my computer and show you. But we did right by you guys. I like you all, and I want to continue working with you. We may have to make some changes, though."

"What type of changes?" Aiden asks.

"Your record label." Dale puts it out there and pauses, watching our faces drop. "They're not thrilled about this considering Serena is also at the same label. I talked to Don over there, and he feels like he might have to drop you. How do you feel about that?"

The guys all let the news sink in. I feel sick. Everything they've worked for is about to be torn away from them all because Derek and I got caught kissing him.

"The relationship wasn't even real," Brent says with a frown.

"I know that. And they do too."

"But they don't give a shit?" Brent asks.

Aiden slams his fist on the table. Derek gets up and begins pacing.

"Isn't there something we can do?" He pauses his pacing. I can see the hope in his eyes, and it kills me that it's come to this.

"There is." Dale pauses, and I see him swallow hard. "They want you to give her up. Break up with her for real and promise to never see her again—romantically. Then they'll be okay with everything. Which I can see isn't going to go over very well."

I look over my shoulder and see that Derek's seething, nostrils flaring, and hands placed firmly on his hips.

"That's not happening." His voice is so low and deadly, it almost scares me.

"Derek," I start to say, but he cuts me off.

"No, Aud. There has to be another way. I took punches to the face for you," he says, gesturing toward Aiden. "I refuse to give you up. You mean more to me than this."

"What about us?" Brent and Aiden say at the same time.

Derek looks over at them. "I'm sorry. I wanna do right by your sister," he says to Aiden. "And Brent, maybe we can get you into another band or something. Or maybe the two you want to go on without me, but I refuse to end my relationship with her."

"Really?" Dale asks. "You've only been together a few weeks and it's already a hard no?"

"Yeah," he tells Dale.

"Let me go make some phone calls," Dale says, rising.

The boys are talking, but I tune them out. I put my head in my hands, feeling the tension building in my neck. The voices are getting louder and louder. I feel like I could pass out. I get up and walk away from them.

On the wall is a picture of the band. It's from their first album, three years ago. They look so young, like babies. It wasn't taken long after they got to LA. Derek and Aiden have a few more tattoos than they used to. Brent used to have a stubble of hair covering his head, but now he shaves it clean. I can't imagine them not playing together. I can't imagine there not being a Crave.

I look over at them all arguing. Aiden is yelling at Derek, Derek is yelling back, and Brent is just plain yelling.

"Boys," I say, hoping someone will hear me. But no one does. "Boys!" I shout.

They all snap their heads in my direction and look at me.

"What's up, Audrey?" Aiden asks.

"If it's Derek and I apart that will keep you all together, then that's what we'll do." I hold my hand up because I see Derek is getting ready to object. "It's not what I want, but I can't imagine the three of you not playing together. I love Crave. I love what you've all built together. It's not fair that I come out of this pretty unscathed and the three of you might be dropped by the record label. That's not fair and it's not right. The whole thing was a lie, sure, but I can't expect you all to pay the price for our happiness."

I turn and only speak to Derek now. "I love you. But I can't be reason that you all are unhappy. You know that and I do too. Besides, we've barely gotten started. How hard could it be to stop?"

"I think I've wanted you my whole life," he says to me. He's not going to make this easy on me.

"No," Brent says, surprising me. "There has to be another way."

"I don't think there is," I say.

"Do you want out?" Derek looks me straight in the eyes.

I hope he can see my pain. I don't want to do this. "You know I don't. But I also don't want you to be the cause of this." I motion around the group.

Aiden gets up and starts pacing. He looks so determined to figure something out. Suddenly, he stops and looks at both of us.

"Are you really serious about her?" Aiden asks Derek.

"Of course. I wouldn't be trying to throw all this away for nothing. I love your sister," Derek tells him.

Aiden shakes his head. "You fucking better after all this shit it's causing us."

"I do," Derek says with more conviction.

"I still don't like this. But if you love her like you say you do, then giving up on her shouldn't be an option. Same goes for you," he says, pointing at me. "If you want to throw grenades like this into people's lives and claim it's for love, you don't get to just walk away."

"There's a song in there somewhere," Dale says, rejoining the conversation. "I can feel it. You should start writing it." He points to Derek. "Come on over here, all, we need to figure this out. See if we can get a way to keep you all playing music."

"What if we agree to never play the song again? What if we give Serena the song? Think that would work?" Aiden is speaking quickly.

"I'm not sure that it would fly," Dale says honestly. "The statement is being sent out. She's taking the brunt of the hate." He points toward me, and I shake my head.

"Why?" I ask. It seems like a silly question, but I'd love to know why I'm the one everyone hates.

"Because you were the one that took Serena's man. You're the one that seduced him. Some of the fans that were at the backstage event say they remember you from the concerts in Cary. That's not helping you." He shrugs like he can't do anything about that. And there's nothing he can, but I still hate the way he puts it on me.

"She's my sister. She's been at things before, and no one has said a word," Aiden tells him.

"Yeah, but she never kissed Serena's boyfriend before that. So that's an issue. That's *the* issue that we are trying to fix."

We all know this. But fuck, this situation is impossible.

Derek turns to me. "I won't let anyone hurt you. I promise you that."

I move over toward him. I need those strong arms wrapped around me. He picks up on it and pulls me near.

"I'll take care of you," he whispers into my ear. "That bitch will not ruin you. We'll make sure of it."

"She doesn't want to ruin her," Dale chimes in. "Serena just wants to say that she was the wronged woman. If she gets that, she'll be happy. She wants to play the victim for a little bit longer."

Aiden screams at the ceiling and faces him. "Aiden, I'm so sorry all of this is happening. I feel responsible and I hate that your life is ruined as a result."

He looks down at me, eyes softening. I see the same concern there that he's shown me my whole life. Whenever another boy broke my heart or when I was cut from the Varsity field hockey team. He's my big brother, and he's always taken care of me. Now I wish I could do the same for him.

"Audrey, it's going to be okay. You did not ruin my life. You just made it a little harder. Being your brother, I've gotten used to the way you make my life harder. You know, with all the bratty little things you used to do."

He's teasing me and I kind of love it. Brings some levity to this shitty situation.

"Plus," he continues, "I'm sure I can throw this at you when I really screw up. Being able to tell you that you have to forgive me because you almost cost me my career is cool."

I shake my head and wrap him in a hug.

"I've got you, little sister." He squeezes me tightly, and I sink into him. It's nice to be able to get a hug from my big brother.

"What do we do now?" Derek asks.

"Now we release the statement. I'm gonna revise it a bit. I'll send it over to you all for your review. Once I have your okay, I'll release it. Then...we'll see what happens. I have a new idea for a spin on this that might help things. Let me work on it. But trust me, I'm going to do my best to take care of you. You're good guys, and I want to fix this for you."

Dale leaves and I slink over to Derek and fall into his arms.

"It's going to be okay," I tell them. "It has to be. You've worked too hard to see this all go away over a girl."

CHAPTER THIRTY-ONE

Things are getting ironed out better than I thought they would be. It's almost like the worst of our trouble might be over. But they're not. I need to talk to Aiden. We haven't really spoken since he found out about Derek and me. That's not like us, either. Normally we talk on the phone or text back and forth. There's a Snapchat picture exchanged here or there. Or we'll comment back and forth on Instagram when Aiden sees my posts.

This silence between us can't go on. I make my way over to the table where Aiden is sitting, a notebook open in front of him. I recognize it as the one Derek has been feverishly scribbling in since I saw him in Corolla. Always working. For rock stars, they sure work harder than I thought they might. It makes me laugh thinking about how Aiden was in high school. Always asking me to do his papers for him. Or trying to bribe the girl he happened to be dating to take care of it for him. Sometimes that works, but I never did his papers for him. My parents would have been so angry at us.

Back when we were kids and I wanted to talk to Aiden, we'd sit at the kitchen table with sodas and pretend we were sipping beer or wine like our parents, trying to make ourselves feel and seem more like adults. We weren't even teenagers then, but we were like any other kids—desperate to grow up. I spot sodas in the glass-door fridge and grab two.

"Penny for your thoughts," I tell him, sliding a can in front of him. It's a peace offering, and I hope he sees it as such.

He looks at the can, then at me, but goes back to the notebook. I'm unsure of what to do. I hope he'll pop it open and drink it with me. I open mine and take a sip. Just like when we were kids, I lean forward and cradle the can in my hands.

Aiden stops what he's doing and watches me. Finally, he pops the top on his own soda and mirrors my position. "What's on your mind, kiddo?"

I smirk, glad that he's treating me like I'm so much younger than him. For once, I don't mind. It seems like he might not hate me forever. "I'm just wondering if you're going to ever talk to me again, or even look at me again without glaring in my direction."

"I'm talking to you now, and there's no glaring. So, I guess I will."

"Aiden," I plead.

"What, Audrey?" Aiden slams the notebook closed and stares at me.

I take a drink and sigh. "How can you keep being like this? We're adults. I thought you would grow up and be a little more accepting of things."

"I know what kind of guy he is. That's what makes this so hard for me," he tells me. "Do you not know what he's like when he's on the road? He sleeps with a lot of women." He takes a long drink of soda.

"You think I don't know that? I've hung around all of you long enough to hear the stories. I've been backstage when you're on tour. This isn't news to me, but I don't think that he'll be like that with me. Can't you give him some credit? He's not any different than you," I throw at him. I can't wait to hear what he thinks about that.

He scrubs his hand down his face. "Maybe that's why I don't

want you dating him. Because I know how I am, and he's a lot like me. I wouldn't want you dating someone like me."

"That's a gross thought," I tell him, crinkling up my nose.

He laughs. "Relax, no one is suggesting we would date. We're twins, dummy."

"I know, I just like giving you a hard time. Gotta make sure you know you're gross. But you've been like this since we were kids. No one was ever good enough for me. Why can't you just let me be happy? We're consenting adults."

"Please don't say *consenting adults*. It makes me think of you doing other things than just dating." Aiden wrings his hands. "I can't think if you doing anything like that with Derek."

"I'm your sister, so I get it. We do those things, though, you know," I tease.

"Audrey," he warns.

"I'm happy, Aiden. I just want you to be happy for me. I finally found someone that makes me happy. Do you have any idea how lonely it's been for me? I've been by myself for six months. Living alone, coming home to an empty house. There are no random hookups on my sets."

"You're lonely?" he asks me.

"Well, I was, until Derek came along."

"Why did you never tell me?"

"Because there wasn't a reason to. No one wants to hear the poor single girl complaining about her life. Besides, you were so happy. There have been a lot of amazing things happening for you, and I didn't want to be a damper."

"Does Emma know?"

I sigh and shake my head. "No, she'd just try to set me up with anything that walks. I don't want that kind of life."

"She does? That doesn't seem like the Emma I knew growing up."

"Focus, Aiden," I tell him. "Unless you wanna shoot your shot with her."

He shakes his head. "No, but it doesn't sound like she's hurting for any action."

"No, she's not."

"Why him?" he finally asks me.

I smile. "Is that what's been bothering you? Is it that I chose one of your friends or the one that I chose? Which one would have been acceptable to you, Aiden? You warned me off all of them. And you threatened the hell out of them. No one came near me in high school. Everyone thought you were going to pound the shit out of anyone who dared to touch me. I had to go to other schools if I wanted to date a boy. And even then, some of them were too afraid of dating me because of you."

"I didn't make life easy on your growing up, did I?"

I scoff. "That's the understatement of the century. But you were my brother and I loved you for wanting to protect me. I love that you still want to do it, but we're adults. It's not like I'm still that little teenage girl who needs protecting."

"I'm always going to try to protect you. That's something that will never go away. I'm your big brother."

"Only by a few minutes," I say, shaking my head.

"Derek is like a brother to me, too, and I never thought he'd cross a line by dating you. He saw the way it bothered me when some of my friends mentioned you were hot or said they had a crush on you." He cringes when he calls me hot, which makes me giggle.

"Seriously, though. Can't we all just grow up and get over this high school shit?" I try to make light of the situation, but I can see it hasn't quite worked.

"If anyone knows how I feel about people dating my sister, it's him. He used to help me; you know. Derek would threaten them too. The guys were just as afraid of him as they were of me."

"He did?" I smile. I should be as irritated with him as I am with Aiden, but there's something cute about it.

"Yeah, he did." Aiden rolls his eyes. "Of course, you would think that was cute. But when I do it, I'm being overbearing."

"Aiden, I'm happy. Can't you be happy for me?"

"I think I'd be happier if it wasn't with him."

"Can you try?" I give him the doe eyes that used to work on him when we were kids. "I'd love it if you talked to him. You'll see he is serious about me."

"You're sure?"

I nod. I think so, but I don't want to say that out loud.

"That nod is all I need to know. You would have answered me with words if you thought he was. Audrey, I know you better than you know yourself."

I sigh again. He's probably right. But still, I don't want to admit my insecurities to my brother. He doesn't want us dating, so of course he's going to sabotage us.

"He chose me, though. He wouldn't break up with me when Dale told him to," I remind him. "Does that count for anything?"

"Have you heard from Mom lately?" Aiden asks me.

He abruptly changed the subject, but I don't mind. Harping on things isn't going to make it any better between us. I just hope he heard me, that he understands that I'm happy. It wasn't easy admitting to Aiden that I was lonely before Derek. I thought that would count for something.

"No, I haven't. Have you?"

"I called the other day to see how things were going. Dad was getting a port put in. I don't know. I just can't wrap my head around it all. I never knew there was anything wrong with him, Audrey. I was talking to him while he was sick—back when you knew and I didn't, but no one felt the need to tell me. It feels like they betrayed me. And you might have, too, a little bit. Then you turn around and screw Derek."

I think about what he's said. He's had a rough few weeks. We all have.

"No one did anything to hurt you on purpose. We were just trying to protect you, Aiden."

"It still sucks. I never imagined that Dad would get sick. You never think you're close to losing your parents. They're young too, Aud—barely even sixty."

I smile warmly at him. "They're like sixty-three, but yeah, it is young for them to be fighting things like this. Cancer doesn't run in our family, does it?"

He shrugs. "I don't think so. Grandparents passed of other things. Grandpa Jack was killed in the war. Grandma Nora died of a broken heart, they say. And mom's parents...well, that was heart trouble and then the car accident."

"Our parents have had some shitty things happen to them too," I remind him.

"They have," he agrees.

Derek and Brent come over and sit at the table.

"Are things okay over here? Or should we leave you be?" Brent asks, lowering himself onto the chair.

"We're fine. Just trying to figure out if this man here has a heart," I joke about Aiden.

Derek laughs and pulls my chair toward him.

"Can't you go ten minutes without touching her?" Aiden snarks.

"She's been over here talking to you for like twenty, so I guess I can," Derek quips. "Are we gonna be okay, dude?"

Aiden scrubs a hand down his face. Looking over at Brent, he says, "Do I have to?"

"Yeah, you do," Brent responds. "Because I'm tired of being in the middle of all of this."

"See what you're doing to Brent?" I chime in.

Brent shoots a glare in my direction. "Oh no, young lady. You can't play innocent here. I tried to explain to you that you needed to let this be, but you couldn't. So, you made your bed, now you have to sleep in it."

Brent is a man of few words. It's one of the things I love

about him. He doesn't need to say a lot to make a person feel better. Sometimes just being near him has helped me. But when he does talk, he's right on the money.

"Listen to, Brent," Aiden teases.

"Shut up, man. Not what I meant," Brent defends. "You could ease up on them, too. I think Derek's serious about your sister. He almost gave up on the band for her. He could have easily thrown her to the wolves in there. I'm impressed." Brent tips his head in Aiden's direction.

"I love her, man. Why can't you just believe me?" Derek pleads with Aiden.

"It's not that I don't believe you. But it's my job to make sure she's safe, loved, and taken care of. But look at all the drama that's come into her life—all the hate she's getting online. And someone like Serena isn't going to let this go so easily. We've seen how calculated and cool she can be. I don't want my sister caught in her crosshairs."

"I wanna protect and help her too," Derek says in a low tone. His head his down. I can't see his face, but his shoulders are slumped like he's feeling defeated.

"I'll get over it," Aiden grumbles out. "It's just going to take some time."

Brent gets up from the table and takes a phone call.

"Aiden, I want to have my big brother on my side. Our father is sick. I'm going to need you..."

He gets up. "I just need some time, guys." He leaves the room without saying goodbye to anyone.

Brent hangs up his phone and shakes his head, looking more devastated than I've ever seen him.

"Brent, I'm sorry," I tell him.

"It's okay. Aud. It'll all be okay...somehow." Brent turns and walks away.

"Do you think he's right?" I ask Derek when we're alone in the room.

"Brent's not one to say things like that lightly. He's not your glass half-full person," Derek tells me.

"I never knew that. I thought he was a positive person," I say. He may speak very little, but I've never heard him so down-trodden.

"Being on the road as much as we are, can be hard on you. I think it's weighing on him. He doesn't have much family to speak of. Just a dad. Mom ran out when he was young. I think he's lonely."

"Jesus, Aiden is the only one with a whole family," I mutter.

Derek pulls me in for a hug. "I am serious about you, you know. Everything I've said is true. I love you and I want to make this work. I wouldn't have thought I would. Aiden's right about the things he says about me. But there's something about you, Aud." His voice trails off and he shrugs. "I've never known anyone like you before. I've never had someone blindly believe in me the way you do. And I don't want to screw this up. He's right about Serena—she may come for us. But I'll be there every step of the way. I promise you."

I stand still and let his words seep in. I don't look up at him, but I feel his arms squeeze around me tighter. "I love you too." It's the only thing I know how to say at this point. It's all I've got.

It must be enough, though. Derek pulls away and looks me in the eye, smiling. Leaning in, he presses his lips to my forehead. "Let's get you home," he says against my skin.

I allow him to pull me out of the building and guide me to the waiting car.

CHAPTER THIRTY-TWO

FOR IMMEDIATE RELEASE
Crave's lead singer was recently seen kissing a woman who's been identified as Audrey Zaks. Audrey is the twin sister of Aiden Zaks, who plays guitar for Crave. Derek was dating Serena at the time of the kiss, and the two have since parted ways.
Derek is extremely sorry for the hurt, pain, and embarrassment he has caused Serena.
Derek and Audrey have known and loved each other since they were kids.
While the timing wasn't great, they've found each other again.
The Zaks family asks for their privacy to be respected during this time, and Derek requests fans to be kinder to Audrey. He takes full responsibility for his actions and wishes Serena well in her career.
Crave looks forward to continuing their collaboration with Serena.

I read the statement over and over again. It's better than I thought it would be. He's playing off the angle that we've known each other all our lives. Making it sound like Derek has always loved me and I've always loved him. Only part of that is true. But I'm not about to argue, because I'm hoping it helps take away some of the hate I'm receiving online.

I have stopped opening up my Instagram account, because when I do, I see message in my DMs calling me a whore or a homewrecker. I wasn't aware Derek and Serena were in that committed of a relationship, but some think they were. There are pictures online of Serena in a wedding dress with Derek in a tux—all photoshopped by fans. Some of them are downright crazy. Which is why Derek has volunteered to get me security.

As long as I'm with him, I feel like I'll be okay. It's when I have to go back to North Carolina that I'm worried about it. I have to head back there in a few days to train the Courage, and that can't be done from here. And Derek can't come with me.

He's at practice right now, but I opted to stay at the apartment to get some laundry done. I feel a bit out of it, and I'm honestly tired of seeing the glaring looks from Aiden. He's not my biggest fan lately.

My phone rings as I'm lying on the couch. I look over at the caller ID and see it's Emma. I smile. We've texted back and forth, but we haven't had the time for a call since all of this started.

"Hey," I say, sinking further into the couch under a blanket that smells like Derek.

"Well, there's America's biggest whore. I was wondering if you were going to pick up or if you had other things distracting you." She giggles at her own joke, and I laugh along with her.

"Very funny, sunshine. I'm here at his place by myself," I tell her. Then I answer the question before she can answer it. "He's at band practice."

"What's his place like? I've never been there, and I've always wondered. Are there bondage walls or tables. Does he have a leather couch? Is it your typical bachelor pad?"

I laugh and give her a rundown of his place. She *oohs* and *aahs* over some of the upgraded things he has in his apartment.

"So how are you holding up, whore?" she teases me. "I've been reading some of those online comments, and people are not happy with you."

I sigh and pinch the bridge of my nose. "I'm okay."

"You know I was only teasing about the whore comments. I love you. I know the truth," she reminds me.

"I know. It's just that I can't open my social media without seeing the hate from everyone. People are going as far as tagging me in things. The PR team at Beachbody has helped me with some of that. So has Derek. He adjusted some of my settings so people can't tag me anymore. It's just weird, Em. I never thought people would be so passionate about it."

"Serena's statement certainly didn't help things. Here's what her press release says: '*I'm feeling very betrayed but understand that this love between the two of them wasn't something that was planned. While I wish them well, I do wish that I wouldn't have been hurt in the process. But that's life and love.*'"

I swear I could recite the damn thing—I've read it so many times. "She could have been worse about it. Derek did break their deal. It's not like he's completely innocent in it."

"How did anyone even find out? Where was that picture taken?" Emma asks.

I forget that this is the first time we've really spoken, so she's bound to have some questions. I try to be patient and reply as normally as I can. When really, it's exhausting having to talk about it. Derek talks about it more than I thought he would. He keeps checking in and making sure that I'm okay. That my work's okay with everything that's happening. That my parents are fine with it.

I have no idea how to answer that last one because I haven't heard from them. As far as I know, they are. But no one has reached out. I make a mental note to do that later today. Maybe after I take another nap. I never used to be a napper, but something about reading things about yourself online that aren't true and being constantly stressed about what could happen when you leave the house will do that to you.

"Outside of a coffee shop, on the way to the studio," I reply.

"How is Aiden handling all of this? I saw a picture snapped of Derek the other day, and it looked like he had a black eye."

"He does," I tell her, and she gasps. "Aiden punched him in the face twice. Got the lip and eye. Derek didn't even fight back. He just let Aiden hit him. I wanted to hit Aiden for hurting him. I mean, it's not like the relationship with Serena was real, and we're both adults. His stupid rule about guys he knows dating me is just bananas, especially considering a lot of his friends are my friends. How would I ever meet anyone?"

She laughs. "Yeah, he does like to keep you on lockdown. How are things now?"

"Things are slowly getting better. Aiden and Derek aren't fighting anymore, which is good. The talk between them is tense, though. I think everything will be fine. He knows Derek loves me. This thing caused both of us to say *I love you* to each other."

"Oh, wow." Emma sounds surprised. "Do you love him?"

I smile. "Yes, I do. I worried that he might not actually love me. That he might have said it because he felt like he was in a tough spot with the media and manager breathing down his neck. But I don't think so anymore. He's been really wonderful through all of this—making me dinners, taking care of me, and holding me all night long."

"Well, that's good. I'm glad he's taking care of you. When are you coming home?" she asks, almost whining into the phone.

I laugh. "Are ya missing me?"

"Weren't you supposed to come home by now?"

"I was, yeah, but Derek asked me to stay here until things calmed down a bit. He's worried about me traveling home alone. I think I'll have to take security."

"Is it because of these crazy bitches online?" she asks. "Because I can come pick you up, if you'd like me to."

"Some of them actually photoshopped Derek and Serena into wedding attire. Like how insane do you need to be to do that?"

"Well, that's probably why he wants you to have security. If those whack jobs are doing things like that, how do you know they won't try to attack you in the airport?"

That's what I've been worried about and why he's worked so hard to keep me in LA. I'm not looking forward to being without him either. I like having him in bed with me at night, then waking up together and preparing meals with him. But that will soon have come to an end because we have jobs to do. That will be the real test to see if he's able to stay true to me while I'm across the country. I believe he will be, but only time will tell.

"Hello, earth to Audrey. Someone please page Audrey to the phone," I hear Emma calling.

I laugh. "Sorry."

"It's okay. Is Mr. Sex On Legs back?" she teases.

"No, I was just thinking about things."

"Uh-huh. Well, how about I pick you up at the airport? Send me your flight information. It's been forever since I've seen you."

"Thank you. That would be awesome."

"Do you have work when you get in, or do you want to hang out?" she asks. "We could do a girls' night at your house or something."

"That would be great. I've missed you and our girls' nights." They're not much, just Emma and I with some ice cream and alcohol. We either watch movies or just talk and laugh the whole time. It's really what I need right now—some levity and girl time. Not that living with Derek hasn't been great. It's certainly had its perks.

I think about this morning when he took me in the shower. I'd been so busy lost in thought after reading a comment that stated if I hadn't been born, then Serena and Derek would be so happy right now. Derek's really good at that. He can tell when I'm getting in my head too much or when things are bothering me. He knows when to pull me out of my funk or let me stew in it. I'm not sure how he's so perceptive. Maybe it comes from knowing me for some long or it could be just some gift he has. Either way, I'm glad he's with me now. I hope things will be back to normal when I'm in Cary. Being here in LA and with Derek probably makes me an easier target. Derek stands out, being so tall and covered in tattoos. His look is very distinct. In Cary, I'll fade more into the background.

"You sound like you might need several girls' nights," Emma says. "Do you want me to stay with you for a bit? Make sure you're okay?"

I love Emma. She's the best friend a girl could have.

"I don't want to put you out. I'll also have my security guy with me if Derek has his way." I'm pretty sure he will. I might as well admit defeat now. It might be nice to have her there, though, because I feel like it will be awkward living with a complete stranger like that. But Derek has assured me that the security guy will be a professional or Derek will break his face.

"Oh, I just might have to live there if he's hot. Then I'll need to see if I can seduce him." She giggles into the phone.

I howl with laughter. "You are something else."

"It's good to hear you laughing."

"Thanks. I had no idea how much I needed that."

"That's what you have me for, babe." She makes a kissing noise into the phone, causing me to laugh again. "Text me when you know your flight information."

"Will do."

We say our goodbyes, and I'm instantly glad she called. I lie back on the couch and doze until the door opens. In walks Derek, Aiden, and Brent. They look tore up. Aiden's clearly been crying.

"What happened?" I spring to my feet as they all walk over to me.

They carefully make their way over like they're approaching a cornered animal. Their steps are light, and even their hands are held out before them.

"Somebody start talking to me," I demand.

"Have a seat, Aud," Derek tells me gently, patting the couch beside him. "Please."

He's been crying too. Brent isn't coming close enough, so I can't tell if he's been crying or not.

Aiden takes a seat on Derek's coffee table, directly across from me. I can't fathom what he could be about to tell me. My mind runs through a million scenarios until it lands on the one I don't want it to be...but I know in my heart it is.

Dad.

"Aiden, just say it." A lump is forming in my throat, and tears are starting to form behind my eyes. I close them, blinking them out.

Aiden sighs and looks up for what I'm guessing is strength. He lets out a sigh and prepares to shatter my world the same way his has been. "Audrey, Dad went to the hospital because he was coughing up blood. There was a tear, and unfortunately, they didn't get to it in time. Dad passed away early this morning." Aiden breaks. He slumps over and sobs rack his body.

"No!" I howl.

I lean forward and lay on Aiden. We sit there sobbing, clinging to each other. I hear another sob break out in the room, and strong hands are placed on my shoulders. It's Derek; he's crying right along with us. I'm not sure how long we're like that, and I have no idea what Brent is doing, but eventually the door opens, and I recognize Dale's voice.

"I got the security and tickets all figured out. A car will be waiting to take you all to their parents' house."

I assume he's telling Brent, who replies, "Thank you."

"Audrey and Aiden," Dale says, "I'm so very sorry. Please know that I'll take care of whatever is needed. Say the word and it's done."

"Thank you, Dale," Derek croaks out.

I don't want to move from this spot. I know we need to get home, but I don't know how to even consider a world where my father is no longer in it. I just saw him. He seemed fine. The thought makes me cry harder. I wonder if he died hearing the awful things that were being spread about his daughter. I never got to talk to him.

My mom is all alone in Cary. I'm sure family and friends are going to see her, but Aiden and I should really be there too.

"We gotta move," I say, extracting myself from Aiden and Derek. "Mom is at home alone, and we need to be there with her."

"Aunt Ellen is there," Aiden tells me.

"Still, we should be with her. Let's get moving." I start heading toward Derek's bedroom, where my things are. I need to start packing.

"Hang on, Aud. I can take care of all of that." Derek trails after me. "Just go sit. Let me take care of you."

I'm not sure that I can sit down. I want to do something to take my mind off my loss. If I sit here and think about the fact that I live in a world where I no longer have a father, I may never get up. Derek may never get me on a plane.

Aiden comes into the room. His eyes are red rimmed, but he looks like he's trying his best to hold it together too. "Let D help you," he rasps out.

Getting off the bed, where I was told stay put, I go to Aiden and put my arms around him. He hugs me back instantly. We just stand there while I hear the sounds of Derek packing up our things.

"What about you?" I whimper out. "Don't you need things?"

"We're going to go there next," Derek says. "I'm not leaving you two alone right now. Brent went to pack up some things, and he'll meet us at Aiden's."

We move as one all the way to airport—no one being left alone or left behind. I don't even get a moment to fall apart by myself. Derek and Aiden stay with me. Thankfully, Dale has arranged everything for us. The cars to and from the airport, the tickets—it's all been taken care of. All I can think about is getting to my mom and being with her. I don't care that Aunt Ellen is with her.

There are so many questions I want to ask Mom, but I can't right now. It'll take time to get those answers. She just lost the love her life, and she needs time to process. Eventually, I'll know all the painful details of why I no longer have a dad.

CHAPTER THIRTY-THREE

Cary, North Carolina—the place I call home. The place I was looking forward to going home to for so long. I needed the comforts of home and not the flashing lights of LA. But now it's the last place I want to be. I don't want my dad's death to be my reality. It can't be. I just saw him. I have no idea how we got here. I say as much to Derek as the car is leading us from the Raleigh-Durham Airport. It's a quick drive, thankfully. I don't think I could have handled it if we were going to be sitting in traffic for hours. It's rush hour, so that's still a possibility, but it won't be too long.

"I don't know, Aud. I'm sure your mom will explain everything in time. Let's just focus on getting to her." He gives my hand a squeeze. He hasn't stopped touching me since we left LA. There's always a hand in mind, on my leg, or on the small of my back. I like it. It's comforting.

I wish Aiden had someone the way I do. I want to be with him too, but he's staying strong and keeping to himself. I haven't really been able to get to talk with him or even hold his hand through this. But he's being Aiden and hiding his emotions—taking everything step by step, worrying about getting on the plane, finding our bags and car, and then getting to Mom.

The car pulls up to our house, and I stare at it. I know that when I walk into that house, it's going to feel completely different. There is no father waiting for me. Only my mom and she's hurting. That's the only thing that helps me get out of the car. Derek is holding onto me. I'm cradled in his arm as I head up the front walk. Aiden has stopped throwing glares in Derek's direction. There are more important things for him to worry about than my choice in boyfriend—or what he sees as a big lapse in judgment.

As soon as we enter the house, I'm happy to see Emma is already here. She's sitting on the couch with my aunt Ellen and Mom.

"Kids." My mom jumps up from the couch and comes over to us. Aiden and I step forward and allow her to wrap us in her arms.

"Mom..." I cry into her shoulder as she holds us. I hear Aiden mumble something, but I can't make it out. I just stand there and cling to her, trying to provide her strength and trying to draw strength from her.

I'm not sure how long we stand there, but I hear Brent, Emma, and Derek talking lowly behind us. I have no idea where they disappear too, but when I pull away from Mom, it's just the three of us standing there.

"What happened?" Aiden finally asks her.

Mom lets loose a heavy, shaky sigh. She's been crying for a quite a while. "I'll explain it later. Right now, I just need you kids."

I nod in understanding, though I can see Aiden wants to fight her. I hope he doesn't push the issue. He has a need to know everything; he wants all of the facts because the thoughts in his head might be worse than what actually happened. But he relents and doesn't push for more details.

"Can I get you some tea, Mom?" I ask her.

"No," she says, her voice quivering from the tears. There's a fresh batch building up behind her eyes. "I'm fine. Emma made me some."

I've never felt so awkward in my own home. I'm not sure what to do or even say to her. I want to crawl in her lap and try, but she's feeling all of this too. I can't put all of my grief on her when she has her own. I look around the room, but Derek and Emma haven't returned yet. I like that they're giving us space, but it still makes me uneasy. I'm not sure what to do or say.

"Sit," Mom says, patting the space on the couch on either side of her. "I've seen the news, Audrey, so I know what's going on with you and Derek."

I figured. I'd sort of been waiting for a phone call from her or Dad. I guess they had more important things going on.

We sit in silence for a while. I don't want to talk about what's happening with me and Derek. There are more important things happening right now. She doesn't need those details or to hear how her own daughter was called a whore in the media. And that's assuming that she doesn't know that already. She has an Instagram account, and she follows me and Aiden. So, she must know.

I can't handle this; I need some kind of answers. I thought maybe it would be okay to sit here and let her tell us when she was ready, but not if she's going to make small talk. This isn't a small-talk situation.

"Mom, how did this happen?" I ask. "Were there complications?"

Aiden sighs heavily beside her, shooting me a glare as if it say, *She told you not to push.*

"He was fine and then he wasn't. He went in to have a port put in for the treatments, which went fine. We got him home and he was resting, then he woke me up in the middle of night, sweating and with a fever. I rushed him into the emergency room, but we lost him a few hours later. Turns out, the port they placed in him had thrown a clot and he also got an infection.

Your father was so prepared to go up against the cancer. Now he'll never get the chance."

She leans forward and a sob breaks through. I place my body on top on hers and try to give her as much strength as I have left. I feel a heavy weight placed on top of me, and I know it's Aiden. It makes me happy that he's here with me, and that even though he's not happy with me, he'll still provide me comfort.

Eventually, Mom attempts to sit up, and we pile off her. She finally turns to me and says, "What's going on with you? I see that you're getting a lot of hate."

Before I can answer, Derek walks back into the room. "I fell in love with your daughter when I was helping her take care of the house in Corolla. Well, if I'm being honest with myself, I fell in love with her long ago when we were teenagers. But I didn't act on it until recently."

My mom looks from him and back to me.

"Things are getting a little better," I tell her. "Beachbody is going to take care of everything with the help of the guys' manager. I still have my job, and it looks like the label may still work with them. There may be some concessions that need to happen with the song with Serena, but I didn't steal Derek from her. I wouldn't do something like that."

"It didn't seem like you."

"Oh God, I hope Dad didn't die thinking I was some cheating whore." My hand flies to my mouth and a sob breaks through.

Derek immediately comes over and wraps his arms around me, rocking me back and forth to comfort me. "I'm sure he didn't think that. He knew you."

"He did, honey," Mom assures me. "Your father was sure there was more to the story than we knew, and we did know that Serena and Derek weren't really together anyway."

"God, this whole week has just been horrible." They all stare at me as I'm laughing like a maniac. "I mean, the whole world hates me. And now my father has died, and he had to hear in the media that I was some sort of homewrecker. This is just so fucking awesome."

Aiden scoffs and shakes his head.

"Don't start," I warn him.

"You're not happy with this?" Mom asks him.

"That's an understatement," I tell her once I get my laughter under control.

"Aiden, stop being such a child," Mom scolds him, which only causes another round of laughter to burst out of me.

I'm not sure what's happening to me. I think it's just the stress of the week. It's caused what feels like an inappropriate reaction to come out of me.

"See, even your mom is okay with this," Derek teases. Aiden doesn't reply.

"I didn't say that." Mom tells him.

"I'm sorry, Mrs. Zaks. I really didn't mean to hurt anyone with this. But I love Audrey, and I'm trying to do right by her. I'm also providing security for her so that no one can hurt her. I will take very good care of your daughter, ma'am."

"I believe that you will," she tells him. "I just don't want my daughter getting hurt by your lifestyle."

"Does everyone think I'm an ass?" Derek asks.

"Well, I know my son, and I'm guessing you're just like him," Mom jokes.

It feels weird and kind of good all at the same time to be joking like this. I hate that there's no chance that my dad will come walking through the door, but that's something I'll have to get used to. Or at least come to terms with. I'm not sure there is any getting used to it.

Emma finds her way into the living room and hands Aiden and I some tea. We all thank her as Brent comes in quietly and takes a seat in the chair across from us.

Emma sits on the other side of me, holding my hand. That's where we stay for a while. Eventually, Aunt Ellen joins us too. We talk about my dad and tell stories about how wonderful he was. There are funny ones, stories of him being a dad and threatening to kick our asses, and moments that are touching. We're in tears from laughter and sadness by the end. It's kind of a great night, considering.

Aiden and I will go with Mom to make the funeral arrangements tomorrow. There's so much to consider and so much to take care of. I can't even fathom it all. Right now, though, I focus on being there for my mom and getting her through the grief, all while trying to process my own grief. To his credit, Derek stays by my side. Brent stays close to Aiden and me. It's great that we have such a great support system. I just wish we were all here for a happier time.

CHAPTER THIRTY-FOUR

I went to Target and bought a plain black dress for the funeral. It isn't something I want hanging in my closet. I want to wear it and then forget I ever owned it. Otherwise, I'll always look at it and remember that tit was what I was wearing when I buried my dad. I may have been able to find something at my apartment, but I haven't been back there yet. I've been staying with my mom, helping her, and sleeping in my childhood room. I had to make sure she wasn't alone. Derek has been bunking with me and Emma. Which is strange, but it's great to have them both so close. Brent has been staying with Aiden in his room.

I put on my funeral dress and sigh, looking at myself in the mirror. My eyes look a little tired and red. Makeup won't help that, and I'm not even sure I'll put any on. What would it matter anyway? I'll only cry it off.

"You look beautiful, Aud," Derek says from behind me, wrapping his strong arms around my middle.

"Thanks," I mumble.

I'm not sure how I would have gotten through these last few days without him. He's been strong when I need him to be, checking on me and making sure we all eat, even taking out tricks from his limited menu and cooking for us, when need be. I appreciate him more than he knows. I know he feels a little like he lost his own father too. My dad was one of the few men in his life who he had to look up to. I know this. He's hurting too, but he's made sure to take care of us instead.

Em has been great, too, staying with me and holding my hand through it all. She's at her house right now getting herself together for the funeral. She said she'll meet us there. Aiden did the same as me and got special funeral clothes from Target. We were both in agreement that we didn't want these clothes anymore. My mom, though, wanted to wear something from her closet. I make a mental note to hide it later on. I don't want her staring at it and reliving the day after we leave.

"You about ready?" Derek asks. "Aiden says we need to go over to the funeral home soon."

I nod and make my way out of my room. Making all of the necessary arrangements for my father's funeral was easier than I thought it would be. It was something my parents had previously talked about, so there wasn't too much to do. My mom insisted on having a quick turnaround with the service. She knows my brother needs to get back to LA, which is partly true, but he would have stayed for as long as she needed him.

I haven't decided how long I'll stay. Derek says I should get back to my apartment and start training again. I pushed that back by two weeks, though—part of my lying low routine. I am a season ticket holder for the Courage, and I do like to go watch them play, but I'm not sure I'll do that. In fact, I just want to sit at home and wallow.

Derek leads me out of my room and into the living room. Mom is in the kitchen. I hear her talking to my aunt. Aunt Ellen has been great. I'm glad my mom has the comfort of her sister being here, and she plans on staying for as long as she's needed. I don't want my mom to be alone. I can't imagine living with someone for the forty years my parents were married and then suddenly having no one. I can't bear the thought. My eyes tear again. Derek rubs my back.

Aunt Ellen comes through and heads upstairs toward Mom's room. She turns, holding a small black purse. "I told her she didn't need one, but she insisted," she says, shrugging in our direction.

"She always felt like she should have one."

"How are you holding up, Audrey? Can I do anything for you?" Aunt Ellen asks.

"No, I'm okay. Thank you for coming, though, and for staying with Mom for so long. I'm sure it means a lot of her. I know it does to me and Aiden."

"I'm just glad I can be here for her. But I'm here for you too, you know. If you want to talk, let me know. I know you have Derek, but I'm happy to listen too."

"Thank you," I say, pulling her in for a hug. "I'm doing alright, I guess. It does help having Derek and Emma here. I worry about Mom. There are all these people here. I feel like she can't be herself or really breakdown with such a full house."

"She has, just in the privacy of her own room. Just the way she would want it. I think it's better for her to have people here. Keeps the house busy and not as quiet as it soon will be."

I nod in understanding.

My mom enters the living room. "We'd better get going," she tells all of us.

Aiden and Brent materialize out of nowhere, as if they could hear her from wherever it is they've been hiding. We all pile into two cars: Mom, Aunt Ellen, Aiden, and me in one. Brent, Derek, and Emma all follow in another. It feels right to be traveling with just family. Even though I wish I still had Derek's hand to hold onto. Instead, I take Aiden's and give it a squeeze.

"It's gonna be okay," he tells me reassuringly.

I nod, unable to say anything. There's a sob getting ready to break through, and I don't want to do it in the car. I don't want Mom to hear me. She isn't crying right now, but I'm sure it would cause her to start too.

"We're gonna get through this. Keeping busy, that's the key," he tells me.

I just nod again. There's nothing wrong with Aiden's way of coping. I just worry that the feelings are going to come flooding out when he's on stage or when he has deadlines to meet. Dale would understand now, but I'm not sure he would later. He almost reminds me of some kind of a pod man, like he spawned out of some hole in the ground and never really had parents. He doesn't have a lot of emotion. Instead, he has ideas and ways to spin things. Just like our dad's death, which he's spun that into a media story. The whole world knows that Aiden and I lost our father. They know that he was a father figure to Derek, too. We're told it works out well because it buys him sympathy with the fans. Serena even made a statement, vowing to send flowers to the funeral. If they are there, I don't want to see them. I want to burn them.

The funeral home comes into view. It's a large old house with a wraparound porch and big black shutters that stand out against the white siding. Our little group is reassembled outside of the home. The funeral director we met with the other day is outside waiting for us.

"Hi, Mrs. Zaks. Everything has been taken care of per your requests. Just like we discussed, we have some time in the beginning set aside for just the family to go in. Who did you want to allow in first?" he asks, eyeing our group.

"All of us. This is all our family," she says, looking around and offering a weak smile to everyone.

"Mrs. Zaks, I don't—" Brent starts to say, but he's cut off.

"Nonsense. You are family, Brent, and you will be coming in with us."

"Yes, ma'am," he replies.

As we make our way in, I'm still holding onto Aiden. Derek is behind me, but this feels like a moment I need my twin brother, not him. In the foyer of the home, I can see the room off to the left holds my father and his body. I haven't seen him yet. The only thing I know is what he'll be wearing. I helped my mom pick out his suit and tie that he would wear. We put the rock star tie on him that Aiden got him for Christmas. On his feet went the socks I got him with Aiden's and my faces from when we were kids. I make a mental note to order my mom a pair for Christmas. I feel like she might like that.

I stop and stare at the room. My feet feel like lead. Aiden has dropped my hand, and he's following my mom and aunt into the room. But I don't want to go in. I don't want any of this to be real. I feel a hand join mine.

"Come on, baby. You've gotta go in there," Derek whispers in my ear. "Trust me, you're going to regret it if you don't."

"I'm not strong enough," I tell him.

"You are. You can do this. I will be right here with you."

Emma and Brent are following everyone in. Emma looks back at me and pauses.

"I've got her, Em," Derek tells her.

She watches for a moment, then makes her way into the room. I catch a glimpse of it and know that my dad is lying in a coffin in that room.

"Derek," I breathe out, gasping for breath. "I don't think I can do this."

He takes me into one of the side rooms. I recognize it immediately as the room where the receptionist sits. I do my best to breathe and in and out.

"Here, sit." He leads me over to the chair. "Now put your head between your legs and breathe."

I do as he asks, and the world stops spinning. I can slowly start to breathe normally again. But the pain in my chest, the ache of losing my dad, is still there. Aiden suddenly comes bursting into the room.

"You okay?" He kneels down in front of me. "Let's go do this together. I'm sorry I left you."

I offer him a smile and accept his hand. He leads me into the room, and we say goodbye to our father. I see the arrangement that Serena sent immediately. I know all the ones with white and blue roses are from the family. That was our gift to Dad. But the lavish one that's much larger than ours and has several different varieties of white flowers on it came from her.

"Make sure you get a picture of that and thank her on Instagram," I snap at Derek.

He squeezes my hand and says, "I'm sure someone from her team already has a picture and will be posting. That girl's all about her image. But let's not worry about her right now

I don't speak at the funeral. Instead, I stand by Aiden while he talks for both of us, his hand in mine the whole time.

"Our father was a great man. He was the cornerstone of our family. Everything he did was in service to my mom, my sister, and me. He made sure we had a great life and always took the time to be at our school events. Most parents wouldn't approve of their son refusing to go to college to be in a rock band, but he did. I never once heard him tell me I needed a backup plan. Music is what I love, and my dad loved that for me. *Follow your dreams*, he'd always say. And I did. So did Audrey. We did it because he taught us it was okay to do so. So now we'll go on in memory of him. Dad, we love you and we'll do our best to honor you and your legacy."

We head back and sit on either side of my mom.

"Beautiful," she says, leaning over and kissing both of us. I love Aiden's words, and I accept the praise from my mom, but I had nothing to do with any of it.

The rest of the funeral flies by in a haze. I keep one hand in my mom's and one hand in Derek's. When it's finally time to say my final goodbye at the gravesite, I lose it. Derek has to hold me up as my body is racked by sobs. I don't even care that there are a few camera crews who managed to find our location. I still broke, and I couldn't care less that it was caught on camera.

CHAPTER THIRTY-FIVE

We arrive back home, and everyone heads out to the back deck to sit around the portable fire pit we got Mom and Dad a few years back. The guys are still in their dress shirts, their ties and jackets long gone, while Mom, Emma, and I are in comfier clothes. It reminds of me of the night we spent in Corolla. Instead of having my dad here, we have Aunt Ellen.

I sigh, leaning back in my chair.

"You okay?" Derek asks me for the millionth time.

"No," I snap at him. I don't mean to snap at him. I'm tired of the question, and I miss my dad. I feel like I would have snapped at anyone who dared to ask me a question right now. Derek doesn't say anything; he just nods and squeezes my knee, then he gets up and heads into the house.

"Be nice," Aiden warns.

"Oh, I thought you would be all for me being mean to Derek."

"I don't want you to be mean to him for no reason, Audrey."

The question that has been on the tip of my tongue since we got home finally comes out. "Did Dale leak the location of Dad's funeral? Is that why all the press was there?"

Brent shakes his head. "He's a lot of things, but no he didn't. He actually had no idea that the funeral was being held there. I'm guessing we were followed. There's security waiting out there for when you decide to go home. And that will stick with you for a while. He made sure of it." Brent gestures at Derek, who's joined us on the deck again.

"Thank you," I say to Derek, hoping it helps with the bitchiness that slipped into my tone earlier. I see he brought his guitar out with him.

"I thought we could play a little bit," he tells everyone.

"I'd love to hear you guys play," Mom says.

"Me too," Aunt Ellen chimes in.

"I'll grab mine," Aiden says before making his way into the house. He returns quickly, holding one of his guitars.

The guys get together and begin strumming a bit. A few are tunes I recognize. They're slower and more somber for the occasion. It's when Aiden begins singing by himself that I realize they're sharing a new song.

You taught me peace.
You taught me to feel comfortable in my skin.
You helped me learn and grow.
I'm a man because of you.
Because of you.

The song is a tribute to my father, and it's beautiful. My mom and I have tears in our eyes when he finishes.

"It's beautiful, dear," Mom says. "Will you play it on the album?"

"I think so," he tells us.

I get up and give him a hug. He squeezes me back tightly. He's been doing that a lot lately.

"Actually," Aiden starts, "Derek wrote it and said I should sing it. I helped with some things, but mostly it's him."

"I just took some things you were attempting to use in your speech and put them into a song. You could have played that for everyone today."

"I didn't want to do that. It seemed like I'd be stealing focus from Dad."

"You wouldn't have been," my mom tells him.

"Either way, I wasn't going to do it. I think we'll release it on our next album. I know Dale is happy about it. I just don't want to make Dad's death about business, and I fear that's what it will do," he says with a shrug.

"I think it's fine. It's about your feelings," I remind him. "You should do it."

"Well, Derek's feelings," he corrects again.

Derek chuckles, shaking his head. "How many times do I have to tell you, I used your words when you were writing drafts of that speech. I just worked with what you were feeling."

"Do it, honey. I really think you should," Mom reassures him.

She rises and hugs each of the men. "Thank you for that. Thank you for playing that here tonight. It reminds me of the last time we were all together, and I needed that. I could almost feel your father here with us. Right now, I'm going to get some much-needed rest."

"Me too," Aunt Ellen says, following Mom.

"I love you, baby girl." Mom comes over and wraps me in a hug.

"You know, I could stay here with you for a few more days. I really don't mind," I tell her.

"No, it's time for you to fly away, my little butterfly. But I know you'll be close, and you'll come and see me for Sunday dinners sometimes."

I did agree that I would come visit and do dinner on Sundays. It's usually a slower day for me. It'll just be weird not having my dad here, but I know it will be harder for her than me. So, I can be here without him for a few hours while she's enduring it every day.

She heads into the house, and we all watch her go.

"When do you guys leave?" I ask the band.

"Day after tomorrow," Derek answers. "I'll take you home and make sure everything is okay, and then I'll come back here and pick up the guys. You're not far, right?"

"Nope, not even a half hour, I don't think."

"I'm gonna hit the hay," Brent says. "I'm so tired."

"Thanks for being here, Brent," I call after him.

"I wouldn't have been anywhere else, kiddo."

"Be there in a bit," Aiden calls after him.

"I think I'm going to sleep on the couch tonight," Emma announces.

"Why?" I ask her.

"I just feel like you two could use some peace and quiet."

"Gross," Aiden says, shaking his head. "We just buried Dad."

"We're not gonna do anything," I try to reassure everyone. Derek, however, stays quiet.

"Oh, come on. Who knows when you'll be able to see each other next," Emma says, heading into the house.

It's just Aiden, Derek, and I now.

"When *will* you two see each other again?" Aiden asks.

It's the uncomfortable question. The elephant in the room. The question I haven't asked because I'm terrified of the answer. So, I do what I do best and avoid the topic altogether.

"I'm not sure," Derek admits. "We haven't really talked about it. The last time I brought it up, she changed the subject."

"You guys might want to have that conversation sooner rather than later." He gets up and heads for the house.

"You're headed in too?" I whine.

"What's the matter, you don't want to be out here alone with Derek?" He watches me as he speaks.

"No, I just thought it was nice with the three of us out here like we used to do."

Both guys nod and take seats back around the fire.

"Does anyone know who bought my grandparents' house?" Derek asks.

I look over at the house he's speaking of. "I'm not sure, but Mom probably does."

"I can't really ask her about that now. I was just wondering what they're like."

I had almost forgotten that this might be weird for him. He grew up right next door and never really got to say goodbye to the house. It was sold out from under him by family who didn't care that Derek wanted to say goodbye to it.

"Are you thinking of asking them for a tour?" Aiden asks.

"Nah, I noticed there was kids' stuff in the backyard, so they probably don't want someone like me hanging around."

I snicker. "Come on, you'd be a great influence on kids."

"Just as good of one as Ace over there."

"Hey, way to take me down with you," Aiden says, then laughs and shakes his head.

"I miss being back here with you two," I remark. "Things were much simpler when we were kids."

"I don't know about that," Derek says. "I remember we got in a lot more shit back then. Boosting alcohol from your parents' stash was always tricky."

"I remember those days. But I also remember how much fun it was having them around when we were kids. All the barbecues and the trips they took us on. Friday night movie nights in the backyard." My eyes tear up as I remind them of all the fun we used to have with them. It doesn't really surprise me that Derek remembers all the shit we got into.

"Yeah, those were some good times," Aiden agrees.

"I loved growing up beside you guys. It was great. The only time I felt like I had family."

We stay up for a bit longer telling stories, and then Aiden goes inside.

"What are we going to do when you leave here?" Derek asks me. "When will I see you again?"

I shrug. "I'm not sure. But I know I can't go back to LA with you. I need to stay here if I want to retain some of my clients." I remind him that I have a job; one that I would still like to keep.

"What if you did your job from there?" he asks.

"What if you did your job from here?" I parrot back.

"Well, mine is a little harder. All my contacts, agents, and manger are in LA."

"New York isn't that far away, and people make that work all the time. Look at Jay Z."

That makes Derek laugh out loud. "Seriously?"

"Yeah, seriously. What if you all stayed around here? Helped out Mom."

"I think we should have this conversation when you're not feeling all nostalgic," he says.

We're quiet for a bit as I watch the yellow and orange flames dance before me.

He finally breaks the silence. "You know, I bet you could train people in LA. I bet there are people who are looking for personal trainers there. It is LA, after all. Look at all the aspiring actresses and the people that need to be in shape because, hello, it's LA. There's even an NWSL team there. What if you trained them? I bet Dale could pull some strings."

I sigh, leaning back in my chair. I had hoped he wouldn't bring this up. "It's like feminism isn't even a thing. Why would you just assume I would follow you?"

"Because it makes the most sense."

"I thought we were doing long distance?" I remind him.

"I want to be with you more than that. Like what if you went on our next tour with us? Wouldn't that be fun?"

He's right, we shouldn't be having this conversation right now. Because I say the thing I don't even believe, but the grief and anger make it come out. "What, so you don't get yourself into trouble? So, you can keep true to your word and not screw around?"

He jumps up and begins to pace. "I can't even believe you

would say something like that to me. Is that really what you think I would do?"

I look at him and sigh. "I told you I didn't want to talk about this right now. You said we shouldn't, but you pushed me, so now I—"

"So now you're just saying shit to be mean? Damn, Audrey, I love you. Remember? I wanna be with you. I haven't felt this happy in a long time and having you with me is a big part of that. I'm sorry that I want to keep you with me for as long as I can. Damn, it's not so I won't fucking cheat."

I feel like I'm two inches tall right now. I shouldn't have said it. I should have just kept my mouth shut. "Can we talk about this later?"

"Yeah, but later is coming quick," he reminds me. "You leave tomorrow."

"I know. But I don't want to talk about it now."

"Okay. But I do not want to end this conversation with a breakup. Understand?"

I nod. "Yes, I understand. I love you too, and that's not what I want either. What are your tour dates?"

He wraps me up in his arms and places a kiss on my temple. "I'll have my people call your people."

I laugh out loud. "Come on, funny man, let's go to bed."

Derek turns off the fire and we head inside. As we're crossing the kitchen and heading toward the stairs, I hear the sounds of moaning.

"What is that?" I ask Derek.

"Someone's having sex," Derek replies. He sneaks into the living room.

"Derek," I hiss at him. "No..." Realization dawns on me that the girl having sex has to be Emma. And I'm not sure if she's fucking Brent or Aiden, but God, I hope it's not Aiden.

Derek comes back over, chuckling.

"What?"

"Aiden and Emma," he tells me. "Aiden is giving it to Emma pretty good in there. I guess that's one form of helping him cope with today. Should we go up and do the same? She particularly encouraged it out there."

"Ew. How can they do that? Come on, that's so weird." I'm sick to my stomach with this. I hope Aiden's not taking advantage of her. I tell Derek as much.

"Leave them be. They're adults, and they have no idea that we saw them. Let's just see how this plays out in the morning." He drags me up the stairs into my room.

"But Derek, we have to..." I'm not sure what we have to do, but I feel like it should be something.

"Aud, think about it. What is so different about what they're doing and what we got caught doing? We can't go down there and bust them. We'd look like hypocrites. As we said, they're consenting adults. Let them be."

"But—"

"Nope, not happening. And as far as they know, we don't know. So, let's just keep it that way. We have no idea if this has been happening since we got here or if this was just a one-night lapse in judgment. Leave them be, Aud."

I sigh. "Fine. But I hope Emma is okay."

"Oh, she sounded more than okay," Derek says with a laugh.

"Gross," I tell him, smacking his shoulder.

"You know, we could have fun too. Get your mind off today." He pulls me in and gives me a deep kiss.

I almost turn him down, but then I remember that this may be the last time we have together for a few months. Derek may have realized the same thing because he makes low and slow love to me. I feel cherished and loved as he looks me in the eye while he drives into me slowly.

When we come back down to earth, he pulls me into his side. "I love you, Audrey," he whispers in my ear.

"I love you too."

He holds onto me and kisses my shoulder and neck. I don't feel like he's pushing for another round here, just memorizing every inch of my skin with his lips. Because who knows when will be the next time we get to lie here just like this, together. The world has a funny way of working out and breaking things that are meant to be preserved.

CHAPTER THIRTY-SIX

I did it. I left him. I'm back now in my own apartment. It felt like a part of my soul was left there on that curb when we said goodbye. But I had to do it, and he knew that. We're not over and it's not a breakup, but it felt like a breaking of sorts. Like a piece of my heart permanently cracked when he hugged and kissed me goodbye yesterday. I promised myself that I wouldn't follow a man around, that I would do my own thing. So that's what I'm doing.

Emma has yet to confide in me about her night with Aiden, and following Derek's lead, I've decided not to say a word to either of them about it. It might have just been a moment of weakness on both of their parts. The next morning, everything seemed fine and there was no weirdness between them. I expected some, but no one was bothered or even seemed hurt or angry. In fact, when Emma left, Aiden just waved her goodbye. She smiled widely at him like normal, and off she went. When she's ready and wants to, she'll confide in me.

For now, though, I focus on training my clients and head to a North Carolina Courage game. It's fun to watch them play. I never played soccer, but I'm always impressed with the speed and finesse that some of them can move the ball with. I can't imagine the thrill of being an adult and still playing the sport you played all your life.

Heading through the gate, I spot a friend I've made since coming to the stadium to train the team. "Hi, Ryan. How's life?" I ask.

He scans my badge and allows me to enter through the side entrance of the stadium.

"They're with me," I motion to the two guys from the security team Derek assigned to me.

"I see that," he remarks. "You really took Serena's boyfriend, huh?"

I shake my head. "Ryan—"

"Relax, I'm only teasing. I saw all the statements and all of the news."

"Has anyone here said anything?"

"Nah, but you're gonna find this interesting. She booked singing the national anthem today."

"She did fucking what?" I ask him. "Perfect. Maybe I should go."

"Just stay. I'm sure she won't even come near you," he tries to assure me. Ryan is probably right; she has no idea that I'm here. When shit went down, the team never even put out a statement.

I make my way to my reserved seating. It's just below the box seats, and I get a nice view of the field, plus shade. Which makes me happy.

"Boys, sit wherever," I tell them, motioning around to the empty seats. "Not many people sit here."

I watch the warm-ups, and it looks like I'll be in an area all by myself. No one is coming near my seats. I buy some popcorn and water from the vendors walking through the arena. I decide to send Derek a picture of my view. I send him the soccer field, with my legs propped up on the wall in front of me.

Audrey: Your girlfriend is singing the national anthem at this game.

I add in a winky face and send it off. It doesn't take him long to reply.

Derek: Funny...my girlfriend can't sing.

Audrey: Well, Serena can.

Derek: You gotta be fucking kidding me.

Audrey: Nope.

Derek: Is your security there?

Audrey: Yes, dear, they are here. And I think they're completely unnecessary.

Derek: I won't have this argument again. They're completely necessary. Now be a good girl or get spanked!

I giggle when I read his last message.

Audrey: Are you going to come here and actually spank me? Because I could get into that.

Derek: Woman, the images you have going through my head right now...

I send him a kissy-face emoji.

Audrey: Your girlfriend is about to start singing, so I've gotta go. Love you. Bye!

I don't have a chance to see his last message because Serena begins singing the anthem. The announcers described her as a "rock sensation." When she finishes, the whole stadium goes crazy.

"Thank you. Thank you very much," she croons. Waving both of her hands in the air, she leaves the center of the field and heads for the tunnel. More security joins the area where I'm sitting, and my stomach fills with dread. This means she's going to sit with me. That's why there's no one else here.

Fuck. I'm not ready for this. I make a move to leave and hear my name called from the field. It's Jess, one of the players. We've talked quite a bit before and after workouts and have even gone out for a drink together.

"Hey, girl!" I call to her. "Good luck today."

"It's so good to see you. Thank you for coming." She comes over closer, and I make my way down to the railing where she is. Thankfully, the stadium isn't very large, and there doesn't appear to be many people around, thanks to my soon to be seatmate. It takes me no time at all to get down to her. "I was sorry to hear about your dad."

"Thank you," I reply. My eyes tear just a bit. I still can't believe people have to say those words to me. His death doesn't seem real, even though I know it is. Hell, I just came from the funeral not even a week ago.

"Catch you after? Wanna grab a drink?"

"Yeah, maybe," I tell her. "I'm beat. It's been a long week."

"Sure, see you after." She smiles and heads back to the field.

I head back up, and sure enough, Serena is making her way to where my snacks are waiting for me.

"Serena," I say to her as I lower myself into my seat. "This can't be a coincidence that you're sitting here with me."

"You're a smart girl," she says with a laugh. "But seriously, I was sorry to hear about your dad."

"Thanks. I read your statement, and we got your flowers."

"I hope people weren't giving you too much hate anymore. I asked my fans to leave you be. Did they listen?"

"As much as a bunch of keyboard warriors can," I remark.

She chuckles. "I see you have security. I really doubt anyone here in Cary will bother you. Do you really think you're big enough for that?"

I don't miss the disdain in her tone, but I try not to let her bait me. "I didn't choose the security. That was all Derek."

"He's so sweet, isn't he? I mean, when we were together, he was so sweet and thoughtful. But then he found you." Her voice trails off and she adds in, "Before you were able to pull him away."

"I didn't pull him away. That relationship was fake. You can't possibly believe that anyone in this section can hear you. We're all alone over here. Which I feel like is your doing."

"Well, I have to be careful," she remarks.

I look around the stadium, wondering if anyone will notice our interaction or figure out who Serena is sitting with. It won't take long to put two and two together. Her security team is doing a great job of keeping guests away from her. I've heard them say a few times that Serena will sign autographs after the event.

"Aren't you worried that someone will see you sitting here with me? There's no way attention won't be on you. I mean, look at the security team flagging off the area. Are you hoping they realize who you're sitting with?"

I look around and make sure my own security team is still here. I find them chatting it up with Serena's team. I roll my eyes, hoping that means they will still protect me even though they're chummy with her.

"You are quite the suspicious one, aren't you? That won't bode well with you and Derek when he's on tour. I still want him to sing that song, you know."

"I heard," I growl out. Not the best news I've heard all week, but certainly not the worst...

"And as for people realizing that I'm here with you, I think that will work well in your favor. Old girlfriend and new girlfriend burying the hatchet and watching a game together. I think those are some pretty good optics."

"Optics, huh? Is that all you care about?"

She shrugs. "My whole life is about optics. Hell, isn't being a woman all about optics? If we appear to be in control, eventually someone will believe that we are. If, when you're with a man and you pretend to need him, he'll eventually believe that you do. If you act sexy, then eventually you'll be sexy. Shall I go on?"

"You really believe the bullshit you spew, don't you?" I ask her, annoyed with her and fighting the urge to admit that she has a point with some of what she's said.

She sits back, and I think our conversation is over. I'm *hoping* it is, otherwise, this will be a long game. Two forty-five-minute periods cannot end soon enough.

"So where is he?" she finally asks me.

"How long have you been holding onto that question?" I look over just in time to see her roll her eyes.

"Still in LA, I'm guessing. I figured you would be here. Your bio says you train the Courage. They were all too happy to have me come out and sing the anthem for them, even if it meant shutting down your usual section. I've sold out plenty of other seats and even agreed to a meet and greet with the team later. Tell me, do they ask trainers to do those types of things, or do you have to be the talent?"

Yep, I hate her. It's official. And not just in the natural *she's touched my man* kind of way. In the *she's the biggest bitch I've ever met* way. "So, you planned this? You wanted us to be sitting here alone?"

"I did," she confirms.

"Why?"

"Because I wanted to talk to you."

"Out with it then," I say. I know for a fact that I'm not going to want to hear anything she has to say. But I've got no other choice. At this point, I'll draw more attention to myself if I leave.

"We have all game. What's the rush?" she says with a laugh. She points over to the jumbotron. "Look at that, we're on the big screen." Serena, of course, loves the camera and egging it on. She stands up and waves. Pulling me by the arm, she gets me to stand too. "Wave," she instructs me.

I roll my eyes, hating that I listen to her, and she pulls me in for a hug and rubs my back. I pull away quicker than she'd like, but still, she maintains that composure and that optic she's so interested in, continuing to please her public.

"Come on, you could at least get something about of this. Make yourself famous since you have a famous man," she comments. "Or do you not know how to use your relationship to your advantage?"

I'm sure my disgust is clear on my face, and she laughs at me.

"Come on, kiddo. You can't be that naive. Use it to your advantage. Make that Beachbody platform you're on even bigger. If you wanna be with Derek, then you better learn how this world that he's in works. And figure out how you fit and how you can get a piece of it for yourself."

I don't like what she's said. I hate how she looks at things and the world as a whole. I don't want anything from Derek. I don't want anything in my world to change. I get that it will, given his position, but I'm not using him for anything.

"I guess that's where you and I are different," I tell her. "I don't want anything from Derek. People have used him his whole life. I won't be one of those people."

"Grow up." Serena shakes her head at me. "The type of things those people wanted from him aren't the same. Couldn't even compare."

"You know about it?" I ask her.

"Sure, we talked about those things."

"I highly doubt that," I snark at her.

"Yeah, well, you don't know him as well as you think you do, honey. Take it from me, you don't fit with Derek. Just give him back to me, and we'll call it no hard feelings."

"And if I don't? Is this PR campaign of niceness going to stop?"

"No, it won't. Seems my friends like it when I'm the bigger person."

We sit in silence. I want to move several chairs away from her, but I can't. Finally, at halftime, I rise from my seat. "I need to use the bathroom."

"Thanks for the notice," she replies dryly.

I'm not sure why I announced where I was going, but it was stupid of me. I hope when I return, she's not here. And if she is, maybe we can sit in silence for some more soccer.

When I return, of course she's still sitting there, holding a smaller version of the popcorn that I have and a beer. She's smiling and waving at fans who have tried to come close to get a picture.

"I'll take pictures when the game is over. Let's keep supporting the Courage."

I roll my eyes behind my sunglasses; thankful she can't see me do it.

"Oh, good your back," she tells me.

"I thought about leaving," I tell her. "But I'm here to watch the players. I actually care about them."

"You don't have to care about them to be here. Please, this isn't all about them. A lot of these people are here filling up their little stadium because I'm here."

"You really are a dreadful person."

"Oh, knock it off. I'm not dreadful. I'm just not naive to how the real-world works. You think Derek isn't like this? Well, think again, sweetheart. Spend enough time with him, you just might find out that you're not with the man you thought you were."

"I don't believe you."

"Believe what you want to believe, but I don't want you to wake up one day and realize you have no clue who the man you're sleeping next to is, Audrey. Hate me all you want and ignore me all you want, but one day, you'll see I'm right."

With that, she gets up and heads up to talk to her security team. It's not long after that they take her to get ready for her big meet and greet. I stay and watch the rest of the game. The Courage wins, but I barely cheer. I just make notice of all the people that are staring at me and the whispers that come along with it.

After the game and the meet and greet with Serena, Jess and I go grab a drink. We're in a hole-in-the-wall bar, sipping on margaritas.

"So, I saw you sitting with Serena." Jess finally brings up the elephant in the room. We've covered the game and how they played, but I'm sure she was itching to talk about this sooner.

"She kind of took over my section. I didn't really have a choice."

"She seems fake," Jess remarks.

"Thank you!" I cry out. "Everyone loves her, but Jess, she's just evil. She made it so hard to enjoy the game."

"If you want to come back next weekend and watch us..."

"I will," I tell her.

"All this crap about you taking her man... it's not true, is it?"

"You could tell that it was fake?" I ask. I'm surprised, but hopefully if Jess saw through it, others did too.

"*She* just seems so fake. I hated having to pose for pictures with her. It was all about the photo op with her. I mean, I'm good at reading people, so I knew something was wonky with her. But a lot of the other girls were all giddy at the thought of her."

I roll my eyes. "She has that effect on people."

I think she picks up on the fact that I'm not comfortable talking about her. I keep looking around and making sure that no one can hear us. So, she changes the subject. We move on to other topics about the upcoming games and my training sched-ule. After about two hours, we're both beat, and I'm headed home.

Glancing at my phone, I realize I never bothered to answer

any of the messages from Derek. I don't know that I want to anymore. It's only a little after ten here and not nearly as late in LA. His night is just getting started, but I don't feel like talking. I shoot him a message letting him know we'll talk tomorrow and turn my notifications off. I can't deal with the world anymore. I go home and take a long hot shower before climbing into bed, where I can ignore the world. A quick peek at Instagram told me that was a great idea. There are pictures of Serena and me all over.

She's such a fake bitch, I think to myself as I drift off to sleep.

CHAPTER THIRTY-SEVEN

Things don't look any better in the morning light. I see I have more voicemails from Derek. They're mostly him telling me he loves me and saying it doesn't matter what time I wake up; he wants to talk to me. But I don't feel right waking him up early in the morning in LA. I decide to wait until it's at least ten o'clock his time, which makes it two o'clock my time.

Thankfully, I have no clients today or any commitments. It's a Monday and it feels like a big one. I just lie around on the couch and watch trashy TV. I text back and forth with the realtor about the house in Corolla. She thinks she might have some offers for me to review by the end of the week. It's great news for my mom. I'll be sad to see the house go, but I know it's for the best. I'll review those offers for my mom, but ultimately, she'll make the decision based on my recommendations.

One o'clock rolls around, and he calls.

"Hey," I say as I answer the phone.

"Hi," he says. He sounds like shit.

"Are you okay? You don't sound so good."

"I'm worried, Audrey. I know what she's like, and I'm worried she filled your head with bullshit ideas and now you're bailing on me. Aiden says you wouldn't do that, but I don't know, babe... This call feels like goodbye."

I sigh.

"That's not a good sound," he tells me.

I laugh into the phone. "Sorry, it was just a very long game. I like going to those games, and I never dreamed she would show up there. But she chose that place because she knew I would be there. I can't even imagine having that kind of power."

"She's a trip."

"Do *you* have that type of power?" I ask him. I want to understand the full weight of his celebrity. Some of the things Serena said to me bothered me more than I'd like to admit.

"I guess, yeah... I could. I could shut down a soccer stadium section and have some alone time with you, if that's something you'd be into."

"No, I wouldn't ask you to do that. But if you ever went with me to see my friends play, I guess you would have to."

"Yeah, maybe. What's going on, Aud? Why weren't you answering me back last night? I was so worried about you. There are all these pictures online of the two of you sitting there and talking. Don't get more wrong, you look miserable in most of them. But they're playing it off like Serena was comforting a mourning friend."

"Wow, she really can spin anything," I remark.

"Audrey" is all he says.

I know he wants more, but I'm not sure what else to say. I'm not sure what else to give him at this point. "I don't know, Derek. She made me feel like maybe we shouldn't be doing this. Like maybe you and I really don't belong together. I might not fit into your world—ever. I don't want to be the reason you're held back from things, and I don't want to wake up one day and find out that you're not who I thought you might be."

"You would never. You wouldn't. I am exactly the same man from that beach in Corolla. The same kid that came up to you and used to steal your Oreos during movie nights. I'm just a little more well-known than that kid used to be."

I don't say anything because I'm not sure what to say to that. He speaks again.

"Come on! I did not just piss off everyone I know for you to end this on me over the phone because of something that spoiled bitch said. We are better than that. Our relationship is stronger than that! Please, Audrey," he pleads with me.

I start to cry, thinking about all she said and all he's saying to me. "I just feel like you could have done so much better than me. Someone like Serena can offer you so much more than I can, Derek. Maybe this shouldn't have ever started."

"No, no, this should have started a long time ago. You are the woman I love and the exact woman that I want. Do not let her twist things or hurt us. That's what she's trying to do. She's trying to see if you'll break up with me and then come back to her, and it's fucking working. How can it be working? You know exactly who I am. You *know me*. Grow a set of those balls I know you have and stay with me."

I'm laughing by the end of his little speech. "Oh, Derek. I do love you," I tell him.

"Then that's it. That's all there needs to be," he says. I can hear the desperation coming through over the phone. I hate that I'm doing this to him, but I'm just not sure. She's made me question everything, and I hate her for that.

"What if she's right, though? I hate that she's made me question everything. I really do, but at some point, she's gotta have a point, right?"

"Audrey." He sighs into the phone. "Don't let her manipulate you the way she has all of her fans. Be stronger and smarter than that. I know she caught you in a rough time, and I know you hate what happened. I know you hate that your dad saw all of this before he died, and you never got to tell him the truth. But trust me, he knew the truth. The same way you do. Come on, Aud. Stay with me."

"It's just so much harder than I thought it would be," I admit. "Being here away from you and having no idea when I'm going to see you again… that's a little hard to take."

"So, what if we make a plan to see each other, will that help? Will you come out here to LA to be with me? Will you come out and go to an event with me?"

"Um, what kind of an event?" I ask him. "I want to see you, but why do I feel like you're about to throw me into the deep end here?"

"It's not the Met Gala, Aud. I wouldn't do that to you."

"You wouldn't be invited," I snark back.

He laughs. "There's my girl. Now you sound more like you."

"I guess I wigged a little bit there, and all I really needed was to hear your voice."

"I wish you would have called me last night and we could have talked this over. I didn't get much sleep, dreading this conversation. Ask the boys. I almost jumped on a plane to show up at your doorstep."

"I'm sorry. It was such a long day, and then I went out for drinks with Jess. It was nice to see her and hang out, but I would have much rather come home to see you at my doorstep."

"You know you could always see me at the end of your long days," he reminds me.

"Let's get back to this event you want me to go to."

"There's this party that the record label is throwing for us in Vegas. You'd just have to come out here to LA, and we would all go to Vegas together."

"That sounds fancy," I say. "I wouldn't have a thing to wear."

"Well, baby, I would take care of all of those things for you. You just get here, and I'll make sure you have an outfit that matches me. It'll be just like prom," he teases me.

"I hated my prom," I remind him.

"That's because you went with that douchebag Scotty Wilson. How could you have dated someone named Scotty?" He laughs and I love the sound of it.

"You and Aiden made sure that no one sane would date me," I remind him. "I had limited options."

"Ha, yeah. It was kind of fun scaring all the boys off you. Aiden and I had fun with that. But I'm sure we didn't make life easy for you." His tone is relaxed now, and he sounds more like the Derek I know. I hate that I caused him hell.

"I didn't mean to make you worry all night long," I tell him. "I would have called sooner if I knew you were like that. But I just needed space."

"Okay, well, next time you're worried about you and me and the future of us, could you maybe just consult me first? I will happily tell you that she's a fucking crazy bitch and you, my dear, are the love of my life."

The words knock me back a bit. Thankfully, I can hear him talking to someone in the background, so I have a few minutes to think of what to say. Finally, I ask, "Who are you talking to?"

"The boys are here. Aiden was worried about me and so was Brent. They stopped over to see if the crazy fog has lifted."

"Aiden came over—that's a good sign. I guess he's coming around to us."

"I guess so," Derek replies, and I can almost hear the smile in his voice.

"Did he ever say anything to you about what we heard, and you saw back in Cary?" I ask. "Because Emma isn't giving me anything."

"Nah, nothing. But I'm sure when they're ready, they will. Or maybe they won't. It's fine either way, remember? We agreed."

"I would like to talk to them about it, but you're right—if they want to talk, they will. Or maybe it was just a one-night thing. Maybe Emma will tell me when I get her drunk enough."

"Don't do that, Aud. It'll be fine." He chuckles into the line. "But seriously, the event with the record label, are you in? I think it would be great if you were here with me. I'll take care of everything. And I'll even give you a better time than Scotty did at prom."

I laugh out loud into the phone.

"I miss you," he tells me.

"I miss you too. When is this event?"

"Saturday evening. You could come in on Wednesday. How's that sound?"

"You're not giving me a lot of time to get this together. You realize that, right?"

"I thought you took a leave of absence from your clients."

I did. I took some time to grieve my dad, so that won't be a problem. I hate the idea of running to LA already. I don't want to start anything or promise anything. But we both know I'm not strong enough to stick to it. I've waited so long to hear someone say those things to me and put me first. How can I not go?

"Alright, I'll be there. Let me see what kind of flights I can make."

"Already taken care of. There's a ticket in your email."

"When did you…? *How* did you?" I ask, astonished.

"I did it right before we spoke. I had high hopes that you would either come around to go to the event with me or that I would need to have you use this ticket to come here and break up with me in person. Either way, I was going to see you again, baby."

I smirk. "Thank you. I would love to see you again. And I love you."

"I love you too. Just do me one favor."

"What's that?" I ask.

"Stop running from me. It's you and me, okay?"

"You and me," I reply. I can't wait for Wednesday.

We talk for a whole other hour about anything and everything. I just want to hear his voice on the line. Finally, though, he has to go.

"I've got band rehearsal, so I need to get going. The boys won't take lightly to me being late. I can call you later."

"Sounds good. I'll be waiting," I say in a low, sultry tone.

"I can't wait until you and I are on the same coast again."

"Me too. Bye, baby. Have fun at practice."

"Bye, sexy. I'll talk to you soon."

CHAPTER THIRTY-EIGHT

The process of getting my butt to LA is surprisingly easy. I let Emma and my mom know that I'm headed to LA to attend some event with Derek. Apparently, my mom has already been made aware of this fact because Aiden called and told her all about it. I love that he did that. I'm glad he shares these things with her. Emma is another story. She just snickered and said she would need my mailing address in LA.

I tell myself over and over again that that's not what's happening here. I don't want to move to LA. I like my life in Cary. I think it's easy and simple. The two bodyguards Derek assigned to me follow me everywhere I go, but I don't think they're necessary. No one approaches me or causes a scene. I'm a pretty perceptive person, and I don't notice anyone slyly taking my picture or staring at me. Then again, I never noticed anyone taking that picture outside of Derek's apartment. But when I've checked online, the only pictures I can find of me in Cary are the ones with Serena at the Courage game. There are more of Derek in LA and people speculating where I am. It makes me laugh because if they were paying attention to the date of the game, they would have known I was in North Carolina. But they would rather speculate that there's trouble in paradise than be factual.

I head down the escalator at LAX and see he's standing there waiting for me, wearing all black and a baseball cap drawn over his eyes. There are three security men standing around him. I walk quickly down the moving steps and rush into his arms. I crash into him, and he takes a few steps back to keep from falling over.

"I missed you too, baby," he croons into my ear. A bit of laughter escapes out while he pulls back to get a look at my face. Laughing, he pulls the NC Courage cap that I'm wearing up a bit. "You're using my way of getting around now, huh?"

I smile up at him. I'm so happy to be here in his arms. "I am. I thought it might be a good idea once we're in LA."

"Well, the Carolina blue may make it stand out just a bit," he points out.

I giggle. "I didn't have a black one like yours."

"We can get you one. I'll get you one made that says, *The Love of Derek Walsh's Life.*"

My whole-body heats at his words. "If I knew we could, I would take you into an airport bathroom right now. But I'm pretty sure you don't want to do that in front of both of our security teams." Although, looking around, I could see that mine has disappeared. Finally able to catch a break, I assume, because Derek's team is on duty now.

He chuckles darkly. "I really wish we could, but no, that would not be a good idea. I think too many people would walk in on us or hear us. You have no idea how busy LAX can be."

"Oh, I noticed, but I just don't care. It feels like a long time since I've been near you." In reality, it's only been about three and a half days. Maybe it's because our relationship is so new. Maybe that's why it's harder to be away from him. Or maybe Emma is right, and I'll be moving out to LA, and she'll need my address here. I push the thought away and allow Derek to lead me to baggage claim.

"You know, if you just gave them your ticket and a description of your bag, they could pick this up for you," he tells me, gesturing toward his security team.

"I know, but I wanna pick it up. It's not nice to make them big up *my* bag."

"They have to come along anyway, babe," he reminds me.

While we wait for my bag, he stays close to me. Our bodies are welded together, his arm draped around my shoulders. I'm holding his hand too. He seems to want to keep touching me; the same way I do him. I guess the time away from me was hard on him too.

"Jesus Christ, how much shit do you need?" he asks when he pulls my suitcase off the conveyer belt. It's heavy. I brought the largest one I had and almost exceeded the weight limit.

"I wasn't sure how much to bring. Plus, I have essentials to help me get ready for the event, like my hair stuff, makeup, some jewelry, and maybe some shoe options.

He smirks and shakes his head. "You know we're being dressed for the event. They've even agreed to dress you. So, you don't need any of this. Shoes, hair, makeup, and jewelry will all be covered."

"Oh," I say. I hadn't realized they would take care of me that much. "I can make myself look nice for you until we go," I quip, trying to make light of it.

"I don't give a shit if you look like a hobo during your time here. I just want to stay as close to you as I can. I'm not letting you out of my sight."

"I love you," I reply. He's so sweet and caring. This thing between us isn't at all what I expected. You would have thought from our gruff first encounter that he wouldn't be saying these types of things. But once you chisel away at that hard exterior, there's a soft, kindhearted man in there.

"I love you, too," he replies, leading me out of the airport and to a waiting car that will take us to his apartment.

I spend a few days hanging out with the guys in LA. I try to spend some time with Aiden, when Derek doesn't have me locked away in his bedroom or when they're not at band practice. And then we're off to the event in LA. I am a bundle of nerves. I can't imagine walking a red carpet.

"It's not going be a big deal," Aiden assures me. He must see the anxiety written all over my face.

The stylist is dressing the band in dark gray suits and black button-down shirts, with motorcycle-type boots on their feet. They look so freaking hot. My hair is half-up, half-down, with loose curls. I have more makeup on than I normally would, but I like the final product. Derek stares at me hungrily, and I'm not even in my dress, just wearing a black silk robe.

"We'll get you into your dress soon," the stylist, Anna, tells me. She has a thick accent. French, maybe. But I just know I love to hear her talk. I could listen to her bark orders all day.

"Is it black?" I ask her.

"No, my dear. I've got you in some black pumps, but I'm doing a red dress for you. We want you to stand out against the band."

"No, I want to blend in," I protest.

She smiles. "Why blend in? You are so beautiful. You should stand out, Audrey. Your namesake would stand out."

I smile. I don't know for sure that I'm named after Audrey Hepburn. I know my dad liked her as an actress, but most people just assume that's who I was named after.

"Okay, whatever you think is best," I say, wringing my hands.

"Relax and take two deep breaths for me," she says. "You've got this. Has anyone told you about the night?"

"Just that it's a red carpet walk with a party," I reply lamely. I know it's silly to be so scared, because it's just a small walk and then we'll head inside. There's a party and the boys have to speak at some point. I get to stand off to the side and say nothing. Derek will be the one giving the speech on their behalf. I listened to them writing it last night. It was comical, and I loved every second of listening to them collaborate. All of them were so serious about it, heads down looking at the computer screen. Trying to get the words in the right order. Making sure it sounded like it came from all of them and not just one member of the band. They made sure to recognize their fans for their support during my dad's death. But in the end, they got a really nice, short and sweet speech out of it.

"Yes, the red carpet is only a small part of it. So just relax and focus on wearing this beautiful red gown with confidence because I know you can, and you will look amazing."

I smile at her. "Thank you for all of your help. I couldn't do this without you."

"I'm happy to help you. Some of the girls I work with aren't as humble as you are. Let's get this dress on you."

"Okay," I reply.

We get me dressed and it takes no time at all. My dress is a fiery red. It's long but form fitting to my body. Thankfully, there won't be any dancing tonight because I'm not sure how I could in this. When I emerge to the see the band, their responses take me by surprise.

"Holy shit," Brent says.

"You look beautiful, sis," Aiden says, coming over to hug me.

"Woman you are making me want to rip that dress right off you," Derek says, hugging me after Aiden and squeezing my ass.

"No, you'll rip my dress," Anna scolds him.

"Yes, ma'am," he replies with a mock salute.

"It's time," Aiden announces.

I feel like I could throw up. My stomach is sick, my hands are clammy, and I can't breathe. I don't want to do this. I'm the only date of the band, and I feel kind of silly. But they've all assured me on numerous occasions that they're happy that I'm here.

I take three deep breaths, hug Anna one last time, and take Derek's hand.

"Sexy, it's going to be okay," he tells me in a low voice. "Just hold my hand and come with me. You don't have to talk unless someone directs a question at you. And if you don't want to answer it, what do you say?"

"No comment," I say, reminding myself over and over again of what we practiced and what will happen, most likely. Although Derek promised he'd do his best to keep the heat off me.

Derek pulls me over to the band, and we huddle together in a circle. Everyone's arms are wrapped around the people beside them, creating a tight circle. I'm between Aiden and Derek. I'm glad I get to draw some strength from the two of them.

"Let's go do this shit," Derek says.

I recognize the words. He says it every time they get ready to perform. True to form, they follow his lead.

"We fucking got this. Let's rock," Aiden replies.

"Let's give them something to crave," Brent replies—a clever play on the name of the band.

"I love you guys," I reply lamely.

"We love you" they all reply in unison. And that's it. We head off to the bright flashing lights.

I hold onto to Derek's hand tightly at first, but as we make our way down the carpet, I get used to it and let up on my grip. They ask him questions about the new tour dates and cities. He says that all the dates should be finalized soon and that he can't wait to see everyone on the road. There are more questions about Serena and if she's coming this evening.

"Sadly, she could not be here tonight. She has a concert elsewhere, so we wish her well," Derek replies. A well-practiced answer that Dale helped with.

I see him in the crowd. He smiles at me when our eyes meet. I smile back and continue to stay with Derek and head down the carpet.

We're almost at the end. We've almost made it when a question is directed at me. "Audrey, how are you doing after everything with your dad?"

I stop and freeze for a moment. I hadn't expected this question. I can see that she thinks she's just being nice, but I would have preferred it if she hadn't said a word.

"I'm doing the best I can," I reply and silently pray that Derek moves on. Thankfully, he does. We make it into the ballroom, and I let out a sigh of relief.

"You were wonderful," he says, turning and giving me a kiss on the lips.

"Anna is going to hate that you messed with her lipstick," I say when we break apart.

"I can take Anna," he teases. "I'm so proud of you." He kisses me again.

"And I am so proud of you. This is your night. Now let's go celebrate you and all the wonderful things you have accomplished. This album is amazing, and I love the surprise track you wrote about my dad. It's going to be really beautiful."

"I love you," he says before getting lost in the crowd. I follow him for some of it. Other times, I stay off to the side and let him talk to the executives of the label. They're here to celebrate his album, after all, not mine. I take pictures of the band in front of the artwork, and one of the snaps gets posted to my Instagram story. I've gone back to posting, back to living my life. The hate and name calling has slowed a bit, and I'm thankful for that.

The lights flicker, announcing that it's time for the speeches to begin. The label executive and Dale are heading toward the podium. Dale motions for the band to follow. I get a quick kiss from Derek, and he's off to stand onstage. I watch lovingly as the executive says nice things about Crave and the newest album they put together. Then Dale takes the stage.

"These extremely talented men before me have had a lot of things to overcome in the past few weeks. But I think they've handled it all with dignity and grace. I'm so proud to represent them and the type of music they put out on the scene. Without further ado, I give you Crave."

They take center stage. Aiden and Brent flank Derek. He clears his throat and beings to speak. "I want to thank you all for coming together to celebrate us and this album. *Lust For* is an album we're all very proud of. It came at a time when we all needed a little strength and push to persevere through some tough spots. But the way it all came together and the emotions that are expressed in it are completely genuine. We are so honored to be touring and providing you all with live versions of these songs. Thank you all for coming out and supporting Crave and thank you all for your continued support. Please enjoy the night. Now, let's hear some music!"

Applause, whoops, and cheering break out. The band standing behind them begins to play music. There's dancing, drinking, and eating. Derek comes over and pulls me into his arms.

"You were wonderful up there," I compliment him, then kiss his neck a bit.

"Thank you, gorgeous. We need to talk about those tour dates," he says lowly, while we sway back and forth to a slow song.

"What about them?" I ask. I have an idea where this is going, and I'm not sure how I'm going to be able to say no to him.

"Come with me," he says. "You don't have to come with me for the whole thing, but for part of it. I want you with me. I want to be able to tour the world with you by my side. I know you have your clients and your commitments, but can you do any of that by Zoom? Can you please come with me?"

I look into his eyes, and I'm not sure how I can say no to him —on his night, celebrating his album. "I need to see those dates," I tell him. The smile I'm rewarded with is worth everything and every moment we've taken to get to this point.

"Are you saying yes?" he asks me.

I nod, and he picks me up and twirls me around.

When he puts me down, I'm laughing. "I just have to let my clients and the team know. But I think they'll be okay with it. I haven't been doing too much this season. It's a winning season, and with my dad, I've severely backed off on those commitments. I think Beachbody is having my program come out after the first of the year, so you may lose me for a bit because of promotional things, but I'll do my best to get back to you."

"You are nothing short of amazing. Who knew if I wanted to find the love of my life, I would just need to look at my best friend's bratty little sister?" he teases, squeezing my ass.

I shake my head. "I was never bratty," I say in my own defense. But we both know it's not true. Sometimes I was a little brattier than I needed to be to get my own way. "Well, you took a punch to the face for me from your best friend, and you almost lost your job because you refused to give *me* up. How can I not do this for you?"

"I would have, you know. You're worth it all. You are what I've lusted for all my life."

"Where you go, I go," I say lovingly to him.

He smiles widely at me again, and his eyes are shining of nothing but love. "About time you figure that out."

He kisses me deeply, until Aiden comes over and taps him on the shoulder before handing us both champagne. "I'm going to need you both to keep it PG, please."

"Yes, sir," we say in unison.

"She coming on tour?" he asks with a shake of his head.

"Yeah, I am."

"Awesome," he says, giving Derek a fist bump. "This is going to be one hell of a party." And I can tell he means it. There is genuine excitement shining in his eyes.

That night, in our hotel room in Vegas, Derek very carefully removes my red dress. He lays me down on the bed. His own clothes come off too, and he joins me on the bed.

Derek rolls onto his back and pulls me on top of him. He begins kissing me passionately, rocking his hips into mine. I can feel myself growing wet just from it. I prop myself up on both hands so that I can face him. He winks at me and captures a nipple in his mouth, and I cry out in pleasure.

"Derek," I moan.

"Hmm," he replies, using a hand to knead the other nipple.

"I need you," I tell him.

"Then you shall have me." He moves off the bed and rolls a condom onto his length. After pulling me back on top of him, he enters me.

"Fuck," I cry out, enjoying the feeling of how deep inside me he is. I begin setting a slow pace, enjoying his moans beneath me. I love being on top of him like this. I like seeing his face as I slide up and down on top of him. I love seeing how much he enjoys the things that I'm doing to him.

I pick up the pace just a bit because I need more friction. His hands move to my nipples, and he begins pinching and twisting. I love the feeling that he's creating, making me wetter and wetter. I can feel the pressure building.

"Go ahead, baby, let go. I've got you." He grabs my hips and begins moving me up and down.

I let out a string of curse words and come apart of on top of him. When I come back down, I rest my body on top of his. We lie there for just a moment before Derek flips us so that he's on top of me. He drives into me with quick, hard thrusts.

"Derek," I moan out, watching him on top of me. "Can you flip me over?" I ask with a wink.

He smirks. "Anything for you, baby."

He flips me and positions me so I'm on all fours. I wiggle my ass at him, ready for what's about to happen. He drives into me, and I scream out with pleasure. Derek continues sliding in and out of me while I do my best to push my hips further and further back. The only sound that can be heard is the slapping of our skin and our moans. The pressure builds, and I can't take any more. I start to come apart. Derek collapses on top of me, laying me flat out on the bed and rubbing at my clit as I moan with pleasure. As I'm coming down from my high, I feel him stiffen and come inside me.

We're both breathing heavily and lying still joined, covered in sweat.

"That may have been the best part of this whole damn night," he tells me.

I do my best to look back at him and capture his lips. "I second that."

"Just imagine doing that on tour," Derek teases.

"My brother is going to hate us."

Derek chuckles. "You don't think we'll hear him? Oh, you're so cute," he says before climbing off me to take care of the condom.

When he returns to bed, he gathers me up in his arms. "Time for sleep, baby. We're both exhausted."

I'm gathered up in Derek's arms, and sleep takes me quickly. The last thing I remember is him murmuring that he loves me before kissing my temple. I don't know that I replied, but I'm sure he knows.

CHAPTER THIRTY-NINE

Opening night of the Lust For Tour opens in LA. The boys have a great venue for it, and the opening act guys seem cool. Once tonight's show is over, we'll hop onto the tour bus, where our things are already loaded, and hit the road. We head to Seattle first and then do a few shows in that area before moving on. I like the idea of snaking down the West Coast until eventually meeting up with Mom in North Carolina.

The house has sold. I spoke to her yesterday, and she sounded like she was in good spirits about it. I just hope she really is, especially since it was purchased by an investment company. But there's more time to worry about that later. Right now, I'm backstage and waiting for him to go.

There's a sort of nervous energy surrounding everyone. I think it's because this is the start of something big. The boys say it's just nerves. They're modest that way. The last time I heard Dale talking about numbers, he was saying that most of the shows were sold out or damn close to it. The US seems to love them. No one seems to care about Serena and how Derek might have cheated on the "Princess of Rock," as she has started calling herself. The song they sing together will still be performed every now and then. They just don't stand so close to each other now. But I don't care, because at the end of the day, she keeps her hands off him.

There's about an hour to showtime and almost all of the preshow checks have been done. The opening band is now performing, and then there will be a slight break before Crave takes the stage. I'll be watching them from the wings. Derek says it's best to keep me hidden because more and more people seem to take notice of me now, especially when Derek is around. They know what I look like, and some of them approach me in the street for autographs. Luckily, everyone has been accepting. There are still those trolls out there that make nasty comments on social media or spreads lies, but Derek and I have learned not to listen to them. We know the truth about us and our relationship, and that's all that matters in the end.

Derek pulls me into the room with the band and says, "I have something to give to you."

"Dude, do you want us here for this?" Brent says cringing.

"A dick pic better not be in that envelope." Aiden smirks before sipping on his beer.

"Nah, and it's something that I want you guys to see too. Here," he says, handing me an envelope. "It only made sense that the house stayed in the family."

I gasp and open the envelope. "You are the one who bought the beach house." I can't believe he thought enough of our family home to buy it like that.

"What good is my money if I can't spend it on you? And besides, we had a lot of good times in that house. I want there to be many more. I plan on telling your mom that she's welcome to go stay there as much as she wants. I'm not sure she will, but it's an option if she'd like it to be."

"Are you serious?" I ask, skimming the document. My eyes are filling with tears.

"Are you kidding me, man?" Aiden comes over and look at

the papers I was just reviewing. "Dude, this is so awesome. I had no idea you were doing something like that."

"In some ways, your parents raised me. They convinced my grandma to stop moving around on me and leave me somewhere stable where you guys were. I feel like I wouldn't be here right now if it hadn't been for your family. So, it was the very least I could do. I've never had a lot of people that I could call family. You guys are it."

Aiden and I hug Derek. While we're hugging, Brent snorts in the background.

"You do realize that out of both of those people that you say are your family, you've slept with half of them."

"Don't make it gross," Derek says, flipping him the bird.

I shake my head. "I love you for doing this."

"I'm happy to do anything that makes you happy." He pulls me in for a hug and whispers low in my ear. "I also happen to remember that the house is where you and I started. I wanted to be able to go back to that place and celebrate anniversaries and other special occasions."

I pull back and he winks at me. "I love that we can do that."

"Maybe make that special time that we had there together an annual thing," he continues. "Or use it for some time to have the band come out for a retreat or something."

"Oh, you know we're doing that," Aiden chimes in.

"You guys are welcome to use it when you'd like to. I want you to feel like it's still your home too."

"That's so nice of you," Aiden says, clapping him on the back.

"Anything for this family, Ace." The two hug and Brent makes a gagging sound.

"Alright, alight," Dale says, coming into the room. "Let's get you boys ready. There's a packed house out there tonight, and everyone is excited to see my boys."

I roll my eyes at Dale's fakeness. He once told them that he has no sons, so he sees the band as his sons. I think that's garbage and just his way of being slimy like other managers in LA. But I have to give him somewhat of a pass because he was a big help when the deck was stacked against the band. He could have dropped them, but he didn't.

"Audrey, you watching from the wings, or should we put you in the VIP area?"

"She'll be in the wings," Derek answers for me.

"Alright, if that changes, just let me know. The view from the wings is cool, but it's also awesome to see them from out there in the crowd. Security will keep you safe either way."

"Thanks, I appreciate it," I say with a smile. At least he tries to be helpful to me at times.

We all make our way to the stage, where the opening act has already finished a little while ago. The fans are chanting their name. They are so ready for my boys to hit the stage. I turn and give Brent a big hug.

"You're going to be wonderful out there," I tell him.

"Aw, thanks, sis." He picks me up and hugs me tightly. "I'll see you after the show."

"See ya," I tell him. I move onto Aiden next. "I love you, big brother. Have a great show."

"Thanks, I love you. I'm glad you're here."

"Me too."

"Makes sense that you're with us for this tour. And not just because of Derek. I like having my little sister around." He picks me up the same way Brent did and twirls me around. "I love you, kiddo."

"Love you more."

I turn to Derek last, noticing that Aiden and Brent kind of disappear a bit to give us our space. "I love you most of all," I tell him before placing my lips to his. Derek deepens the kiss, causing me to moan.

"I can't wait to take care of you tonight in the back of that bus."

I giggle. "They are so going to hate us."

He chuckles. "Oh, I don't know. Sometimes they have their own bus bunnies, and well, that's not always the best thing to listen to either."

"Ugh, what did I sign on for?" I tease him.

"You signed on to be with me always," he reminds me.

"I did. And I will." I kiss him passionately. Just as our kiss is finishing up, the band is being announced.

Dale comes over and taps him on the shoulder. "I don't mean to be a cockblock here, but he's got to get on stage."

"Got it," Derek says, pulling back. "I love you, baby, and I'll see you soon. I gotta go to work."

"I love you and I'll be cheering for you," I call after him.

He turns and shoots me that sexy smile I love so much. Blowing me one last kiss, he heads onto the stage with the rest of the guys, and they launch into the first single from the radio, "Lust For."

I cheer backstage and dance around as the band plays. I've never seen them from this angle before. It's definitely louder, which is why I have earplugs in. But I like that I can see Brent drumming away. I can watch how his hands fly from drum to drum. I have a great view of Aiden and Derek singing. My favorite thing, though, is seeing Derek look over every once in a while and wink at me.

"He's a hell of a rock star," Dale screams from beside me.

I hadn't even realized he was still standing there. The buzzing of my cell phone interrupts my viewing experience. It won't stop. I finally decide to look at it and see that it's Emma. I head away from the stage and pick up.

"What's up, girl? You're interrupting my concert. The boys are playing." I scream into the phone.

"Can you help me? I need to get back there. I'm here too," she says into the phone. "But these assholes won't let me back since I'm not on the list."

"I'll take care of it," I scream back. I head over to Dale and ask that he let Emma in. Like the dutiful manager that he is, he goes and allows Emma into the venue. She joins me and I hand her a pair of her own earplugs. I immediately notice that Emma looks sick. Something seems to be bothering her.

"Do you need to talk?" I ask.

"No," she shouts. "I just want to watch the show for now."

I nod back and the two of us bop around to the music and sing. Emma looks a little better now that she's reached me, but something is still bothering her. I decide to let her tell me when she's ready. And I'm not ready to leave the stage yet. I wanna watch the concert the whole way through. Had this been one of many that I saw, I would have left with her. But this is my first one.

I grab her and pull her into a tight side hug. I vow that no matter what is bothering her, I'll be there for her through all of it.

The concert ends with two encores. The boys were prepared for one, but not two. It's an amazing night and an even better show. They come running off the stage sweating and pumped up.

I move out of the way as the stage crews grabs the drumsticks and the guitars from the guys. They're handed bottles of water, which they all chug. I stay back and wait for Derek to be ready to come over to me. I know when he is, he will.

When he makes his way over, I throw myself into his arms. His black muscle shirt is covered in sweat, but I don't care. I've seen him like this before, and right now, all I want to do is hug him and kiss him passionately.

"You were amazing," I tell him before I grab his face and kiss him tenderly.

When we finally come up for air, he smirks at me and says, "I hope this is the welcome I get every time I come off stage. If so, it's going to be the best fucking tour of my life."

I giggle. "Play like that and you just might."

I pull away and hurry over to congratulate Aiden and Brent.

"You were incredible," I tell each of them when I hug them.

"Thanks," Brent says.

"What is Emma doing here?" Aiden asks.

I look back from him to her. I wonder to myself if he's the reason she looks so freaked out. "I'm not sure. She wouldn't tell me."

"Oh, okay."

"Guys, we gotta talk about that amazing fucking performance!" Dale exclaims.

"I wanna talk to Emma anyway," I tell Derek as he looks unsure about leaving me alone.

"Why is she here?" he asks.

"I'm about to find out," I tell him.

I grab Emma and we make our way to the bus. That's where I assume the guys will be meeting us. There's no after-party tonight. They have to head right to their next stop.

"Come on, we can talk in here." I walk up onto the bus, and Emma reluctantly follows me.

When we're finally situated in the guy's living room, I ask her, "What's going on?"

"This is nice," she says, looking around the bus.

She's right about that. We're sitting on their leather couch, and there are matching leather recliners. There's a small kitchenette with a leather booth that would fit all of us, and toward the back of the bus is storage, closets for each of us, and a pantry that holds all of the food and other necessities. There's a small bathroom and shower. It won't be the easiest to shower in, but I'm sure I'll manage. In the back of the bus, there are four bunk beds—not exactly the best for having sexy time with Derek, but he told me we'll manage. Aiden says they'll all wear earplugs at night to avoid hearing anyone.

I'm not sure how I feel yet about having sex with my boyfriend on the bottom bunk when my brother is sleeping on the set of bunks across from us or the top bunk. But I'm sure eventually I'll either forget about it or I'll be so drunk I won't care.

"It's nicer than I thought it would be. Small, but I'm sure we'll manage."

I want to jump on her and ask what's happening, but I wait and let her talk to me. Finally, she breaks her silence.

"I need you to know that I did not do this to hurt you. Please know and understand that," she begins. Her bottom lip is already shaking.

I reach over and grab her hands. "It's okay, honey. I'm here. Just whatever it is, say it."

"I slept with Aiden." She stares me at as if she was expecting yelling or more of a reaction.

"Derek and I heard you. When we were coming in from the outside, I heard the moaning. Derek peeked, and I did not." I hold my hands up in surrender.

"Were you ever going to tell me you knew?"

"I thought you would tell me about it when you were ready. I figured if you were keeping it under wraps, then you had a reason. Plus, Derek reminded me that I looked like a huge hypocrite if I flipped my shit about it. Which I wouldn't. I'm just worried about you because I know you have a crush on him." I sigh and study her face. She's pale, her bottom lip is quivering, and her eyes are red rimmed from crying. "Did something happen? Are you okay? Is that what brought you out here?"

I hear the boys coming. I know that Aiden will be here soon, and I'm not sure I want him to hear our conversation. I don't even know what's going on yet.

"I'm pregnant," she blurts out.

"What?" I exclaim.

I hear a commotion behind me and turn to see the band is standing there, Aiden's face white as a sheet.

The End

Stay tuned for Emma and Aiden's Story

Long For

Coming February 2024

Thank you for reading *Lust For*. I hope you loved this rock star romance and brother's best friend story.

Find out what happens between Aiden and Emma in *Long For*, releasing February 28, 2024.

And be sure to check out my other book, *Irreversibly Broken*, which has the same steam, spice and forbidden love as *Lust For*.

And you can sign up for my newsletter here:

https://dashboard.mailerlite.com/forms/543405/9642250996285566 9/share

ALSO BY J.L. STRAY

The Broken Series

Irreversibly Broken, The Broken Series Book 1
Fixing the Broken, The Broken Series Book 2
No Longer Broken, The Broken Series Book 3

Standalone Novels

Affliction, A Salvation Society Novel

Tis the Damn Season

Sinning with You

ABOUT THE AUTHOR

J.L. Stray has always enjoyed reading books and writing stories. Finally, she gathered up enough courage to publish one herself. A former Policy Specialist and current Consultant, she spends any extra moment she has writing, outlining and scheming her next book.

Raised in a small town in Pennsylvania, she graduated from Penn State University with a bachelor's degree in Criminal Justice and Public Policy. Most days she uses one of those degrees in either her career or dealing with her children.